The
WARLORDS
—OF NIN—

OTHER TITLES BY STEPHEN R. LAWHEAD

THE
WARLORDS
—OF NIN—

THE DRAGON KING TRILOGY, BOOK TWO

STEPHEN R.
LAWHEAD

THOMAS NELSON
Since 1798

NASHVILLE   DALLAS   MEXICO CITY   RIO DE JANEIRO

Published in Nashville, Tennessee, by Thomas Nelson. Thomas Nelson is registered a trademark of Thomas Nelson, Inc.

Thomas Nelson, Inc. books may be purchased in bulk for educational, business, fund-raising, or sales promotional use. For information, please e-mail SpecialMarkets@ThomasNelson.com.

ISBN 978-1-59554-960-0 (repack)

Library of Congress Cataloging in Publication Data
Lawhead, Steve.
  The warlords of Nin / Stephen R. Lawhead.
    p. cm. — (The Dragon King trilogy ; bk. 2)
  ISBN 978-1-59554-380-6 (hardcover)
  I.   Quentin (Fictitious character)—Fiction. 2.   Mensandor (Imaginary place)—Fiction. I. Title.
  PS3562.A865W37 2007
  813'.54—dc22

                                            2007028411

Printed in the United States of America
11 12 13 14 15 RRD 5 4 3 2 1

For Drake, my shining one.
With all my love.

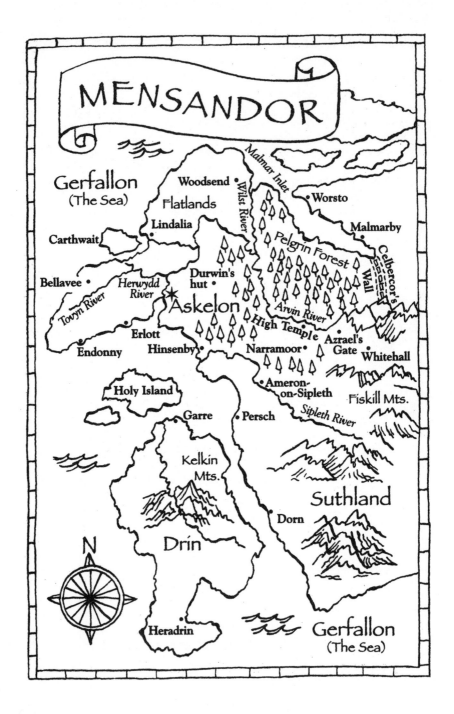

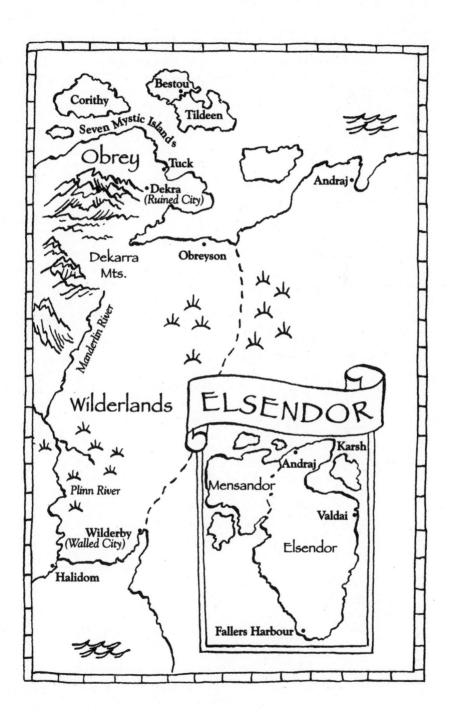

CHAPTER I

Quentin stood at the high parapet overlooking the tranquil forest. His eyes scanned the gently lifting hills clothed in their greens of early summer, all softened in the golden afternoon light by the gathering mists of evening. At his hand upon the cool stone balustrade a thin parchment roll fluttered in the easy breeze. At his feet lay a leather case from which he had drawn the scroll to read only moments before. The case bore the royal insignia he knew so well: the terrible, twisting red dragon of the Dragon King.

The warmth of the late-afternoon sun splashed full on his face, and yet Quentin felt a chill creeping through him. He sighed a heavy sigh and hung his head, shaking it slowly from side to side. Hearing a rustle behind him and the brushing tread of a soft foot on the stone, he turned to see Toli gliding up.

The tall young man settled himself easily on the edge of the parapet and crossed his arms over his chest. He regarded Quentin with a quizzical brown eye and then looked out over the forest, cocking his head to one side. "Listen," he said, after a moment. "It is the sound of a world at peace."

Quentin listened and heard the faraway chirp of birds as they fluttered among the whirtle berries, the breeze nudging the leaves, voices murmuring in a courtyard somewhere below.

"They told me a rider from Askelon had arrived with a message for you. I thought to come and see if you needed anything."

Quentin looked at his friend and smiled. "You mean curiosity moved you from your beloved stables. Yes, a message from the king." He picked up the parchment and handed it to Toli, who began to read.

Presently Toli's head came up, and his eyes found Quentin's studying him. "This does not say what the trouble is."

"No, but it is not a request for a friendly visit. There is some need behind it, and some urgency. If it were but a small thing, Eskevar would have waited. We're due to travel back to Askelon soon anyway . . ."

"And this recommends we leave right away. Yes, I see. But there is something else?" Toli's sharp eyes appraised Quentin, who stiffened and turned from their piercing gaze.

"What makes you say that?"

Toli laughed softly. "Only that I know my Kenta very well. You would not look so if you did not have a suspicion of what lay behind this innocent summons."

"Innocent?" He fingered the leather case that he had stooped to retrieve. "Perhaps, but you are right, Toli; there is something else. I don't know—it just came over me as I was reading."

Toli watched Quentin closely and waited for him to continue.

"I'm afraid if we go to Askelon now, we will never come back to Dekra again."

"You saw this?"

Quentin only shook his head.

"Well, then it may not be. Your feelings may only be a warning of what may come if we do not go at once."

Quentin smiled again; this time a flicker of relief shone in his eyes. "Yes, perhaps you are right. As usual you have rescued me from myself."

"We can leave tonight. It will be good to sleep on the trail again. We have not done that in a long time, you and I."

"We shall, but not tonight. Have you forgotten that tonight we dine with Yeseph? If I am not mistaken, we have only enough time to prepare ourselves and go to his house. He will be waiting."

"We will leave at dawn instead," said Quentin.

"So be it," said Toli, inclining his head in a slight bow. "I will see to our preparations when we have supped with Yeseph and the elders."

Quentin nodded and took the rolled parchment that Toli offered him, then slid it back into its case as they turned and walked back into Quentin's rooms.

Quentin dressed quickly, donning a fresh mantle and tunic, and pulling on fine leather boots. He met Toli at the door, and the two set off for Yeseph's lodgings.

Yeseph lived in a quarter of the ruined city near the library. As they walked along together, Quentin looked upon the home he had come to love. His eyes, long ago accustomed to the tumbled structures that still met his gaze on every side, seemed not to notice the destruction, but instead saw it all the way it had been in the time of the mighty Ariga.

In his mind he saw stones lifted back into place one upon another; arches reconstructed with their colorful tiles, and beautifully carved doors thrown wide in welcome; courtyards once again abloom with flowering plants; streets echoing laughter and song. He saw it all as he imagined it had been. Quentin always experienced the same magical sensation when he moved about the city. In the ten years he had lived in Dekra, he never lost the rapture it held for him, or the feeling that he belonged there, that Dekra was his home as was none other he would ever find.

"It will be once more," said Toli as they moved along the quiet streets, over stones worn and smooth with time.

"What will be?" asked Quentin absently.

"This city. It will be again what it once was: the way you see it in your head."

"Do you think so?"

"Don't you?"

"I believe that it will. I want to believe it. Though it seems sometimes that the work goes so slowly. There is so much to be done. We could use more hands."

"But look how much has been accomplished since we came here. And every year our numbers grow. Whist Orren blesses our efforts with his own."

It was true. The work of restoring the ancient city and populating it with people who shared the dream of rebuilding it to its former glory, of studying the ways of the Ariga and their god—that was going on at a fine pace. Much had been done in ten years. The work of a lifetime, however, still remained. And that was what pricked Quentin's impatience.

They met Quentin's stooped old teacher where he stood waiting for them at the gate of his courtyard. His face beamed when he saw the two young men striding up. "Hello! Hello, my friends!" cried Yeseph, running out to meet them. "I have been waiting for you. You are the first to arrive. I was hoping that would be the case. I wanted to talk to you both."

He drew them into the shady courtyard and led them to stone benches under a spreading tree. The yard was spotless and furnished as nicely as any garden could be whose owner loved plants and flowering things.

"Sit down, please. Sit. Omani!" Yeseph clapped his hands when his guests had seated themselves beneath the tree. A slim young girl appeared with a tray of wooden goblets and a stone carafe. She floated forward with an easy grace and laid the tray at Yeseph's elbow where he sat. "You may pour, bright one," he said gently.

The girl poured and served the beverages around. She turned to leave, and Yeseph called after her. "See that the meal is prepared when the others arrive. It will not be long now, I think." She bowed and retreated into the house, smiling all the while.

The Curatak did not have servants. But often young girls or boys would attach themselves to the households of older Curatak leaders or craftsmen to serve and learn at their hand, until they decided what they wished to do with their lives. In that way those who needed the assistance of a servant did not lack, and young people found useful occupation until they could enter the adult world.

Yeseph watched the girl disappear into his darkened doorway a little wistfully. Quentin noticed his look and commented, "She's a very able helper, Yeseph. You are blessed."

"Yes, and I am sorry to lose her."

"Why would you lose her?"

"Why not? She is nearly eighteen. She wishes to be married soon. Next summer perhaps. She and Rulan, a former pupil of mine. He is a good man, very intelligent. It will be a good match. But I will lose a wonderful cook and companion. I feel she is my own daughter."

"Why don't you get married again?" asked Toli.

Yeseph suddenly looked flustered. "Who has been talking to you?"

"No one. I merely wondered."

"Well, it is true nonetheless. That is what I wanted to tell you. I am to be married. I am announcing the banns tonight."

"Congratulations!" shouted Quentin, jumping to his feet. He crossed the distance between himself and his former teacher in one bound and embraced him, kissing both cheeks.

"Who is the lucky bride?"

"It is Karyll, the cloth-maker."

"The widow of Lendoe, who was killed in action at the forge some time ago?"

"Yes, the same. A fine woman. She has been lonely for so long . . ."

Quentin laughed. "You need not explain to us; you have our permission already. I am sure you will both be very happy together."

"Yes, we shall. I am very happy now—sharing this news with my friends. You know I have come to regard you both as my own sons."

"And you have been a father to us more often than we can remember."

"I wanted you to be the first to know."

"Will we see the esteemed lady tonight? I would like to congratulate her as well."

"She will be here—if that is not her voice I hear even now."

The sound of light voices lifted in laughter came to the courtyard from the street beyond. Yeseph dashed to the gate once more and welcomed his bride and her two companions. Blushing and smiling, he led her toward Quentin and Toli, who stood grinning.

"My friends, this is my betrothed, Karyll."

The short, round-faced woman smiled warmly back at them. Her hair was bound demurely at her neck in an ornamented netting, and among the brown Quentin could see streaks of silver. She was dressed in a plain, white, loose-fitting gown with a bright blue shawl over her shoulders. She was a handsome woman.

As Yeseph drew her close to him with his arm, he gave his future wife a look of such endearment that Quentin felt a pang of longing for his own beloved.

"Hello, Karyll, and congratulations. Yeseph has been telling us that you two are to be married. I am very pleased."

"Thank you, Quentin. We are very happy." She turned and gazed into Yeseph's eyes and added, "Yeseph is full of your praises. It pleases me that he has chosen you to hear of our plans first."

"When will the wedding take place?" asked Toli.

"Yeseph and I thought that a midsummer wedding would be nice."

"Yes," agreed the groom. "There is nothing to prevent us from being married at once. We are both of age." He laughed, and Karyll laughed with him. But the laughter faded when neither Quentin nor Toli shared their mirth. Both had become strangely silent; the light of happiness was extinguished in their eyes.

"What is the matter? Does our plan not meet with your approval?"

"Yes, and more than you know. But I fear that we will not be among the happy wedding guests."

"Why not, may I ask?"

"We were going to tell you this evening. We have received a summons from the king, and we must leave for Askelon."

"Yes? But I thought you would stay until midsummer at least."

"No—at once. A rider came today. We must leave at once."

"Then we will wait until your return," offered Yeseph. Karyll nodded her agreement.

Quentin smiled sadly. "No, I could not ask that. I do not know when we may return. Please, do not wait on our account."

Toli attempted to set the mood in a lighter tone. "Kenta means that if he were in your place, Yeseph, he would not let so lovely a creature escape into the arms of another. You must marry as you have planned. We will return to greet the happy couple before they have been wed a fortnight."

Yeseph sought Quentin's eyes. He, as usual, could read more than his friend intended. "Is it trouble, then?"

"I fear that it is." Quentin sighed. "The message did not say it directly, and the courier did not say more. But he left immediately without awaiting an answer."

Yeseph regarded Quentin as he stood before him. From an awkward, impetuous youth had grown a square-shouldered, sensitive man—tall, lean in the way young men are, yet without the careless air they often have. Quentin had a regal bearing, and yet utterly lacked any self-consciousness of it, or the arrogance that often accompanied such a noble spirit.

A pang of longing ached in the old man's heart when he saw his young pupil and protégé wavering, as if on the brink of a great abyss. He wanted to reach out and pull him back, but he knew he could not. Quentin belonged to Dekra, yes, but he also belonged to Askelon, and neither loyalty could be denied.

"You must go, of course." Yeseph offered a strained smile. "When will you leave?"

"Tomorrow at dawn. I think it is best."

"Of course. Of course. Do not delay. Besides, the sooner you are off, the sooner you may return, and perhaps you will bring Bria with you this time."

At the mention of the name, Quentin started. He smiled warmly again. The cold shadow that had fallen upon the happy group moved away, and in the glimmering of a softly falling twilight, they began to talk excitedly once more of all they would do when next they met.

Despite their desire for an early start the next morning, Quentin and Toli were the last to leave Yeseph's house. There had been much singing and eating and talking. The elders had blessed the young men's journey, and all had listened to stories and songs of the lost Ariga, sung by one of the young Curatak musicians. Then all had made their good-byes, but none more ardently than Quentin.

"Look, Kenta," said Toli as they found their way along the dark and empty streets. The moon shone full upon the city, pouring out a liquid silver light upon all it touched.

Quentin followed Toli's gaze upward to the sky. "What do you see?"

"Oh, it is gone now. A star fell; that is all."

"Hmmm." Quentin retreated again into his reverie.

He listened to their footsteps echo along the streets and felt Dekra's quiet peacefulness enfold him. Then, unaccountably, he shivered, as if they had just walked through a hanging pool of cooler air. Toli noticed the quiver of Quentin's shoulders and looked at his friend.

"Did you feel it too?"

Quentin ignored the question, and they continued on a few more paces. "Do you think we will ever return to this place?" he asked finally.

"The night is not a time to dwell on such things."

The two walked silently back to the governor's palace and made their way to their rooms. "It will be good to see Askelon again," said Quentin as they parted. "And all our friends. Good night."

"Good night. I will wake you in the morning."

For a long time Quentin lay on his bed and did not close his eyes. He heard Toli quietly packing their things in the next room, and the Jher's soft footfall as he left to see to the horses before he, too, slept. At last he rolled over on his side and fell at once to sleep as the moon shone brightly through his balcony doors, peering in like a kindly face.

CHAPTER 2

Quentin met Toli in the stables—the grouping of low stone structures Toli had turned to the purpose of breeding horses. In his time at Dekra, the Jher had become an excellent trainer and breeder of fine horses. In fact, with the help of Eskevar's stablemaster, he was developing a remarkable strain of animals that were a cross between the heavier warhorses, such as Balder, and the lighter, more fleet racing stock that were the pride of Pelagia. The resulting breed would possess strength and stamina enough for battle, but would also have the ability to run fast and far without tiring.

Quentin passed under the stone arch and came to stand before Balder's stall. The old warhorse whinnied softly when he saw his master approaching. Quentin held out his hand and patted the horse's soft muzzle and stroked the bulging jaw.

"You may stay here this time, old boy. Take care of him, Wilton," he called over his shoulder to the youngster who helped Toli. "Give him an extra carrot now and then." Then, patting the horse's white-starred forehead, he said, "We will go for a long ride when I come back."

The stable smelled of sweet fennel and straw and the warm bodies of the horses. The smell reminded Quentin of traveling, and he reflected that he was indeed anxious to be off. He crossed to where Toli stood checking their mounts' tack and gear.

"Good morning, Kenta. I was just about to come and wake you."

"As you see, I am ready to go; I did not sleep much of the night. Is all prepared?" He turned to slap a milk-white stallion on the shoulder. "Ho, there, Blazer! Are you anxious to stretch those long legs of yours?" The horse tossed its flowing mane and rolled a blue-black eye at Quentin as if to say, "Why are we waiting?"

"I have only to charge Wilton with some final instructions," remarked Toli. "Then we will go."

Toli returned and took the reins of both horses and led them out into the quiet streets. Quentin followed at Toli's right hand and listened to the clop of the horses' hooves upon the cobbled stones of the ancient streets. In the east the sky shone with a violet haze that lightened into a golden-red hue as the sun rose higher.

Toli sniffed the air and announced, "The wind is from the west over the sea. We will have good weather for our journey."

"Good. I am hoping to be in Askelon before the new moon. We should be able to manage that, aye?"

"It is possible. With good horses and the king's road restored through Pelgrin . . ."

"We have horses with wings, my friend. And Eskevar's road is now complete as far as the Arvin. We shall fly indeed."

They reached the gates of the city and let themselves out. The gates were seldom tended, since Dekra had no fear of intrusion and no real need for defense.

At the small door that opened within the larger, Quentin paused and took a long last look upon the city he loved. The red stone glowed with the rosy hue of the rising sun. Towers and spires swept majestically into the clear, cool morning air, gleaming and glittering like radiant crystal.

The ordinary sounds of the city waking to life echoed out into the empty streets; a dog barked; a door opened and closed. Behind him Blazer and Riv, Toli's sleek black mount, shook their bridles, impatient to be moving along. Quentin raised an arm in farewell to Dekra and then turned to his horse.

"It is time for speed," he called as he swung himself up into the saddle. "On, Blazer!" The horse lifted his forelegs off the ground, gave a little kick, and leaped ahead to the trail.

Quentin pushed an eager course through the low hills and into the wretched marshlands. They planned to hold north as far as Malmarby, thus skirting the boggy wasteland as much as possible. At Malmarby they would hire a boat to cross the inlet and swing along the shore west past Celbercor's Wall. Then the trail would become easier. They would make for the Arvin River where it came spilling clear and cold out of the Fiskills, ride through the wide foothills above Narramoor along the king's new road, and speed along through Pelgrin to Askelon.

The days on the trail were uneventful. Game was plentiful, and thanks to Toli's skill as a hunter, they never lacked for anything the hills could provide.

They arrived at Malmarby village one bright morning, picking the wider path toward the town out of the maze of bogs and wetlands that surrounded it.

As they approached the village, Toli stiffened in the saddle and reined his horse to a halt. Quentin mirrored his actions, wondering what had alarmed his friend.

"What is it? What do you see?"

"Something is amiss in the village yonder; I feel it."

"It looks peaceful enough. But let us go with caution."

They paced the horses slowly ahead, and both watched the thickets and dense shrubbery that lined the path for any signal that might confirm Toli's apprehension.

They saw no one and heard nothing until just before reaching the village itself. Quentin stopped his horse and stood in the saddle, looking around. The muddy track that served as Malmarby's main street was vacant. No living thing stirred among the rough wooden houses; no sound issued from doorway or window.

"There does not appear to be anyone around. I wonder where—"

He had not finished speaking when four men sprang out of the nearest thicket and grabbed the horses' bridles. Two of the men were armed with spears and the others with short swords. All appeared very frightened, their faces grim with worry and pale from fear.

It was the look upon these sorry faces that made Quentin hold his hand. "Stay, Toli! We need not fear these men, I think." Quentin spoke loudly and calmly so that their would-be attackers would know that they intended no harm.

There was a rustle in the thicket, and another man stepped out, or rather fell, into the road. Quentin recognized the thin, careworn face of the village counselor.

"Good morning, Counselor. Is this the way you treat strangers nowadays? Or perhaps you wished to invite us to breakfast."

The thin, bald man blinked and rushed forward, squinting at the travelers with his one good eye.

"Quentin? Step back, men. It is the prince! Let them go!" Quentin smiled at the appellation. He was not the prince, but his legend had so grown among the simple people of Mensandor that he held that lofty position in their esteem. So they conferred upon him the highest title they could presume; to them he was, quite simply, the prince.

"Yes, it is Quentin. But tell me, Milan, why this rude reception? And where are your townspeople? The village looks deserted."

"I'm sorry, good sir. We meant you no harm." The village chief looked heartbroken. He wrung his hands over each other as he spoke, as if he feared some fierce retribution. "It's just that . . . well, we cannot be too careful these days; there have been stories of evil deeds—we thought it best to post a watch on the road."

"Robbers?" Quentin asked.

Milan ignored the question and asked one of his own. "You your-self have seen nothing?"

"No, nothing."

Quentin shrugged and looked at Toli. Toli studied the faces of the men before them and remained silent.

"Well, perhaps our fears are unfounded. Will you stay with us?"

"No, not this time. If we may have the use of one of your excellent boats, we will put off directly. We are going to Askelon as quickly as we can."

The town counselor fixed Quentin with a strange, knowing look and turned away. "Go on ahead and tell the town. The way is clear; there is nothing to fear," he called to one of his men. Then to Quentin he added, "The boat is yours. You may take mine; it is the largest by far; my son will go with you."

"We are grateful for your kindness," said Quentin as they moved off together.

They passed the simple dwellings that crowded one another all along the path right down to the water's edge. Quentin saw an occasional fleeting face at a window or peering from a doorway, but by the time they reached the great wooden pier that served as a wharf for the town's fish-ing boats, most of Malmarby's citizens were going about their business as though nothing unusual had happened. Many followed them down to the pier, and many more hailed the regal travelers as they passed.

The boats of Malmarby were broad, boxy things—sturdy enough to withstand the anger of the harshest seas, which they never faced, since the bulky boats served but to ply the sheltered inlet from one end to the other along its length.

Milan's boat was more than adequate for their need, though the horses showed some trepidation at being led aboard such a strange-looking vessel.

With Milan's son, Rol, at the long stern oar, they waved themselves away from the throng on the pier. Rol's strong hands worked the oar, and soon they had entered a deeper channel, where a swift current pulled them along. They raised the small sail on its stubby mast and drifted smartly away.

"Where do you wish to land, my lords?" called Rol from his seat at the tiller.

"Anywhere you think best, as long as it is west of the Wall." Quentin paused and regarded the hardy youth, who had strong shoulders and a thick thatch of brown hair. He remembered when the good-natured young man had been a skinny little boy who ran alongside the horses whenever a traveler passed through the village—such as Quentin and Toli had often had occasion to do.

"What is it the village fears?" asked Quentin, stepping close to Rol. "What has come to pass since we have last come this way?"

The young man shrugged a muscled shoulder and continued working the oar. "I do not know. Stories, that is all. It does not take much to frighten such a small village."

"What are these stories you speak of? Why have they frightened everyone so badly?"

Toli stepped in to hear what Rol had to say.

"This spring some people came to us out of the Suthlands, saying they had been set upon by demons and their homes burned."

"Demons do not burn homes," remarked Toli.

Again the tentative shrug. "I do not know if they do or not; that is what the people said."

"Hmmmm . . . that is strange. Did they say what these demons looked like?"

"They are giants. Fierce. Fire spewed from their mouths, and each one had ten arms with claws for hands."

"Where did these demons come from? Did they say?"

"No one knew. Some said they came from beyond the sea. From beyond Gerfallon. Others said they saw the sign of the Wolf Star on their foreheads. Maybe they came down from the sky."

"This is an odd tale," said Quentin to Toli as they drew aside.

"Why would anyone burn a village of peasants in the Suthlands?" Toli asked. "There is little enough there, and nothing to be gained by such doings."

"I cannot guess. The realm is at peace these past ten years. We will tell the king about this; they may have heard something in Askelon."

Rol proved an able seaman, and the day's end found them close to their destination. A faint mist gathered on the water at the shoreline and pushed out into the inlet. Through the gray mist they saw the dark plane of the Great Wall jutting out into the deep water as the shadows lengthened upon the land.

Rol steered the boat around the Wall's looming edge and made for the rocky strand. No one spoke as they passed by the imposing shape. The steady slap and dip of Rol's long oar was the only sound that broke the stillness of the water.

Quentin watched the mist curling around the base of the Wall and thought it made the Wall appear to be floating on a foundation of billowing clouds, while the deepening sky above seemed to grow hard and solid as stone as it darkened with the twilight. He started when he heard a hollow knock and felt the slight jolt that told him they had touched shore.

"Will you stay with us tonight, Rol? We will camp a little way along the trail, up there." Quentin pointed to a tree-lined rise that bordered the shore. "Toli will have a fire going in no time, and we will have some hot food."

"Thank you, my lord. I am tired—and hungry, too. I cannot say which I am the more."

"Well, you have done us a great service, and it shall be rewarded. Here,"—Quentin reached into the soft leather pouch that hung at his belt—"a gold ducat for your trouble, and one for your kindness."

Rol bowed low as he thrust out his callused hand. "Sir, it is too much. I cannot accept so much." He fingered the gold coins and handed them back to Quentin.

"No, you have earned them both, and our praise besides. Keep them and say no more about it. But, look! Toli is already making camp. Let us hurry and join him, or we may be too late for our supper."

The three reclined around the fire and talked as the stars came out in the immense black vault of the heavens. Below them on the strand, the water lapped gently against the smooth, round rocks, and above them, in the trees, a nightbird called to its mate. Tall pines stood over them, and the air smelled of fresh wind and balsam.

Quentin drifted easily to sleep, nodding in his place, until he at last bade his companions good night and rolled himself in his cloak. Toli added another log to the fire and got up to check the horses before he himself turned in. Rol already slept soundly, judging from the slow, even rhythm of his breathing.

Toli stretched and lifted his eyes to the night sky, now sparkling with tiny lights. As he scanned the heavens, his eye caught a curious sight. He stood for a moment, contemplating what he saw, and then he turned and crept softly toward Quentin.

"Kenta . . ." He nudged his sleeping friend gently. "Kenta, I want you to see something."

Quentin turned and sat up. He peered intently into Toli's face, lit on one side by the firelight. He could not read the expression there.

"What is it? Have you at last seen the White Stag?"

"No, nothing so important." Toli dismissed the jest. "I thought you might want to see this." He led Quentin a short space away from the fire and the overhanging boughs of the trees.

"Look to the east . . . there just above the Wall. Do you see it?"

"A star? Yes, I see it—that very bright star."

"See how it shines. Do you think it odd?"

"It is the Wolf Star. But you are right; it does have a different look tonight. What do you make of it?"

Toli gazed upward at the brilliant star and at last turned away, saying, "I do not know what to make of it. I only wanted you to see it, so that we may be agreed about it."

Quentin was not satisfied with this answer. Toli, who was evidently withholding something, declined to speak further. There was no use in pushing the matter further until the Jher was ready to say more. Whatever was tumbling around in that head, thought Quentin, would come out sooner or later, but only when Toli desired it so. He would wait. Quentin sighed and rolled himself once more in his cloak and fell to sleep.

CHAPTER 3

From the sound of the gurgling crash that filled the rock-rimmed canyon, the Arvin's first cataract lay just ahead. Blazer and Riv picked their way among the loose stones on the canyon floor as Quentin and Toli scanned the soaring cliffs above. All around them towered jagged spires of rock. They moved carefully, as through a giant's petrified forest.

They passed between two large outcroppings of dull brown stone upon which rested a great slab forming the posts and lintel of an enormous doorway. "Azrael's Gate," muttered Quentin as they passed quickly through, and then, brightening considerably, "Look! Eskevar's road." He pointed across the Arvin's racing headwaters to the other side, where the road began.

Without hesitation Quentin urged his steed forward into the frigid water. The swift stream splashed around the horse's legs and wet his rider to the knees. Quentin found the icy tingle the perfect tonic to banish the oppressive foreboding that had settled upon him—as it always did—when he rode through the eerie canyon that ended in Azrael's Gate. Now, with that behind and the clear, wide road ahead, his spirits suddenly lifted.

"It won't be long now," he called over his shoulder to Toli, just then splashing into the course. "Tomorrow night we will dine with Durwin, and the following will see us at the Dragon King's table."

"I thought you were the one for haste," replied Toli. "We can do better than that!" At these words he slapped Riv over the shoulders with the reins and leaned into the saddle. The horse spurted ahead, sending torrents of icy water up into the air as he surged past Quentin and clattered up out of the stream and struck for the road.

"A challenge!" shouted Quentin at Toli's retreating figure. He snapped Blazer's reins as they clambered out of the water and dashed after Toli in chase.

High in the lonely foothills, the sound of their race echoed and reechoed from one blank stone face to another. Their jubilant cries sang through the rills and crevices, and rang in rock hollows and caves. The horses' hooves struck sparks from the stone paving as they flew.

At last, exhausted and out of breath, the two trotted to a halt upon a ridge. Below them the foothills dropped away in gentle arcs, fading from violet to blue in the hazy distance. Away to the south stood the lofty, snow-wrapped crags of the Fiskills, where endless winds howled among the sharp peaks.

"Ah!" sighed Quentin as he drew a deep breath. "Such a sight! It is a beautiful land, is it not?"

"It is that and more indeed. My people have a word for the land— I do not think I have ever told you: Allallira."

"No, I have never heard it. What does it mean?"

"I cannot be precise—there is no exact meaning in your tongue. But it means something like 'the land of flowing peace.'"

"Allallira, I like that; it fits." They started down together. "And it certainly is peaceful. Look out across those valleys. These years have been good ones. The land has produced full measure. The people are content. I cannot think but that the god has blessed the realm in recompense for the troubled times when Eskevar was away from his throne."

"Yes, these have been good years. Golden times. I hope we will see them endure."

Quentin cast a sideways glance at his companion. Toli's eyes were focused on some distant horizon. He appeared as if in a trance. Quentin did not want to break the happy mood, so did not pursue the matter further. They continued down the slope without speaking.

The next day dawned fair and bright, warmed by soft winds from the west. The travelers were already well on their way when the sun popped over Erlemros, the Fiskills' highest peak. The road made the going easy, and they pushed at a steady pace, reaching the lowlands by midday.

They ate a hasty meal among moss-covered stones in the shade of an ancient oak and started again on their way; they had not traveled far when Toli said, "Along the road, yonder. We have some company."

Quentin raised his eyes and saw very faintly, and very far away, what appeared to be a group of travelers coming toward them on foot. There was just a glimpse, and then a bend in the road took them from Quentin's sight.

"Merchants, perhaps?" Quentin wondered aloud. Often traders who sold their wares from town to town banded together in traveling companies for mutual entertainment and protection. "I would like to buy a trinket for Bria."

They continued on, and Quentin thought of all the things his love would enjoy. They rounded the side of a grassy hill covered with scarlet wildflowers and approached the spot where they had first seen the travelers.

"Odd," said Quentin. "We should have met them by now. Perhaps they stopped up the road beyond that clump of trees." He pointed ahead to where a bushy stand of trees overhung the road, sheltering all beyond from view.

They continued on with a growing perplexity.

When they reached the shelter of the trees, they could look once again far down the road; there was not a single person to be seen.

"This becomes stranger every step," said Quentin.

Toli swung himself down from his horse and walked along the road, his eyes searching the dust for any signs that might explain the disappearance of the group they had both seen quite clearly only a short while before.

They moved forward slowly. Quentin watched the wooded area to the right of the road. Then Toli stopped and knelt down. He traced his finger around the outline of footprints in the dust.

"They stopped here before leaving the road . . . there." He pointed into the trees.

"How many were there?"

"I cannot say from these signs. But there were men and women, children too."

"Most peculiar," mused Quentin. "What sent them scurrying into the woods? Not the sight of two horsemen, surely."

Toli shrugged and climbed back into the saddle. "Here is something else we must remember to tell the king."

"Indeed we will."

At dusk they camped in a grassy glade just off the road. The sun sent ruby fingers sifting through the gossamer clouds that moved gracefully across the violet arc of heaven. Quentin stood in a meadow dotted with yellow flowers that brushed pollen-laden heads against his legs. With his arms crossed on his chest and a look of dreamy concentration, he contemplated the imposing shape before him: high up on its plateau, the thin trail leading up like a white wisp rising from the lower ground, stood the High Temple of Ariel.

"You miss your old home, no doubt," said Toli, coming up behind him.

"No . . . ," said Quentin absently, then laughed as he stirred and turned away. "No more than one misses a toothache. I was only thinking of the time when I lived in the temple. For me they were days of loneliness and frustration—endless studying, chores, and inscrutable rules. So many rules, Toli. I would never have made a good priest; I could never see the sense of anointing the sacred rock. It always seemed such a waste of time, not to mention expensive oil.

"And the sacrifices—the gold bracelets, silver bowls, and carefully groomed animals—simply made the priests wealthier and fatter than they already were."

"Whist Orren demands more than bracelets, bowls, or flesh. And he lives not only in temples made by men, but in their lives."

"Yes, the God Most High holds out freedom to men; the price is unbending devotion. The lesser gods do not demand as much, but who can know them? They are like the mists on the water—when the sun touches them, they vanish."

They turned and went back to settle themselves for the night. They ate, and Toli turned the horses out to graze in the sweet grass as evening gathered its long purple robes about the quiet glade.

Quentin lay with his head resting upon his saddle with a clear, unhindered view of the spangled heavens. *The stars never change,* he observed. And then, even as he framed the thought, he remembered the conversation he had had earlier with Toli. He turned his head toward the east and saw the strangely glittering star Toli had pointed out to him several nights before.

"The Wolf Star seems to grow brighter," observed Quentin.

"I have been thinking the same thing, Kenta."

"I wonder what High Priest Biorkis would say to an omen such as this. The priests surely have their explanations."

"Go and ask him."

"What? Do you think I dare?"

"Why not? There is no harm."

"I do not believe my ears! Toli tells me to seek an omen from an unholy source! You, Toli, of all people, know I have turned away from tokens and omens. I follow a different god—we both do."

"I do not suggest you ask an omen of Ariel, or discard the truths you have learned. Only that you go to your onetime friend and ask his opinion of a strange event. There is no harm in that. Besides, Whist Orren, who holds the stars in their courses, sometimes declares his will through such portents. Any who will look may see what is written there."

"You are right, Toli. Biorkis is still my friend. Besides, I would like to take a walk. Come along." Quentin was on his feet and striding off across the meadow toward the temple trail, which showed in the bright moonlight as a silver thread winding its way up the side of the steep hill.

They reached the trail and began the circuitous ascent to the top. As they climbed higher, Quentin looked out into the moon-bright night. The valley glimmered darkly; every leaf of tree and blade of grass was traced in spun silver. Away in the distant hills, shepherds' fires winked like stars fallen upon the land.

They gained the top at last and entered the expansive courtyard. In the center of the white, stone-paved yard stood a torch on a carven stone stanchion. Its fluttering flame cast a wide circle of light around its base and reflected on the closed doors of the temple.

"We will see if pilgrims such as we are made welcome by night," whispered Quentin.

They crossed the courtyard and climbed the many steps to the main entrance. Upon reaching the huge doors, Quentin lifted his poniard from its sheath at his belt and rapped upon the solid beams with its handle.

He waited, knowing at this late hour he must rouse some nearby priest from his sleep. As he waited, an uncanny sensation came over Quentin—a feeling that he was once more the skinny temple acolyte of many years ago. For a moment he looked at the dark stone of the temple and the moonlight-filled courtyard through the eyes of his youth.

He knocked again and immediately heard the shuffle of someone on the other side.

"Be on your way, pilgrim. Come back tomorrow. The priests are asleep," came the muffled voice from the other side.

"Yet there is one who will admit us if you take our names to him."

"There is no one who would admit you but the high priest himself."

"Excellent! He is the very man we seek!"

"No, go away! Come back tomorrow; I'll not disturb him tonight."

They heard the footsteps shuffling away again on the other side of the door.

"Well, he means to do us no favors," said Quentin. "But there is another entrance at the rear of the temple. We will try that, since we have come this far."

The two moved like shadows under the high portico of the temple and reached the far south side, that which overlooked the peaceful valley. They walked along the side of the temple, the moonlight falling in slanting rays, forming bands of light and shadow under the mighty eaves.

"Listen," said Toli. "Voices."

Quentin paused and cocked his head to one side. Voices from a little way ahead and below them carried on the still air. The sound was but a dull murmur, barely recognizable.

They continued more cautiously, and the voices grew louder. Soon the travelers were crouching behind the immense columns of the temple, looking down upon a small circle of robed men bent over a shining object.

"They are star searching," remarked Quentin excitedly. "And look— that one in the center. I think I know that shape."

Quentin stepped boldly out of the shadow of the column and descended a few steps toward the group. He took a deep breath and said in a loud voice, "Priests of Ariel, will you receive two curious pilgrims?"

The startled priests turned around quickly and beheld the figures of two young men descending toward them.

The priest in the center of the huddle stepped forward and replied, "Pilgrims are always welcome to the shrine of Ariel, though most choose to make oblations in the light of day."

"We do not come to make oblations, or to inquire of the god Ariel, but of a priest instead."

"Priests are but the servants of their god; it is he who declares his will."

"Neither do we ask for the god's interest in any affairs of ours," said Quentin, approaching the priest. He could see the man's face full in the moonlight now and knew that he addressed his old tutor. "We would speak to you man-to-man."

Quentin smiled as a faint glimmer of recognition lit the priest's visage.

"My heart tells me that I should know you, sir," said the high priest slowly. The old eyes searched the young man's features for a clue that might tell him who it was that addressed him. "But a name does not come to my lips. Have we met, then?"

Quentin moved closer and placed his hands on the priest's rounded shoulders. "Is the life of a priest so busy that he has no time for memories?"

"Memories do not walk the temple yards by night, nor do they confront their bearers face-to-face."

"Then perhaps you will remember this." Quentin dug into his pouch at his belt and produced a silver coin. He handed it to the priest.

"This is a temple coin. Then you must be . . ."

"You gave me that coin yourself, Biorkis, many years ago."

"Quentin? Is this Quentin the acolyte?" the old man sputtered.

"Yes, I have returned to see you, my old friend—for so I always considered you."

"But how you have changed. You have grown up a fine man. You are well—as I can see. What brings you here tonight of all nights?"

The other priests looked upon this reunion in wonder. They gathered close around to see who this returned stranger might be.

"Can we walk a little aside?" asked Quentin. "I have something to ask you."

The two moved off, followed closely by Toli. The priests fell to murmuring their amazement and talking among themselves.

"Your name has grown in the land," said Biorkis as they walked to a rocky outcropping at the edge of the plateau.

"Oh? You hear the tales up here, do you?"

"We hear what we wish to hear. The peasants bring us no end of information. Some of it useful. But you are known as the prince who saved the Dragon King and defeated the monstrous sorcerer, Nimrood."

"It was not I who defeated Nimrood, but my friend Toli here."

Biorkis bowed to Toli and indicated that they should all seat themselves upon the rocks. "They also say that you are building a city in the Wilderlands which rises by magic from the stones of the earth."

"Again, that is not my doing. Dekra is my city only in that the gracious Curatak have allowed me to join in their work of restoring it to its former glory."

"This is what the people say, not I. As for myself, I surmise that the truth of the stories is to be found at the heart—like the stone of an apricot. But I know from this that my former acolyte is doing well and has risen in the esteem of his countrymen. But why should you seek me out now? The temple doors have not been closed these many years."

"We come to ask your opinion of something we have seen." Quentin turned toward the east and pointed out across the quiet, moon-filled valley. "That star rising yonder. The Wolf Star. Has it not changed in some way of late? Do the priests detect a waxing of its power?"

"So you have not forsaken your studies altogether. You still seek signs in the night sky."

"No, I must admit that I no longer study the stars in their courses. This event was pointed out to me by Toli, who remarked on it a few nights ago."

"Well, your Toli is right. In fact, we have been following this star with interest for many months. Tonight, as you have seen, we were once more examining the charts and seeking an answer to this wonder."

"Then you do not know what this sign portends?"

"Does one ever?" Biorkis laughed. "Why do you look so shocked? A priest may have doubts—even a high priest. Ah, but we have our theories. Yes, many theories."

"That is what we have come to hear—your theories. What do you think it means?"

CHAPTER 4

Durwin's long brown robes swept along behind him as he rushed through the darkened corridors of Askelon Castle. Torches lit the way, sputtering in the gusty air as Durwin hurriedly passed. Ahead of him he could see a pair of doors that opened onto a patch of the night sky infused with the moon's radiant beams.

He stepped across the threshold and onto the balcony, then paused. There, a few paces from him, stood the slim figure of a woman; her dark hair tumbled down in shimmering ringlets and curls, and her face was averted, revealing the shapely curve of her slender neck. She was dressed in a loose-fitting gown of white held at her trim waist by a long blue sash that trailed nearly to the ground.

"Your Majesty," said Durwin, softly announcing himself. "I am here."

The woman turned and smiled.

"Good Durwin, thank you for coming so quickly."

"Bria . . . I thought . . ."

"You thought I was the queen, I know. But it was I who sent you the summons."

"You look so much like your mother standing there. With the moonlight in your hair, I thought you were Alinea."

"I will accept that as a compliment, Durwin. For me there is none higher. But you must be tired from your journey. I will not keep you, but I must speak to you a little. Do sit down, please."

She raised an arm and indicated a stone bench a short space away. Durwin took her arm and walked her along the balcony. "The night is beautiful, is it not?" he said.

"Yes, it is—very." The young woman spoke as if she had just become aware that it was night. The hermit could tell she had something on her mind that disturbed her.

"I would not have troubled you, but I could think of no better help than to have you here. Theido is gone, and Ronsard with him."

"It is nothing, my lady. I am only too glad to know that this old hermit may still be of some use to those who dwell in Castle Askelon. I would have come sooner if I had known—your courier had quite a time finding me. I was in the forest, gathering herbs and tending to the illness of a peasant's wife nearby."

"I knew you would come as soon as you could. I—" The princess broke off, unable to say what she felt in her heart.

Durwin waited, and then said, "What is the matter, Bria? You may speak freely. I am your friend."

"Oh, Durwin!" Her hands trembled, and her head sank. She buried her face in her hands, and he thought she would cry. But she drew a deep breath and raised her face to the moon, clear-eyed. In that moment the young woman reminded him more than ever of another woman who bore an immense inner strength in times of great distress—Queen Alinea.

"It is the king," Bria said at last. "Oh, Durwin, I am very worried. He is not like himself. I think he is very ill, but he will see none of his doctors. He laughs at any suggestion I make regarding his health. My mother is worried too. But she can do nothing either. And there is something else."

Durwin waited patiently.

"I do not know what it is—trouble, I think. Somewhere." She turned and fixed the hermit with a smile that, though it graced her mouth, did not light her eyes as it normally would. "Quentin is coming."

"I have not forgotten. We are all going to celebrate Midsummer's Day together."

"No—he is coming now. Eskevar sent for him. Even knowing that he would come for Midsummer, the king sent a special courier to bring him. That is how I know something is wrong."

"It could just be that he wishes to see him sooner—just a whim, that's all."

Bria smiled again. "Thank you for that, but you know the Dragon King as well as I do. He does nothing on a whim. He has some reason for wanting him here, but what it is I cannot guess."

"Then we will wait and see. When will Quentin be here?"

"If he left upon receiving the summons, I believe he will be here the day after tomorrow—the day after that at the latest."

"Good. That is not so long to wait—you will see. In the meantime I will try to discover what ails the king—in body or in spirit. Anything that may be done, I will do. Worry no more on it, my lady."

"Thank you, Durwin. You will not tell them that I sent for you?"

"No, if you would rather not. I will just say that I grew weary of my books and medicines and desired the warmth of fellowship with my friends. I came early to the celebration, that is all."

"I feel better already knowing you are here."

"I am content. Though I imagine you would rather a certain young man stood here right now."

Bria smiled, and this time the light sparkled in her deep green eyes. "Oh, I'll not deny it. But I am content to wait. It does cheer me some-what to know that he comes sooner."

They talked some more and then rose; Bria bade Durwin a good night. Durwin escorted her to the door back into the castle and then turned to stroll along the balcony alone.

He leaned his arms on the parapet and looked into the gardens below. In the moonlight he saw a solitary figure pacing among the beds of ruby roses, now indigo in the moonlight.

He could not see who this person might be, but it was clear from the altered gait that the walker had fallen prey to a melancholy mood. He hunched forward and crossed his arms on his chest, stopped and started continually.

Durwin looked on, and then the figure seemed to sense that he was being watched. He stopped and drew himself up and turned to look quickly into the balcony. Durwin drew away, but he had seen what he had already guessed. In the moment the face swung around, the moonlight illumined it, and Durwin knew that it was Eskevar, the Dragon King.

Biorkis's long, white-braided beard—the symbol of his office—glowed like a bright waterfall frozen in the moonlight. His wrinkled face, though still as round and plump as ever, looked itself like a smaller moon returning its reflected light to a larger parent. He gazed long into the sky and then said, "It may be something, or it may not. The heavens are filled with signs and wonders, and not all of them have to do with men."

"If you thought that, would you be standing out in the night, star-gazing?"

"No, likely not. But this is a most peculiar phenomenon—one does not see such a sign but once in a lifetime, perhaps not even then. To chart its progress would be of value aside from any meaning we might derive from its study."

"You evade my question, Biorkis. Why? Certainly the star is there for all to see and make of it what they will."

An expression of great weariness appeared on the face of the high priest as he turned to regard Quentin. "To the best of my knowledge, this star is an evil sign."

He had spoken simply and softly. But the words chilled Quentin to the bone; he shivered as if the night had suddenly grown colder.

Quentin sought to lighten the remark. "Omens are always either good or bad, depending on the reader."

"Ah, but the greater the sign, the greater the consequence. And this is a great sign indeed. Surpassingly great."

Quentin raised his eyes to the eastern sky and regarded the star carefully. It was bright, yes, but there were other stars nearly as bright. He looked back at Biorkis with a questioning glance.

"It has only begun to show itself," said the high priest in answer to the look. "With every passing night it grows brighter, and so does the evil it portends."

"What is the nature of this evil? Can you tell?"

"Evil is evil; you know that. What does it matter? The suffering will be great in any case. Flood, famine, pestilence, war—all are the same; all destroy in their turn."

"Well said. Your words are true, but men can do much to prepare against an evil time, if they know its source."

"Here is where our theories guide us. Some say that the star will grow and grow until it fills the sky, blotting out the sun and moon and stars. Then it will touch the earth and drive all living things insane before consuming them with fire.

"Others say that each nation has a star and that this Wolf Star represents a fierce and brutal nation that rises against other nations and seeks to extinguish them with its power.

"Still others regard this as the beginning of the end of mankind on earth. This star is the token of Nin, the destroyer god who brings his armies down to make war on the nations of the earth."

"And you, Biorkis, what do you say?"

"I believe all are right. Some part of every guess will be shown in truth."

"When may the truth be evident?"

"Who can say? Much that is foretold does not come to pass. Our best divinations are only the mumblings of blind men." Biorkis turned his face away. "Nothing is certain," he said softly. "Nothing is certain."

Quentin stood, went to the old priest, and placed a hand on his shoulder. "Old man, come with us. You have lived long enough to see the gods for what they are. Let us show you a god worthy of your devotion. The Most High, Lord of All. In him you will find the peace you seek. You told me once that you sought a brighter light."

Biorkis looked at him wearily. "You remember that?"

"Yes, and more. I remember you were my only friend in the temple. Come with us now and let us show you the light you have been seeking for so long."

Biorkis sighed, and it seemed as if all the earth groaned with a great exhaustion. "I am old—too old to change. Yes, these eyes have searched for the truth, but it has been denied them. I know the hollowness of serving these petty gods, but I am high priest. I cannot go with you now. Maybe once I could have turned away as Durwin did, as you have—but not now. It is too late for me."

Quentin looked sadly down on his old friend. "I am sorry."

Toli had risen and was moving away. Quentin turned and looked back at Biorkis, who still remained perched upon a rock, looking out into the peaceful valley. "It is not too late. You have only to turn aside and he will meet you. The decision is yours."

Quentin and Toli walked down the sinuous trail side by side without speaking. When they reached the meadow and the dimly glowing embers of their fire, Quentin said, "You knew the star to be an evil sign, didn't you?"

"Yes, I considered it so."

"But you suggested we go to the temple. Why?"

"I wanted to hear what other learned men might say. For all their spiritual uncertainties, the priests are still men of great knowledge."

"And did Biorkis confirm your worst fears?"

"Biorkis spoke of what might be, not what will be. Only the God Most High can say what will be. His hand is ever outstretched to those who serve him."

"Well, if Biorkis is right in his speculations, then we will have need of that strong hand before long, I fear."

CHAPTER 5

The earth moves through stages, epochs. The ancient legends tell of previous earth ages—four at least. We are living in the fifth age of man. Each age runs its allotted course and then gives birth to a new age." Durwin spread his hands out on the table. Quentin, his chin in his hands, stared at the holy hermit in rapt attention. Around them in Durwin's chambers, candles flickered and filled the room with a hazy yellow glow.

"These ages may run a thousand years or ten thousand. Of course, there is no way to tell how long it will last, but the ancients believed that before the end of each age, the world is thrown into turmoil. Great migrations of people commence; great wars are fought as nation rises against nation; the heavens are filled with signs and wonders. Then comes the deluge: all the earth is flooded, or covered with ice. Then fire burns the earth and erases all the signs of the preceding age. It is a time of chaos and darkness, great cataclysms and death. But out of it comes a new age, both finer and higher than the one before."

As Durwin spoke, an eerie sense of dreadful fascination crept over Quentin. He shrugged it off and asked, "But must the earth be destroyed completely for a new age to be born?"

Durwin mused on this question, but before he could open his mouth to speak, Toli answered. "Among my people there are many stories of the time before this one. It is said that the Jher came into being in the third age, when the world was still very young and men talked with the animals and lived in peace with one another.

"These stories are very old; they have been with us longer than the art of our oldest storytellers. But it is said that the destruction of the world may be averted by some great deed—though what it is that may be done is not known.

"Tigal, the Star Maker's son, is said to have saved the world in the second age by hitching his horses to his father's chariot and carrying off Morhesh, the Great Evil One, after wounding him with a spear made of a single shaft of light. He threw Morhesh into the Pit of the Night, and Morhesh's star was extinguished so the earth did not burn."

Durwin nodded readily. "So it is! As I was about to say, it is believed that not every age must end in calamity. The destruction may be lessened or turned aside completely—usually by some act of heroism, some supreme sacrifice or the coming of a mighty leader to lead mankind into the new age."

"Do you believe this?" Quentin asked.

"I believe in the truth of what has been handed down to us. Those who witnessed it explained it as well as they could with the words and ideas they had available to them. Certainly, much remains unexplained; but it seems strange that each race has somewhere in its past memories of this sort."

Quentin leaned forward and placed his elbows on the table and clasped his hands. "I meant, do you believe that the star in the sky betokens the end of the age?"

Durwin pulled on his chin and scratched his jaw. He looked at Quentin with quick black eyes and smiled suddenly. "I believe a new age is coming, yes, such as the world has never known. A time of mighty upheaval and change. And I believe change does not take place without struggle, without pain. So it is!"

"It all seems very grim to me," admitted Quentin.

"You should not think of the pain involved," responded Toli. "Think of the greater glory of the new age."

Toli and Quentin had ridden from Narramoor to Durwin's cottage in Pelgrin Forest. They had made good time and arrived late in the afternoon, just as the sun slipped into the treetops.

"Durwin is not here," Toli had said as they approached the cottage. They looked around before Quentin went inside. He returned without a clue to where the hermit might be.

"He may be away only for a short while, perhaps tending someone nearby. Maybe he will return by nightfall, but I think not. His cloak is gone and his pouch, though his bag of medicines is inside."

They had then decided to ride through the night, and reached Askelon's mighty gates as the moon set in the west. Not wishing to disturb the servants or awaken the king and queen, they went instead to the chambers kept for Durwin when he was in residence at the castle. There, to their surprise and pleasure, they found the hermit slumped in his chair with a scroll rolled up in his lap. He was sound asleep and snoring.

Upon their entrance, despite their attempts to be quiet, Durwin woke up and greeted them warmly. "You have ridden all night! You are hungry; I will fetch you some food from the kitchen."

He hurried away with a candle in his hand while Quentin and Toli pulled off their cloaks, dipped their hands in the basin, and attempted to wash away their fatigue. They then settled themselves, exhausted, into the chairs and dozed until Durwin returned with bread and cheese and fruit he had filched from the pantry.

"Here, sit at this table and eat while I tell you what I have been doing since we were last together." Durwin told them of his studies and his healing work among the peasants, and at last Quentin told him about their audience with Biorkis and their discussion about the star that nightly grew brighter.

They had talked long and late. At last they rose from the table and turned to curl themselves in their chairs to sleep. Just then a barely audible knock sounded on Durwin's door. Quentin said, "Durwin, you have a visitor, I believe. Do you entertain so late at night?"

"I, as you well know, did not expect a single person in my chambers tonight, and I find not one, but two. So now I entertain any possibility! Open the door and let them in, please."

Quentin stepped to the door and opened it. He was not prepared for the greeting he received.

"Quentin, my love. You are here!"

Quentin instantly threw his arms wide, swept up a young woman in a long, white woolen robe, and buried his face in her hair.

"Bria! I did not know how much I missed you until this moment."

The two lovers clung in a long embrace, breaking off suddenly when they remembered that they were not alone. Quentin gently set his lady back upon her slippered feet. Durwin and Toli smiled as they looked on.

"And what, I might well ask, brings you to this hermit's chambers so late at night?" Quentin demanded, taking her hand and pulling her into the room.

"Why, I was passing by and fancied I heard voices. I fancied one of them was yours, my love."

"Ah! Your lips utter the answer my ears long to hear. But come, I have much to tell you. Much has happened since I was with you last."

"Not here you don't!" replied Durwin. "In a very short time this chamber will ring with snores of sleeping! You two doves must take your cooing elsewhere." He beamed happily as he shooed them out the door.

Quentin and Bria walked hand in hand along the darkened passageway and out onto the same balcony the princess and Durwin had occupied only a night earlier.

As Quentin opened the balcony door, the faint light of a glowing sky met his eyes. Dawn's crimson fingers stretched into the sky in the east, though the sun lingered below the far horizon, and one or two stars could still be seen above.

"I have missed you, my darling," sighed Bria. "My heart has mourned your absence."

"I am here now, and with you. I find my greatest happiness when I am at your side."

"But you will leave again—too soon, I fear. My father has a task for you, and we will be separated again."

"Do you know what it is?"

Bria shook her head.

"Then how do you know it will take me away from you so suddenly?"

"A woman knows."

"Well, then, we will have to make each moment we are together so much sweeter." So saying, Quentin pulled her to him gently and kissed her. She wound her arms around him and rested her head upon his chest.

Quentin looked at the placid sky as its rosy red brightened to a golden hue. The mighty ramparts of Askelon Castle gleamed like burnished gold, magically transformed from their ordinary state of dull stone by the dawn's subtle alchemy.

"Quentin . . ." Her voice was small and frightened. "What is happening? I am afraid, though I do not know why; the king holds his own counsel and will see no one. And when I ask him about the affairs of the realm, he only smiles and pats my hand and tells me that a princess should think of only happy things and not concern herself with mundane matters.

"I am worried for him. Oh, Quentin, when you see him, you will know—he is not well. He is pale and drawn. Some dark care sits heavily upon his brow. My mother and I do not know what to do."

"Hush, my love. All will be well—you will see. If there is anything that can be done to ease his mind, I will do it. And if medicines have any effect, Durwin will know it and avail.

"And yet, I must confess that I am troubled, too. But by nothing so easily explained—though I wish that were the case. I would give a fortune to any who could calm the turmoil I feel growing inside me.

"There is trouble, Bria. I feel it, though all about me appears peaceful and serene. I start at shadows, and night gives me no rest; it is as if the wind itself whispers an alarm to my ears, but no sound is heard."

Bria sighed deeply and clutched him tighter. "What is happening? What will become of us, my darling?"

"I do not know. But I promise you this: I will love you forever."

They held each other for a while, and the new sun rose and filled the sky with golden light.

"See how the sun banishes the darkness; so love will send our troubles fleeing from us—I promise."

"Can love accomplish so much, do you think?" Bria said dreamily.

"It can do all things."

CHAPTER 6

L isten, Theido; I say we should turn back. We have already come too far, and it is past the time when we should have been in Askelon. The king will be fearing our disappearance soon, if not already."

"But we have not seen what we came to see: the enemy, if there is one. We would be remiss if we returned now. Our task is not completed."

Ronsard sat hunched in the saddle, one arm resting on the pommel, the other bent around him as he pressed his arm into the small of his back. "If I do not get off this horse soon, I may never walk again."

"Since when have you been fond of walking? The lord high marshal of the realm should set a better example for his men," joked Theido, swiveling in his saddle to cast an eye upon the four knights behind.

"My men know me for what I am," said Ronsard. "But I do not jest when I say that we should return at once. It is no light thing to keep a king waiting."

"Nor is it acceptable to bring him useless information—the one would foil his purpose as easily as the other." Theido turned his horse and brought himself close to Ronsard. "But I will tell you what we will do, so that I may hear the end of your complaining. We will send one of the knights back with a message of what we have discovered so far, and of our intention to continue until we are satisfied."

"Fair enough. Also relay that we will return as soon as we can, by the most expeditious means, with a full report."

"Agreed." Theido turned his sun-browned face toward the place where the knights waited, resting their mounts before continuing their journey. "Martran! Come up here." He signaled to one of them.

The knight approached his leaders on foot and saluted. "Martran," commanded Ronsard, "you are to ride to the king at once and deliver this message: We are continuing on our mission and are sorry for the delay in returning to him sooner. Tell him we have seen nothing to occasion his concern. Tell him also that we will return to him as soon as we have found what we seek, or have some better report to give him. Do you understand?"

"Yes, my lord," replied the knight crisply.

"Repeat the message," ordered Ronsard.

The knight repeated the message word for word with the same inflection given to the words as Ronsard himself had used. "Very well," said Ronsard. "Be on your way. Stop for nothing and no one."

The knight saluted again and walked back to his horse. He mounted and rode off at once, without looking back.

"Now then," said Theido, snapping his reins impatiently, "let us proceed. We have lingered here too long already."

Ronsard raised himself in his saddle and called to the remaining knights. "Be mounted! Forward we go!"

Since leaving Askelon, they had ridden farther and farther south, first to Hinsenby and then along the coast as it dipped toward the Suthland region of Mensandor. They had passed through Persch and a host of peasant villages unnamed on any map.

Now they approached a rocky stretch of coastland that rose in sharp cliffs at the brink of the sea. This was where the Fiskill Mountains spent themselves in their southernmost extremity. The crags marched right down to the sea, and there the land dropped away as if it had been divided by the chop of an axe. The sea lay crowded with jagged teeth of immense rocks, some as big as islands, though they jutted sharply out of the ocean's swell, bare and lifeless, uninhabited except as roosts for myriads of squawking seabirds.

A narrow, treacherous track climbed upward through the cliffs and entwined itself among the tors. Now it cut through a wall of rock so narrow that a man's outstretched hands touched either side, and now it swung out upon the sheer cliff face, where one misstep would send horse and rider hurtling down into the churning sea.

They halted.

"I suggest we stop here for the night. I would not like to trust that trail by night; it is bad enough in the daylight."

"Very well," agreed Ronsard. "A fresh start at it in the morning would not be disagreeable to me."

They removed themselves but a little way from the trail and set about making camp for the night. As the sun slid down below the dark rim of the sea, the birds fluttered to the roosting rocks, and the evening trembled with their noisy calls.

After a while the moon ascended and cast its pale light all around. The tired men dozed and talked in hushed tones.

"Listen!" said Ronsard abruptly. All lapsed into silence and sifted the soft breeze for sounds. The only sound to reach their ears was the faraway roll of the waves crashing against the rocks and slapping against the cliff walls.

Theido cast a wondering glance toward his old friend.

"Well, perhaps I am hearing things," said Ronsard, but he still peered intently into the night as if listening for the sound to repeat itself.

In a moment he was on his feet, pacing uneasily about the camp, just out of the circle of firelight. Then he walked a short way along the road and stood for a long time, looking toward the cliff trail. Theido watched him narrowly and was not surprised when the brawny knight came hurrying back.

"What is it?"

"Someone is coming! Up there in the cliffs—I am certain of it!"

He ordered his knights in a harsh whisper, "Put out the fire, and take the horses aside. Hide yourselves, and watch me for a signal!"

In the space of five heartbeats, the small camp was deserted, and no sign remained that only a moment before five knights had been encamped there.

Then Ronsard and Theido sat down to wait in the dark alongside the road, hidden from view by a low-lying clump of harts-tongue. Shortly there could be heard the minute sounds of a group of people hurrying along the path, desperately trying to pass unseen: the rattling echo of a stone dislodged by a careless foot, the muffled creak of a wheel upon the rock, a cough.

Then their murky shapes could be seen against the night sky as they drew nearer. They were on foot, and there were smaller shadows among the larger ones. They huddled together in a close knot, rather than ranging themselves along the trail; they evidently feared separation more than detection.

"It is no army," breathed Ronsard between clenched teeth. He let his breath out slowly. "But now to find out who they are and why they risk the cliffs at night—the very thing we declined to do."

"We had a choice; perhaps they felt they had none," replied Theido.

Ronsard rose from his place and stepped near the trail, just ahead of the nocturnal travelers' leader. When the man approached close at hand, Ronsard said in a loud, steady voice, "Halt, friend! In the name of the Dragon King!"

A shriek and a stifled oath came from the main body of the group. But the man stopped dead in his tracks and looked about him for the source of the unexpected command. Ronsard stepped closer, and the moonlight fell on his face. He smiled and held up his hands to show the frightened travelers that he meant them no harm.

"Wh-what do you w-want?" the leader managed to stammer.

"I wish to speak with you—that is all. I will not detain you long." Ronsard still spoke in the same steady voice, loud enough for all to hear.

"Who are you?"

"I am the lord high marshal of Mensandor," replied Ronsard. "Who are you, and what are you doing on this road in the dead of night?"

"Oh, sir!" gasped the relieved man. "You do not jest? You are really a king's man?"

"At your service. Are you in trouble?"

At this all the people rushed forward, drawing close around Ronsard as if to seek the protection of his title, a welcome shield over their heads. They all began to shout.

Theido crept from his hiding place and came to stand beside Ronsard, who held up his hands and called for quiet. "I think I would better hear the tale from only one mouth at a time. You are the leader of this band." He pointed to the man he had first addressed. "You begin."

The man's face shone pale in the moonlight, but Theido got the impression that it would be pale in the bright daylight as well. Deep lines of fear were drawn on the man's countenance. His eyes did not hold steady, but shifted to the right and left and all around as if to warn him of the imminent approach of an enemy.

"I . . . we . . ." The man's mouth worked like a pump, but his words were slow in coming.

"It is all right; you are safe for the time. I have soldiers with me, and we will defend you at need." Ronsard raised his arm in signal, and his knights came forward to stand along the trail, their hands upon the hilts of their long swords.

Their presence seemed to frighten the man rather than calm him.

"Come, you may speak freely," said Theido in a gentle voice.

"We are from Dorn," the leader managed to wheeze at length. "We have left our homes and carry all our belongings with us. We are going to the High Temple of Ariel." He paused, gulped air, and plunged ahead. "We do not know where else to go."

"It is a strange pilgrimage you make, friend," observed Ronsard. "Why do you leave your homes and flee by night?"

"Have you not heard? They are coming . . . a terrible host, terrible. They have landed at Halidom, and they are coming. Why, we are fleeing for our lives to the protection of Ariel! Only the gods can save us now."

"Who is coming? Have you seen anyone?"

The man looked at Ronsard, wide-eyed with disbelief. "Do you not know? How is this possible? The whole land is in turmoil! We are fleeing for our lives!"

The people began to shout again, each pouring out his heart, beseeching the king's men to help them escape. Ronsard and Theido listened and drew aside to confer. "Something has frightened these people; that much is clear. Though what remains a mystery. I can make no sense out of it." Ronsard scratched his jaw.

Theido called the leader over to where they stood. "Tell us plainly, friend, who is it that you flee? What do they look like?"

The man hesitated. "Well . . . we have seen no one. But we dared not wait. Two days ago, men of Halidom in the Suthlands came to Dorn, and they told us of terrible things which had happened there. A mighty enemy has risen up and drives all before him. Their city was burned, and the streets ran with the blood of their children and women. Those that would save their lives fled to the hills. So we flee while we still may."

"This enemy—did you hear a name?"

"It is too terrible to say!" The man threw his hands heavenward in supplication.

"Terrible it may be, but we will hear it. Tell what you know," commanded Ronsard. His authoritative tone seemed to have a calming effect upon the frightened peasant.

He looked from one to the other of them and said, his voice now a strained whisper, "It is Nin the Destroyer!"

CHAPTER 7

Theido looked blankly at Ronsard and then back at the frightened peasant. The man's eyes glittered wide and round in the moonlight. He had scarcely dared utter his enemy's name, and his tongue had frozen in his mouth, but as appalling as the name was to the peasant—enough at least to inspire a whole village to flight at the very sound of it—the name meant nothing to Theido or Ronsard.

"I have never heard of this name," said Theido. Ronsard shook his head and looked hard at the peasant.

"Is there another name by which this enemy may be known? We know nothing of this Nin or his armies."

"No, there is no other name I know."

"Halidom was destroyed? These men that came to Dorn, they saw it destroyed?"

"Yes, so they said. Some of them had lost everything—home and family, possessions, everything."

Theido turned to Ronsard. "There is where we will find our answer—at Halidom."

"So it would seem. We will go there and see what may be seen. The king will want to know in any case." He turned back to the leader of the fleeing people. "This Nin you speak of—he was moving toward Dorn, you say? How did you know if you did not see him?"

"The men of Halidom told us. The enemy ranges the whole country-side. No place is safe from him. That is why we go to the high temple at Narramoor to ask the god to protect us."

"There may be a safer place than even the temple," said Theido. "I have lands at Erlott which need the work of many hands. Go there and present yourself to my steward, called Toffin. Tell him his master sends you to him that he may give you shelter and food and land to work. And give him this." Theido drew a small, round token from the pouch at his belt: a clay tile baked hard, with his signet pressed into it.

The peasant stared at the signet tile and then at Theido. He seemed as much dismayed by it as by Nin himself. "Are we to be sold into slav-ery because we have no place to go? We have left our home to become serfs of the king's men?" He had spoken loudly, and there came a mur-mur from the rest of the group standing a little way off.

"My offer," explained Theido, "is honorable. You may take it or not. I do not withdraw it. I keep no serfs; all who work my lands are free to enjoy the fruits of their labors in equal share. If you doubt my words, go there and see for yourselves. In any case, you are free to leave or stay once you have seen. No one compels you to do as I bid. Only know this: if you stay, you will be required to do your share and to work the land that is given to you. If you do not, your place will be given to another who will."

The man looked at the token in Theido's hand. He reached out for it hesitantly, casting a sideways glance to the others in his band.

"We, too, are honorable, though we are men of low birth." He snatched the tile out of Theido's hand. "We will go to your lands at Erlott and inquire of your steward; we will see how he receives us. If he bears the goodwill of his master, you will find us busy in your fields when you return from your duties." He bowed stiffly from the waist and turned to go. He paused and turned again. "If it is as you say, you have our thanks, my lord."

"I do not ask for thanks, but only that you will do as we have agreed. That will mean more to me than gratitude itself."

The man bowed again and went to where his people waited to learn the outcome of the interview just concluded. Words were exchanged quickly; there were mumbled whispers all around, and suddenly the band was on its way again, but bolder this time and changed in mood. Several of the refugees waved their thanks to Theido as they passed, and all talked excitedly together as they moved hurriedly away down the trail.

"Well, you have done your fellows a fine service this night. I hope you will not have cause to regret your kindness," said Ronsard when they had gone.

"One never regrets a kindness, my friend. But I have no doubt that I have gained as much as they in the bargain."

"How so?"

"Good land needs the plowman's hand to bring it to life, and a husband to care for it. If I did not have men to work my fields, they would soon become barren and worthless. These men do me great service by helping me care for my lands. Rightly managed, there is more than enough for everyone."

"Well, I hope we may see your trust proved true. But why not? The realm has known nothing but peace these many years, and we are at peace still."

"I wonder," replied Theido. "I wonder."

Quentin hastened along wide corridors lined with rich tapestries toward the Dragon King's apartments. Upon rising, he had been summoned to meet with the king in his private council chambers, and had dressed in fresh garments—a new tunic and trousers of forest green and a short summer cloak of blue, edged in green and gold. The finely embroidered cloak, fastened with a brooch of gold at his shoulder, fluttered out behind him as he swept along.

Just as he stepped up to the door that opened onto Eskevar's apartments, the door swung inward, and Oswald, the queen's chamberlain, emerged. "Sir, if you would but come aside with me, my lady would have a word with you."

Oswald smiled as he made his request, but his gray eyes insisted, so Quentin nodded his assent and followed the chamberlain.

They withdrew to a room just across the corridor from the king's chambers. Oswald knocked upon the door and stepped in. "Quentin is here, Your Majesty."

Quentin stepped into the room behind the chamberlain and saw Queen Alinea sitting on a bench in the center of the room, with her hands folded in her lap. She seemed to be staring at something that Quentin could not see: something far away. Quentin saw the lines of worry creasing her noble brow.

When the queen saw him, she straightened, and her face was suddenly transformed by a beautiful smile. Instantly the dim chamber seemed filled with light. She rose as he came to her and held out her arms to embrace him. Quentin hugged her and brushed her pale cheek with his lips; she kissed both of his.

"Quentin, you have come! Oh, I am so glad you are here. Your journey was not unpleasant, I trust? It is good to have you back. The months seem long when you are away." She gripped his hand in both of hers and led him to the bench. "Please, sit with me but a little." To Quentin's glance she answered, "I know the king is waiting, but it is important. I would have a word with you before you see him."

Her sparkling green eyes, deep and serene as forest pools, searched his for a moment, as if deciding whether the hearer would be strong enough to bear the words she had to say. "Quentin," she said softly, "the king is very ill."

"So I have learned from Bria." He blushed. "We met this morning when I arrived. She told me of her concern for his health."

"But I think even Bria does not guess how far he has fallen. She is devoted to her father and loves him with all her heart, but she does not know him as I do. Something consumes him before my eyes; it gnaws at him from within, stealing his strength and sapping his spirit."

Again in answer to Quentin's look, she continued, "Do not wonder at what I tell you; you will see for yourself soon enough. He has greatly changed since you last saw him. It is all I can do to keep from weeping in his presence." She appeared to be on the verge of tears at that very moment.

"My queen, I am your servant. Say the word and I will do whatever you require."

"Only this: take no unusual notice of him when you go in to him. It upsets him when people worry after him. Do not let on that you believe him ill, or that I have told you anything of his condition."

"I promise it. But is there nothing else I can do?"

"No." She patted his hand. "I know that you would if you could. But I have sent for Durwin and have placed a heavy charge on him. It may take all of his healing powers to restore the king—if he is not now beyond them."

"I will pray to the Most High that Durwin's cures have effect."

"That is my course, as well." The queen smiled, and again the room seemed lighter, for a dark cloud had passed over Quentin's heart as they talked. He rose, more encouraged. "Go to him now, my son. And remember what I told you."

"I will, my lady. You need not fear."

Quentin quietly left the room, and when he had stepped back into the corridor, he found Oswald waiting for him. The chamberlain led him to the king's chambers, knocked, and then admitted him.

"Your Majesty, Quentin is here."

Quentin drew a deep breath and stepped across the threshold. In the center of the high-ceilinged chamber sat a heavy, round oaken table, shaped like the room itself, for it was a part of one of Askelon's many towers. Small, round windows of amber glass tinted the afternoon light with a warm hue. Eskevar was standing in a shaft of light from one of these windows, his back turned, gazing out into the courtyard below.

There was an awkward moment when Quentin could not speak, and the king did not seem to have heard the chamberlain's announcement. Quentin hesitated, feeling suddenly trapped. Then the king turned slowly and fixed his eyes upon Quentin. A thin smile stretched his lips. "Quentin, my son, you have come."

If not for the queen's warning, Quentin did not know what he would have done. He bit his lower lip to stifle a cry and then recovered himself and forced a grin.

"I came as soon as I could. Toli's horses are magnificent. I believe they have wings. We flew over the land at an astounding pace."

Still smiling—the sad, weak smile of a dying man, Quentin thought grimly—the king advanced slowly and offered his hand.

Quentin took it without hesitation and could not help noticing how weak the king's grip had become, and how cold the feel of his hand.

Eskevar's flesh had taken on a waxen pallor, and his eyes seemed to burn with a dull, feverish light; his lips were cracked and raw, and his hair—that crowning glory of rich, dark curls—hung limp and lifeless and had now turned almost completely gray.

Quentin found himself staring at the face of a strange man who looked at him intently with sunken eyes rimmed with dark circles. He looked away quickly and said, "This is a cheery room, Sire. Will we be alone, or are others expected?"

"Others will come, but not yet. I wanted to speak to you alone first. Please, sit down." The king lowered himself slowly into a chair at the round table, and Quentin followed. He wanted to weep at the sight of Eskevar, the mighty Dragon King who was now tottering like an old man.

How could this be? wondered Quentin. *How could such a change be wrought in such a short time?* In a scant eight or nine months, the king had deteriorated to a shocking degree. Quentin wanted to dash from the room, to remove himself far away from the creature who sat beside him and who wore the king's crown.

Eskevar gazed into the young man's eyes with a look of inexpressible tenderness; a fatherly compassion that Quentin had never seen before suddenly flowered. Quentin was strangely moved and forgot for a moment the horror of the king's shattered health.

"Quentin," said Eskevar after a moment's contemplation, "as you know, I have no son, no heir to my throne save Bria. My brother, Prince Jaspin, is banished, nevermore to return. I think it is time for me to choose my successor."

"Surely, my lord is mistaken." Quentin gulped. "Now is not the time to think of such things. You have many years ahead of you. You are strong yet."

Eskevar shook his head slowly, frowning slightly. "No, it is not to be. Quentin"—again the sweet, sad smile and fatherly glance—"Quentin, I am dying."

"No!"

"Yes! Hear me!" The king raised his voice. "Slowly it may be, but I am dying. I shall not live to see another spring. It is time for me to set my house in order.

"I intend to choose you as my successor—wait! Since you are not in direct bloodline, it will have to go before the Council of Regents. I expect no problem there. As I have chosen you myself, they will ratify my choice gladly."

Quentin sat gazing at his folded hands, speechless. The king's words had stricken him mute.

After what seemed like hours, he looked up and saw Eskevar watching him quietly, but intensely. "You honor me greatly, Sire. But I am not worthy of such high accord. I am an orphan, and of no noble birth. I am not worthy to be king."

"You, Quentin, are my ward. You have been a son to me as I have watched you grow to manhood these last years. I want you, and no other, to wear my crown."

"I do not know what to say, my lord."

"Say but that you will do as I command; ease my heart in this matter."

Quentin stood up from his chair and then went down on his knees before his king. "I am ever your servant, Sire. I will obey."

Eskevar placed a hand upon Quentin's head and said, "I am content. Now my heart can rest." He took Quentin by the arm; his grip was spidery and light. "Rise, sir! One king does not kneel to another. From this day forth you are heir to the throne of Mensandor."

Just then there came a knock upon the chamber door and Oswald's voice could be heard calling, "The others have arrived, Your Majesty," as the door swung open.

In walked Toli and Durwin. Toli hesitated at the sight of the king, but Durwin did not flinch at all. He hurried to the table and, with a quick bow, began talking of his travels, all the while keeping a close eye on the ailing monarch as if weighing him for some remedy.

"Good, good. Be seated, both of you. We have a matter to discuss."

The king looked at his comrades closely and drew a deep, weary breath before he began.

"For some time I have been of an uneasy mind. Restless, hungry, and uneasy. At first I attributed it to the illness which consumes me, but it is more than that, I fear. It is for Mensandor that my unease persists. There is some distress in the realm."

The Dragon King spoke softly and distinctly, and Quentin realized that Eskevar had so long been the head of his land that he had developed a special feeling for it and knew instinctively when something was wrong. It was as if part of him were hurt, and he felt the wound. He had discerned trouble before anyone else had suspected even the slightest eddy in the current of peace and prosperity that flowed through the kingdom.

It struck him—absurdly at first, but with growing conviction— that perhaps what ailed the land was the cause of the king's distress as well.

"To prove my intuition I summoned the faithful Theido and Ronsard to me and sent them with a small force to discover, it they could, whence the trouble came.

"The time for their return is now past. I have received no word or sign from them, and I am anxious for what may have befallen them. That is why I have summoned you." He nodded to Quentin and Toli. "It becomes ever more urgent that we discover the source of our harm before it is too late. There is evil afoot; I feel it. Each day it grows stronger. If we do not find it soon and crush it out . . ."

"My lord," said Toli, "we have seen portents which would indicate the prudence of your fears."

"And I as well," agreed Durwin.

Toli and Durwin shared with the king the signs they had observed, foreshadows of an impending evil they could not identify. Quentin noted that as his two comrades spoke, and especially when they mentioned the Wolf Star, Eskevar appeared to fall even further beneath the weight of his kingdom's peril.

After a few moments of uncomfortable silence, the king spoke solemnly. "Quentin and Toli, my brave friends, we must discover wherein our danger lies. My people require your courage."

"We will go at once and seek out this evil. And it may be we will find good Theido and Ronsard as well," Toli offered boldly.

Quentin said nothing but stared from one to another of the faces around the table.

"Very well," sighed the king. "You know I would not send you out thus if I thought it were but a small thing, or if another could serve as well."

He turned and looked at Durwin thoughtfully. "You, sir, I did not summon, but as usual, one who knows me better than I know myself has doubtless interceded." He smiled again, and Quentin saw a flicker of the former man. The king continued, "I will detain you, good hermit, that you may remain with me. I may soon have need of your ministrations, and perchance your arts will be better employed here than on the back of a horse."

"So it is," replied Durwin. "I will abide."

The king rose with some difficulty and dismissed them, asking his two warriors, "How soon will you ride?"

"We will leave at once, Sire," said Toli.

"It is well; but stay and share my table tonight, at least. I want to see my friends all together before . . ." He did not finish the thought.

The three arose, bowed, and went quietly out. At the door Quentin turned and was about to speak. He looked at Eskevar, and his eyes filled with tears; no words would come. He bowed quickly, then went out, too overwhelmed to say what he felt in his heart.

CHAPTER 8

The village has been subdued, Most Excellent One." The rider bowed low in his saddle. Behind him black smoke ascended in a thick, dark column to be scattered by the wind blowing in from the sea. His sorrel pony jerked its reins and tossed its head, its hide besmeared with soot and dried blood. "There was no resistance."

Savage eyes watched the messenger from beneath the rim of an iron helm ornamented with black plumes that fluttered like wings in the wind. The warlord said nothing, but turned his horse and started slowly away. The messenger spurred his mount forward and drew up beside his departing commander. "Something has displeased you, my master?" The question betrayed apprehension.

"No, it is well. Our task is complete. I will return to the ships; you will accompany me. I may have need of a messenger." He lifted himself in his saddle and called to several riders who waited a little distance apart. The riders held their helmets under one arm and stared impassively ahead at the smoke curling upward.

"You four"—the commander gestured with his gauntleted hand— "stay with the men and occupy this place. You others will come with me. We ride at once. Follow."

"But what is to be done with the prisoners, Most Excellent One?" called the messenger after the dark retreating form. The warlord did not

turn nor look around, but the messenger heard the words drifting back
to him.

"Kill them," his commander said.

The room hung heavy with the pungent fragrance of burning incense,
and clouds of aromatic vapor drifted about the great figure seated on a
throne of silk cushions. Tiny colored birds fluttered and chirped in cages
nearby, their songs accompanied by the soothing notes of a flute.

Presently, the tinkling ring of a chime sounded in the passageway
beyond, followed by a rustle of clothing. The gigantic form seated on
the throne appeared to be asleep, for he did not move or acknowledge
the intrusion in any way; the huge head rested heavily on the thick neck
rising from massive shoulders and a great barrel chest. The meaty hands
clasping one another in the wide lap remained motionless, thumbs
pressed together.

"Immortal One, I have news," said the minister who had just entered
so quietly. He waited on his knees with his forehead pressed to the floor,
hands thrust before him, palms upward.

"You may speak, Uzla." The voice seemed to fill the small room,
even though the words had been spoken quietly.

"Your warlords have returned. And they bring tidings of victory.
The cities of the coast are subdued."

"Has a suitable residence been found for me?"

"Alas, no, Immortal One, these were but small villages, and none possessed a dwelling worthy of your being. For this effrontery the villages have
been burned and the ashes scattered, lest the sight of them displease you."

Nin the Destroyer looked darkly upon his most trusted minister.
"This land will feel my wrath!" he shouted. The birds trembled in their
cages, and the music stopped. Uzla, the prime minister, cowered below
him on the floor.

"The wretches of this accursed land speak of many castles in the north, and one in particular which may serve your needs while you sojourn here to subject this land to your will."

"What is the name of this palace?"

"It is called Askelon. It is the city of the high king of this land—one known as the Dragon King."

"Ah," said Nin softly. "The sound of these words pleases me. Say them again."

"Askelon is the home of the Dragon King."

"It will be my home, and I will be the Dragon King. This pleases me. I have never killed a dragon before—have I, Uzla?"

"No, my Deity. Not to my knowledge." He hastened to add, "That is, unless in a previous life, of course."

"Then I will look forward to that event with anticipation, and I will savor the moment of its accomplishment." He stood slowly. "Now, where are my warlords?" Nin asked, his deep voice booming.

"They await you on the beach," replied Uzla. "I will summon them."

"No, I will go to them. They have achieved my desires and will be rewarded by the sight of their god drawing near to them."

"As you command, Great One."

Uzla bowed again and raised himself from the floor. He turned and withdrew to the hall, clapped his hands, and shouted, "The Deity walks! Kneel before him, everyone!" He went before his sovereign, clapping his hands and shouting the warning. Nin followed slowly, balancing his immense bulk upon ponderous legs.

As they reached a short flight of stairs that led upward to the deck of the palace ship, Uzla clapped his hands again, and eight attendants brought a throne on poles. They placed the throne before their king, and he lowered himself onto it. Then, straining every muscle, the chair bearers climbed the steps, careful to keep the throne level, lest they incur the wrath of their temperamental god. Soon they moved out upon the deck.

Two more attendants waited on deck with large shades made of brilliant feathers. As soon as Nin's chair emerged out upon the deck, the huge, burly head was shaded from the bright sunlight of a beautiful summer day. The attendants swayed under the weight of their burden, but proceeded down a long ramp that had been erected out over the shallow water from the palace ship to the shore. The ramp terminated in a platform on the beach, forming a dais from which Nin the Destroyer could command his subjects.

At the sight of this procession moving slowly down the ramp, the four warlords dismounted and drew near to the dais, prostrating themselves in the sand. The chair bearers reached the platform and placed the mobile throne squarely in the center of the dais, beneath a broad canopy of rich blue silk. Then they withdrew to await their king's command, kneeling with their faces touching their knees.

The blue silk ruffled in the soft sea breeze. Above the dais, gulls wheeled in the air and shrieked at the spectacle below. Nin raised his hands and said, "Arise, my warlords. You may look upon your Deity."

The warlords, clad in their heavy armor, rose stiffly to their feet and stood shoulder to shoulder before their patron.

"I have seen your victory from afar," Nin continued. "With my own eyes I witnessed the flames of destruction. I am well pleased. Now tell me, my commanders, what is the strength of this land? Is there an army to stand before the Destroyer's blade?" He looked at the four fighting men and nodded to one of them who stepped forward slowly. "Gurd?"

The warrior struck his heart with his closed hand; the mailed fist clanked dully upon the bronze breastplate. His long straight black hair was pulled tightly back and bound at the back of his head in a thick braid.

Quick black eyes set in a smooth, angular red face watched Nin closely. "I have seen no soldiers in the south, Immortal One. The peasant villages were unprotected."

"Amut."

The warrior advanced. His gleaming head was shaved completely bald, except for a short bob of hair that he wore tied in a tight knot.

On his cheeks and forehead were strange blue tattoos, and a ragged scar streaked from the corner of one almond-shaped eye to the base of a thick, muscular neck. "In the north we encountered no soldiers, Great One. The cowardly populace fled before our arrows like leaves before the storm."

"Luhak," called Nin, and the third warlord stepped forward.

Luhak touched his bearded chin with a brown hand. His head was covered in a helm of white horsehide that sprouted a short plume made from a horse's tail at its crest. He was tall and lean, and when he opened his wide mouth to speak, a row of pointed white teeth flashed.

"I encountered but one village in the mountainous interior of this land, named Gaalinpor," the warrior said. "No army could cross those mountains in surprise. We may turn our eyes elsewhere."

"Boghaz."

The last warlord, a towering black man whose features were hidden beneath the veil that covered the lower part of his face, revealing only his large, dark eyes, took his place beside the others. His head was encased in a horn-covered leather helmet, and he wore a breastplate made of flat disks of horn that had been linked together with iron rings. A long red cape fell from his shoulders to the heels of his black boots. At his side he carried, as they all did, a curious curved sword with a thin, tapering blade honed dagger-sharp on both edges.

"And I, too, have seen no soldiers. The villages offered no resistance, the blood of the stubborn ran red upon the ground, and their ashes ascended to heaven in your honor, Immortal Nin." With that the black warrior touched his forehead and bowed low.

"What land is this which builds no walls around its cities and leaves the small villages unprotected? Here is wealth for the taking, my warlords. We will push north to Askelon, and there I will establish my palace, so that I may be comfortable while bringing this land under my rule.

"Go now and bring me word when the castle is mine, that I may come at once and take possession of what I desire. But do not make sacrifice of the king. I will have that pleasure for my own; his blood will flow for me alone. Hear and obey."

The four commanders saluted Nin and backed away a few paces. Then they turned, mounted their horses, and galloped off together. Nin clapped his hands, and the attendants sprang forward to begin the laborious process of carrying their god back up the ramp and into the magnificent palace ship.

CHAPTER 9

Heavy dew still clung to the leaves as the first rays of golden morning broke upon the countryside. Near the sea such dew was common, but it never ceased to delight Quentin when the sun struck each tiny droplet of moisture and turned it into a glimmering gem. Each hillock and bush seemed to acquire inestimable value.

Toli's high-spirited horses, now well rested, pranced and jogged in the cool morning air. Quentin himself lifted his voice in a hymn to the new day. Toli, too, joined in, and their voices rang in the dells.

"Ah, it is good to be alive!" shouted Quentin, more for the joy of shouting than for the sake of conversation.

"This morning the saddle seems a friend to you," called Toli, bouncing along behind. "That is not the impression you gave me last night."

"In the morning the world is re-created. All things are made new—including saddles."

"It is good to see you in such high humor. For the last three days one would have mistaken you for a growling bear—not that I noticed."

Quentin seemed to ignore the remark, and they continued on as before, the trappings of the horses jingling brightly as they cantered along. "I have been under a shadow," Quentin said at length. "It is good to be doing something—at least, I feel better for moving."

"That is well for both of us," replied Toli in his usual elliptic style.

The two riders approached and mounted the crest of a long, sloping hill. Here they paused for a short while and contemplated the road before them and the valley beyond, in the center of which lay the village of Persch.

"See how quiet it is," remarked Quentin as he gazed at the scene below. "So peaceful. This is how it has been for a thousand years . . ." His voice trailed off.

"We will pray that it may remain so for another thousand," answered Toli. He flicked the reins and started down the road, a thin dirt trail barely scratched in the long, thick green grass of the hills.

As they drew nearer to the seaside village, Toli grew tense with concentration. Quentin noticed the change in his companion's attitude and asked, "What is it? What do those eagle eyes of yours see?"

"Nothing, Kenta. And that is what worries me. I see no one—no activity in the village at all."

"Perhaps the people of Persch are late abed and late to rise," Quentin said carelessly, attempting to maintain the mood of tranquillity that had just been shattered by Toli's observation.

"Or maybe they have a reason for remaining behind doors on such a day as this, though that reason is certain to be born of fear."

Quentin sighed. "It will not be the first time we have encountered such this trip." He placed his free hand on the hilt of his sword and shifted it slightly to bring it into readiness. His eyes scanned the breadth of the town drawing slowly closer with each step. He saw not a sign of life, either human or animal, in the streets or on the road before them. Certainly that was strange. Ordinarily, the first rays of morning light would find the narrow little streets busy with citizens going about their daily chores. The merchants would be opening their stalls in the marketplace and the craftsmen their awnings. Farmers would be offering cheese and melons and eggs in exchange for cloth and various metal utensils. Wives would be carrying water from the well in the town square, and children would be scampering around corners and darting to and fro in noisy play while the village dogs barked and dodged their bare, sun-browned legs.

But this morning there was no such bustle and fuss. The empty streets seemed haunted by the echoes of childish laughter and the eerie absence of the villagers.

The riders entered the main street of the town, and Quentin heard the soft crush of horses' hooves upon the tiny fragments of shells with which the people of Persch paved their streets. Quentin always thought that this gave all the seaside towns a fresh, clean appearance. This day, however, the whitened streets looked desolate, sepulchral.

No face appeared even fleetingly in a doorway or a darkened window. No sound could be heard, except the soft sea breeze blowing among the eaves; it whispered a note of utter loneliness.

"Everyone is gone," observed Toli. His voice seemed to die in the empty air.

"I do not believe it. Everyone cannot have left. Someone must have remained behind. A whole village does not disappear—not without good cause."

They reached the village square. It was an irregular rectangle formed by the fronts of Persch's principal buildings: the inn, which was rumored to serve a most remarkable fish stew; the communal hall (since no nobleman dwelt in Persch, the citizens had erected their own great hall in which to observe feasts and holy days); the marketplace and the stalls of the vendors; the small temple and shrine to the god Ariel; and the dwellings of the craftsmen.

In the center of this rectangle stood a large well, and on a mound beside it an immense old cedar tree spread forth its shaggy limbs to offer shade to all who gathered there. Quentin and Toli drew up to the well and dismounted. Toli picked up a shallow wooden bucket which lay beside the stone rim of the well and dipped out water for the horses. Quentin filled a gourd and drank his fill of the cold, fresh water and then offered some to Toli.

"Hmmm," Quentin mused, "not a sound, nor a sight. And yet, I feel that we are not alone."

"Yes, I feel someone close by. I also feel their fear." Toli replaced the gourd carefully and then motioned for Quentin to mount up again. Quentin did so with a questioning look, and the two rode the rest of the way through the village.

When they reached the last dwelling, Toli led them aside and whispered, "We were not entirely alone back there. I felt someone's eyes upon us. Let us leave the horses here and go back by another way."

They crept quietly along a pinched alleyway between buildings and soon made their way back to the square. There was nothing to be seen; it all looked just as it had only moments before.

"Well, it appears we should look elsewhere. Perhaps we should try one of the dwellings."

"Wait but a moment and I will join you."

Toli had no sooner finished speaking when they heard a slight scrabbling hiss, like that of a snake moving through dry sand. It stopped and started with a measured pace. They listened for a moment, and the sound seemed to diminish rapidly. It was then Quentin realized that someone had been very close to them, perhaps just around the corner of the same wattle-and-daub abode where they now crouched waiting in the shadows. The sound was the light, shuffling footfall of someone treading gently, cautiously along the shell-strewn path.

"He is getting away!" whispered Quentin harshly, and he dived around the edge of the dwelling in time to see a leg and a hand disappear behind an overgrown yew thicket.

"He is making for the basin!" shouted Toli. "We will catch him this way." He pulled on Quentin's arm and pointed behind them to where the narrow alleyway turned and started down as it became a path, like so many in the sea town, which led to the waterfront where the villagers kept their fishing boats.

Toli bounded away, and Quentin followed in his fleet steps. They tumbled down the path together and jumped down the rock steps placed in the side of the sandy hill that separated the town from the strand below. Ahead of them lay the basin, the small cove that formed the harbor of Persch; there, between two fishing boats resting with their black hulls skyward, a small skiff with a white, triangular sail had been thrust upon the sand. And hurrying nimbly along the sand toward the skiff ran the slight figure of a young man.

Quentin darted out onto the beach in pursuit. He ran a few paces, then stopped, raised his hand, and shouted, "Hold, sir! Stop! We mean you no harm! We only wish to talk."

The figure half turned and only then saw the two men watching him. Though Quentin and Toli were still too far away to make out the features of his face, the effect of Quentin's words was quite obvious. "You have frightened him!" called Toli as the figure on the beach lurched forward, stumbled, fell, picked himself up, and ran deerlike for the skiff. "Come on!" cried the quick-footed Jher, skimming over the sand.

The young stranger had reached the skiff and was shoving the boat into the water with all his might. It seemed to have caught on something, thought Quentin, or perhaps the tide had withdrawn somewhat since the boat had been left here, making it harder to push free.

But with the strength of desperation, the stranger succeeded in launching the small sailing boat and was thrashing through knee-deep water to turn the boat around before clambering in, fishlike, over the side.

Toli reached the water's edge first and jumped in. Quentin plunged in after him, and both waded toward the boat. The stranger, paddling furiously with a long oar, cast a terrified look over his shoulder. Quentin noticed the compact frame and slim shoulders dressed in the leather vest and coarse-woven brown trousers worn by fishermen. The shapeless, floppy, soft hat, also traditional among the seaside dwellers of southern Mensandor, was pulled down low over the young face.

Quentin waded toward one side of the boat, and Toli splashed toward the other. The boat, despite the prodigious thrashings of its occupant with the oar, was not moving into the deeper water rapidly, and they had no trouble reaching it in quick strides.

Once they were within range, the oar whistled above their heads. Quentin tried to reassure the stranger, saying, "Be still, good sir! Desist! Ow!" as the wildly flailing oar came dangerously close. "We mean you no harm."

As Quentin occupied the boy's attention, Toli moved behind him toward the bow. The youngster turned and brought the oar down on the gunwale with a crack in the exact spot where Toli's fingers had been only an instant before. Quentin, seeing the stranger momentarily off balance following the delivery of the blow, seized the stern with both hands and gave the boat a mighty, twisting shove. The young stranger gave a surprised yelp and, with arms flung wide and fingers clawing the air, toppled over the side headfirst into the water, the oar clattering to the bottom of the boat.

Quentin ducked the splash, and Toli swung himself around the side of the skiff to face Quentin. Between them floated the fisherman's hat. Quentin reached into the shallow water, snagged a hold on the stranger's collar, and hauled him sputtering to his feet.

"Well, what have we here?" asked Quentin amiably. "Toli, I think we have caught ourselves a . . ." He stopped abruptly. Now it was Quentin's turn to be surprised.

"A girl!" cried Toli, finishing Quentin's thought.

Quentin held the dripping hat, now a soggy black bag in his hands, and looked in wonder at the long, dark tresses, now wet and ropy, glistening in the sun. The young woman's dark lashes blinked over clear, ice-blue eyes as she shook away the water streaming down her face. She had soft, well-shaped features, and her cheeks bore the ruby blush of excitement.

"Let me go!" she cried. "I am nobody. I have no money. Let me go!"

"Peace," Quentin said softly. "We will do you no harm, my lady."

The young woman looked from one to the other of her captors, eyeing them suspiciously. "We are not robbers, if that is what you are thinking," replied Toli. "We are king's men."

"Since when do king's men arrest innocent citizens and abuse them for no reason?" she challenged them haughtily.

"Innocent citizens have nothing to fear from us. Why did you run?"

The woman threw a furtive glance toward the village and murmured, "I was frightened. I found the village deserted and . . ."

"And then you heard us coming and hid."

"Yes," she said sullenly. She drew a soggy sleeve across her face and threw a defiant look at Quentin. "Now let me go!"

"We will let you go in good time. But you have pricked our curiosity, and we wish answers to our questions first. Now," said Quentin, offering her his hand, "we needn't remain standing in the water; let us all dry out on the beach."

He turned and began sloshing toward the shore. Suddenly he felt his knees buckle, and he pitched forward into the water with a strange yelp. His back and shoulders were pummeled with fierce blows. He twisted underwater and was trying to haul himself back to his feet when the attack was broken off. He surfaced sputtering and shook the water out of his eyes. Toli was gripping the young lady by the arm, having pulled her off Quentin. Toli then pushed her, clawing and kicking, toward the shore.

Toli's face wore a strange, ridiculous grin.

CHAPTER 10

"How is this possible?" Theido shook his head in disbelief. His eyes scanned the black plain where the village of Halidom had been.

"There must be something left, though it does not look promising." Ronsard motioned to his knights, and the party started down the gentle hill above the flat valley of Halidom. Each man's face wore a look of grim wonder, and each man's mind echoed Theido's thought: how was it possible that an entire village could be annihilated so completely?

There was nothing left of Halidom but a blackened spot on the earth. Not a timber stood; not a stone was left standing upon another. The entire area where the town had been was now a razed jumble of destruction.

"Even the birds have finished with it," observed Ronsard as they approached the perimeter of the scorched circle.

"Not quite. Look over there." Theido gazed a short distance away. Ronsard followed his look and saw a large, flapping buzzard settle himself on the remnant of a tree trunk. Three scolding ravens flew up from where they had been busily feeding on the ground.

"Let us see what draws their interest." Ronsard turned to his men. "Spread out and search the ashes for any signs of who this enemy might be." Then he and Theido reined their horses toward the place where the buzzard was now hopping along the length of burned trunk. The bird was eyeing something on the ground below. What it was could not be determined.

They moved through the midst of the destroyed village. Scattered among the ashes were the charred remains of the everyday life of the simple villagers: an iron tripod with its battered pot nearby, a small stone statue of a household god, the blackened shards of a wine jug. And here and there lay the remains of hapless villagers: a sooty skull staring vacantly skywards; a long, clean length of shinbone; the curved hull of a rib cage rising from the desolation.

The vulture took disgruntled flight at the approach of the horses and lifted itself slowly into the sky to circle high overhead with the ravens.

"By the gods!" cried Theido, drawing near the spot.

"What . . . ?" began Ronsard. Then he, too, saw what Theido had seen. "By Orphe—no!"

Theido had already thrown himself from his mount and was tugging at the lashings of his saddle for his water skin. Ronsard, entranced by the sight before him, dismounted slowly and stepped closer. He placed a hand on the hilt of his sword and was drawing the blade when Theido touched his arm. "No need for that, I think. He is beyond pain, beyond suffering."

As Theido spoke, the object of their attention—a badly burned torso of a body—jerked convulsively, and a yellow eye rolled toward them. Upon seeing them, the mangled half-corpse uttered a pitiful moan. Theido knelt gently down beside the carcass and offered his water skin.

"Peace, friend. Here is water for your parched tongue." Theido was on his knees, gently bringing the tip of the skin within reach of the cracked mouth. He allowed a few drops of water to seep out and dampen the man's lips. The black tongue poked out and moistened itself with the water. The cracked eyelids fluttered, and the dry eyeballs rolled in their sockets. Miraculously, the water seemed to take effect, and the eyes cleared with recognition.

"How is this poor creature still alive?" wondered Ronsard, bending close to Theido's ear.

"I do not know." The knight paused to let some more water trickle out. "But perhaps he may tell us something of what happened here before Heoth claims him."

"Can you speak, friend? We are king's men, and your answers would do your king service."

Ronsard turned away from the stench that assailed his nostrils. The man was burned horribly. Great areas of his chest and arms were charred black; the lower part of his body had been crushed by the tree when it fell. He lay in a shallow depression in the ground, half-twisted on his side. His hair had been burned off one side of his head; on the other, a few dark strands still clung to the bare scalp to trail in the breeze.

The birds had fed on the man where he lay and had laid open a fair portion of his shoulder and back. White bone could be seen gleaming from the raw, red wounds.

"Let him die in peace," said Ronsard, turning back. His voice was tight and choked.

"No-o-o." The voice was little more than a whisper on the wind. Both men looked down into the eyes and saw a glimmer that held them. The man was trying to speak.

"Easy. We hear you. Let me come close to listen." Theido leaned forward and placed his ear directly above the man's lips. He spoke softly and with a serenity Ronsard found hard to believe. "Tell us what happened, if you can."

The words formed themselves in the air, though Ronsard could not see how; and, however faint, they could be understood. "I have been waiting for someone to come," the man whispered. His voice was a dry rasp—the sound of a withered leaf blown over the sand. "Waiting . . . waiting . . ."

"We are here now; your vigil is over. Can you tell us anything?"

"All killed . . . All destroyed . . . burned . . . everything."

"Yes, we see. Who did it? Do you know?"

"Ahh"—a long, raking gasp—"the destroyer god . . . ten feet tall . . . fire spewed from his mouth . . . everything destroyed."

"Just the god alone?"

The words were growing ever fainter and more tenuous. "N-no . . . many soldiers . . . they say . . ." The man coughed violently, and the torso was racked with another convulsion.

"What did they say?"

"Ahh . . ."

"Tell me, and then it is over. The god will take you to your rest."

"Beware . . . Nin the Destroyer . . . Ahh-hhh."

The yellowed eyes grew cloudy and still. There was not enough breath left to make a last gasp, but Ronsard fancied he felt the last remnant of life flee the broken form that had held it so long against its will.

Theido stood slowly. "Let us bury this brave one at once."

The birds squawked overhead as if they knew that they would be denied their meal.

When the pathetic corpse had been buried with as much kindness as the knights could render, Ronsard and Theido went a little apart to talk. "Have you seen enough, my friend?" asked Ronsard, leaning on his sword.

"Here—yes. But I would like a look at this enemy that strikes helpless villages and kills the defenseless."

"That we shall have ere long, I believe. But now is not the time for it. We should return at once with word of what we have seen. When next we ride, it will be with a thousand at our backs."

"I think you may be right . . ." Theido paused; he seemed to regard something on the far horizon.

"What is it, Theido? Does something trouble you yet?"

Theido drew a long breath, and when he turned back to Ronsard, a strange light shone in his eyes. He turned again to the horizon, and his voice sounded far away. A shadow moved across the valley.

"I am afraid, Ronsard."

"You, afraid? How little you know yourself, sir!"

"Don't you feel it?" His look was quick and sharp. "No? I wonder . . ."

"Speak your mind, Theido. You have a foreboding, and I would know what it is. Out with it! Let there be nothing between us, my friend."

"Very well—you are right, of course. But it is not so easily put into words. Just now, as we were talking, I had a feeling that we were riding down a narrow path whose end lay in darkness, and darkness was falling all around. That is all, just that. But it made me fearful."

Ronsard studied his friend carefully, and at last spoke in a firm but quiet voice. "We were together, you and I? Well, come what may, that is enough for me. It will be a dark path indeed that daunts these two knights.

"But come, this is an evil place. Let us return at once to Askelon for the king's counsel. I tell you, we have been away too long already."

"Let us return, then. I have seen enough." Theido squared his shoulders and clapped Ronsard on the back with his hand. "But I wish we had seen this mysterious enemy and knew somewhat of his strength in numbers. I would feel better if we could see his face."

"So would I, but perhaps that time is not far hence. We may yet encounter him before reaching Askelon—though we are ill prepared for battle."

"I have no wish to engage an unknown enemy—only to search him out. All the more since this one seems too fantastic to believe."

They had been walking back to their horses, and upon reaching them, Ronsard swung himself up and called to his knights, "Be mounted, men! We are away for Askelon!"

The knights took their saddles and began riding back up the hill the way they had come. But this time they gave the charred circle on the plain a wide berth.

Theido stood for a moment beside his horse, gazing far away. Behind him he heard Ronsard call; he shrugged, mounted his big, black palfrey, and hurried to catch the others. As he gained the crest of the hill, the late-afternoon sun caught him full in the face, and he felt his melancholy flow away in the flood of golden warmth that washed over him. He spurred his horse forward and did not look back.

CHAPTER 11

Durwin hiked his robe over his knees and waded into the reed-fringed pool. The afternoon sun fell in slanting shafts through broad oaks and silver-leaved birch to glint in shimmering bands upon the clear water. Tiny fish flashed away from Durwin's intruding feet. The liquid, crystalline call of a lark on a nearby branch split the forest's green silence into two quivering halves.

Durwin stepped carefully into the deeper water, scanning the pebble-strewn bottom as he splashed along. He thought for a moment to throw off his robe and submerge himself in the pool's cool depths, as was his custom on a warm summer's afternoon in Pelgrin Forest.

But he thought better of the notion, inviting though it was, and continued his browsing. He soon had reason to be glad he had kept his robe, for as he worked his way around the pool, dipping now and then into the water, he noticed something white shining there. He glanced again and realized that it was a reflection on the mirrored surface of the pool. With a start he looked up and saw a woman clothed all in white standing on the shaggy, grass-covered bank above him.

"My lady!" he exclaimed. "You made me jump! I did not know that I was being watched."

"I am sorry, Durwin. I did not mean to alarm you," laughed Alinea, her voice ringing in the hollow. It had been a long time since he had heard her laugh. "You appeared so deeply engrossed, I feared to disturb your thought. Forgive me!"

"Your consideration is most thoughtful, but unnecessary. I am only gathering some biddleweed for a tisane."

"Water hemlock? That is a deadly poison, is it not?"

"You know the plants of the field and forest?"

"Only a few. My mother, Queen Ellena, knew many remedies and made our medicines for us. As a child, I helped her gather herbs."

"Well, then you know that a plant is neither deadly nor dangerous, but the intent of the healer makes it so. Yes, some are very powerful. But in wise hands even the most poisonous may make a wonderfully potent cure."

"Your hands are surely the wisest in the realm, kind hermit. Your medicines are most efficacious."

"Oh, my lady! You do not know how sorry your words make me."

"Have I said something wrong? Please tell me." The queen drew a few steps closer to the edge of the bank. Durwin waded toward her.

"No, you intended no wrong. But your words mock my lack of skill. For the one patient I would above all heal with my humble craft lies abed—no better now than when I first began his treatment. His malady resists my utmost art."

"Surely it is a most subtle cachexia."

"So it is!"

Durwin peered into Alinea's deep green eyes and read the heavy burden of care that grew there; every day added to the weight. He felt powerless to help her, as he felt powerless when he stood over the birth of a peasant baby born too soon and dying before it had begun to live. He would have taken the burden upon himself though it was a thousand times greater. But there was nothing he could do, save stand aside, humbled by his own uselessness.

"Do you think the Most High God hears our prayers for the sick?"

"He must, my lady. He hears all prayers and answers each in its own season."

"Then prayer will do what potions cannot."

"You shame me with your faith. In my search through all my medicines I have sorely neglected that remedy. But no more."

The queen sighed and raised her eyes to the sky shining soft and blue and bright in the afternoon light. Clouds fair and far away drifted slowly on the breeze that rustled the trees gently from time to time. The little pond was a polished glass reflecting all that passed above. Alinea plucked a tiny purple flower from a cluster at her feet. She gazed into it as if seeking a sign from its maker.

Durwin continued wading, stooping now and then to snatch up a plant by its roots. When he had collected enough, he strode through the water and climbed the bank where Alinea had settled to wait in the shade.

"What is happening, Durwin?" Her question was softly spoken, but the uncertainty in her voice and the worry lurking behind her eyes gave it the impact of a shout. Before he could speak a reassuring word, she continued. "It seems to me that something very bad, some dark evil, is growing, drawing nearer. Sometimes I stop for no reason, and a cold fear passes over me. It is gone again as quickly as it came, but afterwards it lingers in the air like a chill, and nothing is the same."

"I, too, have felt it. But I am at a loss to explain it. Something, I believe, is moving in the land—something evil, yes. It is unknown now, but will not so remain. Too soon we will know what it is."

"To hear you speak so does cheer me, though your words are not happy ones. At least I know that a dear friend feels as I do and understands."

"I would reassure you if I could."

"You have done your service well. I came here hoping to find you and to rest a little. I have seen naught of the hills and woods of late, and the summer is waxing full."

"It is peaceful here. When I come here, I can almost imagine I am in the heart of Pelgrin itself, it is so quiet. I take heart that even in a storm-blown sea of troubles, there are still islands of serenity to be found. Nothing can touch them, and nothing will."

The queen moved to rise, and Durwin offered his hand. "Stay a while longer if you wish, my lady. I must go and begin with these." He shook sparkling drops from the biddleweed.

"No, we will return together. I must look in on the king once again."

They moved to their horses and then rode back to Askelon Castle in the quiet warmth of each other's company.

"Where do you come from, changeling?" Quentin asked, squeezing the water from his jerkin. "And what is your name?"

"I'll not tell you until I know who it is that asks." The young woman's eyes flashed defiantly.

"Very well, a name for a name. I am Quentin, and this is my friend Toli." As he said their names, Quentin thought he saw a flicker of recognition cross the girl's comely features. "Do those names mean anything to you?"

"No. Should they?" she shot back.

"There are some who would have heard them spoken before, that is all."

"I suppose there are some who have heard of most anyone as loud and quarrelsome as you two are."

Quentin rankled at the girl's sharp tongue. "You have not told us your name, though we have given ours," he said crossly.

"I give my name to whom I choose. And I choose to be known only by my friends." She shook her limp, wet hair and turned her face away.

"If you knew who it was that spoke to you . . . ," Quentin began hotly. His temper was rising at the haughty spirit of this obstinate young woman.

"If you knew who it was you mistreated . . ." She turned on Quentin again and, quick as a cat, leaped at him with claws extended.

Toli caught her by the arms once more, saying, "Peace! What Quentin is trying to tell you, my lady, is that we are sworn to protect all subjects of the realm. We are at your service." He spoke softly and released her when she grew quieter.

"Well, you need have no care for me," she returned in a more subdued tone. "I am not one of your king's subjects."

"Not of Mensandor? Ah, now we are getting somewhere," Quentin remarked sourly.

The girl looked up at each of them from beneath dark lashes, as if sizing them up. "Very well, I will trust you—but only because Toli has a mannered tongue." She glanced darkly at Quentin. "I am Esme. My home is Elsendor."

"Then you are very far from home. What brings you to Mensandor and to this modest village yonder?"

"The village was not my destination, I assure you, sir. But my tale is not for your ears, worry me though you will."

"And who might best hear your tale if not king's men?" Quentin asked.

"The king himself!" She folded her arms over her chest and glared at them both.

"Then allow me to offer you the king's protection until you shall obtain audience with him," said Toli, bowing low. Esme smiled triumphantly and nodded. Quentin rolled his eyes heavenward.

"I accept your protection; it seems a woman needs it in this rough land." She straightened her clothes and looked at them squarely. "Take me at once to the king, I charge you."

"Toli is right to offer you the king's protection, and we will ride to the king—but not yet. We have a charge placed upon us by the king himself and cannot return until it is accomplished."

The young lady frowned and seemed about to lash out angrily once more, but again Toli interceded. "Quentin speaks the truth; were it not for the urgency of our errand, we would gladly conduct you directly to the castle itself. We return there ourselves as soon as we can."

"Then I will go myself. With or without your protection, my mission must not wait."

"How will you go? In your boat? That would take far longer than you might think. The current of the Herwydd is strong; going against it is not easily done, and Askelon is far. Or perhaps you would walk all the way?"

"Or you could give me your horse," she answered.

"Quentin is suggesting prudence, my lady. Our errand is perhaps of an end not many days hence. We have good horses that can reach Askelon swiftly at need. Come with us"—he hesitated—"for your protection and so you may reach the king the sooner."

The fiery young lady stared from one to the other of them before she made up her mind. "Very well, I will go with you. There seems no better choice." With that she turned and began walking back toward the abandoned village of Persch.

Toli and Quentin followed behind, and upon reaching the village square, Esme turned to them and announced, "I will attend directly." She then disappeared into one of the dwellings.

"I will wait here for our proud companion," announced Quentin. "Fetch the horses, and we'll leave as soon as she returns."

Toli brought the horses and set himself to redistributing small items of their traveling effects.

"What are you doing?" asked Quentin, looking on.

"I assumed that you would not care to have the lady share your mount, so I am making ready mine."

"I will take responsibility; it is my place."

"How so? It was my tongue which placed this burden upon your back. Therefore, I will help bear it."

"If it pleases you, Toli, you shall carry her in your arms all the way. Have it as you will."

"I am ready," called a voice behind them. They turned to see a very different young woman from the one they had fished from the sea. She had gathered back her hair and bound it in a leather thong. She wore riding trousers, but of a finer cut and fit than a man's, and embroidered with intricate designs along the seams. She wore a short cloak thrown over one shoulder; it, too, was carefully embroidered and matched her trousers. The cloak was a deep blue, as was the soft tunic under it. A thin belt of new leather held a long dagger at her waist. Soft leather boots covered her feet and reached almost to her knees.

A more remarkable transformation could hardly have been anticipated. Toli and Quentin blinked in wonder. Esme looked like a warrior princess, but such things were unheard of in Mensandor.

"Which horse will I have?" she demanded.

"Toli has agreed to share his with you."

Without another word they climbed into their saddles. Toli reached a hand down and drew the lady up to sit behind him on Riv's broad back. They soon left the silent village behind.

As the declining sun lengthened their shadows upon the green hills, they stopped for the night in a stand of thin aspens near a trickling brook. Quentin and Toli routinely began making camp, while Esme planted herself on a grassy knoll and drew her knees up to wait. Only when Toli had meat on the spit and broth bubbling in the shallow pot did she approach.

"We will eat better tomorrow, perhaps," remarked Quentin. "We did not have the opportunity to gather provisions as we would have liked." He inclined his head in the direction of Persch.

"It appears a banquet to me," said Esme, her eyes glowing as she watched Toli turn the spits. "I have not eaten in two days."

The confession shamed Quentin, who colored deeply. "I . . . I must apologize for my behavior back there, my lady. It was not right of me to judge you so."

"And I have misjudged you," she admitted. "But perhaps you will grant me my error. A woman must sometimes discourage untoward advances by strange men. I thought you would take advantage of me."

"I would pity the man who tried."

"No harm will come to you while you remain with us, my lady," said Toli earnestly.

"I thank you, good sir." When their eyes met, Toli looked away quickly and finished preparing the meal.

When it was ready, they sat down together. Toli handed a plate of meat around and filled their bowls with broth. He broke some crusts of hard bread that they each dipped into the broth to soften it for chewing. Esme ate with a most unladylike appetite that Quentin and Toli made certain not to notice.

"You are most kind not to scold my ill manners. The food does so warm an empty stomach."

"How could we scold what we ourselves indulge?" asked Quentin. "Have more; you are welcome."

"I have eaten quite enough, thank you. Toli, your way with simple fare is praiseworthy. I would care to see what you could do with more exotic victuals."

Toli said nothing, but merely smiled mysteriously.

"Would you now tell us what you were doing in the village alone?" Quentin asked after some time.

Esme looked into her bowl of broth as if the answer might be read there. She cocked her head to one side and said, "That I was alone was no fault of my own. I went there, as you would surmise, to obtain the clothes you first saw me wearing. I found the village empty as you did; so I helped myself to the garments."

"You wished to disguise yourself—why?"

"I have already told you—a woman cannot be too careful when traveling alone. It was a poor disguise, I know. But I thought it might serve until I could discover another or until"—she smiled broadly—"disguises were no longer necessary."

"Do you know so little of Mensandor, then, that you think every man a rogue?"

"It is not Mensandor's subjects that I fear, though I did not propose to put them to the test. But tell me of your errand. Something tells me that we may be of closer purpose than seems first apparent."

"We go to see comrades long overdue," offered Toli. "They were sent to——"

"To derive the truth from certain rumors now growing in the land," said Quentin tactfully.

Esme's brow became suddenly troubled. "They rode to the south, your friends?"

"Yes; south along the coast. Why?"

"Good sirs, I greatly fear for your friends." Her voice held a note of sharp concern. "I do not wonder that they are long overdue. It is possible they will not return at all."

Quentin leaned forward in keen attention. Toli laid aside the utensils as he watched Esme carefully. "What do you know about this?" asked Quentin calmly enough, but there was no mistaking his anxiety.

"Only this . . ." Esme saw the effect her words had had on them and chose her way carefully. "It was between Dorn and Persch that I lost my companions two days ago."

CHAPTER 12

There you are," said Quentin softly as he moved quietly up to stand at Toli's shoulder. "I should have known you would be stargazing."

"I could not sleep, Kenta. The star is growing." The light of the late-night sky gleamed on the Jher's upturned face.

"It looks the same to me," Quentin said without conviction. "It will be dawn soon; perhaps we should make ready to leave. Our new companion's words have troubled me; it would ease my mind to be on our way. I would not like to think that Theido and Ronsard were trapped because we didn't warn them and prevent it."

"Yes, the star grows each night, and evil increases," replied Toli. He turned and looked at Quentin, his large, dark eyes filled with a light Quentin had rarely seen. "I will make ready the horses and wake the lady. I fear the day is already far spent."

He slipped away noiselessly to leave Quentin pondering his words and peering up at the star glowing brightly in the east. Quentin heard a soft tread behind him, light as a shadow, and Esme came to stand beside him.

"So you know about the star too," she said.

"We have been watching it, yes—though what it betokens is not certain."

"There is no need to spare me your worst suspicions. Our priests

84

are well acquainted with heavenly signs and the reading of portents. I know what they say about the Preying Star. But I am not afraid."

"Then you are braver than I, my lady. For I must admit that I sometimes feel very much afraid when I look upon it."

Toli brought the horses, and the three mounted up. They left the shelter of the aspen grove, slipped out into the waning night, and moved across the starlit hills. Behind them rose the cragged walls of the Fiskills and the narrow trail beside the sea. They had come through the pinched corridor late in the afternoon and had pushed up into the sloping foothills on the other side to find their camp for the night.

Although extremely curious about his new charge, Quentin had not pressed her for details of her story. She did not seem inclined to talk about the loss of her companions, nor about the mission that took her to King Eskevar. But her fearful thoughts on the safety of Theido and Ronsard had unsettled him, for he had been feeling a vague uneasiness regarding them himself. She had put words to his doubt and had made it real and urgent.

"They must have gone south toward Halidom," Quentin had reasoned as they sat around the campfire after their supper. "Otherwise, Esme and her party would have met them on the road between Dorn and Persch."

"But why would they go so far?" Toli had asked.

Quentin had shrugged. "I will ask them that when next we meet. Perhaps they saw something which took them there. These empty villages are mystery enough for me."

They had lapsed into silence and uneasy rest. Quentin's restive mind gnawed at his unanswered questions like a hound with a twice-picked shank. He felt better now that they were moving again.

He listened to the cadence of their passing in the deepest part of the night. Soon the horizon would begin to lighten in the east as the sun rolled back the darkness for another day. But now they rode as night's children, slipping unseen through the sleeping world.

Quentin struck out once more along the coastal road, a wide, rock-strewn path that linked the seaside villages. If Ronsard and his knights were to be found, it would likely be along this road, although there were other, more infrequently traveled routes to the north through the brown Wilderlands. These were tracks that the traders used to traverse the vast and empty Suthlands and bring them to the more populated regions of the north.

The empty villages—first Persch, then Yallo and Biskan—had greatly troubled him; though he sought time and again for a logical explanation, none was forthcoming. He wondered if Theido and Ronsard had discovered them as well. They must have if they had passed through, or the towns might have been abandoned after the knights had ridden on. There was no telling how long ago they had traveled the road, where they might have stayed, or who they might have seen.

Quentin hoped, though reason told him six armed knights were a match for anything, that they had not encountered whatever it was that had overtaken Esme's party.

They rode for an hour or more, following the rising and falling trail as it climbed and descended the gently undulating hills along the coast. At each crest they could see the great sea, lying dark and still in the distance. Gerfallon was not troubled by the mere vexations of mortal men; he slept in his deep bed, and his creatures with him. Quentin stopped at the crest of the next hill and waited until Toli, with Esme sitting behind, hands on thighs, had drawn up beside him. Blazer jigged sideways, impatient with the delay.

"What do you think it could be?" asked Quentin, nodding in the direction of the northern hills. A faint, leaden smudge could barely be seen glowing in the sky far away. "If I did not know better, I would say that the sun was coming up in the north today. A false sun that would be."

"I have seen such false sunrises, and you may suspect some misfortune is at hand."

"What is it?" asked Esme.

"Fire," said Toli.

"Are you certain? It does not look like fire to me," said Quentin, leaning forward in his saddle for a better look. "Why, it would take a pile of wood the size of a—"

"Village." Toli supplied the missing word.

"You do not think . . . ," cried Quentin with growing alarm. "Illem lies in that direction!"

"Yes, a league to the north, I would say."

"Then we waste time talking," said Quentin as he turned his horse toward the glow in the sky. "We may be of some help. Let us go!"

"Hold tight, my lady," said Toli as he snapped the reins. Riv leaped from the track and bounded after Quentin's gliding shape.

As the horses galloped at full speed, the glow on the horizon brightened and spread. At half a league it covered the far hills and deepened with an ugly, reddish hue. The hanging gloom of smoke could be discerned against the darker curtain of night.

In the east the sky had grown pearly with the coming of the dawn, making the glow ahead seem ever more ominous and unnatural.

Quentin reined to a halt at the bottom of a deep ravine. In the spring the thaw from the Fiskills filled the dry bed with icy water. Now it was filled with weeds and brush, the waters having long since emptied into the sea.

"I think Illem lies just beyond the ridge," said Quentin. The ravine curved its way through a long trough of a valley bounded on three sides by low ridges. From the bottom of the dry streambed, the sky to the north shone as rust, and the smoke rolled away on the landward wind.

"The fire rages," said Toli. "I advise caution until we discover what caused it—or who."

"I agree," said Esme. "We are only three against—who knows how many."

Quentin looked at her with surprise. She evidently counted herself as one of the protectors rather than the one protected. "Why must there be an enemy? Surely you don't think . . ." Quentin stopped; he knew Toli's uncanny instinct well enough to know that even his slightest whims should be taken seriously. He had seen them proven true too often to dismiss them lightly. "Very well, we will continue along the valley until we draw even with the town. Then we can climb out below it in the shelter of the ridge."

They started off again, but at a more measured gait. Quentin led the way, scanning the tops of the hills for any signs of unusual activity. They had proceeded only a little way when the course wound around a sharp bend. "Wait!" said Toli in a sharp whisper. "Listen!"

Just around the bend could be heard an odd muffled sound, as if a large animal were rooting in the soft soil of the dry streambed. It shuffled along, breathing heavily, with an airy, bristling sigh. Blazer and Riv lifted their ears at the sound.

"What can it be?" wondered Esme, her whisper almost lost in the quickly growing intensity of the sound.

"Whatever it is, it is coming this way," said Quentin. "Over here!" He spurred Blazer toward the near bank to escape the path of the oncoming beast.

But he was too late. As Blazer jumped forward, the thing came churning around the bend. Quentin had a glimpse of a vast, rippling body— shapeless and ill defined. The creature saw him too, and let out a yelp that seemed to come from a dozen throats at once. It was then that Quentin knew what it was.

"Hold!" shouted Quentin, laying the reins hard to his mount's side, so that Blazer reared on his hind legs and wheeled about. His command echoed from the far bank. Toli was instantly at his side.

The beast screamed and broke into a hundred separate pieces, each one darting in a different direction. The strange beast was, in fact, the townspeople of Illem, fleeing their burning homes en masse. The sound had been that of many feet hurrying through the dry brush and the murmur of fear as they fled.

"Hold!" Quentin called again. "In the name of the Dragon King."

The people stopped. The sight of the instantly appearing horse and rider rooted them to the spot. For a moment no one dared to move. Quentin judged them to be as many as fifty in all: men, women, and children.

One brave man stepped forward. "Do not hinder us, sir. Whoever you are, if you call yourself friend, let us go." The man approached Quentin slowly. The others behind him were too frightened to speak or move.

"We will do you no harm; have no fear," said Quentin.

The man looked over his shoulder and cried, "The Destroyer is upon us! We have only escaped with our lives—let us go! Even now he comes for us!"

"Who is the Destroyer? We will meet him and—"

"No, it is too late!" He made a quick motion to his followers, and as they started to move on, the man suddenly threw his hand in the air. "Ahh! They have found us!"

Quentin looked behind the man and saw something moving by torchlight down the sides of the ravine. He drew his sword from its place behind his saddle and heard the ring of Toli's blade at the same time.

"Run for it!" Quentin cried to the townspeople. "We will protect your escape."

Toli charged ahead, and Quentin saw more torches boiling down the side of the ravine. Quentin leaned forward on Blazer's neck, darted toward the embankment, and drove straight to the nearest of them. He heard Toli's blade sing in the air and the crash of metal followed by a stifled cry. With his own sword held high, he leaped across the flat bed of the stream and caught a confused group of mail-clad soldiers as they tumbled down the bank. Two of them felt the bite of his blade, and two others fled back up the bank.

Turning, Quentin found his way barred from behind. Blazer reared and lashed out with flying hooves. Quentin's sword became a lashing shield before him as he fought to Toli's side. Twice a lance head thrust out of the darkness, and each time the sword sliced through the shaft. Now a buckler was cleaved in two, and then a helm.

It was clear that the soldiers had not anticipated finding men on horseback. They were uncertain what to do and ran into each other in an effort to stay out of range of Toli's well-trained steeds. This led Quentin to believe that, though greatly outnumbered, they would prevail.

But once over the initial surprise, the soldiers quickly regrouped and surrounded the riders. "We are cut off!" cried Quentin as he raced by Toli. "We must break through the line. Where is the weakest point?"

"There—see that gap?" Esme called. Quentin saw her point past him with her dagger.

He looked and saw a space between two soldiers who were hurrying toward them. "Good eye! Follow me!" He threw the reins ahead, and Blazer sprang for the spot. Closer, he saw that a wall of low bushes stood in the gap. Before he had time to think, Blazer was up and over it.

Toli was not so lucky. Riv, with the weight of an extra rider, charged up and cleared the shrubs with his forelegs, but his hind legs became tangled in the branches. Quentin saw all three go down as soldiers instantly converged on the spot.

Blazer thundered to a churning stop, and Quentin pulled him around and headed back into the fray. "Whist Orren, protect your servant!" he cried in desperation.

In the scant few moments of battle, the sky had lightened enough to see the soldiers distinct from the darker background. Quentin sounded a battle cry and prepared for the shock of the inevitable collision. He saw Riv thrashing his head as the horse regained his feet. Toli and Esme were lost beneath a dozen black shapes of soldiers swarming over them.

Quentin bore down and slashed out at the jumble of lances and swords. He heard the gasps of pain and felt the sword strike deep. He thrust and thrust again, and the roiling mass of bodies parted.

Then he felt something tugging at his cloak, yanking him backward. Hands reached out and grabbed his arms; his sword was struck from his hand. Blazer reared and jumped, but the grip on Quentin's arms held firm, and he was hauled from his saddle.

As he tumbled to the ground, he saw Esme leap out of nowhere and dart past him. For one heartbeat their eyes met. In that same instant Quentin thought she would come to his aid. But she turned away and was instantly in Toli's saddle. Then Quentin was on the ground, and a foot smashed into his throat.

As the world spun sickeningly before his eyes, he heard the sound of Riv's hooves pounding away.

CHAPTER 13

Heavy draperies were hung across the windows of the Dragon King's chamber. The barest thread of light shone through a chink in the gathered cloth to fall in a single shaft upon the king's high bed. Otherwise, the room was as dark as a cave deep under a hill.

Durwin entered quietly and stood for a moment by the door. He pressed a finger to his chin and then moved closer, listening to the irregular and shallow breathing of the still form on the bed. He stepped nearer the stricken king and stooped to peer into the sleeping man's face. It was then that he detected the faint, putrid odor of death.

The holy hermit spun around and laid the wooden goblet he carried on a nearby table. He went to the high, narrow window and seized the draperies in both hands and pulled with all his might. There was a tearing sound and a crash as the stifling folds came tumbling down beneath an avalanche of dazzling morning light now streaming into the gloomy chamber.

Fresh air swept fair and warm into the night-chilled room and banished the foul stench. The man on the bed, pale and wizened amid his mounds of thick coverings, stirred feebly. A breathless moan passed his lips.

"My king, awaken!" shouted Durwin, bending close. "Do you hear me? Awaken, I say, and throw off the sleep of death!"

Durwin snatched up the goblet and, slipping his arm beneath Eskevar's head, brought it close to the invalid's lips. He poured, and the yellow liquid ran down the king's chin and neck, staining his bedclothes.

But some of the medicine seeped into his patient's mouth. The king gasped weakly, and the hermit poured again, emptying the goblet. In a moment the gray eyelids flickered and rose, revealing dark eyes filmy with stupor.

"Awake, Eskevar. Your time is not yet." The eyes stared unmoving in their milky gaze. "Oh, have I come too late?" Durwin muttered to himself.

"What is it? Durwin? What has hap—" The queen appeared in the open doorway. She took two steps into the room, then saw her husband staring upward, motionless. "Oh!" she cried, rushing to the bed.

"He is with us still, my lady. But for how long I cannot say." As he spoke, Alinea clutched his arm for support, then threw herself upon the bed, burying her face deep in the bedclothes. In a moment her sobs could be heard, muffled and indistinct.

Durwin stood aside, regarding the queen and her dying king. His own heart swelled with pity and grief. "God Most High," he prayed, "you give men life and receive it back from them when their span is done. All things grow in their season as established by your command. Surely it is to you a hateful thing when life is cut short.

"An evil malady afflicts our king and crushes him in a deadly embrace. Release him from it. Turn his steps back from their downward path, and restore him once more to his loved ones and to his realm."

Durwin's quiet prayer lingered in the air like a healing balm. The breeze blew softly, carrying the scent of roses from the garden outside. It whispered softly in the stillness of the room. Then all was silent.

"Durwin—look!" Alinea exclaimed. In her hands she clasped one of Eskevar's as she knelt at his side. The king was now gazing quietly at both of them; his eyes were moist with tears.

"Oswald!" Durwin called. The queen's chamberlain, hovering near the doorway, stepped fearfully into the room. "Fetch me the jar from my worktable!" The worried servant disappeared at once and was back before Durwin could add, "And hurry!"

The hermit once more administered the liquid, pulling the seal from the stoppered bottle and pouring it down the king's throat. This time Eskevar coughed deeply, closed his eyes as if in pain and said, in a voice barely audible, "Have I fallen so low as to be poisoned in my own bed?"

"The king complains—that is certainly a good sign." Alinea turned anxious eyes to the hermit, who replaced the stopper in the jar. "My lady, he is safe for the moment, but not out of danger yet."

Durwin moved about the bed and began throwing off the coverings of wool and fur. "I have been foolish and slow-witted, however. Perhaps the king would not have sunk so far, almost beyond return, if I had been more observant. Come, my lady, we must get him up."

Alinea looked doubtful. "Do you think—"

"At once. He must save the strength he still possesses. He must use it to gain more. Help me to get him on his feet."

They took the unresisting body of the king, now light as feather down, between them and raised him carefully. Supporting him by the arms, they pulled him from the bed gently and placed his bare feet upon the floor. "Ahhh!" Eskevar cried out in pain. The queen threw a worried glance at Durwin, who only nodded as if to say, "Continue; it must be done."

Carefully they walked him step by halting step back and forth across the room, stopping to stand before the window each time to allow him to catch his breath. On and on they walked, the king with his head lolling on his shoulders, barely conscious.

By midday Eskevar could move freely, though he still required the arm of his queen for support. His brow was damp with sweat and his shrunken frame shaken by racking spasms of violent coughing. He swooned with exhaustion.

Durwin and Oswald carried him back to bed as Alinea looked on, wringing her hands. "He will sleep soundly now, I think. We will wake him again in a while to eat. And he must walk again before the sun sets. I will watch him through the night."

Durwin turned away from the bed and shook his head back and forth slowly. "How could I have let him slip so far?"

"In truth, it is not your fault. You have done all that could be asked, and even now you have saved his life." Alinea patted Durwin's arm gently and smiled with calm assurance.

"The god has opened my eyes in time, my lady. That is something indeed to be thankful for. But we must not slacken our vigil again or he will be lost. He is very weak and his strength very fragile."

"Come to the kitchen, Durwin, and refresh yourself. You, too, will be needing your strength in the hours to come, as will we all."

Quentin twisted on the ground. A sharp pain seared through his side. One eye was swelling shut; and his mouth, tasting of blood, throbbed with a dull ache. He raised his head slowly and looked cautiously about.

Smoke from the burning town still drifted in hanging clouds that rolled along the ground, stinging his eyes and making his nose run. The sun was barely up, a fierce red ball burning through the black haze that filled the air and seeped down the slopes of the ravine where he lay.

A soldier nearby saw Quentin's slight movement and jabbed him in the shoulder with the butt of his lance. Quentin put his head down again and lay still; he had seen what he wanted to see. The main force of the soldiers had moved off; only a few remained to guard the prisoners—if prisoners there were, for Toli was nowhere to be seen.

Quentin tried to wiggle his fingers, but they were numb; the ropes that bound him had been tied tightly and efficiently. Both hands were thrust behind his back and lashed together; a loop passed around his neck and one around his feet. To move hands or feet tightened the noose around his neck and strangled him. But periodically Quentin wormed this way and that in an attempt to better reckon his surroundings.

It was only by the hand of the god that he was still alive. In the chaotic moment of his capture, he had been instantly beaten senseless. As he lay bleeding on the ground, a scowling warrior had raised a double-bladed axe over him. Quentin had seen the blade flash on its downward arc toward his heart.

He was saved at the last heartbeat by a hand that had caught the axe-man's arm in midstroke. An argument had broken out then. Although Quentin could not understand the slurred words of the rough speech, he knew that it concerned him and his probable fate. The soldier with the axe wanted to kill him at once. The other apparently insisted upon wait-ing, probably for a superior's approval. Quentin was then bound up and left to wonder what awaited him.

He did not have long to wait.

He heard the hollow sound of a horse's hooves. There was a sud-den scurrying around him, a harsh voice barked out an order, and he was jerked urgently upward to his knees by two grim warriors grasping him by the arms. The voice uttered another command, and Quentin's head was snapped sharply back by a hand thrust into his hair. His eyes squeezed shut with pain.

When he opened them again, he was looking into the cold, hard-ened eyes of a warlord of Nin.

The warlord regarded him coolly. He was wearing a strange form of battle dress made of bronze, which glowed in the rising sun with a red-dened luster that matched the tone of his flesh. His arms were covered in sleeves of mail from his shoulders to leggings. He wore no helmet, and his long black hair was pulled back and bound in a thick braid that hung down his back. A long, curved sword hung from the pommel of his sad-dle, its thin blade besmeared with crimson ribbons of blood.

The warlord's horse, wide of shoulder and heavy of flank, shook its braided mane and snorted loudly. One of the soldiers supporting

Quentin began speaking. The speech was strange to Quentin's ears; he could not think what language it might be, for he could not catch a word of it. But, he guessed, the soldier was telling his commander about how the prisoner had been captured.

The warlord listened intently, interrupting the discourse to ask a question at one point. Quentin then thought he saw a spark of interest light the savage countenance. He spoke a quick command, and two soldiers rushed forward and untied his legs. Then Quentin was hauled to his feet and marched away. The warlord watched him go, then spurred his horse and rode off down the ravine.

Quentin was pulled up the steep bank of the dry streambed. In the smoke blowing across the field he saw soldiers, all wearing the same coarse, dark clothing and carrying brutal-looking double-bladed battle-axes, clustered around several great wagons. At one the soldiers gave up their weapons, which were collected and placed in the wagon. At another they were given large baskets. They then hurried back into the smoldering remains of Illem.

Quentin was taken to one of the nearer wagons and placed up against one of the huge wheels, so large that it was fully as tall as he was. He was untied and then lashed to the wheel by his wrists and ankles. He had no choice but to watch the strange activity taking place in the ruins.

A line of soldiers emerged from the curtain of smoke, carrying sacks of grain and casks of wine. These and other foodstuffs, the provisions of the entire town, were heaped up into a great pile and then loaded into hand-drawn barrows that carted the provisions away.

Then soldiers with baskets began filing past, two by two, moving off into the hills. Quentin could not see where they were going, but knew the general direction to be north. The men carried the baskets on their shoulders, some bent low by the weight of what they carried. Quentin wondered what the baskets contained.

But as he watched the activity around him, his mind returned again and again to the one thing he feared most. More than about his own

safety, he wondered what had become of Toli. His friend and companion was gone. There were two possible explanations, he knew. Either Toli
had been killed in the attack, in which case his body lay unattended back
down in the ravine; or the crafty Jher had managed somehow to escape
in the confusion of the battle. Quentin prayed that Toli had escaped.

He heard a signal—a long blast on a horn—and a rank of men on
horses moved past the wagons. Each carried an axe and a shield as well
as the peculiar curved sword. The horses, too, were armored. Large discs
of hardened leather attached with rings of iron and woven into strips
were slung over the animals' withers and rumps, trailing almost to the
ground. Upon their hooves were bands of sharpened spikes; and two
long, cruel spikes sprouted from each horse's headplate as well.

Whoever they were, thought Quentin, they had come prepared for
war.

When the riders had passed, he heard another blast on the horn,
and to his horror, the wagons began rolling. Quentin, thinking they had
forgotten about him, cried out as the wheel to which he was tied rolled
forward. His cries brought nothing but laughter from the soldiers
nearby. He knew then that they had not forgotten him. He was intended
to travel with them in this torturous manner, battered slowly to death
on the turning wheel.

CHAPTER 14

Yeseph sat on a bench in his courtyard, head nodding toward his chest. All around him the gentle sounds of evening crept into the air. The sun had slipped behind the hills of Dekra, and though the sky was still a brilliant blue, streaked with orange clouds, long evening shadows cast the clean-swept courtyard of the esteemed elder into deep gloaming.

Beside him a young laurel tree rattled its fragrant leaves in the fitful breeze. The feathery notes of a lilting melody drifted over the wall and fell into the courtyard like delicate petals of a flower. His cup sat untasted near his hand. He sighed heavily.

There was a slight pit-a-pat and the rustle of clothing, and Karyll, his wife, was beside him. Yeseph could feel the warmth of her presence as she stood looking down on him.

"My husband is tired from his day's work," she said. "Dear one, awaken. Our evening meal is ready." Her voice was as light and soothing as the breeze that played in the tree.

Yeseph raised his head, and she saw his eyes gradually take in his surroundings as awareness returned. She saw the deeply etched lines of concern furrow his brow and crinkle around his eyes. He smiled when he saw her, and she noticed that it was a sad smile with no light in it.

"Husband, what is wrong?" She waited for him to tell her.

"I have had a dream," Yeseph explained simply.

"And your dream has troubled you, for it was a dream of darkness instead of light."

"How much you women see. Yes, it was a dream of darkness—a vision. I saw . . . ," he began, and then stopped. "No, I must not tell what I have seen just yet. I must ponder it in my heart for a time."

"Then you may eat while you ponder. Come. Your supper will be getting cold."

She turned and padded back into their dwelling. Yeseph watched her go, thinking how lucky he had been to find one so wise and understanding to share his old age. He breathed a prayer of thanksgiving to Whist Orren for his good fortune. Then he raised himself slowly and followed her in.

As they lingered over their meal, Karyll watched her mate closely. He did not eat with his usual fresh appetite, but dawdled over his plate. In the lambent glow of the candles on the low table, Yeseph sank further into pensive reflection. Twice he brought a morsel of food to his mouth only to return it to the plate absently.

"Yeseph," Karyll murmured gently, "you have not eaten well tonight. Your dream has upset you. If you will not tell me, perhaps you will tell the elders instead."

"Yes, that is what I must do." He got up from his stool at once and went to the door, where he paused and turned toward her, his form a dark silhouette against the evening sky. He seemed suddenly to come to himself once more. "I am going to call together the other elders. We will meet tonight. Do not wait for me, my love. It may be very late."

"I do not mind. I have some work with which to occupy myself while you are gone. Now, away with you. The quicker you go, the quicker I will have my Yeseph back."

In an inner chamber of the great Ariga temple, Yeseph waited for the elders to join him. It would not be long, for he had sent runners, three of the young men who served in the temple, to fetch the other Curatak leaders. He had merely to wait for their arrival, and the meeting could begin. Yeseph busied himself with lighting the many candles that stood on their long holders around the bare room.

In the center of the room, four straight, high-backed chairs sat in a circle facing one another. When the candles had been lit, Yeseph took his place, folding his hands in his lap in quiet meditation. In a few moments the curtains that overhung the chamber's entrance parted and the familiar form of Jollen entered, smoothing his council robes.

"Good evening, Elder Yeseph. Your summons saved me from quite a distasteful chore—I had promised to begin translating a song for some of the children."

"That, distasteful? Surely, you do not mean it. If you do, perhaps it were better you went back and got right to work."

"Oh, do not misunderstand. I love the children and would give them anything. But the song they have chosen is of the old Ariga dialect. A very dreary piece about an unhappy youngster who is changed into a willow because of his complaining. I tried to persuade them to choose something happier, but their hearts were set on this one and none other."

"You will be better for it in the end, I am sure," laughed Yeseph. "An excursion into the old dialect will sharpen your wits."

Jollen made a wry face. "If I did not know better, I would suspect you of having put them up to it. It would be just like you."

The next to enter was Patur, the unofficial leader of the group. It was he who most often took it upon himself to inform the Curatak of the elders' decisions in matters of public import. He was a most able and influential orator and often led the worship in the temple. He was well studied in the religion of the vanished Ariga.

"Greetings, my learned friends," he said, adjusting the robe he had just donned upon entering the chamber. His eyes gleamed in anticipation of the evening's work, for, whatever it was, it would involve him in close communion with other sharp minds, a thing he dearly loved.

"Greetings, Patur. Thank you for coming along so quickly. We only have to wait . . . ah! Here he comes now." Yeseph nodded to the curtain, and Clemore, the most recent addition to the group upon the death of Asaph, the oldest member, entered, bowing low.

"Good evening, brothers. I pray you are well." The others nodded, and they all took their places.

Yeseph looked from one to the other of their familiar faces. These were his most trusted friends; yes, Clemore was right: his brothers. He could tell them his dream, and they would shoulder the burden, no matter how small or great it would prove in the end. He felt better just being in their presence and wondered if any of them ever felt the same way about him. He supposed they did, as often they had sought his counsel singly or with the others. Now it was his turn to put a problem before them.

"Good Yeseph, do not keep us in suspense any longer. Tell us what disturbs you, for I see in your eyes that your spirit is distressed by something," said Patur.

"You are right; I am troubled." He paused as he collected his thoughts and looked at each of them in turn. "This evening I had a dream. Very brief it was, and very strange."

"You believe it to presage something of significance?" asked Clemore.

"I do."

"And have you an interpretation for us?"

"No, that is why I have asked you to come here tonight. I thought perhaps together we might seek understanding."

"Very well," said Jollen, "tell us your dream as it came to you. We will ask the Most High to enlighten us with its meaning."

Yeseph nodded slowly and, closing his eyes, began to recite his dream.

"I had just stepped into the courtyard when a great drowsiness came over me, even though I had not eaten. I quickly fell asleep where I sat and began to dream. And the dream was this:

"I saw a river running through the land, and wherever the river touched the land, it sprang forth abundantly with green shoots and trees and food for all living things. And the water was clear and good; men came to the river's edge to drink, and the wild creatures drank and were satisfied.

"But then a dark storm came out of the east and began to blow. The river still ran, but the water began to change, becoming the color of blood. At first just a trace of red clouded the clean water, but it deepened until the water ran black and the river became foul.

"Now no one could drink from the river and live; men who drank of it died, and animals too. And all the trees and grass and flowers which had sprung up along the river's banks now withered and died. The land became desolate, for all things depended upon the river for their life. The winds came and blew away the dust, and dust filled the air in great clouds, covering the land, and the river dried up."

Yeseph paused, drew breath, and continued. In the silence of the inner chamber, his words sounded like the toll of a bell.

"Darkness fell upon the land, and I heard a voice crying out. It was the voice of a terrified child, saying, 'Where is my father? I am afraid. Where is my protector?'

"The darkness rolled up in answer to the child. It spoke with the voice of the night and said, 'Your father's bones are dust and scattered to the winds. Your protector's sword is broken. You will live in darkness all your days, for now you are a child of the night.'

"I wept to hear those words. My tears fell like a mighty rain upon the earth. And the rain of tears washed over the land, which had become a bowl to catch the tears and hold them all.

"Another voice, mightier than the first, called out and said, 'Where are my servants? What has become of those who are called by my name?'

"I answered, saying, 'I am here, and only I—all others have perished.' I fell on my face in my grief.

"The voice answered me and said, 'Rise up and take the bowl and pour it out.' I took the bowl in my hands and poured it out, and it became a sword of living light which flashed in the face of the darkness, and the darkness fled before it. 'Take the sword!' the voice commanded.

"I began to tremble all over, because I knew I could not take up the sword. 'I have never touched a sword and do not know how to use it,' I argued.

"Then give it to the child,' the great voice answered. 'He will use it, and you will guide his hand.'

"But when I looked for the child to give him the shining sword, he was gone. The night had swallowed him up, though I could hear him crying as the darkness carried him farther and farther away."

Yeseph opened his eyes once more and looked at his brothers in their council robes. They sat unmoving as they pondered his words. Their eyes were grave, and their faces reflected the concern they all felt at hearing Yeseph's dream.

"Brothers," intoned Patur deeply, "this is a most unsettling dream. I hear in it a warning of some urgency. Let us now ask the Most High to guide us in our interpretation, for I believe it is given us this night to oppose the power of darkness bespoken in the dream."

At that the elders of Dekra joined hands and began to pray.

CHAPTER 15

The sleek black stallion seemed to flow down hills and through valleys like water. Esme had only to press with her knees or move a hand to the right or left and the horse responded, as if to her very thoughts. The animal was remarkably well trained—so much so that Esme began to fear for its welfare. Riv would run until his heart burst before slackening his pace in disobedience to his rider's command.

The scene of the ill-fated flight lay far behind her now, and still the horse flew on, the lather streaming off his neck and shoulders in flecks whipped away by the wind. Esme saw the dark line of a creek snaking through the lowland valley ahead. Where the creek rounded the grassy base of a hill, there rose a stand of young birches, shimmering white in the morning light. That, she thought, would be a good place to rest.

"Whoa, Riv!" she called, leaning forward in the saddle. She pulled back the reins with the lightest touch, and the horse slowed to a canter and then a trot. Esme let him cool down before reaching the quiet stream, knowing that it would not be good to let him drink his fill while still hot from the chase and winded. She would need this horse to reach Askelon.

The birches ringed a shady hollow where long grasses grew, fed by the stream. It was secluded and invisible to any who might come after her. The stony feet of the hill lay exposed at one side of the hollow where the stream formed a shallow pool.

She slid from the saddle and led Riv into the shady grove, walking him slowly. The hollow was cool and silent and full of golden spatters of sunlight and green shadow. Warily, she advanced toward the running water heard spilling blithely over a rank of stones set in its course. She heard the call of a meadow bird above her on the hill and the swish of the horse's legs moving through the grass. That was all, apart from the bubbling water. Yes, she was safe.

Esme led her mount to the edge of the pool and watched as he plunged his nose into the water. He drank deeply and pulled his head out of the stream to shake his gleaming mane in the sunlight. Glistening pearls of water were flung into the air, then splashed back into the crystal pool. She watched as the horse repeated the procedure several more times, and each time she was a little closer to forgetting that she had just barely escaped with her life.

Riv snorted and turned away from the water to stand looking at her calmly, as if to say, "You may drink—I will keep watch." Esme knelt in the long grass, cupped her hands, and brought the clear water to her mouth. When she had finished, she led Riv to a patch of wild clover and let him eat his fill. She did not tether him, knowing that a horse as well trained as Riv would not abandon his rider to wander off.

She left the horse to crop the clover and turned her attention to the hill nearby. It presented to her the highest vantage for viewing her surroundings. Having left the fray at the ravine with little more thought than to come away with her skin, she had almost no idea where she might be. As much as possible she had tried to hold the direction whereby they had entered the ravine in the first place, her object being to regain the road they had been following. Once on the road, she would turn north and then hurry to Askelon.

Esme climbed the steep slope of the hill as it rose out of the vale and above the trees. Out of the shade, the air was warmer and alive with bees and butterflies beginning their daily chores. A fresh wind blew ruffles along the tall grass; the sky billowed bright and blue, unconcerned with the darker deeds of night and desperate men. Here she could almost forget what had passed just a few hours earlier.

But she could not forget the two gallant men who had so courageously flown to the aid of the helpless townspeople and who had, without question, offered her protection as well. As she reached the crown of the hill, she turned her eyes back toward Illem, now leagues behind her. There was nothing to be seen; not even a smudge of smoke on the horizon remained to mark the place.

For a moment she stood in indecision—should she return and try to discover what had become of her friends? Or go on, to complete her charge and deliver her message to the king?

It was an empty choice, she knew. The enemy that had overcome them in the ravine at Illem was the same that had surprised her and her companions on the road. Now the lives of two more had been added to the sum, for there was little doubt in her mind that by now Quentin and Toli were dead. And were it not for the importance of her mission, she would have stayed to share their fate.

There was nothing to be done but go on.

She gazed out over the land, her dark eyes sweeping the horizon for any recognizable landmark. Away to the south, she saw a thin slice of spangled blue that merged with the sky. *The sea*, she thought, *I have not gone far wrong*. By squinting up her eyes she could almost see the road itself as it hugged the coastal hills. She cast one look over her shoulder to see if the dark enemy had followed her, but saw nothing except the radiant sky and the hills of summer. So she turned with heavy heart to leave.

Clambering back down the side of the hill, Esme heard the excited whinny of a horse. Was it Riv, or some other? She stopped, her heart now fluttering in panic. She listened.

From beneath the leafy canopy directly below her she heard again the shrill scream of a horse in distress. In the tangle of leaves and branches, she could not see the animal, nor its assailant. As quickly and as quietly as she could, she slipped the rest of the way down the hill, careful not to show herself openly.

Once below the treetops she saw Riv, legs splayed, head down, backed against the rocks, shaking his mane and baring his teeth. But she could see nothing at all that should so upset him. All was as she had left it. Not a single intruder, man or beast, was in evidence.

Esme dropped to the ground and crouched in the grass for a moment. Hearing nothing and seeing nothing disturbing, she rose and went to the frightened animal to comfort it.

"There, Riv. Easy, boy." She patted his sleek jaw and curled a slim arm around his neck. "Easy, now. What is it, Riv? Hmm? What has frightened my brave one?"

The horse calmed under her touch and soothing voice. He nickered softly, low in his throat, and tossed his head. But he continued to look away across the creek—at nothing Esme could see.

"There, now. See? All is well. There is nothing—"

Before Esme could finish, Riv tossed his head, eyes rolling white in terror, and broke away from her. She snatched at the dangling reins, but the horse leaped away and ran through the long grass to stand whinnying across the hollow.

"Riv!" Esme shouted impatiently. "You perverse creature! Come back here!" She stood with her hands on her hips as the horse bucked and shied, spinning in circles of fear as she watched. What had gotten into the animal? wondered Esme. She had seen nothing like it before.

"Away, foul beast!
And take your rider—
Or be ye still,
And stand beside her."

At the strange, singsong words spoken in a rasping babble of a voice, Esme whirled around. Her hand flew to the long dagger at her belt.

"Not a hangman's knot.
Nor blade of knife
Prevail against
This sibyl's life!"

Esme could not believe her eyes. For there, in a huddle of rags on a rock in the middle of the creek, stood a humpbacked old woman. She held a long staff in one hand and waved the other before her as if warding off bees. As Esme watched in mute astonishment, the old woman hopped as lightly as a cricket from stone to stone and so crossed the stream without so much as wetting a single tatter.

Upon landing on the bank, the old woman shook her rags in a flurry and stamped the ground three times with her staff. Then she proceeded to hobble toward the spot where Esme stood gaping in amazement. Where had she come from?

"Who are you, old mother?" asked Esme warily. The withered creature did not answer but drew closer in her peculiar hopping gait, swinging the staff and puffing mightily. Her hair hung in a mass of tangled gray snakes bedecked with bits of leaf and twig. The shriveled face looked like a dried apple, a mass of lines and creases browned by the wind and baked by the sun. When the woman moved, Esme imagined she could hear her brittle bones rattle; she appeared as old as the rocks under the hill.

"Who are you?" Esme repeated her question.

The hag made a pass in front of her with her wavering paw. Esme saw the rough hands and blackened nails and noticed, too, the scent of smoke and filth that billowed from the old woman.

"If rock and hill
And laughing water

Be hearth and home,
I'm Orphe's daughter."

She turned her weathered face slyly toward Esme and grinned a leering, toothless grin. It was then that Esme saw the sunken sockets where
once eyes used to be. The old woman was utterly blind.

"You live here . . . in the hollow?"

"So ye say
And speak ye truth
And I would ask
The same of you."

"Me? I am Esme. I did not mean to disturb your home. I heard the
horse . . ." She turned and noticed Riv had calmed and now stood watching and cautiously nodding his head as if spellbound. "I will trouble you
no further, but will leave at once."

"Of leaving let
No more be spoken
Till I have known
You by your token."

The ancient oracle held out her hand and propped her chin on her
staff and waited. She looked like a bent and gnarled tree on a withered
stump, offering a lonely branch. Her ragged clothing fluttered in the
breeze like leaves.

"I do not have a token, old mother," said Esme, thinking fast. It
did not do to upset an oracle. Especially one of the caste who called
themselves the Daughters of Orphe, for they were very powerful and
wise. "But let me offer a blessing in your name when next I come to a
shrine."

The hag threw back her head and laughed, and Esme saw two lonely brown teeth clinging like lichen to their place in the elderly jaw. The old seeress's laughter rang like the clatter of hail in an empty pot.

"Of blessings I
Have little need
Bless me instead
With a noble deed."

Esme started at the old woman's use of the word *noble*. She asked suspiciously, "What deed would you have me perform?"

"The rabbit caught
Within your briar,
Tastes the better
When aroast with fire."

The old woman crooked a knobby finger along the stream behind them. Esme followed it with her eyes and saw a hawthorn thicket rustling vigorously as if something were indeed caught within it.

"You would have me cook you a meal? This is the deed you require?" Esme did not like the idea; she was anxious to resume her journey. The country was not safe; the enemy prowled the hills at will. She had had two encounters already and did not welcome a third. She wished she had some item of value she could give the hag and be on her way. "Very well," she said slowly, and reluctantly went to retrieve the rabbit she knew she would find caught among the thorns.

Orphe's daughter turned and followed her with sightless sockets. She smiled, and the wrinkled old face contorted in a shrewd, lipless grimace. She mumbled happily to herself and fluttered like a crippled bird to perch herself upon a nearby rock to wait.

Esme had no difficulty catching the rabbit. She could see it struggling in the thicket. Reaching in carefully, she pulled it out by the scruff of the neck. She could feel its tiny heart beating madly as she held it close. It gave a terrified kick and leaped out of her arms. Esme watched as it bounded away, afraid that she had lost it and would now be cursed by the oracle for failing in her deed.

But the rabbit, a plump hare, gave two faltering jumps, then pitched forward—dead. Esme ran to it and picked it up. The racing heart was still. She took her dagger and cut off its head to bleed it. She left it dangling by its hind legs from a branch while she went in search of wood to make a fire.

When at last the fire was crackling and the skinned rabbit gutted and roasting on a spit, Esme went to the seeress and announced, "Your meal will be ready soon, old mother. And I have found you an apple to eat with your meat." The apple she had thoughtfully peeled and diced into a wooden bowl that she had retrieved from Toli's pack behind the saddle. She had then ground the large golden globe to mash with the handle of her dagger.

The hag said nothing but hopped nearer the fire and seated herself. Esme went to the stream and filled a second bowl with water.

"Perhaps Orphe's daughter would care to wash her hands before eating," Esme said gently, holding the bowl before her.

The old woman nodded regally and dipped her hands daintily into the bowl and rubbed them together. The water turned murky with dirt. The old woman then wiped her wet hands on her filthy clothes and smiled.

Esme fetched her another bowl of water, took the cooked meat from the spit, and cut it into strips that she shredded and chopped. "Your meal, my lady," said Esme, for the oracle had assumed a queenly air as she was presented with the bowl of apple and rabbit, thoroughly minced.

Esme withdrew to watch the old woman dine with obvious pleasure, licking her fingers and smacking her lips. When she had finished, she held out the bowl for more. Esme filled it again and sat down beside her to wait.

The sun reached its zenith, dwindling the shadows in the glade to nothing, and still the old woman hunkered over her bowl. Esme clasped her hands around her knees and forced herself to wait as patiently as possible.

At last the old woman had eaten her fill. She placed the bowls on the ground beside her and rose up with much creaking and snapping of joints. She shook herself forward to stand before Esme and leaned once more on her staff. This she did with such surety of motion and without hesitation that Esme realized for the first time that the hag saw as much with her inner eyes as others did with perfect vision. She shuddered to think that as a child the woman had probably had her eyes put out to further enhance her strange gift.

> *"The deed was done*
> *And with thoughtful art.*
> *As best befits*
> *A most noble heart.*
> *By this I know*
> *As by a gold ring,*
> *Princess ye are*
> *And your father king."*

Esme gasped and jumped to her feet. The hag had spoken rightly, but it frightened her to have her secret so easily known.

"You see much that cannot be seen with eyes alone, Priestess. Since I have served you as you asked, allow me to leave with your blessing."

> *"A blessing ye ask*
> *And this ye receive,*
> *Your secret safe*
> *If none ye deceive.*
> *Full rare is she*
> *Whose safety would spend*

In risking death
For love of a friend.
But this ye do
And this will be found:
Your errand done
When two are unbound."

The old woman turned and scuttled away. Esme felt a nudge at her elbow and realized that Riv had come to her and was anxious to be off and away from the strange old woman.

Esme climbed into the saddle and watched the shapeless bundle of rags hop from stone to stone back across the stream. "Thank you for the blessing, Daughter of Orphe. May your prophecy be true."

At that the hag stopped and turned once more toward Esme. She raised her crooked staff overhead with both hands and turned around three times very fast. Esme wondered that she did not fall off her precarious perch in the middle of the stream.

The old woman's rasping voice rose to fill all the hollow.

"I speak what is,
And not what may be.
But since you ask,
Hear my prophecy!"

The oracle raised her face toward the sky and muttered a long incantation while the staff waved back and forth over her head. Then she brought the knobby head of the rod down with a crack upon the stone where she stood. Her hand shot into the air, fingers spread like a claw. Her words echoed in the dell.

"See ye the sword
And do not yield it!

If foe be slain,
A king must wield it."

With a skip and a jump, the hag disappeared as quickly and as mysteriously as she had come. But long after she was gone, her words rang in Esme's ears like the clear peal of a bell.

CHAPTER 16

Quentin hung limply from the wagon wheel, his mind benumbed with the pain drumming through every extremity of his broken body. He whimpered softly, unaware that he was making any sound at all—unaware of anything but the throbbing, insistent agony.

All day long the wheel had spun—over rock and root, through dust and deep water. And Quentin, lashed to the wheel, had been slowly tortured into insensibility. He did not notice when the wheel finally stopped, nor when the sun set, nor when the night brought an end to his torture.

He hung on the wheel and whimpered softly and pitifully as darkness deepened around him.

Amid the ordered confusion of Nin's army making camp for the night, the moon rose fair and full, and with it the Wolf Star. Quentin gazed unblinking at the moon with unseeing eyes. Some small part of his mind watched it curiously, a frightened animal peering out from a cave where it had retreated to escape the hunters.

After a long time it seemed to Quentin that the moon was coming toward him, leaving its course in the black dome of heaven to come closer and closer. He could see it weaving over him, shining with a gentle light. It had two dark eyes that watched strangely. He wanted to reach out and place his hand against its smooth, luminous surface, but his hands would not obey. Then the moon disappeared.

Years passed, or were they moments? Quentin next felt something cool touch his forehead. He opened his eyes and saw that the moon had come back. It was looking at him and whispering to him, but he could not hear the words, though they buzzed softly in his ears. He struggled to lift his head to speak, but lacked the strength, so simply allowed the moon to comfort him with its cool touch.

"Kenta, can your hear me? It is Toli. Kenta . . ."

Quentin blinked his eyes and peered dully back at the round, shining face of the moon. He opened his mouth to speak, but could not remember how to form the words.

"Do not try to speak. Just listen to me. I have come to free you. Kenta, can you hear me?"

Quentin moaned. Why was this moon so persistent? What did it want? He wanted only to drift back into the soothing void of unconsciousness.

"Here is some water." He felt something press against his lips, and cool liquid spilled gently into his mouth. He swallowed feebly and then again. "Drink it slowly," came the whisper.

Next Quentin felt something tugging at his hand. He felt it, though it seemed to him that his hand was far away and no longer a part of him. When the hand was free, it fell limp and useless to dangle at his side. He watched as the moon stooped to slice through the cords that bound his feet. Then the other hand swung free, and he pitched forward onto his knees and into the solid arms of the moon, who whispered in his ear, "Can you move?"

Quentin made no answer. He felt himself rolled to the ground gently and then half lifted, half dragged under the shelter of the wagon. His head was raised, and the cool liquid poured into his mouth. Then he was laid back down, and Toli fell to rubbing some life back into his friend's mangled limbs. He sank once more into peaceful oblivion.

"Kenta, wake up." The voice was the barest of whispers. Warm breath tickled his ear. "It is time to go."

"Toli?" The word was a slurred moan.

"Shh! Not so loud. I am here. Thank the God you are alive. I thought I had lost you."

"What has happened! Ohhh . . ." His shoulder had begun throbbing again mercilessly and the pain and the night chill revived him somewhat. "Where . . . where am I?"

"There is no time, Kenta. It will be morning soon. We must get away now. Can you move?"

"I—I do not know. I do not think so."

"You must try. Come, I will help you." Toli gently lifted his master to a sitting position, but even this effort caused black waves of dizziness to wash over Quentin. He moaned again and could not restrain it.

"I think your right arm is broken, Kenta. Hold it close to your side, and try not to move it."

"I cannot feel anything. But my shoulder . . . ahh!" Toli had placed his hands under Quentin's arm to drag him from beneath the wagon.

"The soldiers are asleep, but there are sentries around the perimeter. They are careless, for they are not expecting an encounter this night. We have a chance. Can you stand?"

"I . . ." With Toli's help he struggled to his feet, then swayed uncertainly. The pain took his breath away.

"I will hold you, but we must move now." Toli guided his first faltering steps as Quentin stumbled helplessly forward, trying to make his legs move in harmony. It was no use—he collapsed not two steps from where they started.

"Good," grunted Toli. "We try again. Lean on me." He raised Quentin back to his feet, and they started off again.

Quentin tried to raise his head, but searing fireballs of pain burned through his brain with the effort. He let his head wobble upon his chest as Toli propelled them forward. The earth felt strange beneath his feet, as if it were rolling away from him with every step. His legs kept entangling themselves and tripping him, but somehow Toli kept them both upright and moving.

"Ahead is a gully—maybe fifty paces. We will be hidden there. We can rest before moving again. But we must be as far away from here as possible before daylight."

They lurched through the darkness as Toli's night-hawk vision kept watch for signs of discovery. They were moving away from the camp; the wagons stood between them and the huddled masses of sleeping enemy soldiers. But ahead lay the circle of sentries at their posts.

The gully, little more than a weedy depression carved in the ground, opened before them, and Quentin slid down the side to lie panting on his back when they reached it. His head ached, and dark shapes, like the wings of ravens, swarmed before his eyes.

"Listen," Toli said. He crawled to the rim of the gully to look back toward the wagons. "I think they have discovered our escape. Someone is moving around the wagon. We must move on quickly."

He lifted Quentin to his feet, and crouching as low as could be managed, they staggered off again.

Quentin concentrated on putting one foot in front of the other and staying upright; Toli bore the responsibility for keeping them moving. It was all Quentin could do not to cry out in pain when his shoulder was jostled.

"There are trees up ahead. If we can reach them, perhaps we can rest again."

As Toli spoke, they heard a shout behind them and the rattle of men running. "They know!" cried Toli, pulling them forward.

The trees loomed up as a black mass hurled against a black sky. The moon had set long ago; Toli had chosen this, the darkest hour of night, for their escape. Twice Quentin stumbled and fell full length to the ground, and Toli could not prevent it. Each time Quentin gamely hauled himself back to his feet, though the agony blinded him.

Somehow they reached the trees. Toli propped Quentin up beside a formless trunk and left him there holding his arm with his good hand. Though the night was cool, Quentin swam in his own sweat and tasted its salty tang on his lips. He fought to remain conscious when he saw the black wings fluttering closer. He felt as if he did not have a single bone that had not been wrenched out of joint.

Toli was back beside him in an instant. "They are looking for us. They know you have escaped. They have not yet turned toward the trees, but it is only a matter of time. They will find the gully, and they will follow it as we have. We cannot stay here."

Quentin gasped and nodded. His temples pulsed with the pain as it twisted deeper and deeper into him. He could feel his strength slipping away. With Toli beside him he started off again, blindly, for between the sweat running in his eyes and the darkness of the wood, he could see nothing.

There were torches wavering over the landscape now. The soldiers were searching for them in knots of three or more, spreading out over the land. Soon Quentin could hear their voices echoing behind them as they dodged and floundered through the trees. Once he thought he saw the flare of a torch off to his right, moving even with them. The voices of their pursuers, excited by the chase, sounded closer.

"I have a horse waiting," Toli said, "down there."

Quentin realized dimly that they were standing at the top of a low bluff whose slope was clothed in brambles. Before he could speak Toli had them plunging down the slope and into the thickets, heedless of the barbs tearing at their flesh.

Quentin fought his way through and, with Toli ever at his side, had almost reached the bottom when his foot struck against a root, and he was flung headlong down the slope. He landed hard, unable to break his fall with his hands, and heard a sickening snap as he felt something give way in his injured shoulder. Daggers of pain stabbed into the wound. A startled scream tore from his throat before he could stifle it.

Toli darted past him, and Quentin felt a rush of movement just in front of him and realized he had landed almost underneath the horse Toli had somehow acquired and hidden for their escape. Then he felt Toli's strong hands jerking him once more to his feet. He was pushed into the saddle to hang like a sack of barley, head on one side and feet on the other. Toli was instantly behind him, holding him on with one hand and snapping the reins with the other.

The horse jumped away, and Quentin saw the earth spin aside in a jumble of confused shapes: branches, rocks, sky, and ground. He saw a light and then another. He heard a shout close at hand and an answer not far away. His teeth ground against each other as he clung helplessly to the saddle.

Now the shouts of the enemy were all around. A dark shape rushed at them from out of the brush. Toli slashed down at it with the reins. Suddenly the copse was ablaze with torches. Toli jerked the reins hard and turned the horse toward the slope, but it was too steep for the frightened animal. The horse struggled, slid, pawed the air, and then fell back, legs pumping furiously.

Quentin was flung to the ground and Toli on top of him. In an instant they were ringed by soldiers and seized. Quentin saw the flash of a torch and the awful scowl of a face leering over him; then black hands grabbed him and began dragging him away. He heard a voice shouting in desperation and realized it was his own, but he could not make out the words.

He jerked his head around to see what had become of Toli, but could only see the swinging torches behind him. *How bright the flaming brands are,* he thought. It hurt his eyes to look at them. *Run, get away!* another voice told him, this one inside his head. Yes, he must escape. If only they would release him, he would run and run and not stop running until he was far away.

Where were they taking him? he wondered. What would happen to him? The questions framed themselves in his mind, but no answers came. Very well, it did not matter. Nothing mattered anymore. He had ceased to feel anything at all. He felt consciousness slipping from him; he heard a furious buzzing sound loud in his ears.

There was a rush of black wings, and suddenly he was soaring, falling, tumbling, floating high above the earth. Quentin looked down and saw a strange procession of torchbearers marching through the wooded dell. They carried with them the bodies of two unfortunates. Who could they be? Quentin was sorry for them. Sadly, he turned his eyes away and saw the dark edge of the night sweeping toward him.

It was as if a silken veil had passed before his eyes, removing all from view. He let it touch him and enfold him in its dark embrace. Quentin felt the last fine threads of strength and will leave him, and he knew no more.

CHAPTER 17

The candles burned low in their tall holders; several had sputtered out, and the inner chamber of the elders smelled of hot beeswax and tallow. The elders sat stonelike, each one hunched over, head bowed and hands clasped. All was silent but for the rhythmic sigh of their breathing.

The night had drawn full measure, and still they sat. Waiting. Listening. Searching within themselves for an answer to Yeseph's dream—a most disturbing dream.

Then at last the waiting was over, for Clemore raised his hands and began to sing. *"Peran nim Panrais, rigelle des onus Whist Orren, entona blesori amatill kor des yoel belforas,"* he sang in the ancient tongue of the Ariga. "King of kings, whose name is Most High, your servant praises your name forever."

The three others slowly raised their heads and looked at Clemore. His eyes were closed and his hands raised to either side of his face.

"Speak, Elder Clemore. Tell us what has been revealed to you," Patur said quietly. The others nodded and leaned back in their high-backed wooden chairs; the vigil was over.

Clemore, eyes still closed, began to speak. "The river is Peace, and the water Truth," he said. "And the river runs through the land, giving life to all who seek it, for Truth is life.

"But the storm of war descends, and its evil defiles the water. Truth is poisoned by the lie and is choked off. When Trust perishes and Peace dries up, the land dies. And the gales of war blow over the land, filling the sky with clouds of death, which is the dust. Then darkness—Evil—covers all, blotting out the light of Good.

"The child who cries out in the darkness is a Child of the Light, who has lost his father, the ways of righteousness. His father's sword is the knowledge of the Truth, which has been destroyed.

"But there are some left who do not go down to death and darkness, who still remember the River and the Water and the Living Land. They are the man who weeps. The tears are the prayers of the Holy who mourn the coming of Evil.

"The prayers are poured out and become a Sword of Light, which is Faith. The Sword flashes against the darkness of Evil, because it is alive with the Spirit of the Most High. The Sword is to be given to the Child, but alas! The Child has been overcome by the Night and is carried off."

When Clemore had finished his retelling of the dream, they all spoke at once, joining in agreement with the interpretation. Yeseph's voice rose above the others. "Brothers! We must not forget that dreams may have several meanings, and all of them are true. I do not doubt that the interpretation we have just heard is truly of the Most High. But I am troubled by one thing."

"What is it?" asked Jollen. He opened his hand toward Yeseph, inviting him to speak freely. "It was your dream, after all."

"I feel as if there were some more present danger yet unspoken."

"Certainly the dream is dire enough, Yeseph," said Patur.

"And its interpretation is clear warning," added Clemore.

"Yes, a warning of something to come," said Yeseph slowly, "but also a reflection of something even now taking place."

"Well said, Yeseph. I think so, too." Jollen reached across and touched his arm. "The interpretation was given to us that we might be ready for what is to come. The dream was given to us that we might know there is peril even now upon us."

Clemore nodded gravely, and Patur pulled on his gray beard. "What does your heart tell you, Yeseph? What are we to do?" asked the latter.

"I hardly know, Patur. But I feel a great torment in my spirit. It has grown through the night as we have sat here." He glanced at the others. "I feel that we must even now pray for the Child of Light whom we have sent out from among us."

"Who is that, Yeseph?" asked Clemore.

"Quentin."

"Quentin? But he is in Askelon."

"Quentin, yes, and Toli too. They are in desperate need; I feel it."

"Then it may be," replied Jollen, "that our prayers are needed at this moment if the dream is to have an ending." He turned to the others. "I, too, am troubled about Yeseph's dream. It does not suggest an end, which means that the end is still in doubt. Therefore, we must unite our spirits, and those of our people, to bring about the ending which the Most High will show us."

"Your thoughts are mine," said Yeseph.

"Then let us not waste another moment. Our prayers must begin at once." Jollen raised his hands and closed his eyes. The others followed his example.

In moments the temple chamber filled with the murmur of the elders' prayers ascending to the throne of Whist Orren. Outside the temple the silvery light of dawn was tinting the gray curtain of the night in the east.

Dawn brought with it a sudden chill. The horizon was an angry red, dull and brooding, though the sky seemed clear enough overhead. The wind had changed with the coming morning; Toli had noted it as he lay bound beside his master. Quentin hardly breathed at all. He clung to life with a tenuous grasp. Several times before dawn, Toli had had to place his ear against Quentin's chest to see if he still lived.

In the camp the soldiers were busy making ready for their day's march. Toli, whose eyes missed nothing, had a presentiment that he and Quentin would not be making the trip with them, for he had seen a group of soldiers readying the ropes and harness, and the three guards who now stood over them laughed and pointed at them. Toli knew that the means of their execution was prepared.

The cooking fires sent white smoke drifting through the camp. The guard on the prisoners was changed, so those who had watched through the night could be fed. When all the soldiers had eaten and were ready to march, reckoned Toli, they would be assembled to view the execution as an entertainment, something to dwell on as they marched that day.

Toli spent his last moments of life praying for Quentin, who could not pray for himself.

He was roused with a sharp kick to his back. The blow rolled him over, and Toli looked up into the hate-filled face of a giant who held a battle axe with a blade as wide as a man's waist.

The giant, whose face was seamed with crisscrossing scars, pointed at the captives and growled. The guards seized them and dragged them out into the meadow where the army had camped, pushing through the mass of thronging soldiers who formed a solid wall around some object that held their attention.

Toli and Quentin were pushed through the assembled host and thrown down at the edge of a wide ring formed by the shields of the soldiers. In the center of the ring stood two horses, one facing east and the other west. Between the horses lay a tangle of ropes and two heavy yokelike objects. At the farther side of the ring stood the warlord's black steed, tossing his head and jerking the arm of the soldier holding his bridle.

As Toli watched, a ripple coursed through the ranks at the edge of the ring, and a wide avenue opened, through which came a man wearing a breastplate of bronze and a helmet of bronze that had two great plumes like wings affixed to its crest. A cloak was clasped at one shoulder, beneath which protruded the thin blade of his cruelly curved sword. Toli had no doubt that he was seeing the warlord.

The warlord approached his courser and paused momentarily while two of his men dashed forward and flung themselves at his feet. One lay prostrate, and the other crouched next to him on his hands and knees. The warlord proceeded to climb into his saddle upon the bodies of his men. He then raised his hand in signal.

Toli swallowed hard, inwardly shuddering. He cast one last look at Quentin, unconscious on the ground beside him. "Stay asleep, Kenta," he whispered to himself, "and fear nothing. I will go before you."

But it was not to be. Two soldiers came forward at the warlord's signal; one carried a gourd full of water. They rolled Quentin over on his back none too gently; a moan escaped his lips. Toli struggled against his bonds and was struck on the head by a guard.

The soldier with the gourd knelt over Quentin and placed the vessel against his nose and poured.

"You will drown him!" shouted Toli, receiving another blow on the head for his trouble. He lunged at the soldier and was kicked in the ribs.

Quentin coughed violently and choked. Water spouted from his mouth and nostrils, and he awoke sputtering. His eyelids flickered, and he turned cloudy eyes upon Toli, who now knelt over him. "My friend . . . ," Quentin gasped, "I am sorry."

Quentin seemed to know what was about to happen.

Both prisoners were jerked to their feet; Quentin was made to stand supported between two scowling soldiers, one of whom grasped a handful of hair in order to keep the captive's head erect.

The warlord gave a second signal, and there was a sudden scuffle behind the two captives. A third prisoner was flung forward into the ring. He was a soldier, bound hand and foot as Quentin and Toli were. "One of the sentries of last night," whispered Toli. He guessed the warlord would make him the first victim.

The man's face was gray; he trembled all over. Sweat soaked his hair and ran down his face—a hideous mass of purple welts, for the man had already received a sound beating. The luckless trooper was quickly wrenched to his feet by two other guards, who then stripped him naked, cutting away his clothing with their knives. The soldiers looking on laughed.

The unfortunate was marched to the center of the ring, where the giant with the broadaxe waited between the two horses. He was pushed to the ground, where he writhed in anguish as his arms and legs were securely tied to the heavy wooden yokes. Then, upon a signal, the two horses, harnessed to the yokes, were led slowly away in opposite directions.

The ropes pulled taut. The giant stepped into place over his prey. The victim was lifted off the ground to hang in agony while his body stretched by slow degrees. The horses leaned into the harness, and the man screamed terribly. The awful popping sound of joints and ligaments giving way seemed to fill the ring. As the victim screamed his last, the giant, quick as lightning, spun the broadaxe in a flashing circle about his head and with one hand brought the blade down with a mighty stroke.

The jolt of the blow almost felled the horses, who stumbled to their knees as the ropes suddenly went slack. The poor wretch was hewn neatly in half as the host wildly clamored their approval, rattling their weapons and cheering.

Toli glanced fearfully at Quentin, who stared emptily at the horrible spectacle; though Quentin's eyes were open, Toli could not tell if they saw what had been played out before them. His look was vague and far away.

The warlord ordered the corpse to be removed from the yokes and then led his steed across the ring to where Toli and Quentin waited. Toli gritted his teeth and stared stubbornly ahead. The warlord glared down at his prisoners for a moment. He spoke something in an unintelligible tongue. Toli raised his eyes, snapping with defiance, and for a brief instant their gazes met. The warlord grasped his reins and struck down at Toli and slashed him across the face—once, twice, three times.

Blood spurted from a gash over his eye and ran down his face. The warlord barked at him and shot a quick glance at Quentin, who still seemed not to know what was happening around him. Then the warrior chief swung his mount around and trotted back to the center of the ring.

He looked slowly around the entire circle of faces in his army and then spat out a short speech to them which, from the somber mood that suddenly fell upon the host, Toli guessed to be on the order of an official reprimand. When he finished, the warlord nodded, and the soldiers began readjusting the yokes and harnesses. Toli believed the moment to be his last. He closed his eyes and sent aloft a prayer for strength and dignity in his moment of trial.

Across the ring a blast of a horn sounded. Toli opened his eyes to the far hills and trees, intent that his last memory should not be of his executioner or the grotesque corpse lying in two pieces beside the wicked blade. He felt a twinge of regret that he would not be able to comfort his master in his last moment, nor even say his leave as a man would, but he doubted whether Quentin would know or understand anyway.

The soldiers on either side of him tightened their grasp, and suddenly he was being dragged forward. His heart raced madly in his chest, and his vision suddenly became remarkably acute. He saw every blade of grass under his feet, and every leaf on every branch of nearby trees stood out in breathtaking clarity.

Time seemed to swell, expanding to immeasurable dimensions. He moved step by step, wonderfully aware of each moment as it slid by; he held it, savored it. Now he was raising his foot, taking a step—how long it took—now the other foot swung up. There were twenty more steps to go before reaching the axe-man, and each step seemed to last forever.

He was conscious of the air as it filled his lungs: the taste of it, the tingling freshness as it rushed in. He felt the sun on his neck and thought that if he tried he could count each single ray as it touched him. How strange, he thought, that every nerve and fiber of his being should be so fully alive this close to death.

Then he was struck with a horrible thought. In this heightened state, he would be able to see the executioner's blade as it glittered in the air in its lazy arc. He would be able to feel each tiny fiber of muscle strength and pull; he would feel his bones wrenched leisurely from their sockets; he would hear his own spine snap.

He would see in that most hideous of moments—stretched out far, far beyond its normal length—the cruel blade bite deep into his flesh, cleaving bone from muscle. And he would see himself severed in half and feel the awful rush of his organs spilling out.

He would know his death in its most terrifying aspect. He would die not instantly, as it would seem to those who looked on. He would die with torturous slowness. Gradually. Bit by excruciating bit.

CHAPTER 18

You look better this morning than you have in weeks, Sire." Durwin had seen the king from across the garden and had watched him for some moments before approaching. Eskevar sat quietly on a small stone bench amid a riotous splash of color from flowers of every shade and description. Every variety of flowering plant and shrub from the farthest ends of the realm and beyond had a place in the Dragon King's garden.

A shadow vanished from the king's brow as he looked up and saw his physician coming toward him. "Thanks to the ministrations of my good hermit, I think I will yet trouble this world with my existence."

Durwin cocked a wary eye at Eskevar. "How strangely you put it, Sire. I would have thought that today of all days, you would rejoice in your improved health and put gloomy thoughts far behind you."

"Then little you know me, sir. I may not make merry when my— when men of my bidding are still abroad."

"It is Midsummer!" said Durwin. His gaiety was a little forced; he, too, felt uneasy about Quentin and Toli and the others being so long away. "I would not wonder if they were enjoying the hospitality of one of the happy villages by the sea."

Eskevar shook his head gravely. "You contrive to cheer me, but your words fall far short of the mark, Durwin—though I thank you for the attempt. I know too well that something is wrong in Mensandor. Something is very wrong."

Durwin stepped closer to his monarch and laid a hand on his shoulder. The king looked up into the hermit's eyes and smiled wanly. "Sire, I, too, feel a dread creeping over the land. Sometimes my heart flutters unexpectedly, or a chill falls upon me as I sit in my chamber before the fire, and I know something is loose in the land that does not love peace. Too soon, I fear, we will face a most loathsome enemy.

"But I also know that we stand in the light of the god's pleasure, and no darkness can extinguish it."

"I wish I had faith enough to believe in your god. I have seen too much of religion to believe." Eskevar sighed and rose slowly to his feet. Durwin reached out a hand and steadied him.

The two old friends walked the garden paths side by side in silence for a long time; Durwin kept his hand under the king's arm.

"I do not think I could survive another campaign, another war," said Eskevar after they had walked the entire length and breadth of the garden.

"You are tired, Sire. That is all. You have been very ill. Take your time, and do not let such thoughts trouble you. When you have regained your strength, you will feel differently, I assure you."

"Perhaps." The king grew silent again.

The sun shone down in a friendly way, and all the garden seemed to shout with the exuberance of life. A fountain splashed in a shady nook near a wall covered with white morning glories. A delicate song floated on the perfumed air as the men strolled slowly by. They stopped to listen.

"How sweetly your daughter sings, Sire."

"She cannot do else." The king laughed gently, and the light seemed to rise in his eyes. "She is a woman, and she is in love."

Seeing how his patient brightened at the thought of his daughter, Durwin turned aside and directed their steps toward the fountain and the young woman dressed all in white samite, glistening like a living ray of light.

"My lady sings most beautifully," said Durwin when they had drawn close. Bria, her hands busily plaiting a garland of ivy into which morning glories were woven, raised her head and smiled.

"I would have thought my lords too preoccupied for a maiden's vain utterings," Bria laughed. Music filled the air, and shadows raced away. Eskevar seemed suddenly to become young again, remembering perhaps another whose laughter enchanted him. "Come, Father. And Durwin, too. Sit beside me, and tell me what you two have been talking about this morning."

"We will sit with you, but it is you who must tell us what occupies your thoughts," said Durwin.

They sat on stone benches near the fountain; Eskevar settled next to his lovely daughter and did not take his eyes from her. Bria began to relate the trivial commonplaces of her day, and her excitement at the approach of the evening's Midsummer celebration. There was no hint in her voice of anything but the most joyful anticipation of delight.

How very like her mother, Durwin thought. How wise and good. Her heart must have been filled with thoughts of Quentin and consumed with longing for his presence in this happy time; yet she did not let on that she felt anything but the most perfect contentment and happiness. She was doing it for her father, he knew.

After a little while, Durwin slipped away and left his patient for the moment in the hands of an even more skilled physician, one whose very presence was a healing balm.

Arriving at the road, Esme had faced a hard decision. To the north lay Askelon and her goal; to the south, danger and the likelihood of being captured again. But she guessed that any help she might bring must come out of the south, too. That was the way her protectors, Quentin and Toli, had been heading when they encountered her. That was the way their friends were expected to return.

The choice had occupied her the greater part of the afternoon— ever since leaving the oracle. And upon reaching the seaside track, she was no further decided in her mind. Very likely Quentin and Toli were dead. And it was almost certain that their friends—whoever they were—had been ambushed and killed, as had her own bodyguards. It seemed a futile gesture to turn away from Askelon now; there was nothing to be gained by wandering farther afield.

And yet, the words of Orphe's daughter still whispered in her mind:

> But this ye do
> And this will be found:
> Your errand done
> When two are unbound.

What else could it mean but that Quentin and Toli—the two— were still alive but would not remain so unless she went to free them? If she believed the prophecy at all, it would mean that her errand would only be accomplished in securing their release.

It made no sense. But when, thought Esme bitterly, did the gods ever make sense to mortals?

So, against all reason, she had turned Riv to the south. As their shadows deepened and lengthened in the late afternoon, they set off in search of friends in a friendless land.

A long night fraught with lingering chills had passed into a sullen morning in which an angry red sun glowered upon the horizon. Esme was up and shaking the leaves and dew from her cloak when she heard it: the crisp jingle of horses moving on the road. It was thin and far away, but it was a sound she knew well—the sound of men-at-arms moving with some speed and purpose, their weapons and tack clinking with every step.

She slipped from the bower that had been her bed for the night, slightly below the road and down an incline so that it was well hidden, and crept to the road's edge to peer along its length. She could see no one coming, and for a moment the sound drifted away; she wondered if she had imagined it. But the road hereabouts ran over and around the many humps of this hilly region, and presently the sound came again.

She ducked away again into her leafy refuge and led Riv out and along a route parallel to the road. They descended into a small valley and rose again to the top of a little, tree-lined hill. From there Esme judged she would have a clear view of the road below without fear of being seen.

She waited. The resentful sun rose slowly, throwing off a sulky light; the air seemed dank and stale. The sky held the feel of a storm, though not a cloud was to be seen. Such days did often betoken ill, thought Esme, hoping that its end would not leave her with cause for regret.

Into the stillness of the morning came once more the jingling refrain she had heard before. This time it was closer and more distinct. Listening very hard, she thought she could hear the thump of horses' hooves as the party, not large, moved along. Presently Esme saw the ruddy glint of a blade or helm as it caught the sun for a brief instant. Then, jouncing into view below her came two knights, three more following close behind.

Though she watched them for a while as they jogged along, Esme knew at once she had nothing to fear from these men. They were not of the destroying horde she had twice encountered. And from her secret perch she could barely make out the blazon of one knight's shield as it hung beside him on his horse's flank—the twisting red dragon of the Dragon King.

When the company of knights had drawn even with her hiding place, Esme urged Riv out gingerly and hastened down to meet them in the road. One of the knights saw her racing toward them, said something to his companions, and then broke away, galloping to intercept her. He did not speak as he joined her, but eyed her cautiously as he conducted her to where the others had stopped and were now waiting to receive them.

There was an awkward moment of silence when she finally reached them; the two foremost knights exchanged glances quickly. It was clear they did not know what to make of her, a young lady riding out of the hills alone.

"I am Ronsard, lord high marshal of Mensandor. I am at your service, my lady." It was the knight whose blazon she had recognized.

The young woman spoke up without hesitation. "I am Esme—," she began, but was interrupted by the second knight, a man of dark aspect whom she thought seemed somehow familiar.

"I used to know an Esme," he said, "though she was but a slip of a girl and shy as a young deer."

"It is a common name, sir," she said guardedly. Who was this man? She was certain she had seen him before.

"Of course, you are right. The Esme I knew lived away in Elsendor and was never fond of horses, as I see you must be to ride as you do." A secretive smile played at the edges of the knight's mouth. Was he laughing at her? Esme wondered.

"Elsendor is a realm of some size," she said. "Perhaps you would remember whose house it was wherein you saw the girl that bears my name."

"I remember it well," laughed the knight. "Often it was that I found lodging there and hospitality of the most royal kind." He lingered on the word "royal" and gave it a peculiar emphasis.

Ronsard looked from one to the other of them curiously. "It is well that we have naught to do but pass the time wagging our tongues. Or perhaps there is some hidden jest which this dull head does not apprehend."

"Sir, if it is a jest, it is not mine," she said, a little confused. "I am on an errand of some importance concerning friends of yours, I think."

"Then, my lady, I suggest you tell us plainly what you require of us. We are charged with an errand of importance as well."

"Now, now, good Ronsard. Be not so hasty with this young lady. For though she is a stranger to you, I think her father is not."

"You—you know my father?" She peered at him closely. "Your words addle me, sir. But there is something about you which seems not altogether unfamiliar."

"Yes," said Ronsard, growing impatient. "If you think you know something, then out with it!"

"Very well," sighed Theido. "It may be that I am indeed mistaken. Yes, I'm certain I am. For any of King Troen's offspring would know one whom they called Uncle."

The young lady's dark eyes opened wide in disbelief. Her head shook dubiously, wagging the sleek braid at the back of her head. "Theido?" A look of happy relief flooded her face as she saw the dark stranger throw back his head and laugh deeply.

Ronsard clucked his tongue and rolled his eyes. "What a meeting this is. It is not to be believed."

"Believe it, Ronsard. Allow me to present Princess Esme of Elsendor. Far from home she may be, but far from friendless she is."

"Theido! I do not believe it either, sir," she said to Ronsard. "Upon my word, he is the last man I would have expected to meet this day."

"Well might I say the same of you, Lady Esme. You see, Ronsard, I spent much time in the halls of King Troen when that craven Jaspin seized my lands. I was made an outlaw in my own country, but Queen Besmire took me in, though her husband was away in the wars of Eskevar."

"However did you know me? I scarce but recognize you."

"You have much of your mother's look about you, and much of your father's boldness. The name Esme is not so widely used as you would have us believe. When I saw you, I knew there could be only one."

The other knights murmured their surprise. Ronsard turned to them and said, "Why do you wonder at this, sirs? You well know Theido is kith to every family in the realm, be they plowman or prince."

They all laughed, including Theido, who said, "Friends I have many, and it is true few men in Mensandor have not heard of Theido— though that is more of my father's doing than my own.

"But let us be once more on our way. Join us, my lady, and tell us of your errand while we ride. We are for Askelon at once."

"That suits me well—"

"I believe you spoke just now of friends of ours? What news would you bring us of them?" The party started off again.

"Dreadful news, sir. I wish it were not mine to tell. If you are friend to ones called Quentin and Toli, then you must prepare for the worst." She glanced fearfully at her two companions. Their faces clouded with worry when she pronounced the names.

"I see I am right."

"You are. Tell us what you know."

"We were riding in search of you, my lords, traveling by night. We saw a fire—they said it was Illem, burning—and we rode to give aid. We were met by a fierce enemy, and Quentin and Toli were taken. I escaped."

Tight lines appeared around Theido's mouth, and Ronsard's jaw bulged. "I marvel at your fortune," said Ronsard. "And more at the directness of your speech."

"My father has often said that bitter news does not grow sweeter on the tongue, and is better said quickly. If I thought that you would have been offended by my manner, I would have spared you."

"No, don't spare us. But tell us if we may hope for them."

"Yesterday I thought not, but I chanced to meet an oracle by a pool. She gave me reason to hope, and reason to try to find you."

"An oracle, you say?" Theido shrugged his shoulders. "Where need is great, any hand will serve, I guess. But we must not linger one moment longer; I fear my idle jesting has caused too much delay already. We will pick up the trail at Illem. We will have to wait for the rest of your story, my lady. I do not wonder but that it is most remarkable."

"We ride for Illem!" shouted Ronsard to his knights. Reins snapped, and spurs bit into flanks, and the horses raced off into the hills toward the burned and blackened ring that had once been Illem.

CHAPTER 19

Evening light lingered golden in the trees as Durwin stood out on the great bartizan overlooking the king's magnificent garden, now ablaze with a thousand lanterns. The music of the assembled minstrels floated over all, a delicate tapestry of melody woven as if from the petals of summer flowers.

Nervous young men escorted radiant young ladies along the garden paths. Children frolicked among the leafy bowers, their laughter clean and clear, sounding like music played on silver instruments. Fine lords and ladies in bright costume moved gracefully among blue-and-yellow-striped pavilions wherein dainties were served. The Midsummer celebration at Askelon Castle was a feast for the senses, thought Durwin, sniffing the fragrant, flower-scented air. A thing of rare beauty.

"Why so heavyhearted, good hermit?" The voice was as light as the breeze that gently lifted the leaves in the garden. Durwin turned and bowed to his queen.

"My lady, you are a keen observer. I'll not deny it," he sighed.

"What can trouble your thoughts on an evening such as this? It is the night when all good things are dreamed—and you know that dreams may sometimes come true."

"I wonder. Good does often seem so fragile against evil, the light so powerless against the darkness . . ." His voice trailed off without finishing the thought.

"That is not the Durwin I know. You sound as if you have been taking the king's counsel."

"Ah, so it is! How fickle a man's mind, ever prey to his emotions. A weathercock for whatever winds may blow." He smiled gently, recovering something of his former cheer. "Ah, yes. You are right to reprove me. What good is a physician who does not take his own cure?"

Alinea smoothly linked her arm in his and turned him toward the sweeping steps to the garden below. "Walk with me, kind friend. For I, too, have need of some good word." A shadow moved across her lovely face. Durwin felt it like a pang.

"If words can help, then rely on it that I will say them."

"I have been troubled today myself. A subtle unease disquiets my inmost soul, and most elusive it is. No cause seems readily apparent. Often, I discover myself to be thinking of Quentin."

"I would calm you if I could, but these are not the words for it. I, too, have been thinking of Quentin this day—and of little else. When you came to me just now, I was thinking again of him, and of Toli, though even then I did not know it."

"Do you think they may be in some trouble? It seems silly, I know—"

"Not at all, my lady, not at all. The Most High often joins our hearts with our loved ones in times of distress as well as joy. I have been praying for them all this day, though my prayers are uninformed."

"I wish that I had the knowledge of the Most High that you possess. Then I would not feel so disposed to the foolishness of a woman's fears."

"But you have something else that serves as well. You have the ability to believe without the need for reasons, or for great signs and wonders. Yours is a faith to endure."

"And yours?"

"Mine will endure, but it is born of years of struggling and vain striving. I have come to my belief over a most circuitous and rocky path, and I cannot say which is better. I think the god gives each soul what it requires, and there is the difference."

"Still, I would know more of what you have learned in your quest. It cannot hurt to be informed."

"Aye, my lady. You speak aright. I will gladly teach you what little I know. But do not be surprised if in your heart you already know the truth of what I would instruct. It is often thus."

They were silent as they reached the last step and entered the festive world of the Midsummer revelers. Alinea turned and looked earnestly into Durwin's broad and weathered face.

"What can be done for Quentin and Toli?"

"Nothing that has not already been done. Pray. It is no little thing."

"Let me come to you when the celebration is over. We will pray together. If one heart alone may have effect, then two will speed the remedy. And your sure prayers will guide my own more directly to the mark."

"As you wish, my queen. I will await you."

Just then the blast of trumpets rang out above them from the bartizan they had just quit. They turned to see the king's pages, their long trumpets in hand, snap to attention. Then King Eskevar himself was leaning on the stone balustrade, looking down upon the merrymaking. Silence descended slowly over the garden as all eyes turned toward him. Then the giggling children grew quiet as they sensed something important was about to happen, though they regarded it more of an interruption in their fun than an occasion of state. Their elders exchanged puzzled glances—it was not usual for the king to address his guests like this. But all waited to hear what he had to say.

"Citizens of Mensandor, my friends. I will not keep you long from your merrymaking, and I will join you soon. But I would tell you some things which have been on your king's heart of late."

There was a murmur of concern; some for the words, and some for the appearance of the king, whose haggard features were not at all disguised by his festive apparel.

"What I am about to tell you may cause you some concern. Please know that it is not my intention to worry you, nor cause you needless alarm."

"What is he doing?" whispered Durwin.

"I do not know." Queen Alinea shook her head. A line of concern appeared on her brow. "He discussed nothing like this with me."

"But as your king," Eskevar continued, his solemn tones descending like a leaden rain into the garden, "I would be less than just if knowing of the danger to our realm I did not at once warn my people to look to their safety."

Now there was a general clamor, and a voice called out, "This is a poor jest for Midsummer!" Another said, "Let the king speak! I would hear him out in peace!"

"It is not a jest, my loyal friends. But my heart can no longer abide rejoicing while across fair Mensandor the wild, angry clouds of war are gathering." He held up a hand to silence the outburst that followed this revelation. "Even now my marshals scour the land to bring me word of our enemy, that we might know his strength and so arm against him. We shall fight for our land against any foe, and we shall win!"

The king's voice had risen to a rant; he sounded like a madman, though his words were sane enough. A stunned silence fell upon the Midsummer revelers. Eskevar seemed to come to himself again and realized what he had done. His hand trembled slightly as he said, "Return now to your pleasure. It may be the last we will know for many dark days." He turned and walked away from the balustrade and disappeared into the castle, leaving his guests to mumble in confused alarm.

"What can he mean by this? Oh, Durwin . . ." Alinea turned to the hermit, eyes filling with tears. "Is he . . . ?"

"No, no. Do not be alarmed. He is as sane as you or I, perhaps the more. I believe that his great heart feels deeply for the land. Somehow it is part of him; when it hurts, he hurts. I am certain that I am telling you nothing you do not already know."

"That may be, but it is good to hear another say it. I have long known him to be unable to enter into gaiety when there is any unhappiness he may cure. But he has never taken it to this extreme."

"Pray that I am wrong, my lady. But it may be that we will have cause ere long to look upon Eskevar's ill-timed warning as the act of a most brave and noble soul. I think he senses something that is not yet apparent to us. I fear we will share his forebodings too soon."

"You will excuse me, Durwin. I must hurry to attend to him just now. He will be wroth with himself for his outburst. He will want a cool hand to soothe his brow."

Durwin bowed, and the beautiful Alinea hurried away with a rustle of her silken skirts. He turned and saw that all eyes had been upon the queen in the moments following Eskevar's strange address. Durwin smiled as broadly as he knew how, held up his hands, and shouted, with as much cheer as he could command, "Friends, let us enjoy our celebration! There may be trouble to come—so be it! But it is a good day, and we may have need of such joy ere long. So let us fill our hearts with happiness and let care belong to the morrow!"

His hand flourished in the air, and, as if waiting for his cue, the music swelled and filled the garden as the minstrels began to play once more. The children, sensing the momentary ban on their fun had been lifted, burst forth with pent-up high spirits, and their laughter sounded from every corner. In a short while the garden was transformed into a scene of mirth and merriment. The ominous cloud, so sudden and unexpected in appearance, had just as suddenly passed.

Night came on like a dream. Quentin had some vague recollection of a day that seemed to stretch out forever without end. He and Toli had been thrown into the back of one of the wagons to wonder at their fate. There was not a heartbeat throughout the interminable day that he did not relive the horror of their sunrise ordeal.

He had been pulled across the execution ring at the signal of the war-lord. Halfway to the bloody spot, he had seen the deathman turn away. He looked around as the warlord was riding through the scattering throng of his soldiers; the ring was melting away. Suddenly he understood that the warlord's order had been one of dismissal. The executions were over. For some reason, which he would not know until later, he and Toli had been spared. Relief, however, was slow in coming as he watched the giant axe-man walk away rubbing the cruel head of his broadaxe with shreds of the dead man's clothes.

Shortly after the wagon had begun to rumble and jostle away, Quentin had slumped into a deep sleep, broken only by Toli's persis-tent nudging and admonitions to eat. They had, by some chance, been bundled into a wagon bearing provisions taken from Illem. Toli, after managing to loosen his bonds somewhat, had gathered a few foods for them. He was adamant that Quentin eat and regain some small part of his strength for whatever lay ahead.

After a meal of dry grain, strong goat cheese, and hard bread, Quentin had fallen asleep again. It was nearly sunset on Midsummer's Day before he stirred.

"You have decided to remain a little longer in this world?" Toli asked as Quentin's eyes opened. They were now sitting amid a careless jumble of food stores in the half-light of the covered wagon.

"We have stopped!" Quentin struggled to sit up, but hot knives shot into his shoulder and arm. He ached all over. "Ow!"

"Rest while you may, Kenta. Yes, we stopped some time ago. I think they are making camp for the night. Soon they will come for provisions."

"What will happen to us then, I wonder?" He shook his head as he looked at his ever-resourceful friend. "I thought you were dead. You should have escaped while you could."

Toli smiled brightly back at him. "You know that was impossible. There could be no escape without my Kenta. It is *fiyanash*—unthinkable."

"Well, we may both pay with our lives tomorrow, but I am glad you are here with me, Toli. At least Esme escaped."

"Yes," Toli said flatly, and Quentin felt as if he had touched an open wound.

"I thought—ahh!" Quentin's face contorted into a grimace.

"Is there much pain?"

"It comes and goes. I feel as if my bones have been taken out, rumbled together, and replaced one at a time whichever came to hand."

"I feared you dead when I saw you lashed to the wagon wheel." He smiled again, and Quentin wondered how he could be cheerful at such a time. "But you were displaying more wisdom and restraint than you usually do. I would have had us free and away from here if not for that wretch of a guard."

"His life was forfeit for his error." Quentin paused, thinking again of the hideous spectacle he had witnessed and only narrowly avoided taking part in. "Perhaps it was meant to be a warning to us; perhaps he did not intend to put us to death—just yet anyway."

"What is important now is that we have time to try again to escape. Tonight will be an excellent opportunity."

"Tonight?"

Toli nodded. "Midsummer—they will occupy themselves with their revelry. The watch will be relaxed and inattentive. We may have a chance."

Quentin's head ached remembering their previous attempt at escape. He seemed to remember something else about Midsummer, something that stirred a brief flutter of pleasure, but it faded even as he struggled to grasp it. "Midsummer. Do you think these . . ."—he did not know what to call them—"these barbarians mark such occasions?"

"There is a fair chance, I would say. Even the Jher observe the Day of the Long Sun. It is so with most peoples; these would be no different."

"Who are they? Why have they come to Mensandor?"

Before they could ponder the question further, two soldiers

appeared at the back of the wagon and pulled out the gate board. The prisoners were yanked out of their nest and each one dragged to a wheel and lashed securely in place, arms outstretched, legs spread and bound to the wheel at the knee. They could not move, except to turn their heads and look at one another helplessly.

The two guards then took up a position close by to enable a tight watch to be kept on their charges. The guards sat a little way off upon a log and stared at them with cold malevolence. It was plain that neither of the guards relished the duty; possibly it was too risky, considering what had happened to one of their own that very morning.

With both soldiers watching them closely, Quentin decided that no movements to free themselves could take place, so he ignored the guards and tried to make sense out of the frantic activity taking place around them.

The army had chosen a flat lea overlooked by a long, low bluff of poplars and beeches on which to camp. Soldiers were busily dragging fallen trees down the hill and pitching them into a great heap in the center of the meadow. Small fires for cooking had already been lit, and the silvery smoke hung in the unmoving evening air. Other soldiers led horses away to a stream somewhere out of sight. Twice Quentin caught a glimpse of the warlord as he rode through the camp, directing the work of his men. He did not so much as glance toward his prisoners.

Soon the bustle throughout the camp decreased as the smell of cooking food wafted from the fires. Soldiers grouped around the fires in tight knots that slowly broke apart into smaller groups. The men sat on the ground with trenches of wood and dipped their hands into their meal. Quentin and Toli could hear their smacking lips and noisy slurping as they licked their platters.

Quentin decided to try to count the number of soldiers in the party. There were twenty cooking fires scattered across the lea, and by his best estimation each served a hundred or more men. There were more moving about the perimeter, employed in tending horses, gathering firewood, and various other chores. In this body there were at least two thousand soldiers, possibly many more.

He also noted that the warlord maintained a special bodyguard of fifty or so men who occupied themselves near his circular, dome-shaped tent. They sat apart from the others and did none of the menial duties of the rest of the soldiers.

As Quentin watched, a man emerged from the tunnel-like opening of the tent and came toward them. Even from a distance Quentin could see that there was something different about the man; he was vaguely unlike the other soldiers thronging the wide meadow. There was something in his bearing, something in his appearance that set him apart.

The man, tall and dressed in a loose garment of deepest indigo bedecked with chains of gold, wore an unusual soft, flat hat of a kind Quentin had never seen before. Beneath the hat a long face protruded, rimmed by a short, bristling beard. The beard was black as pitch, contrasting boldly with the lighter, somewhat sallow complexion of the emissary.

He strode with purpose directly to the wagon to stand with hands on hips, glaring the two prisoners. Quentin stared boldly back into the snapping black eyes as the warlord's chief emissary—for so Quentin now considered him—spoke quickly to the two guards. He did not turn his head to speak to them, but kept his eyes on the captives alone.

The guards grumbled back an answer to the bearded officer. He barked at them once more and tossed them a hasty look over his shoulder. At once they jumped to their feet and, still mumbling, began to untie the prisoners from the wheels of the wagon. Then he turned and began walking back to the tent.

Quentin and Toli were jerked to their feet and pushed forward to follow him. Their guards seemed none too pleased to be about this duty. Quentin wondered what this summons could mean. Toli returned his questioning glance with one of his own as they marched through the camp. Quentin noticed that the eyes of the soldiers they passed followed them with looks of mingled fear and awe.

At the warlord's tent the approach of the emissary and prisoners brought two soldiers to their feet to hold back the entrance flap. The tall man stooped and entered without a word; Quentin and Toli were pushed forward to follow him. Their guards, glad to be done with the detail, hurried away to find their supper.

Stooping so low brought a gasp of pain from Quentin, who stumbled and caught himself uncertainly. His hands had grown stiff and numb from his bonds. When he picked himself up, he saw that the inside of the domed tent was like the canopy of the night sky and just as dark. Tiny golden lamps suspended from golden chains burned brightly, each one a flaming star in the vault of the heavens. The robed emissary turned to them and held up his hand, indicating that they were to remain where they were. He turned and disappeared behind a richly embroidered hanging curtain.

"This is like no commander's pavilion that I have ever seen," said Quentin as his eyes took in the strange, slightly fantastic furnishings of the abode. Everywhere he looked, the soft glisten of gold and silver met his gaze.

"It is a king's palace made to travel." Toli, too, registered surprise at the contrast between the fierce warlord and his men, and the surroundings of his tent.

Just then the bearded emissary stepped back through the curtain and motioned them forward, and as he did so, the warlord's seneschal cuffed Quentin sharply on the neck as an indication he was to bow in the warlord's presence.

Quentin entered the inner sanctum with eyes lowered. He and Toli stood side by side for some time in silence. No one moved or spoke. Before them and a little above they could hear the slow, even breathing of the warlord, and Quentin imagined he could feel his cool gaze upon them as he pondered their fate.

The warlord grunted a command, and his servant came forward and bowed before him. The warlord spoke a low rumble in his unfathomable tongue. The seneschal bowed again and said, his voice smooth and cultured, "My lord has decided that you may sit in his presence. He wishes you to eat with him, but you are not to speak—unless he asks you a question, and then you are to answer without hesitation. If either of you do not answer at once, he will know that you are contemplating a lie and will have your tongue cut out that your friend may eat it and remember not to follow your example."

He clapped his hands, and two servants brought cushions and placed them at the prisoners' feet. "Sit," came the order.

When they had seated themselves, with some difficulty in Quentin's case, the bearded emissary said, "You may raise your eyes."

When they had done so, he cried, "Look upon the immortal Gurd, commander of Ningaal, warlord of Nin the Destroyer!"

Quentin was not prepared for the sight that met his eyes.

CHAPTER 20

They camped here last night, by the look of it," said Ronsard, rising from the cold ashes he had been examining.

"And by the look of it, there must have been close to three thousand men with wagons and horses." Theido's gaze swept the wide meadow where the army had camped. All that was left now were scattered traces: matted grass where men had slept, charred patches where the fires had burned, broken turf where wagons had passed, and the crescent indentations in the earth where horses had walked. But the army had moved on.

"It will not be difficult to follow them; the signs are clear enough," said Ronsard. He looked toward the westering sun. "How far do you think an army of that size could travel in a day? Four leagues? Five?"

"Four leagues, perhaps. Not more. They do not seem to be in a great hurry. It is strange . . ."

"What is?"

"That a force of such size should move through the land, driving all before them and yet . . ." He paused, seeking the words.

"Not appear afraid of being met and challenged." The voice was Esme's, who sat upon her mount, watching the two knights and following their conversation.

"Yes, that's it. If I were invading a strange country," said Theido, "I would have a thought for the resistance which must surely come sooner or later. There is an arrogance here which chills me to the bone."

One of Ronsard's knights hailed them from across the meadow. "He has found something," replied Ronsard. He led them to where the knight knelt. Drawing closer, they soon noticed the look of frank disgust that contorted the soldier's features.

"What is it, Tarkio? What have you found?"

"Lord Ronsard, I think someone has been killed in this place."

The soldier was right. The deep red-black stain upon the earth could have been made in only one way.

Theido eyed the evidence, his lips pressed into a thin, colorless line.

"It could have been a stag," suggested Esme. Her words lacked conviction; she, too, feared the worst.

"What would they do with the body?" Ronsard's voice was strained and tight. He turned away from the ugly splotch in the grass, and Esme noticed the dark flame of anger that leaped into his eyes.

"I think I know what they did with the body," said Tarkio in a tone devoid of all expression. He spoke so oddly the others looked at him and then followed his gaze to the nearby trees.

"By Azrael!"

"The fiends."

"Avert your eyes, my lady. It is no sight for a woman," said Ronsard. He glanced at Theido, and his look was one of keen distress. For two heartbeats a question hung unspoken between them. "We must," he uttered softly. "For I would know."

"I will go with you," said Theido quietly. "Stay here with Tarkio, Esme. We shall return at once."

Theido dismounted and started off with Ronsard toward the tree, a great, spreading oak wherein hung the dangling corpse of the unfortunate soldier.

It did not so much resemble a human body as it did that of some animal carcass hung up to age. The birds had been all day at its face, and the entrails were but ragged shreds. It was hung from a low branch, both halves side by side, twisting slowly on the cord that passed through the bound hands and feet.

"One of their own?" Theido's voice was thick and his features a tight grimace.

Ronsard nodded. "This one was never born in Mensandor." He turned away from the gruesome token. "I am satisfied. Quentin and Toli may still be alive, but that is all I can say. I wish there were some clearer sign; I am not at all heartened by what I have seen here."

"Nor am I. But it is enough, I think, to continue the chase." Theido cast his gaze to the sky, now radiant with the gold of the lowering sun. "We still have a few hours' daylight; we can go far."

"And we will ride tonight. We should catch them before morning."

Without another word they walked back to where the others were now waiting. Esme and Tarkio had been joined by the two remaining knights. "Be assured, my lady. Yonder wretch was never friend to us. One of their own, most likely." Ronsard shot a questioning glance at the two who had, like Tarkio, been scouring the area for any signs as to the fate of the captives. Both knights merely shook their heads from side to side; they had seen nothing.

"Then we ride on. The trail is an easy one to follow. We shall stop at the next water to rest the horses. Nobren and Kenby go ahead, and then Tarkio and Esme. Theido and I will follow." As the others took their mounts, he said to Theido, "We must have a plan before we reach the camp."

Theido offered a nod. "We will pray that something presents itself along the way. For now, I am eager to put this cheerless place behind me."

Two human skulls stared vacantly back at Quentin from where they stood affixed to long poles on either side of Gurd's low dais. The warlord himself seemed only a slightly more animated skull. He sat unmoving, the soft lamplight filling the hollows of his keen face with shadow. That he was aware at all of their presence was shown by the two glinting orbs of his black eyes.

The warlord was seated, as were his reluctant guests, upon a cushion. His chest was bare, for he wore a short jacket open to the waist. It was of a very ornate pattern, brocaded in delicate figures foreign to Quentin's eye. But it was the man's chest that caught and held Quentin's attention. For even in the glimmering light of the oil lamps, he could see that it was a mass of scars—long, jagged, nasty-looking scars. No accident or wound of battle could have produced them in such profusion; some were obviously more recent, for they overlaid the others, and some were freshly healed.

Quentin realized with a start that the wounds, these horrible mutilations, were self-inflicted.

The seneschal, now seated at the warlord's right hand between the prisoners and his master, clapped his hands, and slaves bearing large bowls of food came hurrying in. Another slave set down smaller bowls, which the food bearers proceeded to fill from the larger bowls. When this was completed, the bowls were left before the diners, and the slaves withdrew hastily.

The warlord picked up his bowl and fell to eating at once, without another glance at his guests.

The food, an unfamiliar kind of boiled grain heavily spiced with chunks of meat in a thick sauce, was steaming hot. It tasted exotic and otherworldly to Quentin's uninitiated palate, and once swallowed it left a lingering warmth on the tongue. They ate with fingers, bowls held to their lips. Quentin contrived to balance his bowl on the inner part of his knee, dipping with his left hand, his useless right arm cradled in his lap.

Midway through the meal, a slave appeared with a jar and began to pour out an amber liquid into golden cannikins. These, too, were placed before each one, and the slave departed. The beverage was a wine of some kind. Quentin recognized the slight metallic tang, but it was of a kind he had never encountered: smooth, almost thick, and wonderfully

sweet. He found that a sip banished the warm tingle on his tongue produced by the spice of the food.

The warlord ate two bowls greedily without looking up. When he
had finished, he laid down his bowl and placed his hands upon his
knees. He belched once, and then said something very quickly.

"The meal is over," the seneschal informed the prisoners. And
though Quentin's bowl was still half-full, he put it down and rested his
hand upon his knee in imitation of his host.

"Lord Gurd wishes you to know that he only eats in the presence
of those he respects, and that he will only share food with those he
admires." The emissary nodded to them, indicating that some response
of like nature was intended.

"Who are we that he should respect or admire us, his enemies?"

The emissary translated Quentin's question, and the warlord chuckled
deeply and made a short reply.

"Lord Gurd says that your spirit has ennobled you. You, fair-skinned
one, have survived the ordeal of the wheel. Had you been a coward, you
would have died. You," he addressed Toli, "risked death to rescue your
friend. This deed has value, even though it is the act of a fool. The Lord
Gurd admires such courage. He will be sorry to kill you when the time
comes, but your blood will flow through him—as a most satisfying obla-
tion for his immortality. This pleases him."

This answer mystified and angered Quentin; he started to make a
reply, but felt Toli's light touch on his arm. Instead he said, "Why do
you invade our land? Who are you?"

The seneschal spoke to the warlord, who smiled thinly, like a serpent. "I informed the Lord Gurd that you were honored that he should
deem you worthy for such service." To Quentin's sharply angry look, he
added, "It would not serve to anger him just now. He would have you
disemboweled to return the food you have eaten with him."

"What does he want with us?" asked Toli.

"He alone knows."

Gurd picked up his goblet and drank deeply of the sweet liquor. When he had done, he rumbled a long discourse to his emissary, who interpreted. "Lord Gurd wishes to know how far is the great city—this Askelon—and how is it fortified and by how many soldiers is it guarded."

"How is it that he believes I know the answers to such questions?" Quentin replied.

After a brief consultation with his lord, the man replied, "Lord Gurd knows that you have horses and therefore are not insubstantial men. He has seen your weapons and clothing and believes that you are of favored rank. The fact that you attacked his soldiers, the two of you alone, tells him that you are not unfamiliar with military matters and are in fact well trained for such purposes."

Quentin hesitated. Toli's thoughts could not be discerned.

"If you are wondering whether to answer or not, please allow me to remind you that Lord Gurd perceives any answers following such reluctance to be a lie, as I have already told you. Give me your answer at once, and he will be appeased."

"Askelon is a far distance from here, many leagues. And he is right to call it a great city, for it is. There is none like it. No host has ever conquered Castle Askelon, and none ever will."

"And how many soldiers defend this palace?"

"Tell your Lord Gurd that the Dragon King's army is sufficient to any need."

The warlord watched this exchange closely, not entirely pleased with Quentin's response. But he nodded with satisfaction when his interpreter had finished his reply. Gurd beamed at Quentin and Toli and in his thick, incomprehensible speech addressed them both.

"The Lord Gurd is pleased with your answers. He has decided to allow you to live until we reach Askelon, where you will be sacrificed in order that he might win the city more quickly. He wishes to assure you that your blood will flow for him alone. This is a very high honor."

"It is an honor we would rather forego," Quentin said in a voice edged with subtle sarcasm, "but perhaps we may reciprocate the distinction at some future time."

The emissary smiled slyly and began to offer Quentin's remarks to his master, who bowed faintly and then yawned. He waved his hand toward his servant, who stood, saying, "The audience is now at an end. Bow to him and retreat; do not show your back to him."

They backed away from the warlord's presence and through the curtain. They crossed the tent and stepped once more outside. The evening was deepening, and Quentin felt the atmosphere in the camp pulsing with a barely contained excitement. The soldiers clustered together in knots, and coarse laughter could be heard on every side. The sun was well down, and the sky blushed crimson in the west. *When the light finally disappears*, thought Quentin, *these barbarians will deliver themselves to frenzy.*

As if reading his thoughts, the seneschal said, "This night there will be wild celebration, for it is Hegnrutha—the Night of Animal Spirits."

"You speak our language well, sir," said Quentin cautiously.

A sly look came into the dark eyes. "I speak eleven languages very well."

"What did you say in there?" asked Quentin as his former guards hurried up to take them away.

The warlord's personal servant smiled, revealing a row of fine white teeth that seemed to glow in the fading light. "I told him that it was an honor you would gladly repay in kind. He was flattered."

"Why should you protect us?" asked Toli as the guards retied their hands. "What is it to you if we live or die?"

"There is no time to explain. I will come to you tonight when the chaos is at its peak." The emissary spun on his heel and went back into the tent. Quentin and Toli were marched away to the wagon once more, but this time Quentin felt as if they moved in an aura of increased respect. The looks they received from the soldiers they passed were frankly awed to the point of reverence. He guessed that most who were summoned to the tent did not walk out, but they had.

CHAPTER 21

Durwin remained long enough with the guests to ease their fears over the king's odd behavior. He had walked about and greeted all, as if he were the king himself, and his presence seemed to calm any feeling of disquiet created by the king's speech. The music trilled and eddied, a rippling river to carry away concerns of the moment.

The minstrel master called a cotillion, and the couples began choosing the leaders from among the best dancers present. Durwin chose this time to sneak quietly away, as neither Eskevar nor Alinea had returned. He was vaguely worried that something more serious might have transpired.

He hurried up the stone steps and fled into the castle's gallery entrance; the wide wooden doors were thrown open, and rows of bright torches illuminated the corridor. A few curious guests strolled the gallery to marvel at the interior of Castle Askelon. Without appearing in haste, Durwin nevertheless hurried along to the king's apartment. He had little doubt he would find Eskevar there.

Oswald was at the door when Durwin came bustling along. "Oswald, is all well?"

Oswald ducked his head in a shallow bow and said, "Aye, m'lord. The king is inside and the queen with him. He has a messenger."

Durwin's eyebrows arched. "Who?"

"I do not know. I did not see him arrive. The warder brought him here at once."

"Very well. Let us see, then, what is afoot."

Oswald opened the door and went in. As Durwin made to follow the old chamberlain, he felt a light touch on his arm.

"Bria, I thought you were in the garden."

"I followed you." Her smooth brow furrowed with worry. "What is it?"

"A messenger has come; that is all. Wait here but a little, and I will come and tell you all I can."

"No, I would go with you." So saying, she stepped through the doorway and pulled Durwin with her.

"Ah, Durwin! I was about to send for you." Eskevar sat in a great carved chair; Alinea stood beside him with her hand on his shoulder. Both were looking intently at the knight, bedraggled and exhausted, his clothing and light armor grimed over with the dust of the road. The soldier stood swaying with fatigue before them.

"It is Martran." Eskevar indicated the man with an open hand. "One of Ronsard's knights. He was just about to tell us his message."

The knight bowed and said, his voice rough from the dust he had swallowed, "Lord Ronsard says, 'We are continuing on our mission and are sorry for the delay in returning to him sooner. We have seen nothing to occasion his concern. We will return to him as soon as we have found what we seek, or have some better report to give him.'"

"Is that all, sir knight? You may speak freely."

"That is all, Sire. That is my message."

Eskevar, his eyes displaying concern, stroked his chin with his hand.

"Why did he send you with such a message, brave knight?"

"I believe that he was worried that his long absence would cause you alarm. Theido suggested a message be carried back that they might continue their errand."

"Why was that? Had you seen nothing to render an account?"

"No, Sire. We saw nothing out of the ordinary. But——" He hesitated, as if unsure of his place to speak further.

"But what, good fellow?" asked Durwin, drawing closer. "Have no fear. There is nothing you can say that will incur your king's displeasure. Withholding your thoughts, however, could be a mistake. Please speak and allow us to judge."

"Yes, sir." The knight bowed to Durwin. "It is this. I sensed that something was bothering my lords. They were looking for something and not finding it. This upset Theido greatly. He pushed a furious pace; he wanted to ride all night on occasion. But Ronsard would not let him. They often had words with one another over it.

"But I saw something that puzzled me on the way back. I think that if Theido had seen it, he would have been even more adamant in his ways."

"And what did you see?" Eskevar asked softly. His eyes were eagle's eyes as he watched the messenger.

"One of the villages we had passed through only a day or so before was empty when I rode back through. I thought it strange that I did not see anyone, though I did not stop to look further into the matter."

"Empty?"

"Yes, Sire. It was completely abandoned."

"Anything else? Anything to indicate why that should be so?"

"Not at all. It seemed as if it had been deserted very quickly, though I could see no cause. But, like I say, I did not stop to wonder at it. I came on."

"I see. Very well, Martran; you may go to your bed. You have well earned your rest.

"Oswald, take Sir Martran to the kitchen and feed him, and then find him a bed in the castle where he will not be disturbed." To the knight he added, "Stay close about; I may wish to question you further. Now go and take your ease."

Oswald led the knight away; the man reeled on his feet. "Just one more thing, sir," said Durwin as Oswald swung open the door. "You did not say that you met Quentin or Toli on the road. Yet you must have passed them at some point. They left here in search of your party a fortnight ago."

The knight shook his head. "I passed no one at all. And I thought that strange as well, for until I reached Hinsenby the roads were mine alone."

"Thank you, Martran. Sleep well."

Durwin fixed a wondering look on the king. "His tale is odd indeed. I do not know what to make of it."

"It is as I have said—there are strange happenings in the land. An evil grows, but we do not see it."

"But what has happened to Quentin?" Bria was suddenly concerned.

"We do not know, my lady," answered Durwin. "But the land is great. They may have traveled by another route." His tone was not as reassuring as he would have liked.

"At any rate we will soon know," Eskevar offered. "I propose to go myself in search of them." The Dragon King was on his feet, striding forth as if he would leave at once.

"My lord, no!" pleaded Alinea. "You have not yet recovered enough strength to abide the saddle."

"Go if you would, Sire. It is your pleasure. But in going you risk missing the return of your envoy. And where would you begin searching for them?" Durwin asked.

Eskevar threw a wounded look at the hermit. "What am I to do? I cannot remain here forever, waiting while the enemy grows stronger."

"No one has seen an enemy," pointed out the queen.

Eskevar turned on her with a growl. "You think he does not exist? He does!" He thumped his chest. "I can feel him here. He is coming—I can feel it."

"All the more reason to wait. Gain your strength. The action you seek will come soon enough if you are right."

King Eskevar fell back into his chair in frustration. His noble countenance seethed with dark despair. He thrust his hands through his hair. "Mensandor cries out for her protector, but he sits abed and quakes with fear. Who will save us from our weakness?"

"Leave him now," said Alinea, taking Durwin and Bria aside. "I will tend him. This is the duty of a wife and queen."

"By your leave, my lady. I will withdraw to my chambers. Send for me should you need anything." Durwin took Bria by the arm and drew her from the room.

"I have never seen him thus," said Bria, her voice quivering on the edge of tears.

"It is a most difficult time for him, and he is not a man much accustomed to difficulty. But it is well. For I see signs of his former spirit returning. He will be the Dragon King once more."

The great hand closed over the small white body of the bird. There was a flutter of tiny wings and a surprised chirp as the hand withdrew from the cage. The dove struggled weakly, its head poking through the circle formed by the giant thumb and forefinger. A small red-ringed eye stared in terror at the contorted face of the mighty Nin.

Nin the Immortal felt the swift beating of the tiny heart and the dove's soft, warm body filling his hand. Then he squeezed. The bird squirmed and cried out. Nin squeezed harder. The yellow beak opened wide; the tiny head rolled to the side. Nin, whose fleets stretched the breadth of Gerfallon, opened his hand slowly. The bundle of feathers shivered and lay still.

With a cry of delight, Nin the Destroyer flung the dead bird across the room, where it landed with a soft plop near the door of his chamber. A flurry of white down floated gently to the floor to settle like snowflakes around the lifeless body.

As Nin sat gazing at his handiwork, a chime sounded in the passage-way beyond, followed by the ludicrous sight of Uzla's head peering around the edge of the door.

"Immortal One, I bring news." The minister's eyes strayed to the small, white lump of feathers on the floor beside him.

"Enter and speak," Nin's great voice rumbled.

Uzla tiptoed quietly in and prostrated himself before his master.

"Rise. Your god commands you. Speak, Uzla; let your voice utter pleasing words of worship to the Eternal One."

"Who is like our Nin? How shall I describe his greatness? For it is more brilliant than the shining deeds of men, and his wisdom endures forever." Uzla lifted his hands to his face as if to shade his eyes from the piercing rays of the sun.

"Your words please me. Tell me, now, what is your news? Has Askelon also been taken? I am becoming impatient with this waiting. Tell me what I wish to hear, Uzla."

"My news is perhaps better suited to a different time and place, Most Noble Nin. I know not of Askelon, but may it be as you say."

"What, then? Tell me quickly—I grow tired of your foolishness."

"The commander of your fleet below Elsendor sends word of victory. The ships of King Troen have been destroyed, and the battle on land is begun."

The great hairless face split into a wide smile of satisfaction; the flesh of his cheeks rolled away on either side like mountains forming alongside a deep chasm. His dark, baleful eyes shrank away to tiny black pits, and his chin sank into the folds on his neck. "It is well! How many prisoners were sacrificed to me?" The room shook with the ringing joy of the thunderous voice.

Uzla's look transformed itself momentarily into one of dismay. "I know not, Infinite Majesty. The commander did not say, but we may deduce, I think, that it was a very great number. It is ever thus."

"True, true. I am pleased. I will have a feast to celebrate!"

"May I dare remind the Supreme Light of the Universe that it is Hegnrutha? There is already a feast tonight; it is being prepared even now."

"Ahh, yes. How suitable. Go, then, and bring me word when all is ready. And command the slaves to ready my oil bath; I will be anointed before the celebration begins. My subjects will fill their eyes with my splendor tonight. It is my will for them. Hear and obey."

Uzla fell on his face once more and then backed out of the room. His brittle cadence could be heard moments later calling the slaves together to prepare fragrant oils in which to bathe their sovereign.

Nin raised his round moon of a face and laughed; the deep notes tumbled from his throat to reverberate to the farthest corners of the enormous palace ship. Those who heard it shuddered. Who among them would be asked to provide for the Immortal One's amusement tonight? Whoever chanced to serve that honor on the night of Hegnrutha likely would not see another morning.

CHAPTER 22

The tower of flames leaped high into the night, pouring itself onto the vast darkness above, blotting out the stars with its scarlet glow. Quentin and Toli, tethered to the wagon's wheels, could feel the heat of the enormous bonfire on their faces, though they were well removed from the blaze. As the flames soared skyward, the wild revel rose on its own wicked wings, taking the form of a thing fevered and inflamed.

The tumult had grown steadily through the evening hours, and now the surrounding woods echoed with the crazed ravings of the celebrants. The raging mass seethed about the fire in gyrations of ever-increasing frenzy. To Quentin and Toli, looking on in mute wonder, it seemed as if something had taken control of their spirits and played them as a maddened minstrel striking his instrument in tortured ecstasy.

Quentin saw, in the glare thrown out by the fire, something moving in the darkness beyond the perimeter. Through the shimmering sheets of heat loosed by the fire, he could see it lumbering slowly, like a colossal beast, a dark shape that seemed to form itself out of the darkness surrounding it.

"Look yonder—there across the way," he whispered to Toli. Quentin did not know why he had bothered to whisper—their guards were not even making a show of watching them. They had given themselves over to the festivities of their comrades, though they still sat at their posts, long-ing to join in the turmoil.

"What is it? I cannot make it out."

"Wait, it is coming closer." No sooner had Quentin finished speak-ing than the creature emerged from its dark captivity into the roiling circle of light. It loomed large in the dancing light, the glow of flames glittering on its hideous black skin. It was a creature of terrible beauty, awful and tremendous; it looked a very denizen of Heoth's forsaken underworld, a thing distilled out of a thousand nightmares. And it came lurching out of the forest into the midst of the celebrants, as if it had been called up from the depths of its underworld home to reign as lord over the foul Hegnrutha.

At first Quentin believed it to be alive, but as the thing moved closer, he saw that it was in fact pulled along with ropes by a hundred or so of its keepers, who clustered about its feet. At last they brought it to the fire's brink, where it stood with hands outstretched in a perpetual bless-ing or curse.

It was a statue—an immense carven image of a beast with the legs and torso of a man, the head of a lion, and the maw of a jackal. Two great, curving horns swept out from either side of its head, and its mouth was open in a snarl of rage.

"It is their idol," said Toli, his eyes filled with the sight before him. He fairly shouted, for at the sight of the towering idol, the frenzied scene below had erupted in a climax of pandemonium. Their two guards jumped up and began dancing where they stood, waving their arms and screaming with enravished abandon.

Now more wood was being thrown around the base of the statue, and it was being introduced into the flames. As Quentin and Toli watched the flames encircle the monstrous idol, a shadow detached itself from among the myriad flickering projections and crept toward them along the perimeter. In a moment, without sensing anyone was there at all, Quentin heard a rasping whisper in his ear.

"I am going to cut your hands free. Do not move."

Quentin did as instructed and felt his bonds fall away. His right arm swung limply down; he gathered it up with his left hand and held it close to his chest. Without waiting for further instruction, he rolled to cover beneath the wagon.

The three met, heads together, under the shelter of the wagon box. Toli rubbed his wrists and asked, "Why are you doing this?"

There was a brief flash of white in the darkness as the warlord's emissary smiled. "They are my captors, too. I have long planned to escape, but if I am to survive, I will need the help of those who know this country." He looked at both of them, his eyes glinting in the firelight. "Time is short. We must go."

Away from the wagons, there was little chance of discovery. There were no sentries on this night, but there were several smaller groups of revelers gathered around smaller fires at the edges of the camp, and others could be heard crashing through the woods in hysterical rapture. Their screams tore through the night, leaving little doubt in Quentin's mind of the reality of the animal spirits to which this night was devoted.

The three crouching figures worked their way around the rim of the camp, darting furtively through the mingling expanses of light and darkness. In the trees around them, the huge, elongated shadows cavorted in grotesque mummery as the savage rites progressed unabated.

It was slow work threading through the circle's outer ring, but at last they managed to reach the shelter of the wood, where the shadows gathered over them like a cloak. "I have hidden our horses just there." The seneschal nodded into the darkness beyond. "I was able to retrieve your steed," he said, looking at Quentin, "but your friend's could not be found."

Toli grinned and replied, "It was not my horse—I took it from among the others at tether."

Even in the dark Quentin could see their guide's eyebrows arch upward in surprise and his eyes shine in amused disbelief. "Then I was right about you two after all. You are not without considerable resources yourselves. I have chosen my partners well."

The air seemed cooler in the woods, and they moved with increased confidence, though the dell rang on every hand with the howls and shrieks of the celebrants of Hegnrutha. The familiar woodland seemed now a desolate place given to the homeless shades who wandered the nightlands.

Quentin shivered inwardly and fought to keep pace with the others. By the time they reached the horses, waiting patiently in a small gorse-covered draw, Quentin was panting and weak. The small strength he had rationed through the day was nearly exhausted.

"I know a way out of this wood, if you will follow me," said the emissary. "Then it is I who will follow you."

"Very well," said Toli. "Lead on."

The two mounted quickly and wheeled their horses to the north and away from the camp behind them. Toli cast a quick look over his shoulder and saw Quentin hanging from the saddle with one hand, too weak to climb onto his horse.

"Wait!" shouted Toli, slipping from his mount. "Oh, Kenta, I am sorry. . . . I should have realized . . ."

"No—I will be all right. Just help me into the saddle."

In the moonlight softly filling the draw, Toli saw the film of sweat glistening on Quentin's brow. "Ride with me; I can take us both."

"Once we are away from here, I will be all right," insisted Quentin. "Hurry, now. Help me into the saddle. There is no time to argue."

Toli caught Quentin's foot and hoisted him onto the mount. He could see that Quentin's right arm dangled uselessly from his shoulder. Quentin grabbed the reins with his left hand and drew his right across his lap to tuck it beneath his cloak.

"Let us away," he said hoarsely.

Toli sprang to his mount, and they were off, the horses clipping over the furze and heading into the wood. Blazer seemed none the worse for his adventure, thought Quentin, relieved to be in his own saddle again.

At least with Blazer he did not need two hands to ride—the horse would anticipate the commands of his master. Quentin had only to hang on; that was something he desperately hoped he would be able to do.

In a moment they were in the deep wood where the thick columns of trees broke the silver moonlight and scattered it in slivers all around them. Behind them, like the voices heard in dreams, the cries of the revelers wailed on, diminishing rapidly as distance and the thick growth of the wood cut them off. *It is a dream*, Quentin imagined, as he chased the elusive shapes before him, flitting in and out of shadow and light—*an awful dream that will be forgotten upon waking.* But the sting of the occasional whopping branch and the bracing freshness of the night air on his face were only too real. He knew this was one dream that could not be shaken off in daylight. The nightmare was real, and it had come in force to Mensandor.

CHAPTER 23

It is time something is done," the high priest of Ariel said to himself as he paced his bare cell. "It is time to act." The thick candle guttered in the swirls stirred up by Biorkis's passing to and fro. A stack of parchment scrolls teetered precariously upon the table, clustered and rustling like autumn leaves in the breeze.

"It is time . . . It is time," he said, heaving himself through the door of his cell and into the darkened passageway through a side entrance used only by the priests. He hobbled across a moonlit courtyard and through a narrow portal in the wall, then stood at the edge of the plateau and looked out across the silent valley below. He turned and cast his old gaze, still sharp as blades, toward the eastern sky.

The moon was overhead, but in the east a star blazed brightly—more brilliant than any of its sisters. And around the glowing star a film of light seemed to gather, streaming out from the star's core. The portion of the night where that star was fixed shone with pale radiance, and wherever the eye roamed in examination of night's black dome, it was drawn back to that star—the Wolf Star.

"Yes! It is time to act!" shouted Biorkis. His voice was echoed back to him from the empty courtyard and the temple colonnade beyond the wall. He turned, fled over the jumble of rocks, and swept back through the courtyard and into the temple once more. He made his way, puffing along on short, stout legs, to one of the temple's many summons gongs. He picked up the striker and, pausing one final instant for reflection, banged it into the gong several times in quick succession.

"That will bring them running," he said, and he was right.

In a moment the vestibule was filled with sleepy priests who rubbed their eyes and groaned at the disturbance to their slumbers.

"Brother priests!" Biorkis's voice sounded loudly in their sleep-dulled ears. He shouted on purpose to bring them fully awake. "My bed has remained empty these two nights running; you can bear with me just this little while. I wish to speak to you." There were groans among the general body of priests.

"What is this, Biorkis? Why have you called us from our devotions?"

"Your snoring vespers are not important," Biorkis snapped at his insolent questioner. "It is time to act! The star which shines without, growing bigger with each passing night—I know what it means."

"And this could not wait until morning?" The speaker was Pluell, the under-high priest, his own assistant. He, at least, had the privilege, as Biorkis had once had, of questioning the high priest.

"I think not. It has waited too long already. While we have blindly contemplated its meaning at our leisure, the star has grown large, and with it the strength of the evil it betokens. Mensandor is under siege by forces from far countries. The world we know is trembling on the brink of destruction."

There was a murmur among the priests. Pluell bent to confer with several of his brothers. "I am surprised to hear that you are so concerned, Biorkis. It is not like you at all. You are the one who has ever instructed us of the folly of considering the commerce of mortal kings and their petty concerns.

"It does alarm me to hear you speak so now. Should we not draw aside, you and I, and discuss this together?"

Biorkis bridled at the suggestion. "Why, Pluell, do I sense in your tone the shriek of ambition? Why should not our brothers hear what I have to say?"

The under-high priest stepped toward his mentor, placing a hand on his arm as if he would lead him aside. "This is not the time to display such ill-founded airs before our assembled brothers. Come aside. You are tired, and your vigil has made you somewhat—shall we say, irrational."

"Irrational, indeed! I have never been so lucid in my long and eventful life. But I do not understand your manner at all. Why do you look at me so?"

"It is late, brothers. Return to your cells and to your rest. We will no doubt have a more fruitful discussion tomorrow."

Some of the priests made as if to leave; others stood hesitantly, uncertain whether to stay or go as instructed.

"I am high priest!" shouted Biorkis angrily. "Have you forgotten? All of you stay where you are and hear me! I propose to send King Eskevar word of our discovery."

"Your discovery, Biorkis. You cannot expect us to endorse it, surely." Pluell's voice was smooth, and there was not a trace of sleep or fatigue in it.

Suddenly Biorkis realized what was happening: Pluell's overreaching ambition, long held in check, was now released. He was making his move to take over the high priesthood. Biorkis trembled with rage as the realization knifed though him. *What a fool I have been*, he thought. *While I have lain awake seeking an answer to the riddle of yonder star, he has been scheming for my rod.*

"It shall not be, viper!" Biorkis shouted. His unexplained outburst brought wondering stares from the assembled priests. "Take your hand from me! Hear me, brothers. I am high priest, and long have you known me. When have I ever proposed a thing unwisely, or brought dishonor to the god whom we serve?"

There were doleful looks all around and much foot shuffling. No one ventured to speak. Pluell fumed silently at Biorkis's right hand, his eyes narrowed with hate.

"Why should the suggestion of a message to the king cause such concern for some of our brothers?" As he spoke, the high priest gazed about him and recognized some who must belong to Pluell's faction. He knew he was fighting now at a great disadvantage, but his heart warmed with anger, and his thoughts became crystalline.

"What does anyone have to fear of my sending word to our monarch? Unless there is a reason why they would keep all knowledge of events to come to themselves. Unless they would remove the high temple from its place as servant to the subjects of the realm."

Pluell laughed, but there was no mirth in his voice. "How you do go on, Biorkis. There is nothing at all to prevent your communication with the king if you like."

"Of course not. I am high priest. A journey to Askelon is within the authority of my sacred vows, for I will it to be so. I would grant this same authority to any who served me in the matter."

"Why not go, then, and make the trip yourself?" Pluell hissed.

"I? I am too old, and a younger man could travel faster. I will set my seal to a letter to be carried by one whom I will choose."

"I do not think you would find any who would as eagerly cast aside their vows as you would have them."

"They would not violate their vows. I have already said as much—why do you persist in this?" Biorkis felt suddenly weak and sick. Somewhere—though Biorkis had not seen it—the crafty Pluell had turned the discourse to his advantage. The high priest knew he was doomed, though he could not see how.

"Who better than the high priest to go and speak to a king? Let your own lips bear your tidings."

"Very well," said Biorkis angrily. "I will go. Who will come with me?" He glared around the circle of bewildered faces.

No one volunteered.

"What? Will no one accompany the high priest on this arduous journey? I could order all of you to go!"

"Maybe now we should come aside and talk," suggested Pluell once more. He seemed to glow with satisfaction.

"I have nothing more to say to you!" Biorkis raised his rod and brought it down with a crash upon the stone floor at his feet.

"As you will, brother. Then I have no other choice but to inform the priests of Ariel of the transgressions committed by the high priest and ask for their recommendation."

"What transgressions? Name them—I am not afraid. In all my life as a priest I have ever been faithful to my vows and to the god."

"You force my hand. Hear then, all priests," Pluell said, nodding to a priest who had drawn close. The priest handed over a scroll that Pluell took and made a great show of unrolling. In a strident, accusing voice, the under-high priest began reading off a list of imaginary crimes that Biorkis was alleged to have committed against the temple and his vows. The priests looking on appeared divided; some nodded their agreement with the charges; others wore looks of astonishment and disbelief.

When Pluell was finished, he turned to Biorkis. "What do you have to say to these indictments?"

"Azrael take your indictments! There is no truth in them; any who know me can tell you that. But I do not think it matters at all what I say; you have already made up your mind how this will end. Get on with it."

Pluell turned to the assembly and with his easy and unperturbed manner said, "You have heard with your own ears that he will protest the charges no further. There is but one recommendation we can bring: Biorkis is to be stripped of his priesthood and a new high priest should assume his duties. Biorkis is to be cast out from among us. Are there any who would gainsay these recommendations?"

The room was silent as a grave. No one moved a muscle.

The moment passed, and Pluell, speaking with calm assurance in a voice tinged with false sadness, turned to Biorkis. "I am sorry it had to end this way. It would have been better for you to have gone away alone while you had the chance. I would have spared you this indignity."

"Don't spare me, foul friend! I will go at once, but hear me before I leave, all you priests of Ariel." He gazed at each man, many of them close friends who turned away from his burning stare in shame for their silence. "Evil has this night entered this temple. It will destroy each one of you if you do not pluck it out and cast it aside at once."

In response to a signal from Pluell, four temple guards came forward with torches. They took Biorkis by the arms.

"I am going," the high priest shouted. "But remember my words, all of you. The land is fallen under a shadow. Soon no place will be safe—not even the High Temple of Ariel. If you will not follow me and do what must be done, at least look upon the one whom you have chosen, and know him for what he is.

"The people of the realm will seek your protection and bid the gods to defend them. You will not be able to do it, for your prayers will not be heard."

"Take him away!" shouted Pluell. "He is raving again."

The guards moved to take Biorkis out; the great wooden doors of the temple were already swinging open. The night air blew in among the assembled priests as a sudden chilling reminder of Biorkis's dire predictions.

The temple guards hauled their former leader down the long stone steps of the temple and pushed him into the courtyard. Biorkis stumbled a few steps away and then turned toward his accusers, who had spilled out upon the steps to watch him go. The white-haired old man raised his rod of office, which the guards had neglected to wrest from him, and said in a voice strong as cutting steel, "The end of this age is upon us. Look to yourselves for your salvation; the gods will not help you. This temple will not stand!"

So saying, he threw the rod to the ground, where it burst into a thousand pieces. Then he turned and hobbled off into the night.

CHAPTER 24

I f ears do not deceive, the enemy lies encamped in yonder wood."
Ronsard leaned heavily on the pommel of his saddle, staring down onto
the wooded plain below them, black and forbidding in the moonlight.

"I cannot think what else would raise a clamor like that," replied
Theido; he, too, was tired and arched his back to stretch weary muscles.
Ronsard's knights had dismounted and now walked to draw the stiffness
from their legs. Only Esme seemed as fresh as when they had begun so
early that morning.

"What rites require such observance?" wondered Esme as she listened
to the horrific din emanating from the wood. The rattling screams pierced
the waning night like the cries of the tortured and dying.

"We can but guess, my lady. But perhaps it is the better for us. We
may creep closer while they spend themselves in savage revel."

"If Quentin and Toli are down there, we will find them," said
Ronsard resolutely. "We may as well make a start." He tried his sword in
its scabbard; the blade slid easily, flashing a glint of silver in the moonlight. He turned to Esme. "My lady, would you care to remain here until
we return for you? It would ease my mind."

"Have no fear for me, brave sir. I will do my part. You might need
what little service I can render. My arm is not as strong as yours, but my
blade is sharp as a serpent's tooth and quicker still."

"As you wish; I shall not discourage you. It does seem most apparent that you can take care of yourself. Follow, then, and do what I direct." Ronsard flicked the reins and called to his knights, "Be mounted. We will approach the wood single file. Keep blades and shields covered. We will leave our horses in the wood and come to the camp on foot. If all goes well with us, we may escape undetected."

"Lord Ronsard!" shouted one of the knights. "Someone flees the wood as you speak. See—there. Along the gully beyond those trees."

"I see it!" replied Theido. "Yes! There are three of them. Do you think . . . ?" He looked at Ronsard hopefully.

"It would do to find out who they are, at least." He watched the three figures riding away from the wood with some speed; they were pale shapes floating over the gray sea of long grass just above the black line of a dry watercourse some distance away. "I think we may meet them just there." He pointed with a gloved hand toward a bed where the gully swerved around the base of a hill. "Come, let us see who it is that flees the foul host by night."

Quentin clung to the saddle by force of will. He felt drained and used up. All strength had been wrung out of him in the escape. Now he let Blazer have his head and concentrated merely on keeping himself upright in the saddle, knowing he could not go on much longer; soon he would have to stop and rest. But he thought if he could last until daylight, they would be far enough away that stopping would not endanger them.

So he clutched at the horn of his saddle and hung on as Blazer jounced and jostled along. To his dazed mind it seemed as if he had entered a dream in which hills and sky and woods became his pursuers, crying after him with shrieks of rage and fury. He fled them through gray mists on a horse that flew like the wind, but could not outpace the pursuit.

In his waking dream he saw an army emerge from the hills above them to come sweeping down upon their flank. The dream-knights came thundering to intercept them; he could see their faces hard in the moonlight, and could feel the hot breath of the horses on his face as they drew nearer as if by magic.

But there was something odd about the dream; he shook his head to clear it and looked again—the dream remained. Quentin peered intently, forcing himself to see clearly. But again he saw the force of knights moving down the hillside toward them.

"Toli!" he cried, lurching in his saddle as he flung his good arm out to his side. The Jher glanced quickly over his shoulder and dropped back to Quentin's side. "They have found us!" he shouted. Toli jerked his head to where Quentin was pointing, and his startled look confirmed at once that it was not a dream. They were being chased.

He gave a shrill whistle that brought the seneschal around, and at once all three riders turned their horses to the shoulder of the hill beside them.

Blazer's hooves bit into the soft earth and flung it skyward as his powerful legs churned. The horse stretched its back and fought its way up the slope of the hill. Quentin threw himself down along the horse's neck in an effort to maintain his precarious balance.

Now he could hear the hooves of the strange knights' horses thundering closer, and he thought he heard a shout. Bending low, he looked along Blazer's flank behind him and saw that two riders descended into the shallow gully. Another leaped it and came on.

In that moment of inattention, Blazer spurted ahead and stumbled over a rock protruding from the hill, throwing Quentin sideways as he fought to regain his feet. Quentin's fingers, so tightly wrapped around the pommel, were wrenched free, and he felt himself sliding backward over the rump of his mount. His injured arm flailed uselessly as his good hand grabbed for the bridle strap. He was not quick enough. Almost before he knew what was happening, he tumbled out of the saddle and landed on the hillside.

On impact the air rushed out of his lungs, and the night suddenly flashed in a blaze of brilliant stars, their scintillating rays stabbing through his brain. He rolled over, breathless, fighting to force air back into his lungs. He pushed himself up on one knee and threw aside his cloak, which had wrapped itself around his arm. With a shock he realized that he did not have a sword or a poniard with which to defend himself.

He heard someone shouting and looked up the hill to see Toli wheeling around to come after him. But it was too late. When he turned again, the first of their pursuers came pounding up. The horse reared, and the knight looked down on him. In the pale moonlight Quentin thought he knew the face that sought his; there was something familiar about it, but he could not be sure. He shook his throbbing head slowly, and he heard the whinny of his own mount behind him.

"Are you hurt?" said the knight towering over him. Quentin could not believe his ears—here was a tongue he recognized. The knight leaned down to look at him closely.

Yes, the face seemed familiar, like one he had seen in a dream long ago. But it was real, and it peered down on him intently, eyes shining in the soft light.

"Quentin? By the gods' beards! Quentin!" the knight shouted, jumping from his horse.

Quentin shook his head dazedly. He passed his hand in front of his eyes. "Who is it?"

There was a shout behind him. "Theido. Is it true?" The voice was Toli's, and in an instant the Jher was beside him, tugging at him.

"Theido? How . . . ?" Quentin could speak no more. He sank back as heavy vapors of darkness covered him, his consciousness receding swiftly. He heard many shouts and voices close at hand and the sound of horses galloping in. He struggled to keep his eyes open, but his lids had grown leaden, and there was no fight left in him. It seemed that he had grown light as down, for he felt himself borne up as on a sudden gust to ride on the wings of the wind, which now roared in his ears.

CHAPTER 25

The touch of a cool hand on his brow brought Quentin out of the deepest sleep he had ever known. He heard a voice somewhere above him say, "See there! He has come back. Heoth would not have him!"

He opened his eyes to see a ring of faces grinning down on him. Esme's pretty brow wrinkled in concern quickly giving place to relief.

"There seems to be no escaping you," remarked Quentin as he strained to sit up. There was laughter all around, and hands reached out to clap him on the back.

"We knew you could not elude us," said Ronsard. "Oh, but it is good to see you alive."

"Ronsard, Theido . . . I must be dreaming still. How did you find us?"

"It is no dream, my friend. But if not for this young woman"— Ronsard nodded to Esme kneeling next to him—"we would never have found you, nor even known to search. She showed us where to look."

"You came back," Quentin said.

"I had to protect my protectors, did I not?" Esme answered. Her sudden smile seemed to warm him from within. "Besides, I had already lost one escort, and I was determined not to lose another." Her dark eyes suddenly welled with tears. "Forgive me for leaving you, sir. When I saw you pulled from your horse, I wanted to help you, but I could only think of my errand. I am sorry."

Toli thrust his head in among those gathered around him. The smell of food that he brought with him reminded Quentin how hungry he was.

"Eat, Kenta. We have already done so. We will talk while you breakfast." Toli set a steaming bowl before him, and Quentin fell to with a ready appetite.

"Myrmior has been telling us of your captivity. You have much to thank him for," said Theido.

"Myrmior?" The name was strange to Quentin.

"You mean he has risked his life to bring you out of the enemy's camp and you do not know his name?"

"There was not time enough for such pleasantries. We were quite busy with staying alive. And only half succeeding at that."

"This one has a strong will to survive." The deep rolling voice was the seneschal's. "I am glad to know you, Lord Quentin."

"I am no lord, Myrmior."

"Better than that," said Ronsard. "He is the king's own son."

"His ward," Quentin corrected.

"Ward or son, I see I have chosen well the man to save. From now on, my lords, I am at your service. It will be an insult if you do not allow me to serve you in whatever ways you will." Myrmior bowed low and touched his forehead with his fingertips.

"You have done service enough for the Dragon King. Your reward is yours to name once we reach Askelon and King Eskevar hears how you have rescued his own from certain death."

"I was looking out for myself, sir. I, too, was held against my will by the terrible Ningaal. The risk was but a small one for me, even at that." Myrmior beamed at Quentin and added, "Whatever gods rule this land, they have poured out their favor upon this one. I have never seen a man survive the wheel, and it was that which allowed me to convince Gurd to spare your life.

"And you"—he turned to Toli—"your failed attempt at rescue nearly cost my head as well as your own. But Myrmior is nothing if not resourceful. I turned it to advantage, though you had to endure the anguish of seeing the guard's execution—and fearing the imminence of your own."

"It was at least less severe than the execution itself would have been," replied Toli.

"How did you come to be in the company of the—what did you call them?—the Ningaal?"

"The name Ningaal means 'the Terror of Nin,' his army. It is no secret how I came to be among them, but it is a story I would rather tell to your Dragon King."

"There is much that you might tell, I would wager," Ronsard put in. "But the sun is well up, and I think we must put as many leagues between us and the Ningaal as may be. The Dragon King awaits in Askelon, and we must not forget the fearful tidings we bring. There will be much to discuss when we sit down together. For now, it is enough that we reach the king as quickly as possible."

"My thoughts exactly," said Theido, rising to his feet.

"Quentin cannot ride in his condition, surely. If you like, I will remain with him and come hence on the morrow when he is more able to withstand the journey," Esme offered.

Ronsard pulled on his chin. "I did not think that he would be unable to—"

"I can ride; I am well enough." To show he meant what he was saying, Quentin fought to his feet, where he swayed uncertainly. He took two steps and pitched forward. Theido reached out a hand to catch him, but Quentin collapsed on the ground.

"It is your arm, is it? You cannot move it."

Quentin rose to his knees, cradling his arm. "It will be all right. It is nothing."

"It is enough. Why did you not say something?" Theido bent to examine the injured limb; it was swollen and discolored and hot to the touch.

"Well, we can do nothing for it here, but I do not like the look of it. Perhaps Toli and Esme should remain behind with you, though I must confess I like that even less."

"No one will remain behind, and Kenta will not ride," said Toli. "Ronsard, send two knights to bring me two young birches. I will fashion a *deroit* for him."

"Excellent!" cried Ronsard. "I might have known you would have a solution—a litter. My knights will fetch you whatever you need."

Despite Quentin's protests, which grew feebler with time, the litter was constructed after a style used by the nomadic Jher. The finished deroit was strapped to Blazer, and before the sun had traveled an hour's time, the party set off once more toward Askelon. Esme rode Blazer.

Quentin fumed at being trundled off like so much baggage, but his fussing was mostly for show. Inwardly, he was grateful to Toli for providing him with a means to rest along the way. For despite his assurance to Theido, Quentin was deeply worried about his arm. When he had fallen in the underbrush on the night of their unsuccessful escape, something had snapped—he remembered it vividly—and all the feeling had fled, and with it the ability to move the limb.

The weary party quit the forest they had been traveling through all day. The sun was lowering in a scarlet haze among flaming clouds as they stepped out of the sheltering boughs upon the hard-packed trail that would lead them to Askelon's gates.

"Tonight we will sleep in proper beds with fresh linen," said Ronsard. "And we will dine in the Hall of the Dragon King."

"I wish that it were with lighter hearts than our own that we came here," Theido replied darkly. "I rue the tidings we must lay upon his shoulders. It is a burden I would not wish on any man."

"There will be a burden for all of us, I think," mused Ronsard.

Presently the travelers rounded a bend in the road and came to the edge of a broad, shallow valley. Across the valley rose the great dome of rock upon which stood Castle Askelon, transformed in the gloaming into a city of light. The shadow stretching across the length of the valley had not reached the foundation rock of Askelon; the castle rose out of the purple shadow and glinted in the ruby light, a jewel with soaring spires and towers and graceful bartizans perched upon high walls.

"Oh, it is beautiful," said Esme, her voice awed and breathless with admiration. "I never dreamed . . ."

"A god's very palace! It is a wonder mortals dare intrude," said Myrmior. "It far outshines even its own legends."

Quentin, sprawled on the deroit, craned his neck to see the familiar shape of his beloved Askelon—a sight he never quite got used to, and one that always moved him strangely. *It is far different from Dekra*, he thought, *but the Dragon King's castle is also home to me.* He gazed proudly upon the magnificent structure, rosy in the deepening blue of the twilight sky.

Toli, riding beside Quentin all the way, sat on his horse unmoved and stared at the twinkling jewel across the fair valley.

"What do you say, Toli? We are nearly home."

Toli did not look at Quentin when he answered, and when he finally spoke, his voice was far away. "It does appear now to be as far as ever it was when we began this journey."

As usual, Toli was seeing something very different from the others. And Quentin had learned it was no use trying to find out what the Jher meant by these mystical pronouncements.

Ronsard, at the head of the party, urged his mount forward. The others followed him down the gentle slope as the feathery wisps of evening mist began rising in the cool valley. The air was still and silent, a soft sigh upon the land. No one could have described a more perfect picture of peace as they gazed down into the valley growing green with the crops of the peasants, and to the east along the broad expanse of plain already falling to dusk.

From somewhere in the stillness, a bird trilled a poignant farewell as it winged homeward to the nest, and all at once a sadness came over the party. To Quentin, it seemed that some final word had been spoken, and he was indeed seeing Askelon as it would never appear again.

CHAPTER 26

Y ou have returned none too soon, my young man." Durwin scowled as he examined Quentin's swollen arm. "It appears your arm has been broken and has begun to set."

"That is good, is it not?" asked Bria anxiously. She held Quentin's left hand and snuggled close to him as the hermit poked and prodded Quentin's injured right arm. Quentin's filthy tunic had been removed and a soft robe draped across his chest. His arm rested on a cushion on a low table which had been pushed up to his couch.

"It will heal, Durwin—yes?" Quentin forced himself to ask the question he feared asking the most. Durwin ignored it and answered Bria's instead.

"I feel it is not good, my lady. Ordinarily, yes. But not this time. As it is, the arm will never heal properly."

"Oh!"

Durwin hastened to reassure them both. "But I have seen this before. The arm will heal"—he paused to assess the effect his next words would have—"but I must break it again and reset it correctly."

Quentin winced, and a tear formed in the corner of Bria's eye. "It hurts me to see you in pain, my love," she said.

"There is but little pain. At first, yes, but not now. I can bear it."

Durwin bent once more to his examination of the arm and shoulder.

"That is what worries me, Quentin. There should be pain—a great deal of pain. I have never known it otherwise. I fear something of greater consequence than a broken bone is involved here. But what it is I cannot say."

A knock sounded on the chamber door, and Theido stepped into the room. "What say you, Durwin? Will our young warrior's wing heal to fly again?" Catching Durwin's troubled frown, he added, "If I have misspoken I beg your pardon, sir."

"No, no. You are right," Durwin blustered. "I am being a silly old man. Of course the arm will heal. We will reset it at once."

"At once?" Quentin closed his eyes.

"It would be best."

"After we dine, at least?" offered Theido. "In the hall the meal is being laid. Better to face it on a full stomach, eh?"

"There is no harm. I had forgotten you all have ridden very far. Yes, there is a wonderful meal in honor of your safe return. We can attend to our business after we have eaten."

"Then let us go directly," said Theido. "I, for one, stand in need of some rejoicing this night. There will be little enough in the days to come."

"Meaning what?" asked Durwin.

"Eskevar has announced a Council of War. It begins tomorrow."

"So soon?"

Theido nodded gravely and left.

Durwin and Bria helped Quentin to his feet and pulled the robe around him after putting his injured arm in a sling. Then they all made their way to the Dragon King's great hall.

The hall, shimmering in the light of a hundred golden torches, was even larger and more glorious than Quentin remembered. It seemed as if it had been many years since he had been in the hall. Steeped in its own kind of emotion and majestic drama, it was his favorite place in all the castle, and had deeply intrigued him since he had first seen it as a boy.

A crackling fire roared in the massive hearth, and the flames on the ranks of black stone columns marched the entire length of the hall. Long tables had been set down the center of the hall, and these terminated at the dais where the king's table stood. A royal blue baldachin edged in silver and bearing the king's blazon arched gracefully above his table.

The great hall was filled with people. Servants rushed here and there carrying huge platters of meat—fish, fowl, venison, pork, and dozens of roasts on spits. Knights and lords, some with their falcons on their arms, strolled with their ladies. Minstrels wandered through the crowd or played for smaller groups on request. Maidens with flowers in their hair flirted coyly with passing youths. The hall was a riot of color, a meandering current of gaiety.

Quentin's heart swelled within him as he beheld the splendor of the Dragon King's hall.

Two servants carrying a basin came hurrying up as the three entered. The basin was in the shape of a dragon and contained warm water scented with roses. Quentin dipped his good hand, while Bria washed it for him and then dried it with a soft linen cloth offered by one of the servants. Durwin dipped his hands, and the two young servants dashed away to offer the courtesy to other newly arrived guests.

As they moved into the stream of the jovial guests, trumpets sounded from the far end of the hall.

"Ah," said Durwin, "we are precisely on time. Let us take our seats."

He moved at once to the high table, and Quentin and Bria followed. Toli and Esme met them as they ascended the dais to find their places, while servants scurried around, filling goblets of onyx with wine and ale. Esme fairly glowed in her bejeweled gown. For once, thought Quentin, she looked the princess she really was.

"This is most wonderful," she cooed. "You are so kind, Bria, to lend me one of your beautiful gowns. I feel like a woman again, after all those days on the back of a horse." The two young women laughed; Quentin and Toli looked on, smiling.

"Toli has most kindly conducted me all through the castle, and I am much impressed. I have long heard stories of Askelon's wealth, but the stories do not tell half."

"You are a most welcome guest, Esme," said Bria warmly. "We must have a talk together soon. I think we may become very good friends."

"I would like that. I have grown up among my brothers, and female friends were rare—I think my brothers scared them away. When my business here is at an end, perhaps I will tarry here with you."

"Please, I can think of nothing better."

"It seems our two young women are cut of the same cloth, eh, Toli?" Quentin had stepped close to his friend while the ladies talked happily together.

"Our women?" Toli suddenly blushed.

"Bria and Esme, of course. Do you think I do not see the way you look at Esme? I saw that look once before on your silly face—the day we fished her from the sea."

"It is not your arm that is ailing; it is your head. You begin talking strangely; perhaps I should call Durwin to take you away. This atmosphere has addled your mind."

"My head is whole, and my eyes are not deceived, my good friend."

Toli blushed again. The trumpets sounded a final call, and Bria said, "Let us all be seated. Toli and Esme, you must sit near us. I will arrange it."

After a bit of fuss, they sat down together. Quentin looked down the table—past the platters of meat and pastries, trenchers of pewter and silver, baskets of breads, and tureens of vegetables—to examine the guests who shared the high table. Ronsard, who sat with Myrmior on one side and Theido on the other, caught his eye and waved; an instant later he was once again deep in conversation with the lanky knight at his side. Durwin sat to the left of Toli and on the right of the king, whose exquisitely carved chair remained empty. The queen's chair, smaller but equally handsome, was next to it and empty too.

Quentin peeped behind the trailing baldachin, expecting the king to emerge from behind it at any moment. But even as he did so, a hush fell over the noisy hall. The trumpets sounded a ringing flourish, and in swept King Eskevar and Queen Alinea. They moved slowly through the hall toward the high table, stopping to offer a greeting to their guests along the way.

Quentin was much relieved to see that Eskevar, though grave and gaunt, moved with a spring in his step and with head erect; the crown encircled his head with a ring of fiery red gold. If anything, the king's recent illness had given him an aspect of determined strength, of invincibility.

The royal couple moved to the dais, stopping at Quentin's place at the far end of the table before moving on to their own chairs. "I am glad to see you safely under my roof again, my son." The king placed a hand gently on Quentin's good shoulder. "Let me say again that I am sorry for your hurt."

"It is ever my joy to sit at table with you, my lord. And we have said enough already of Toli's and my trials. I am assured that my arm will be as fit as ever in no time."

"That is good news, Quentin," said Alinea. She smiled with a warmth that made all feel welcome and at ease.

"Come to me tonight after the games and we will sit and talk together," said Eskevar. Quentin was about to speak, but Alinea broke in quickly.

"My lord, you have forgotten that young people have more amusing pursuits than to sit in a chamber on a pleasant summer's eve."

"Of course!" Eskevar laughed. "Forgive me. Yes, I had forgotten. There will be time enough for talking. Enjoy your evening, my young friends. I will see you on the morrow."

They moved off, and Bria leaned near to Quentin and whispered, "Your first night back and I was afraid you would become my father's captive." Her green eyes held his for a moment. "Oh, do not ever leave again."

"There is no place I would rather be than right here with you. But I think Durwin has plans for me this night, even if Eskevar does not. You have forgotten so quickly?"

"My poor darling, forgive me. I am a selfish woman. I would have you all to myself always. But may we not walk once around the garden? It is so lovely, and I have missed you so."

One turn around the garden gave way to another, and then another. The two young couples had started off together, but Quentin soon lost sight of Toli and Esme among the winding paths.

The air was soft and warm and full of the perfume of the flora glowing softly in the moonlight in pale pastel hues. They had spoken of nothing and of nonsense and had laughed at their intimate jests, but now strolled in silence.

"Was it very bad for you?" asked Bria suddenly, but in an abstract way that made Quentin wonder what she meant.

"Being captured? Yes. I hope never to endure it again."

"There is another kind of captivity which is terrible."

"And that is?"

"Not knowing. When someone you love is far away and you cannot go with him, be with him, when you do not know what may happen to him . . . I was worried about you. I knew something horrible had happened."

They walked along without speaking again for a long time. Bria sighed heavily, and Quentin murmured, "There is more on your mind, my love. What is it? Tell me."

"I am ashamed of myself for thinking it," Bria admitted reluctantly. "I know there is going to be a war—"

"Who has told you that?"

"No one, and no one need tell me. I just know it. Ever since you got back, I have seen nothing but Theido's dark looks, and Ronsard has been sending messengers far and wide. You do not deny it, so it must be."

"Yes, war is a fair possibility," agreed Quentin.

"A fair certainty," she corrected him. "I do not want you to go. You are injured. You would not have to go. You could stay here with me."

"You know as well as I that would not be possible."

"Too well I know it. The women of my family have long sent their men into battle—some have even ridden by their side. That is what makes me so ashamed. I do not care about any of that; I only want you safe."

"Ah, Bria. How little I know you. You are possessed of an iron will and a spirit that shrinks from nothing under the heavens. I do not doubt that you could launch a thousand ships and send whole legions into battle; yet you tremble at the thought of just one soldier going away."

"Yes, how little you know me if you think you are nothing more to me than just one soldier." She sounded hurt and angry. Quentin, disappointed at his bungling comment, was about to make another attempt at soothing her when Durwin's bellow boomed out behind them.

"There you are! I thought I would find you here in the only place lovers may be alone respectfully. I do not blame you for wishing to put off the ordeal at hand, but the sooner it is over, the sooner healing can begin."

"You are right, Durwin, though I little welcome your remedy. Let us go." He turned to Bria to take his leave.

"I am going too. You may need a woman's touch. Besides, if someone does not watch you very closely, Durwin, you may break the wrong arm."

"Have a care!" Quentin implored. "It is my arm you are talking about."

"Come along," Durwin instructed.

Bria leaned close and gave Quentin a quick kiss. "That is for courage," she said. She kissed him again. "And that is for love."

"Lady," Quentin said, "I need them both tonight."

CHAPTER 27

Quentin, are you sleeping?" Toli crept to the high, wide bed on which his friend rested. Quentin opened his eyes when Toli came near.

"No, only resting." Both looked at his freshly bandaged arm, set with splints of bone and wrapped in new linen. A sling of forest green—to match his cloak—was bound around his arm, which rested on his chest. "Is it time?"

"Yes. The council will sit within the hour. Would you have me attend in your stead?"

"No, I feel much better. We will both go. Has everyone arrived?" Quentin raised himself up off the bed and swung his legs over the edge. Toli placed a hand under his arm and helped him.

"The lords of the flatlands have not arrived, but are expected to be late. Theirs is a far journey. But Eskevar thinks it best not to put off beginning.

"The others are here, or will arrive shortly. Rudd, Dilg, Benniot, Fincher, Wertwin, Ameronis, and Lupollen—those I have already seen."

"Those are enough to ratify any decision the king might make, though I do not believe there will be dissent."

"Do not be too certain of that. Mensandor has been long at peace, and men grow soft. Some will wish to avoid conflict at any price."

"Then we must make them see that is impossible." He looked at his friend sadly. "Toli, I do not love war; you know that. But I have seen enough to know that it has come to us whether we will or not. We have no choice if this land is to remain free."

They walked from Quentin's apartment to the round, high-domed council chamber in the north tower, passing through the walled court-yard where the king sometimes held vigil when weighty matters were bearing on his mind. The courtyard was clean and fresh and the sun directly overhead.

As they entered the yard, Theido and Ronsard, deep in discussion with another, waved them over. "Ah, Quentin! It looks as though Durwin has done his worst on you. How do you feel?"

"Fit enough. He wanted to keep me abed with a potion of his, but I declined. It would have meant missing the council."

"Do you know Lord Wertwin?" Theido introduced the man stand-ing with them.

"He has some interesting tales to tell in council," added Ronsard.

"Yes, your lands lie to the south of here, do they not?" inquired Quentin.

"That is correct. Just beyond Pelgrin, above Persch." The man smiled warmly, and Quentin noticed he was missing a tooth in his lower jaw; but that and his leathery, weather-beaten visage gave the lord the rugged appearance of a tenacious fighter.

"Sir, if you do not mind my asking, however did you come so soon? It would take a messenger two days to reach you."

"Ordinarily, yes. But I was already on my way here—as I was telling Theido and Ronsard just now."

Quentin did not need to ask what had prompted Lord Wertwin's trip, but he did note its timeliness. They talked a bit longer until a page came out from the tower entrance across the courtyard to ask them to come in and take their places.

They filed into the tower and up a short flight of spiraled stairs to an upper floor. The arrow loops cast a dim light in the narrow passage, which gave out onto a great, round chamber with a polished wooden floor. Shuttered windows were thrown wide to let in the sunlight, giving the chamber an open, airy feeling, though it was hollowed out of massive tower walls sixteen feet thick.

In the center of the room, a ring of chairs had been established, one for each member of the council. But there were others among them, and Quentin wondered who would occupy them. Behind each chair a stanchion raised a banner bearing the device and blazon of each participant. Some of the council members were already seated, and behind their chairs stood a squire or page ready to do his lord's bidding. Other council members stood apart, with heads together, and talked in low tones; the room buzzed with the murmur of their conversation.

Quentin found his chair, marked by his own blazon: a flaming sword over a small dragon emblem. He smiled to himself when he saw it. The only time he ever saw his device was when in Askelon. Next to his chair sat Toli's, whose device was a white stag running on a field of forest green. He identified Ronsard's, a mace and a flail crossed and raised in a gauntleted hand. Theido's was the readily recognizable black hawk with wings outstretched. There were others he had never seen before, and several chairs had no banners.

In all there were fifteen chairs in the ring, but a few more stood along the wall to be added if the need arose. One by one the remaining council members took their places, and the room fell silent in expectation of the king's entrance.

Presently a side door opening into a private chamber creaked on its iron hinges, and Durwin stepped in without ceremony, followed by the king. *How tired he looks*, thought Quentin. *Not a king to inspire his nobles with a stirring call to arms.*

Eskevar took his chair and Durwin the chair beside him, which was unmarked by a banner. The king began at once.

"My noble friends, thank you for coming." He looked at each one around the circle. "My heart is heavy with the thought of what must be accomplished this day. I am no stranger to war and no coward. Some of you have stood with me in many glorious campaigns, and some where there was no glory for either side.

"Prudent men do not seek war, for it brings nothing good. But men of valor do not shrink from it if called to defend their homeland against a rapacious foe.

"Such is now the case. Mensandor is under invasion. At this moment foreign armies are burning our cities on the southern coast. The people there have no lords to protect them, so they flee to the hills and to the mountains."

This last statement sent a ripple of surprise and outrage coursing through the assembled nobles. Lord Lupollen, whose lands were in the north, below Woodsend, raised his voice above the others and asked, "What enemy is this? I have heard nothing of an invasion."

The king answered when all had quieted down once more. "As I bore certain suspicions regarding such activity, I sent the lord high marshal and the noble Theido, a trusted friend of the crown, to discover the source of my unease. I will let them tell you what they have found."

Ronsard spoke first. "My lords, with an accompaniment of four knights, Theido and I rode out, striking first to the south. We saw nothing unusual until we reached the sea pass below Persch, where we met a band of villagers fleeing to the north by night.

"These villagers told us of an enemy moving northward along the coast. They also said that Halidom had been destroyed completely. We proposed to ride to Halidom to see with our own eyes the veracity of this report. The villagers seemed frightened and given to exaggeration."

"Was Halidom destroyed?" asked one of the lords.

"Yes sir. There was nothing left of it but a charred spot on the earth."

"What? Surely you jest?"

"Not at all, sir." The voice was Theido's. "It is as he said. And not only Halidom. Illem is gone as well."

"But did you not see the enemy?"

"We saw no enemy, and only one survivor of the destruction, who died as we stood over him."

"This is ridiculous! You ask us to believe—," sputtered Lupollen.

"Believe what you will, sir," snapped Ronsard. "We say only what our eyes have seen."

"I must voice my dismay at this news, Sire," said Lord Ameronis. "It does seem most unlikely. We have been at peace for over ten years, and it has been far longer since an enemy dared set foot on the soil of Mensandor. Are we to think that a raiding party has landed and terrorized the villages? That surely can be dealt with forthrightly, and no Council of War need stand to ratify such a move."

"Yes," agreed Lord Rudd, "it sounds very like the time when the Vrothgar came up the Lower Plinn into the Wilderlands. Once opposed, they left readily enough."

Eskevar held up his hands for silence. "Please, my countrymen, if I thought that a stout body of knights would serve against this new menace, I would have dispatched them at once. But I have reason to believe the danger we now face is greater than that of a handful of barbarians raiding our cattle and crops." He nodded to Lord Wertwin.

"Noble friends, I came here today of my own volition, meeting the king's courier on the road. I agree with Eskevar—there is something here deserving more serious consideration. For the past half month or more, I have been receiving a steady traffic of refugees into my defenses. Some from as far away as Don: villagers, merchants, peasants. They have come begging protection and refuge from a terrible foe which has come against them—though 'tis true few of them have ever seen him."

Lord Rudd loudly challenged him. "It is not so strange an occurrence to have a few peasants stirred up over nothing at all. That no one seems to have seen this awesome and mysterious enemy is proof enough for me that if he exists at all, he is no more than a band of ruffians to be crushed with a single blow." When Rudd had finished speaking, there were murmurs of approval and nods of agreement.

"I have seen this enemy!" said Quentin boldly. All eyes turned toward him. "And I can say he is no mere band of ruffians or barbarians seeking meat and seed. Toli and I were captured at Illem on the night that town was sacked and burned."

He waited for his words to sink in.

"For two days we were held prisoner, escaping only with the help of one of the enemy's own officials." He paused to measure his words carefully.

"What we saw in that camp gave us to know that the army of Nin is no thieving tribe of barbarians, nor raiders after spoil. The Ningaal are a highly trained and disciplined army, and they are moving against Mensandor."

"I do not believe it!" shouted Lupollen angrily. "If such a foe exists, we would know it."

"Obviously he is cunning beyond belief!" snapped Ameronis with cold sarcasm.

"Believe it!" the high-pitched, cutting tone was a woman's. The assembly turned in their chairs as one to see who dared invade the king's council chambers.

Quentin saw Esme standing before the door to the inner chamber. She had entered undetected and had heard what had been said.

"Who is this woman, Sire? Send her away! The Council of War is no place for a female." There were other complaints of a similar nature.

"My lords, she will be heard. I have asked her to join us, and it seems that now we may hear her story. Continue, my lady, but let me inform this assembly that before them stands Princess Esme, daughter of King Troen of Elsendor."

Esme, looking every inch the princess that she was, with a thick circlet of silver on her brow and sheathed in a gown of deepest vermilion— Bria's no doubt—approached the king's chair to stand before the council. Her dark hair hung in rings to her shoulders; her black eyes sparked with an intense flame.

"I have come to Askelon at the behest of my father to deliver a message of warning and a plea for help. What I have heard this day makes me fear for both our lands.

"Late this spring, one of my father's ships was attacked at sea, but managed to fight off the attacker and return to port. Troen sent to discover who this enemy might be and ordered the commander of his personal vessel to search out and engage the pirateer. The ship never returned, but an answer came—for two days later, fivescore enemy ships were sighted off our southern coast by a fishing boat. My father issued forth the fleet to engage them; my brothers took command of our ships. I was dispatched here with the warning that a very great and powerful enemy has risen and would seize our lands. I have also come to ask King Eskevar to send help in our time of need."

Nothing was said following Esme's account until Eskevar asked, "Have you, then, nothing to say regarding these tidings?"

They must believe her, thought Quentin, *even if they do not believe my own story. Esme has spoken with such strength and assurance.*

"As you tell it, my lady, it makes a very convincing tale. But are we to understand that you believe the supposed enemy within our borders is the same that engages your father's fleet? I find that quite unlikely." With that speech Ameronis gained a few more nods of assent.

Eskevar exploded angrily. "You seem bent on disavowing any evidence we bring before you. Why is that, Lord Ameronis?"

Ameronis was cool in his reply. "The realm has been at peace for many years. I do not wish to see this hard-won peace so easily discarded. I, for one, do not see cause for mustering troops to oppose an enemy which no one has seen and whose intentions are inexplicable."

"Ah, we strike the heart of the matter at last!" said the Dragon King. A high color had risen to his cheeks and brow. His eyes, sunken and dark-rimmed from his long illness, blazed brightly. He nodded to one of the pages, who disappeared into the inner chamber to reappear a moment later with a tall stranger. The stranger, swathed in a loose-fitting blue garment, with chains of gold around his neck, entered and bowed low before the assembled lords. His black beard bristled like the quills of a hedgehog, and his eyes were sharp and direct.

"I present to you Myrmior, prime minister to the high suzerain of Khas-I-Quair. He it was who made possible the escape of my ward and his friend. Tell us what you have to say, brave sir."

Myrmior bowed again and touched his fingertips to his forehead. "It was not my intention to come before you in this way, but the king has willed it so, and I obey." He spoke smoothly, and his words had an edge that cut at the pride of the assembled lords who glared at him.

"I was captured four years ago when the home of my people was brought under subjection to Nin, called the Destroyer. The high suzerain was beheaded like a thief in the village square after a long, bloody war that lasted five years. I, his minister, became a slave to one of Nin's warlords.

"I have seen much in the years since my captivity began. Nation after nation has fallen; the realms of the mighty have been crushed; lands have been laid waste before Nin and his horde. Each victory makes the Ningaal stronger and pricks their leader's insatiable hunger for greater conquests. He has extended his empire from Sanarrath to Pelagia, and from Haldorland to Artasia. He will not stop until he rules the world, until all lands are his and all men his slaves.

"Now he has turned his eyes upon the west and the nations of the mighty kings. If he succeeds here, as he has in every other land where he has loosed his warlords, there will be no stopping him. He will achieve what his evil heart contemplates: Nin will be the god before whom all men bow and worship."

Myrmior's voice had risen steadily throughout his speech, and now the last words rang in the council chamber. No one moved or breathed. All eyes were on this mysterious messenger of doom.

"Do not deceive yourselves, lords of Mensandor. You cannot hide in your castles behind your strong walls. He will search you out and destroy you as surely as the snake catches the rat.

"Hear my words and beware! He has turned his eyes upon your kingdom and will have it for his own. There is nothing he cannot do and nothing he does not dare, for his star is growing in the east, and soon all men will know the terror of his name."

CHAPTER 28

There is naught to your discredit, Sire. You have done what a man can do. We will try again," Theido said soothingly.

They all sat gloomily around a large oaken table in the king's private chamber. Eskevar stared dully at his hands clasped before him. He had raged and fumed and threatened to no avail. The Council of War had ended in a deadlock. Lords Lupollen and Ameronis openly stood against raising an army, Wertwin and Fincher pledged their support, and the rest were undecided.

"I should have waited for the others to come; they could have made the difference. I was too hasty . . . too hasty."

"No," objected Durwin. "You did the right thing. The others will not arrive until tomorrow or the next day. We need to move at once. Who knows what a delay of two days might mean? Kingdoms have fallen in less time."

"Meanwhile, Lupollen and Ameronis have ample time to sway the others to their side." Eskevar sighed, and the room seemed to grow darker.

"They will all come 'round when they see the danger," offered Ronsard.

"But will it be too late?" wondered Theido. "I say we should send the king's knights out now to engage the invaders and hold them until an army can be raised. We must not let them reach Askelon unchallenged."

"Noble sirs, may I offer an observation?" It was Myrmior, who had been sitting in silence since the private council had begun. His impassioned appeal before the council had been to no avail, and he had retreated into a sullen mood, as had most everyone else.

"Nothing short of total strength will dismay them. Nin's armies are well trained and battle-ready. And there are more of them than you know. The force which Quentin and Toli met with was only one of four which are within Mensandor's borders. They are all moving toward Askelon by various routes."

"Why would they?" asked Ronsard. "Why not come en masse?"

"Nin long ago learned it was best when invading a strange land whose strengths were unknown to move in smaller forces, thus dividing the defense.

"A few valiant men may stand against many given a tactical advantage—is this not so?"

Nods around the table affirmed it was indeed. "But it is almost impossible to defend on four fronts at the same time. That is what you propose to do."

"And with few enough knights to do it," noted the king sourly. "Our cause is lost before trumpet has been blown or blade drawn."

"Say not so, Sire. There is much we may do with the men we have. The others will fall in line when they learn the threat is real and not imagined." Ronsard struck the table with his fist. He looked around to the others for support of his view.

"Ronsard is right," said Durwin slowly. "There is much we may do. And the sooner we begin, the better. It would be in our interest to—"

Just then there came a rap on the chamber door. A sentry stepped in and, bowing low, said, "Sire, there is a priest without who would speak to you without delay. He has been told you are in council, but will not be put off."

"Will he identify himself?" asked the king.

"He is Biorkis, as he says," offered the sentry.

"The high priest? Here?" Quentin looked at Toli, who only nodded mysteriously.

"Allow the high priest to enter. We will admit him."

The door was thrown wide, and an instant later Biorkis, dressed in his coarse brown robes, swept in to stand before them, a rueful smile upon his wrinkled, white face.

"Ariel has not forsaken his servant," the priest said. "All is as I would have wished."

Durwin leaped from the table so quickly, he sent his stool crashing to the floor. "Biorkis! Have you given up your vows at last?" The hermit strode to his old friend and clasped him by the arms.

The priest shook his head sadly; his white, braided beard wagged from side to side. "It seems as if I have been released from my vows whether I would or no." Durwin's eyebrows arched upward. "I mean," said the priest, "that I have been expelled from the temple."

"But why? Certainly it cannot be for any but a most serious offense— and what that would be from you I cannot imagine."

The former high priest turned to the others as Durwin drew him to the table, giving Quentin a special greeting. "It was for the most serious offense, my lords. I have been guilty of standing in the way of gross ambition. The charges were trifling ones; I persisted in seeing danger where none could be seen, in reading omens in the stars which threatened the security of the temple."

Durwin nodded knowingly. "We have been cast out this day for roughly the same reasons. But more of that later. I know that what you have come to tell us has not been watered down by your troubles. High priest or no, your heart will remain steadfast once it has decided on a course."

"Well you remember me, Durwin. You were ever one who could read a man's inmost soul. Yes, I have come with a message, but seeing you all here leads me to believe that I have come too late for my message to be of any great service to you."

"Say it, by all means," said Eskevar, "and let us judge its worth. That it has cost you your place in the temple is no small thing; rather, it speaks for the importance of your errand. What would you say to us?"

Biorkis bowed to them all; Durwin righted his stool, offered it to the priest, and went himself in search of another. When he had been seated, Biorkis spread his hands on the table and began.

"My lords, in my position of high priest, I worked tirelessly in the sifting of elements to discover the destinies of men and nations. It is my belief that religion should serve man in this way.

"When an omen presents itself, it is studied carefully to determine its import and consequence. I say that to say this: an omen has arisen the like of which has never been seen. It is a star, known to all by its common name—the Wolf Star. Unchanged since time began, it has recently begun to wax with unaccustomed brilliance. It has grown so quickly as not to be believed by any who have not followed its course as closely as I have."

"This is the star you spoke of, is it not?" Eskevar turned toward Myrmior, who merely dipped his head in assent.

"I see you know of it. Then I need not tell you how curious a thing it is. I have searched through the records of the temple. Back and back—as far back as records have been kept—thousands of years and more." Biorkis smiled and inclined his white head toward Quentin.

"This I did after your visit to me that night. Your curiosity about the star proved to me that there was something beyond novelty that study might reveal."

Quentin answered, "As I remember, you were very gloomy in your predictions even then. It was evil, you said, and more."

"Ah, that I was. Now I know I was right to believe as I did. The sacred records of the temple reveal that such a sign is not unknown. Twice before, long ages ago, such stars have been seen to grow in the sky. And though the old writing is hard to discern, and the meaning of the words is now unclear, it may be said with certainty that such omens betokened the very worst catastrophes for mankind."

"The end of the age!" said Durwin.

"The end of the age," agreed Biorkis. "In chaos and death. Destruction such as no man nor beast can survive. Nations are swept away; kingdoms vanish in a single hour, never to return. The face of the earth is changed forever. Lands rise up out of the sea, and continents submerge. All that was shall be changed in the mighty roar of the heavens rending apart. The stars fall from their courses, and the seas rise up. The rivers burn, and the earth crumbles away.

"Thus is the end of the age, and it is at hand."

The midnight conversation that he and Toli had had in Durwin's chamber when they had first come to Askelon leaped vividly to Quentin's mind, inspired by Biorkis's pronouncement. Conversation continued around the table; the voices of Ronsard, Theido, Eskevar, and Durwin sounded in his ears, but Quentin did not attend to them. They receded farther and farther from him, and then he heard them no more.

It seemed to him that he now entered a waking dream.

A dark, limitless horizon stretched before him, the darkness brooding and seething as a beast hungering and lying in wait for its prey. Quentin saw a small, bright figure laboring up a rocky slope to stand at last on the top of the hill.

It was a knight in armor, and as he looked more closely, he saw that the armor shone with a cool radiance, scattering light like a prism. The knight faced the brooding darkness and placed his hands to the hilt of his sword. He drew forth his sword, and it flashed with a burning white fire.

He raised his sword, and the darkness retreated before him. Then, with a mighty heave, the knight flung the sword into the air, where it spun, throwing off tongues of fire that filled the sky. As he did so, the knight shouted in a resounding voice, which seemed to echo in Quentin's ears, *"The sword shall burn with flames of fire. Darkness shall die: conquered, it flees on falcon's wings."*

The talking at the table ceased. All eyes turned toward Quentin, who stood before them, shaking his head and blinking as one awakening from a dream. The surprise on their faces, their open mouths, let Quentin know that he had not heard those words only; he had spoken them aloud before everyone there. The voice echoing in his ears was his own.

"What did he say?" Ronsard wondered.

"It was—I am sorry, excuse me," Quentin blurted. Toli peered at him through squinted eyes. There were stares all around.

"Where did you hear that?" demanded Durwin, jumping up.

"Why, I heard it just now . . . in a dream. I seem to have had a dream while everyone was talking. I do not know what it means."

"I do!" Biorkis fairly shouted. "It is from *The Chronicles of the Northern Kings.*"

"Yes, it is. 'The Prophecy of the Priest King.'" Durwin towered over Quentin, staring down upon him, eyes sparkling with a fierceness Quentin had never seen. Quentin squirmed uncomfortably on his stool, feeling foolish and light-headed.

"Tell me that you have never read that anywhere, nor heard it spoken in our presence, and I shall believe you."

"I tell you the truth, Durwin, I never have. The words mean nothing to me, whatever you say. I know them not."

"It is possible that you may have heard them in Dekra," mused Durwin. "But I think not. You would remember if you had."

"What is this?" asked Eskevar, his voice brittle with amazement.

Theido and Ronsard merely gazed in surprise at what was happening before them; Myrmior rubbed his hands absently over his bearded chin, eyes narrowed to slits.

"My lord, it is a wonder! A most powerful sign." Biorkis closed his eyes. His head began to weave with the cadence, and the old priest's voice swelled to fill the room as he began to recite the ancient prophecy.

"The stars shall look upon the acts of man. They shall bring forth signs and wonders. Cities of old are still to be seen; the cunning work of giants, the skillful shaping of stone. Wind is the swiftest messenger.

The clouds shall fly free forever. Thunder speaks with a mighty voice; the temples quake upon their foundations. The sacred rock shall be cloven. The spear struck upon shield shall make war. The eagle shall ascend on wings of strength; his offspring shall be honored among men. Courage shall be in the warrior. The jewel in the ring shall sit high and broad. The good man in his country shall do deeds of glory. The snake in his chamber shall be pierced. The valor of the knight shall be strong iron; his name is sung in the halls of his fathers. The wolf in the forest shall be craven. The boar in the wood is bold in the strength of his tusks. The king shall have a throne. The priest shall wear a crown. The sword shall burn with flames of fire. Darkness shall die; conquered, it flees on falcon's wings.

"The dragon under the hill shall be ancient; lordly, bold, and unafraid. The gods of high places shall be thrown down; theirs shall be the rage of death. The Most High shall suffer them no more. From out of the temple he has called his servant; his ways shall be exalted."

CHAPTER 29

Esme and Bria were waiting for them as they emerged from the council chambers. Quentin smiled when he saw them, though he did not feel like smiling. The two young women had become such fast friends, they were seen together everywhere, and it pleased Quentin to think that, though very different in many ways, they shared much in common, especially the same iron resolve in matters that touched them deeply. They were, he reflected, the living idea of the word *princess*.

Quentin had not spoken upon emerging from the chamber. He felt weak and a little frightened of what he might say next. The vision and prophecy had unnerved him, making him feel he could no longer trust himself to behave normally. Toli had ushered them all away to a quiet spot in the kitchen, where they could sit and munch apples and be alone.

After a while Quentin recovered some of his usual good humor and began to talk about what had happened. He told of the talk around the table, and of his dream, and the prophecy he had uttered, and how excited Durwin and Biorkis had become after hearing it. It was then that Esme related her own experience with the daughter of Orphe, and the prophecy that had been given to her in exchange for the meal she had cooked for the oracle.

Esme recited the strange prophecy, and Quentin was struck with how similar it was to the one he had himself spoken. Both spoke of a sword of power that would vanquish the invaders with a stroke. When Esme had finished her story, they had all fallen silent for a long time, not daring to break the spell that had descended upon the little group.

For Quentin the time of silence was welcome. He turned the words over in his mind, sifting them, holding them as they tumbled through his consciousness. His vision, so long ago received in his Blessing of the Ariga at the temple of Dekra, seemed now to be taking form, unfolding before him and pulling him along. His vision. Long had he pondered it and held it in his heart. Part of him wanted to run to it, embrace whatever lay ahead, knowing that he would never know true peace unless he did. Another part of him wanted to hold it off, to turn away from its terrible, fierce glory. And Quentin was torn between the two.

Quentin and Toli stood in the night-darkened passageway and knocked. They heard a shuffle on the other side of the heavy door, and it was drawn open slowly. Ronsard's broad, handsome face grinned back at them.

"Enter, friends," he said. "We have been waiting for you."

"What is the meaning of this summons? Ronsard, Theido—have you nothing better to do than keep tired men from their beds?" Quentin stepped into Durwin's chamber, made bright by the clustered lights of tall candletrees placed around the room.

"You will regret those harsh words soon, sir," said Theido quietly. Quentin had spoken in fun, but though Theido smiled, Quentin could tell there was an uneasiness in the knight's manner.

"You are going away!" said Quentin in dismay. He glanced quickly at their faces and knew that he had guessed correctly.

"Yes," said Ronsard gently. "Before sunrise."

"But—I do not understand. Why so soon?"

"It must be," explained Theido. "We are leading the king's own knights against the Ningaal. We must move at once before they have time to draw their strength together."

"Come in and sit down. We have a little time to part as friends ought," said Durwin warmly.

Quentin moved woodenly to a chair in front of the empty hearth. Toli settled on the arm of the chair beside him. What the dark-eyed Jher was feeling could not be read upon his face, though his eyes had gone hard.

"I know it comes as a shock to you, Quentin. But this is the way it must be." Theido's tone was smooth and assured. "I know you had your heart set on coming with us, but I assume you also know that cannot be. With your arm, you would not last the first clash of battle."

Quentin was mildly flattered to think that Theido had so high an estimation of his courage. Actually, he had no wish to encounter the brutal Ningaal again.

"That is not the cause of my misgivings, though you do me honor. You cannot go against the Ningaal with the king's retinue alone; it would be disastrous! There are too many, and they are disciplined soldiers every one. I have seen them."

"We dare not wait any longer," said Ronsard. "Every day we delay may mean much in time to come. But do not worry overmuch; we do not go entirely alone. Lord Wertwin will meet us with his troops—he will raise a hundred sturdy knights and arms for all."

"But four hundred or five hundred—what is that against Gurd's thousands? And he is but one of four, if Myrmior speaks true."

"I think we may say that Myrmior speaks true," laughed Ronsard. "He is going with us. He will help us to plan our strategy against the warlords."

"It is no small thing," agreed Theido. "His help shall prove invaluable; I have no doubt of it." He leaned forward and searched Quentin's face with earnest, dark eyes. "We must go, Quentin. We must gain this time for Eskevar to bring the other lords around.

"We did not expect such a poor show among our peers. But that is the way of it. They will see that war has come, and they will join us in the end. Of that I have no fear."

"But in the meantime, while they are making up their minds, you will all be killed!" said Quentin bitterly. "No. there must be some better way."

"This is how it will be," said Ronsard. He stood and walked to Quentin and put his hand upon his shoulder. "Do not fear for us, for we do not fear for ourselves. A knight can have but one death, and that one with honor or he is no true knight. I have seen enough battle that it holds no terror for me. I am content.

"We have no intention of moving foolishly. In truth, you will not see two more cautious and prudent men as we. But we must give the king time to pull the lords together, or our cause is lost before it is begun. Myrmior has shown us that, at least.

"Besides, I do not think you will be idle yourself. If I understand Durwin aright, he means to employ you most strenuously. You will have no time to think about us."

Quentin threw himself out of his chair and grabbed Ronsard by the arm with his good hand. "I will always think about you! Both of you have been more than comrades to me. I wish I could go with you and share your portion. I would gladly take my place on the battlefield with you once again."

"And so you shall. There will be enough battle for all of us, I'll wager." Theido came to stand beside a tearful Quentin.

"The injury that keeps me here was more hurtful than I knew," Quentin told them, embracing them both in turn. "Go, then, and may the Most High go with you and grant you his unfailing protection."

"And you," the two knights said in unison.

They moved reluctantly toward the door. Toli, coming up behind Quentin, shook both their hands and wished them, in his native tongue, singing blades and shields that never fall. And turning to Durwin he said, "Good hermit, will you say a prayer to the Most High for our brothers?"

"Of course—I was about to suggest it myself." The hermit of

Pelgrin came forward and raised his hands before the two knights. Ronsard sank to one knee, and Theido knelt down beside him.

"God Most High, who ever guides our steps and hears our prayers," he said softly, "hear us now. Be to these our stout companions the sharp edge of their blade, the strength of their arm, and the protection of their shield. Show them mighty among the enemy; show them dauntless and unafraid. Go before them into battle as a lance to drive the evil from our shores. Be to them a comfort and a guide; refresh them when they are weary, and bear them up when strength is gone.

"Banish fear from their hearts, and give them wisdom to lead their men to victory. Be to them the glory which will shine through the darkness, and bring them home to us once more."

The knights rose slowly. "This god of yours, Durwin, can he do so much?" asked Ronsard softly.

"He can do all things, my friend. Do not fear to call upon him in any need. He is ever quick to aid his servants."

"Then from now on I will serve him—this God Most High." He grinned at Quentin. "See, you are not the only one who listens to this prattling hermit. I have a care for my spirit, too."

"Truly, this is a time of wonders unceasing." Quentin advanced and offered his hand to them. "Farewell, my friends."

"Farewell, Quentin. Farewell."

CHAPTER 30

Quentin and Toli had been too preoccupied with their own preparations to think beyond what lay ahead. They had spent two days following the departure of the knights gathering supplies and making ready. Then early, before the sun had risen above the dark line of Pelgrin, Toli led the horses and pack animals out across the inner ward, through the inner curtain, and into the outer ward where Durwin and Quentin waited.

There they had been met by Alinea, Bria, and Esme. The women pressed gifts of food into their hands and exchanged kisses all around.

"Eskevar wished me to bid you farewell," Alinea said. "He would have come to see you away, but a king does not say good-bye. So, for him and myself, farewell. Travel swiftly and return safely. Our hearts and our prayers go with you."

Then Bria and Quentin had removed a little apart to speak the special feelings between them. Esme, with flowers in her hair, took one and gave it to Toli, who carried it over his heart beneath his baldric.

The three women had accompanied them across the drawbridge and stood there, tears splashing to the ground in a gentle rain, waving them good-bye until the narrow streets of Askelon had taken them from view.

The sadness of that parting settled heavy on Quentin's spirit. It brooded over his waking hours for the better part of three days following.

He spoke but little and moved about as one asleep. He did not notice that Toli, and to some extent Durwin, behaved in exactly the same way.

In his lonely meditation, Quentin turned again and again to the events of the hurried last days in Askelon, and especially the meeting in Durwin's chambers that had lasted far into the night. It now seemed shadowy and indistinct, as if he were watching smoke trails curling and rising in the night air. But it seemed real enough then, and it was that particular event that was now speeding them on their way.

As they moved through the darkened pathways of Pelgrin Forest, now heavy with verdure, summer sitting full on every bough, Quentin rehearsed once more the happenings of that night.

After Theido and Ronsard left Durwin's apartment, almost before their footsteps had diminished in the corridor, Biorkis had swept in with an armful of scrolls and parchments and map skins. Since the private council with Eskevar the day before, he had disappeared; Quentin had not seen him since he heard the old priest recite the ancient prophecy that still rang in his ears.

Biorkis, they were soon to discover, had busily buried himself in the castle's athenaeum and there, stopping neither to eat nor sleep, scratched together the odd assemblage of material he now carried with him.

"I have found what we need, Durwin. It was not easy—the king's library is not at all as orderly as the temple's, but that is to be expected. Some of these writings are barely discernible—even to a knowing eye— and quite incomplete. But my memory, and yours, of course, Durwin, will serve where the parchments fail us."

The old priest bustled and fretted so prodigiously in getting his texts arranged that Quentin laughed out loud. "Do not tell me we are to endure one of your interminable lessons! Spare us!"

Biorkis cocked his head to one side. "Do not think that it would harm you, sir. You have probably forgotten all I ever taught you."

"Biorkis and I put our heads together upon leaving the king's council," Durwin explained. "I think you will be interested to hear what we have learned." Although Durwin did not say it, Quentin knew by the glint of the hermit's eye and the mood of high excitement that suddenly bristled in the room that the subject of the meeting had something to do with the prophecy and his strange utterance of it the day previous.

"Yes, it is all here. Enough at any rate to allow us to act, I think, though I wish I had access to my books at the temple." Biorkis sighed sadly.

"And I my own at the cottage," agreed Durwin. "Still, I have read them enough to know them from memory, I daresay."

"Are we to understand," said Quentin, indicating Toli and himself, "that you believe this . . . Prophecy of the Priest King, or whatever— this has something to do with us?"

"Not us, Sire," said Biorkis blithely. "You!"

Quentin had almost succeeded in putting off the feeling of awe-some responsibility that went along with the thought that he might be chosen for some great task. He had almost settled into feeling his nor-mal self again—almost, but not entirely. For the inexpressible notion that he was caught up in the swiftly running stream of history, that he was moved by an unseen hand toward an unknown destiny, and that all this had something to do with his vision of the flaming sword—this notion haunted him, lurking behind his thoughts like a shadow, or the lingering presence of a dream.

"There are many signs by which these things can be judged, as you well know," the priest burbled on. "Let us just say that I have spent a day and a night in sifting through all that is known about the prophecy and the events surrounding it, and that I have no good reason to doubt that the signs point to you."

"There are also very good reasons to believe that now is the time in which this prophecy will be fulfilled," added Durwin.

Toli spoke up. "Though I have never heard of this prophecy—before it was spoken in the king's chamber, that is—the Jher, too, have a legend that a king of the white race will arise who will usher in the age of light.

He is to be called Lotheneil, the Waymaker. That is because he will lead men's minds toward Whinoek, the God Most High." Toli fixed Quentin with a knowing look and crossed his arms upon his chest, as if satisfied that the matter was settled.

"Do not think that I am unwilling," said Quentin. "But you must show me how these things pertain to me. I know nothing of this prophecy—"

"And yet you quoted it word for word, or nearly. In the original it goes something like this: *'Thee sword sceal byrnan with fyr flaume, Deorcin sceal dhy; deffetyn hit fleon winge falcho.'*

"I would have been quite astounded if you had spoken it in the old tongue. Still, it was surprising enough. There are fewer than five men in all of Mensandor who know and can quote that obscure prophecy. That two of them should be in the same room together at an utterance—well, it is quite remarkable. Incredible."

"I did not tell the whole prophecy, only part of it." Quentin fidgeted in his high-backed chair, while Toli perched like a bird of prey beside him. "It might have been a coincidence."

"Quentin," Durwin reproached softly, "you know as well as I that for the servants of the Most High, there are no coincidences. And for a prophet to quote the merest portion of a prophecy is the same as to invoke the whole. The elders at Dekra should have given ample instruction in that."

It was true; he had often heard and understood the elders to make reference to various events and happenings in the sacred texts, quoting portions of the text and implying the rest. He knew Durwin could see through any attempt on his part to distance himself from the events that were forming on all sides. It seemed to Quentin that a web of circumstances was weaving itself around him, pulling tighter and tighter. Soon he would be trapped by a destiny he had not foreseen and was not certain he could fulfill.

But he also felt that aside from his personal reluctance, which sat like a lintel stone upon his back, if what Biorkis and Durwin said was true, he had a responsibility to follow wherever the trail would lead. If he did have some part to play in saving the realm, he had to accept it and do whatever was required, aside from how he felt about it.

It was this other, more rational Quentin who answered.

"Very well. Let us see what you two rumormongers have schemed up for us. There seems to be no denying you."

"You are beginning to think beyond yourself, eh, Quentin? That is good. Yes, very good." Biorkis pulled on his long, white, braided beard. "Now, here is what I have found."

The hours that followed had seemed but the flicker of a candle flame. A wink, a nod, and they were gone. From the moment his old teacher had begun to speak, Quentin was gripped in the spell of enchantment, transfixed by the unutterable mystery of the story of strange events, long forgotten, having passed from the minds and hearts of men long ages past. It was remembered only by a few learned men, and now it was revived in his presence. He listened intently, seizing every word as a thirsty man opening his parched throat to the sky to drink in the drops of rain.

They told of the sword, a sword unlike any other and possessed of a mysterious holy power; of secret mines beneath hidden mountains in half-remembered lands; and of the forging of the mighty weapon upon an anvil of gold. Biorkis and Durwin, their round faces flushed with the excitement of their tale, spoke of the ache of the people who for generation upon generation had waited, believing that they would see the coming of the sword and he who would carry it. They told of songs sung and prayers prayed in all the dark, hopeless times for the hand worthy to possess the sword to arise and deal deliverance at its point.

Zhaligkeer—that was the name the ancients had given the sword. The Shining One.

Quentin rolled the name on his tongue, knowing the name linked him to those who had lived and died waiting to see the sword. He wondered how many men had breathed that name in their hour of need; he wondered how many had despaired of ever seeing it and had given up hope and turned away.

When at last the story was told, Quentin rose to stretch and pace the room in quick, restless strides. "Are you suggesting that we just go and find this sword? That it lies hidden in some cave in the high Fiskills?"

Biorkis shook his head wearily. "Not find it; the sword does not exist. You must make it. Zhaligkeer must be forged of the hand that will wield it."

Quentin sighed hopelessly. "I do not understand. Forgive me, what was all that about anvils of gold and secret mines and all? I thought that it was all part of the legend."

"Oh, it is, it is," said Durwin. "But it is our belief that the legends indicate the manner in which the sword must be made, not how it was made. I do not think that anyone ever actually made the sword."

"Well, why not? It does not seem at all clear why they would hesitate. What was to stop them from trying?"

Durwin cocked his head to one side and smiled smugly. "Nothing and . . . everything. Undoubtedly, many tried. They applied the prophecy to themselves and their own times. But two things are needed for the sword to become Zhaligkeer, the Shining One: the one is from the secret mines, but the other is the hand of him whom the prophecy names. Even if they found the ore, which perhaps some of them by some means accomplished, they still lacked the thing that would make the sword Zhaligkeer: the hand of the chosen one. You see, it is not the blade alone but the hand of the Most High which endows the sword with its power."

"If, as you say, men have long sought the Shining One, why have I not heard tell of it before now?"

"There is nothing unusual there, sir!" laughed Biorkis. "It is ever thus. In good days men think not of the hand that helps them. But when evil days come upon them, they cry out for the deliverer. In Mensandor, the years have brought prosperity and peace to the people as often as not. Men have forgotten much of the old times, when their fathers struggled in the land. They have forgotten the sword; but for a few the prophecy would have been lost completely."

Quentin brushed his good hand through his hair. His eyes burned in his head. He was tired. The night was old, and he needed sleep.

"I know nothing of making swords. Neither do I know the way to the secret mines in the high wastelands of the Fiskills. And even if I already possessed such a sword, I do not know what I should do with it; I do not even have the arm to raise it."

Durwin crossed the room and placed a firm hand on his shoulder. "You are tired; you should take your rest like Toli there." Durwin nodded toward the Jher, who had curled himself up in an empty seat and was now sleeping soundly. "Go to bed now. We have talked enough for one night. We will talk again tomorrow. Believe me, there is much more to discuss before we set off."

Quentin believed him. There were a thousand questions flapping around in his head, like blackbirds over a new-plowed field. But he was exhausted and could think of nothing but sleep.

"Does anyone else know about all this . . . this. . . ." Words failed him; he could think no more.

"No, not as yet—Ronsard and Theido know we will be busy while they are away. To Eskevar I have mentioned my suspicions regarding the events before us, but he knows nothing of the sword. No one beyond we four knows anything about what we have talked of this night.

"Good night, Quentin. Go and find your bed. We will talk again in the morning."

As if on signal, Toli rose and slipped to the door to lead Quentin away. In a few moments Quentin felt himself sink deeply into bed, collapsing full-length upon it without even removing his clothes. To Quentin it seemed as if he had plunged into a warm, silent sea. He was asleep as the waves closed over him.

The next day was a blur of maps and scrolls—so dusty and brittle with age, one scarcely dared breathe on them—and dizzying conversation. Toli, sensing that the time for riding was drawing swiftly nearer, had begun selecting animals and provisions for the journey. Several times Quentin saw Durwin and Toli head-to-head in a corner as Toli checked some detail of his plan with Durwin.

Quentin wondered why he was not consulted about the preparations, but at the same time he was glad to not have to think about them. His mind had more than enough with which to occupy itself; his head fairly throbbed with the things he was taking in. Also, he missed Bria. He had not seen her but for fleeting moments over hurried meals.

He could tell that she knew he was going away soon. Her silent gazes, her bittersweet smiles and furtive gestures told him she knew. But she did not mention it to him; she did not cling. It was a mark of her high character that she, as much as was humanly possible, put her own feelings aside and tried to make his last days at the castle easier. And Quentin loved her for it.

When he finally mustered enough courage to face breaking the awful announcement of their departure, Bria placed her fingers to his lips, saying, "Do not say it. I know you must leave me now. I knew that from the moment I saw you emerge from the council chamber. You have much to do, great deeds to perform, and I will not bind your heart with promises.

"Go, my love. And when you return, you will find me waiting at the gate. The women of my kindred are accustomed to waiting. Do not worry after me, my darling. I will pass the time the better knowing your mind is settled."

Despite his broken arm, Quentin hugged her to him for a long time, wondering whether he would ever see her again.

In the haste which overtook them, there was little time for brooding or sadness—that would come later; there was simply too much to be done. In two days they accomplished what would normally have taken a week.

Long hours were spent in consultation with the king. Their plan had won his approval outright, although not without certain misgivings. With the hills and countryside become harborage for the Ningaal—no one knew precisely where they were—Eskevar was loath to allow the party to leave without an armed escort.

They at last convinced him that such would only make their errand more difficult. It would be better to pass unheralded through the world and unencumbered by the chores of moving many men and horses overland in secret.

Quentin, Toli, and Durwin went. Biorkis, too old to withstand the rigors of such a journey, stayed behind in Askelon to give aid and counsel where he could. If battle drew near, he would be needed to attend as physician to any wounded. Also in Durwin's mind, though he did not voice it aloud to anyone, was his apprehension that Eskevar, not wholly recovered from his mysterious malady, would require competent care in his absence. Were it not for that, Durwin would have taken his leave of the castle with a lighter heart.

The dark, cool pathways of Pelgrin, overhung with leafy boughs that blotted out all but the most determined of the sun's rays, soothed Quentin's mind as he rode along. His sorrow gradually left him, and he became filled with the excitement of the quest. Though it was still hard for him to accept the fact that he seemed to have a central part in it— he felt the same old Quentin, after all—he allowed himself to linger long in a kind of rapture over the tale of the mighty Zhaligkeer, the Sword of Holy Fire.

CHAPTER 31

W here will we find the master armorer to help in forging the sword? I do not recall having mentioned that. Surely, you do not contemplate that we will undertake that task without guidance?" Quentin rested with his back against a mossy log in a green clearing deep in Pelgrin's wooded heart. Toli was busily poking among the bundles of the pack ponies to assemble a bite for them to eat. They had been riding since sunrise, and this was the first time they had stopped.

"I have an idea where we may find someone suited to the task," said Durwin. His hands were clasped behind his head, and his eyes were gazing skyward. "Does the name Inchkeith mean anything to you?"

"Inchkeith? Why, he is said to be the most skilled armorer who ever lived. He fashioned the armor for the first Dragon King, and it was he who designed Eskevar's battle dress, which he wore in the war against Goliah. Everyone knows that name! But is he still alive?"

"Oh, very much alive, though you make him older than he really is. It was his father, Inchkeith the Red, who made the armor for the Dragon King, and for several kings before that. He is many long years in his grave.

"But his son has continued the work begun by his father, and has increased the renown of the name. It is no wonder legends abound whenever men strap on greaves and gorget. The armor of Inchkeith is known as the finest made by human hands."

Durwin smiled and winked at Quentin's look of unalloyed amazement. "Well, what do you say? Will he do to make us a sword?"

"A slingshot fashioned by master Inchkeith would do as well. Of course he will do!"

They ate their meal and talked of the trail. Toli said little, and Quentin guessed his friend was concentrating upon reviving his dormant trailcraft—it had been a long time since the wily Jher had had an opportunity to practice the storied skills of his people. The little journeys back and forth from Askelon hardly counted, for there was a good road. But where they were going they would have need of his animal-like cunning, for there were no roads, no pathways, nor even trails. Man had not set foot in those high places in a thousand years.

Quentin was thinking on these things, realizing that just as he did not know how they would fashion the sword, he did not know exactly where they were going.

"These mines, Durwin—where are they? How will we find them?"

"I have brought along maps, such as they are, taken from the old scrolls. This is as good a time as any to show you. Here." The hermit moved to one of the ponies and withdrew a long roll of leather.

"This is the way we shall go," he said, unrolling the map. "It is very old, this map. And the land is much changed: rivers have slipped from their courses, and hills have worn away; forests have vanished, and cities have come and gone. But it shall serve to guide us nonetheless."

Quentin fingered the skin on which the map was painted. "This does not appear as old as you say, Durwin. It looks as if it were made only yesterday."

"It was!" laughed Durwin. "We did not dare bring the original, or originals, I should say, for this map is made from scraps Biorkis and I have found over the years. The very age of the scraps made bringing them out of the question. They would have blown away on the first breath of breeze.

"No, this map was made by the combined resources of Biorkis and myself, and it is a better map for it. He had information which I did not.

It is a lucky thing he came when he did. If he does nothing else, he has already helped greatly."

"Durwin," Quentin chuckled, "do you not know that where the servants of the Most High are concerned, there is no such thing as luck and coincidence?"

The hermit laughed and raised his hands before him. "So it is! Give me quarter! I submit. The pupil has instructed the master."

"I am not always so dull," Quentin said, looking again at the map, which seemed little more than a bare sketch. "Be it as you say, there is still precious little here to follow. I do not even see any mines indicated on it."

"Very rough. But it is all we have—besides the riddle."

"Riddle?" Toli spoke up. He stood over them, looking down at the map.

"Did I not tell you of the riddle? Oh? Well, I will tell you now. There was so much to do and so little time, I do not wonder that you feel ill equipped to begin this journey. I thought I had told you.

"The riddle goes like this:

'Over tooth and under claw wend your way with care.
Where mountains sleep, sharp vigil keep; you shall see the way
    most clear.
When you hear laughter among the clouds and see a curtain made
    of glass
Take no care for hand nor hair, or you shall surely never pass.
Part the curtain, divide the thunder, and seek the narrow way;
Give day for night and withhold the light
And you have won the day.'

"It sounds simple enough," said Quentin. "Where did you find it?"

"That we shall see. I am certain that it will seem more than difficult enough when the time comes to unravel its meaning. As to where I found it, you should know that already."

"How so?"

"At Dekra. That is where I discovered most of what little I know of this affair. Yeseph himself translated it for me."

"He never told me about it."

"Why should he? It was years ago, and I was a pestering young man digging through his library like a mole. I chanced upon the riddle in a book which made mention of the mines of the Ariga."

"Those are the mines we seek?"

Durwin nodded. "You see, the blade is to be made of lanthanil."

"The stone which glows," said Toli. "My people have heard of it. It is said that of old the Ariga gave gifts of glowing stones to the Jher for their friendship in the time of the white death. Whoever touched the stone was healed and made whole. They were called Khoen Navish—the Healing Stones."

"Yes, that, at least, I have heard of, too. But I assumed that like much of the lore of the Ariga, the lanthanil had passed from this earth."

"I think not, though we shall see," Durwin said. "The Most High will show us aright. We must remember that it is he who guides us to his own purpose. We need not fret ourselves overmuch about the things we cannot foresee. The things we see too well will require our utmost attention, I have no doubt."

Theido and Ronsard, with a force of three hundred mounted knights behind them, rode southward as far as their coursers could take them. They wanted to reach their rendezvous with Lord Wertwin on the third day and then undertake to engage the enemy before he had a chance to travel very much farther and strengthen himself on the spoils of Mensandor.

At midday on the third day, they reached the prearranged place of meeting. The knights dismounted and walked the wide greensward while they waited for Wertwin's army to arrive. Squires in attendance watered the horses and saw to their masters' armor; some polished breastplates and repainted devices erased by use, others set up their sharpening stones to hone blades long unused, and the smiths at their wagons pounded out dents in helm and brassard upon their anvils.

The day was filled with the clatter of an army looking to its armament. Theido and Ronsard had withdrawn under a shady branch to await their comrade. Ronsard dozed, and Theido paced while the afternoon came on in full.

"He has not come yet?" asked a sleepy Ronsard as he rose to his feet, stretching.

"No, and I am beginning to wonder if we should send a scout ahead to see what may have become of him. He should have been here waiting for us. Instead it is we who wait for him, and he shows not."

"I will send Tarkio ahead a little and see if we can discover what has become of our tardy friend. Perhaps it is nothing. You know it is no small task to mobilize a force of knights in a single day. He may have made a late start."

"Let us hope that is what has happened," said Theido. He did not mention the other explanation that came to his mind. Both of them knew what it was, and neither wanted to hear or believe it.

Ronsard sent a squire to fetch the knight, and they waited for the courier to ready himself. "Be easy, Theido. You are wearing a path in the grass. See here, your pacing has bared the earth."

"I like this less and less, Ronsard. I do. Something has happened. I feel it here." He smacked his fist against his stomach.

Ronsard stared at his dark friend as Theido continued. "Your instincts in the ways of battle are ever keen. You must feel it, too." Theido paused and stared, his gaze almost fierce with impatience. "Well?"

Before Ronsard could answer, they heard a battle horn sound in the wood; it seemed to surround them as it blasted a note of alarm. They turned and looked out across the greensward and saw a knight on a charger come crashing out of the wood. They watched as one of their own apprehended the man; there was a wild waving of arms, and then the knight looked toward them and spurred his mount forward. In an instant he was pounding toward the spot where Theido and Ronsard waited.

"Noble knights, brave sirs! I come from Lord Wertwin," the breathless soldier said as he flung himself from his saddle. "We were on our way here and were joined by the enemy." He gulped air; sweat ran down his neck and into his tunic. His armor was battered and dashed with blood.

"How far?" asked Ronsard.

"No more than a league, sir," the knight wheezed.

"What was the disposition of the battle when you were sent to find us?"

The knight shook his head slowly; his face was grave. "There is little hope. The enemy is strong, and there are many of them. My lord was surrounded on three sides, his back to the lake that lies at the edge of the forest."

"There is no time to lose!" shouted Ronsard. "Marshal, sound the trumpet! We move at once!" He dashed to his charger and began shouting orders to the men who had gathered around to see what the commotion foretold.

In three heartbeats the greensward was a confusion of knights buckling on armor and clamoring into their saddles. Out of chaos emerged a ready-mounted, fearsome host. Theido and Ronsard each took their places at the head of the column, and the army moved off at a gallop, leaving the armorers and squires to lead the wagons and follow along behind.

The clash of battle could be heard long before it was seen. The king's forces dropped down the wooded slope into a broad, grassy bowl, which formed the higher end of the lake's basin. Once below the level of the lower trees, they could see that the enemy had indeed surrounded Wertwin's troops and were attempting to push them into the lake.

Theido and Ronsard ranged their army along the rim of the bowl and, when the knights were in position, sounded the attack. They came swooping down out of the wood and encompassed the field, driving straight into the thick of the enemy.

The startled Ningaal turned to meet this unexpected charge and found themselves blade to blade with a fresh foe. Ronsard half expected that the sight of the king's knights descending in numbers upon them would send the horde scattering into the wood, where they could be driven to earth like cattle.

But the warlord Gurd's men were seasoned to battle. They dug in and met the flying charge head-on. Many Ningaal lost their lives in that first surge. But dauntless and seemingly immune to fear, those who survived the onslaught merely stepped over the bodies of their comrades and fought on.

Theido forced a passage through to the shoreline of the lake and struck toward where Wertwin labored in the thick of the battle. When Theido reached him, the brave commander's horse's hind legs were in the water. Several valiant knights, having been unsaddled, had drowned along the strand in shallow water, unable to right themselves.

The fallen were everywhere. The blood of friend and foe alike stained the gray shingle a rusty red.

Ronsard led his contingent around to the rear to begin a pinching action upon the enemy caught between Theido's forces and his own. By sheer force of weight—the knights being mounted, and the enemy on foot—Ronsard was able to join Theido in short order, successfully dividing the Ningaal into two isolated halves.

"We are outnumbered!" Ronsard called when he had driven to within earshot of his comrade.

"Our horses and armor will sway the balance!" Theido retorted.

The blades of the knights flashed in the sun; their shields bore the shock of fierce blows. On horseback the knights were almost invulnerable—living fortresses of steel—their beveled armor shedding all but the most direct strikes against them. On foot, however, the slow-moving, heavy-laden knights were disadvantaged by the lightly protected but more agile Ningaal.

The tide of battle ebbed and flowed for both sides. The clash of steel and cries of the wounded and dying filled the air, and carrion birds, having tasted blood on the wind, now soared overhead. With a mighty shout the Ningaal, at some unknown signal, suddenly rushed the mound that Theido and Ronsard had managed to gain. The tactic allowed them to rejoin the two halves that had been divided.

"We cannot hold them long," said Ronsard through clenched teeth, his blade whistling around his head. "We must break through now, or we may be trapped against the lake once more."

"Aye, well said. Have you any suggestions?" Theido grunted as he slashed and wheeled in his saddle, thrusting and thrusting again.

"A charge along the shoreline and then back into the woods!" shouted Ronsard.

"Retreat?" asked Wertwin. "I would rather fall with my men."

"Let us say that we are moving the battle to more favorable ground," cried Theido. "If we stay here much longer, we will be pushed into the lake once more. They are too strong for us!" He turned and shouted his order to the marshal, who obediently sounded the horn.

The knights of the Dragon King drew together and pushed along the shoreline of the clear blue lake; those scattered further afield disengaged themselves and followed in their wake. Several riderless horses joined the retreat, and knights on foot ran alongside, not to be left behind.

When they had reached the shelter of the wood, where the ground sloped upward, Ronsard halted and turned his men to face the foe once more. Theido's and Wertwin's knights streamed past and continued deeper into the wood. Ronsard called to his knights to be ready to dismount after meeting the first attack. He had decided in the close quarters of the wood it would be better for his men to fight on foot and use the higher ground to their advantage.

But the Ningaal did not follow them into the wood.

"What is this? They withdraw," Ronsard cried in disbelief.

Instantly Theido was beside him. "I do not understand. It is hours to sunset, but they are leaving."

"We will give chase!" cried Wertwin.

Ronsard cautioned against this, saying, "Let them go. Whatever moves them, I do not think it is fear of us. They were giving blade for blade down there. They are not fleeing. It may be a trap."

"We could crush them!" objected Wertwin.

"No, sir!" said Theido. "A moment ago we were in difficulty to hold our own. That will not have changed because they choose to withdraw. Ronsard is right—they do not leave the battlefield out of weakness."

Theido cast his gaze across the tufted field now bearing the bodies of the dead and dying. Upon the mound they had just left he saw a lone figure mounted on a sturdy black charger. The figure raised the visor of his plume-crested helm and turned his face to where Theido, Wertwin, and Ronsard stood at the edge of the wood. Then he lifted his sword with its cruel curved blade high above his head in salute.

"It is the warlord," said Theido.

"He taunts us!" hissed Wertwin.

"It is a salute, perhaps. A warning," said Ronsard grimly.

The warlord lowered his sword and turned aside to follow his army, now moving away along the opposite side of the lake, leaving the field to the birds and the moans of the wounded and dying.

"Send a party to bind our wounded and retrieve the armor of our fallen. We need not fear another attack today," said Theido. "Then let us go back to camp and hold council. I would hear what Myrmior has to say about what has happened here today. He may have much to tell us."

CHAPTER 32

Under their banners of blue and gold and scarlet in the council ring, the lords of Mensandor sat in their high-backed chairs. Eskevar glared down from this throne upon the dais, his thin, knotted hands clutching the armrests like claws.

"The foe does grow each day stronger. How long will you wait, my lords? How long? Until your castles are burning? Until the blood of your women and children runs red upon the earth?

"And to what purpose? Do you think that by hiding within your gates you may save your precious gold? I say that you will not! The enemy comes! He is drawing closer. The time to move is now!"

The Dragon King's words rang with surprising force and vigor, coming as they did from a man who appeared only half of what he had been, so wasted was he by his illness. The gathered lords, now all accounted for—aside from Wertwin, who had made his decision and was with Theido and Ronsard—sat in silence. No one wished to be the first to go against the king.

"Do you doubt the need?" asked Eskevar in a softer tone. "I will tell you how I perceive the need: I have sent my personal bodyguard, my three hundred, to stand against the Ningaal. Lord Theido and the Lord High Marshal Ronsard lead them, and they are joined by Lord Wertwin and his standing army of a hundred.

"These are gallant men and brave; but there are not enough. We must send tenfold knights and men-at-arms to stand with them if the Ningaal are to be crushed and banished from our shores."

Lord Ameronis, in a voice of calm reason, said, "That is precisely the point we would question further, Sire. This enemy . . . this Nin, whoever he is . . . we have heard nothing of him. How do we know that he is so strong and his numbers so great? It would seem to me that we would be more prudent to send a scouting force to ascertain these and other details before embarking upon all-out war with an imagined enemy of unknown strength."

"How well you speak, Ameronis. I would imagine, as you have had ample time to compose your thoughts, that you are quite settled in your mind as to how you will go." The king paused to let his sarcasm hit its mark.

"Lord Ameronis opposes the call to arms!" shouted Eskevar suddenly. "Who else will defy his king?"

Eskevar's sudden unmasking of Ameronis's subtle opposition shocked the assembly, and in that moment several of the lords who had agreed to join a coalition of nobles against raising and funding an army now wavered in their opinion. It was a dangerous thing to defy a king outright, especially one as powerful as Eskevar. It might not be worth the gold they would save in the end.

But Ameronis recovered neatly. "You misunderstood me, Sire. I do not oppose action where it is plainly necessary. When the time comes to stand upon the battle lines, I will be at the head of my knights and at your side."

Lord Lupollen, Ameronis's neighbor and friend, his closest ally in the council, spoke next. "If this enemy is as great as you say, Sire, would we not have heard of him before now? That is the puzzling thing."

There was a murmur of assent at this question. Eskevar looked sharply at Lupollen and said, "You also I know, my lord. That your king has sent his own knights into battle should be proof enough for anyone loyal to the crown that the need exists. Why do you doubt your king?"

Eskevar stood in the silence that followed his remarks. He looked at each one of his lords in turn, as if he would remember the exact set of each chin and the expression upon each face.

"I have said all I can, lords of Mensandor. And I have allowed others to speak where I thought most advantageous." He was speaking of Esme, who had again pled her request for help before the council earlier that day. "I have nothing more to say. It is up to you. If Mensandor is to survive, we must not tarry."

He stepped down from the dais and moved out of the circle of the council chairs. He spread out his hands imploringly—hardly a characteristic gesture for the Dragon King, and it was not without effect.

"I leave it in your hands. Do not wait too long."

He left the Council of War deep in hushed silence. No one dared speak until he was far away from the room, and then the arduous debate began: Ameronis and Lupollen and their friends in opposition; Benniot, Fincher, and several others just as strongly in favor of supporting the king's call to arms.

The argument was bitter, loud, and long, lasting the length of the day. Eskevar returned to his apartment in the castle to brood darkly upon the stubborn blindness of his independent, self-sufficient lords.

With every league the foothills of the Fiskills marched closer, changing in color from misty violet to blue above the mottled green of the forested hills. The party had set out due east cross-country toward the lofty heart of the rugged mountain range. In this part of Mensandor the Fiskills seemed to rise sharply out of rolling hills gently sloping upward to their very feet. They were a wall, as Celbercor had intended them, a soaring fortress against all save the most foolish and determined. It was this fortress Quentin, Toli, and Durwin dared to assail.

Each day the land rose higher. Quentin fancied he could feel the wind freshen and the cool air of the mountain heights waft down to breathe upon them in unexpected moments. In the happy countryside, with its small, well-groomed villages, it became increasingly harder to believe the ominous events that had loomed so large when in Askelon. Even his own experiences in the camp of the Ningaal seemed as if they had happened to someone else and Quentin had merely heard about it. If not for his injured arm dangling from the sling, Quentin would scarcely have believed the tale.

Only at night did the sharp reminder prick him; it came in the form of the star, growing slightly larger night by night. It now seemed to out-shine every other star in its quadrant. Hard and bright, it sent a corona of milky rays outward from its hot, white core. *Everyone must see it now,* thought Quentin, lying rolled in his cloak at night. *Everyone must surely feel the evil it portends.*

But by the morning's light, the Wolf Star faded, as did all the other lesser lights of heaven. The spell of the glowing star was broken by the coming of dawn.

"How far before we come to Inchkeith's abode?" asked Quentin as they made ready early one morning to get under way.

"No great distance, I think. If the trail permits," Durwin replied, "we will sleep in feather beds tonight."

"Are we close, then?" Quentin had no idea where the home of the legendary arms maker might be. But the rocky highlands they were now traversing did not strike him as the sort of place a master armorer would be found.

Durwin walked up the slope of the little hill where they had camped. Quentin followed, squinting as he moved out into the light of a crimson sunrise.

"Do you see that ridge of bare rock beyond the near valley?"

Quentin nodded. The ridge was a ragged gray wall that cast a black shadow across the green blanket of the pine-covered valley. "He lives beyond the ridge?"

"Not beyond it—within it!" laughed Durwin. "Or very nearly, as you shall see. Inchkeith is a strange man; he has many strange ways. But he is the man for us."

"You know him, Durwin? You have never mentioned him in my hearing until most recently." Quentin regarded his hermit friend with something approaching suspicion. Not that there was anything at all unlikely about Durwin's being acquainted with such a man.

"There is much I do not mention in your hearing, my young man. Only half of what I know will fit in my head at any one time!" He winked and laughed, his voice booming in the clear morning.

Toli whistled from below. When they joined him, all was ready.

"If we are to sleep on feathers tonight instead of pine needles, we had better away. See how long the shadows grow already." Toli's dark eyes flashed with good humor. He was once more in his native element. Every day he seemed to slip more and more into the quiet enigma he had been when Quentin first met him years before. Give him back his deerskins and bone knife, thought Quentin, and he would be once more the Jher prince.

"You would prefer pine needles, I would wager, Toli. But lead on! The day, as you say, is speeding from us!" Quentin, with difficulty but unaided, swung himself up into Blazer's saddle and turned his face to the warmth of the rising sun.

Toward midday, towering banks of clouds sweeping down from the north in a long line, gray as smoke beneath and white as new-bleached wool above, rolled high above them. The churning mass swelled and billowed, spreading a great flat anvil at its soaring crest as the fierce upper winds took the bank and flattened it.

"There will be rain soon," said Toli.

"Do you think it will hold off until we have reached our destination?"

"Possibly," replied Toli, squinting his eyes into the sky. "But the air is already growing cooler. Thunder whispers on the wing. The rain may hold and it may not."

Quentin could hear no thunder, but since Toli had mentioned it, he did seem to notice that the feathery breeze lifting the leaves in the trees around them now bore a cooler touch.

"Then let us not tempt it further by stopping to wag the chin!" cried Durwin. "Let us ride dry while we still may. A hot supper will make up for a meal missed on the trail."

"I am for it!" called Quentin. "Let's away!"

Durwin urged his brown palfrey forward, followed by Toli with the two pack horses; Quentin brought up the rear and kept a wary eye on the gathering clouds overhead. They had made good time that morning, stopping only to refresh the water in their skins at a rushing brook in the heart of the valley. Every time Quentin chanced to look up, the great gray wall of rock, glimpsed as a looming rampart between the shaggy branches of pine, seemed to have advanced dramatically closer.

Presently Quentin heard the splash of a nearby stream as it tumbled over rock. The party left the sheltering pines and came to a wild and rocky channel carved out by a shallow river that bounced and frothed over black stones, round as loaves of bread. The tumbling water, for all its activity, rose barely to the horses' fetlocks, but it was broad as a ward yard. Durwin struck along the loamy band and turned upstream parallel to the face of the ridge.

Standing pools of water along the bank mirrored the bulging blue-black clouds overhead. The wind had freshened, and Quentin could smell the musty earth scent of rain.

The stream angled along a sweeping bend lined with tall, finger-thin, long-needled pines that whispered in the rising wind. "The rain is on the way!" shouted Durwin.

"Our destination is not too much farther, I hope," called Quentin as he came abreast. "Perhaps we should find shelter and wait until the first downpour has passed."

"If I remember correctly, we have not far to travel. Look ahead." The hermit pointed to the gray cliffs directly before them once more. "See where the water emerges from the base of the ridge wall? It is just ahead."

"It appears a seamless wall," said Quentin.

"You will see. You will see."

"Unless we hurry, Inchkeith the armorer will greet three very soggy travelers," remarked Toli. As he spoke, the first fat drops of rain began plunking into the pools around them and plopping onto the trail, where they raised tiny puffs of dust.

They spurred their mounts ahead with renewed vigor as the ripe droplets splattered around them and made dark splotches upon their clothing.

As they came nearer the place Durwin had pointed out, Quentin could see a fold in the ridge wall he had not noticed before. Where the stream emerged, the left face of the cliff angled away sharply as the right face overlapped it. From a distance it gave the eye the impression of a continuous, unseamed wall. Closer, it began to open to them as they followed the river to the vast stony feet of the rock face.

The ground rose slightly as it met the ridge; pine trees grew right up to the very face of the gray wall. The horses' hooves clattered over a stone embankment, and then they were through the cliff and gazing on a breathtaking sight. Despite the raindrops pelting down around them, Quentin stopped to marvel at the vision before him. A vast, rolling meadow of rich mountain green spread out on either side of the stream, here narrower and more deep. Enclosing the meadow and towering above it on all sides rose smooth, flat walls of stone, now blue under the black sky. At the far end of the meadow, which Quentin adjudged to be fully a league wide and half a league long, stood an enormous house of white stone, glimmering like the white sails of a ship on an emerald sea.

"That is Inchkeith's home," said Durwin, "and we are just in time."

A clap of thunder rolled across the ridge to echo its booming voice throughout the meadow. The long grass began to dip and rise like the waves of Gerfallon in the fitful wind.

They galloped out into the wonderful meadow, the rain, sharper now, stinging their cheeks. Quentin felt a thrill of excitement as lightning tore the sky in a jagged flash. The resounding roar filled the blue canyon and rumbled out across the valley behind them.

Inchkeith's house was as large as a small castle, an impression strengthened by the single stately tower that served as entrance and gate-house before a generous, stone-paved courtyard. Several smaller structures clustered close about the main house; these were also of the same white stone. The stream, running deep and quiet in its course through the meadow, formed a graceful waterfall as it spilled out over the sheer rock face behind the master armorer's manor. At the farther end, where the water ran down into the meadow, a large wheel turned slowly in the swift current.

There was no one to be seen as the travelers pounded to a halt before the tower. A portcullis of finely wrought iron barred their way into the courtyard beyond.

"He keeps no gateman," observed Durwin, "because he expects no travelers and has but few guests."

The hermit slid down off his palfrey and strode to the archway. In a nook in the stone hung a knotted rope. Durwin grasped the rope and pulled twice very quickly. A bell pealed in the courtyard.

"That should bring someone running," said Durwin. The rain was falling harder; in a few moments they would be soaked to the skin. Out across the meadow, back the way they had come, great white sheets of shimmering rain were wavering toward them, driven like sails before the wind. Water was pooling up around the horses' feet and streaming down the walls of the manor.

"Who seeks admittance to my master's house?" Quentin had not seen the slight young man dart out of a doorway across the courtyard. He held his cloak over his head and peered at them through the iron grillwork of the portcullis.

"Tell your master that Durwin the holy hermit of Pelgrin and his friends Quentin and Toli are here to see him on king's business. Tell him we respectfully request the hospitality due travelers. And you had better tell him quickly, or we will be in a most unhappy disposition." He wiped away the trickle of water sliding down the side of his nose.

The young man seemed to weigh a decision carefully. "You do not seem disposed to be unruly. Come in out of the rain while I fetch word to my master." He disappeared into a recess beside the portcullis, and instantly the heavy iron gate began to lift, smoothly and without so much as a squeak or creak. It was obviously made with the utmost skill.

The damp travelers hurriedly stepped under the arch of the gatehouse to wait until the young servant returned. Quentin and Toli dismounted and stood dripping in the dark tunnel of the archway.

Quentin was struck by the spare simplicity of all he saw around him. Not a post nor a portal possessed an inch of ornamentation. Around the perimeter of the courtyard, not an item was out of place, and the yard itself was spotless. The edifice of Inchkeith's manor house was all clean lines and square corners; clearly it had been erected with exacting care. Not a crack or crevice was to be seen anywhere.

To Quentin's eye the effect was reminiscent of the architecture of Dekra, though not at all derivative of it. He was impressed with the clean appearance of all that met his eye; it spoke of a hand that left nothing undone, and a mind that saw to the smallest detail.

He heard a shout and saw the young servant waving to them from inside the arched entrance to the manor hall. They dashed across the corner of the courtyard and joined him under the sheltering portico. "Come along with me. Take no heed for your horses; I will send someone to care for them and bed them. My master asks that you join him at table in the great hall if you are so inclined."

"Indeed we are!" Quentin fairly shouted. He was hungry, cold, and wet. A hot meal seemed like the most wonderful thing he could have dreamed at the moment. "Lead on!"

The skinny, long-boned young man led them along the short passage to the hall's entrance, pushed open the ironbound wooden door, and ushered them in. The hall was ample and gracious, but marked with the same unadorned, almost severe style as the exterior. Quentin gazed around in admiration. Several servants were moving about in preparation for the meal. A single long table with benches along either side overlooked a wide and generous hearth in which a well-made fire burned cheerily. It spoke of a well-drafted chimney, for there was, Quentin noted with pleasure, not a trace of soot on the walls or ceiling of the hall anywhere. Everything was as clean as if it had never been used, and yet it was warm and homey.

The appearance of Lord (for so Quentin now considered him) Inchkeith's abode drew a picture in Quentin's mind of a stern and exacting personage of regal bearing, a man of quick temper and a will as strong as the iron gate at his door, a man of precise and flawless judgment, one who would never suffer imperfection or blemish lightly. A man of power, strength, and grace. A man of relentless, fervent perfection, obeyed by all around him with unspoken efficiency and unfailing courtesy.

"Durwin! You old mumblebeard!" a hearty voice boomed out behind them. "Welcome! Welcome, fair friends! Welcome to Whitehall!"

Quentin turned, expecting to see the man of his imaginings. The picture so carefully drawn in his mind collapsed utterly as Quentin, with a rude shock, beheld the lord of Whitehall.

CHAPTER 33

Y ou should have allowed me to accompany you today," said Myrmior. "I could have helped you against them."

"No." Ronsard shook his head sternly. "You are too valuable an ally. You will help us more with your knowledge of the Ningaal ways than with your strong sword arm. If you had been killed today, as many good men were, we would have had no one to guide us in preparing against them."

"I submit to your will, Lord Ronsard. I will obey. But I wanted you to know that I am not afraid, and that when the time comes to lift blade against my former enslavers, I will do so with all courage."

"We do not doubt your valor, Myrmior. Truly. You will ride with us in due time, no doubt. But Ronsard is right. You are worth more to us as a guide to the Ningaal's mind and heart than as a sword wielder. You are unique; stout blades we have many."

Lord Wertwin sat nearby and did not speak. His heart was heavy with the loss of many fine men that day; he had borne the brunt of the battle and was now bereft of almost half his company.

After the daring rescue of Wertwin's troops by Theido and Ronsard's forces, they had all returned to make camp for the night upon the greensward. As they sat huddled in a consultation, the ring of the hammer upon the anvil and the moans of the wounded could be heard throughout the camp as smith and surgeon saw to the repairs of weapons and men. Sentinels had been posted, and fires had been lit for the night's vigil. Theido, Ronsard, Myrmior, and Wertwin turned once more to the brutal events of the day.

"We cannot go up against them again as we did today," said Ronsard grimly. "They are too strong, and too well disciplined."

"Disciplined!" snorted Myrmior. "They simply fear their warlord more than they fear you. You can only kill them, but he has power over their souls!"

"Is he really so powerful? I have heard of such things in my time," said Theido.

Myrmior shrugged. "Whether it is true or not, I do not know. But the Ningaal believe it, so it is for them—and for you—the same thing. They will fight to the death rather than surrender. And each foe they kill becomes a step on the long stairway of immortality, or so they believe."

"Whatever gives them their ferocity, it is indomitable. I do not see how we can stand against such a foe. Though they are but lightly armed and our own men well protected, they wear us down by sheer crush of their numbers. We have lost near seventy-five brave knights this day."

"Do not forget that you have only seen but a fraction of the total. Three other warlords with their armies are abroad. When they have joined together once more, nothing will stop them." As Myrmior uttered this gloomy pronouncement, Wertwin glared under his brows and cursed.

"By Azrael! What would you have us do, you savage! Are we merely to fall upon our swords and be done with it? If you know so much, why do you not give us guidance? Instead you torment us with your lies."

Myrmior suffered this outburst in silence. His countenance showed nothing but sympathy for the commander's plight. "I have said what I have said in order that you will not build any false hopes of standing against the Ningaal in battle," he said quietly. "They cannot be beaten in that manner. At least not with our numbers."

He paused, and all was silent in the tent of the commanders. Outside the twilight deepened, the sky blue-black with the coming night.

They could hear the clear ring of hammers on steel and the crackle of a fire nearby. The shadows of men were flung against the walls of the tent, making it seem as if they were surrounded by the shades of their fallen comrades.

"I have not been idle in my long captivity. I have seen much of the ways in which men make war. I have studied those who have fallen against the Ningaal and observed the things which offer the greatest hope of victory, though few enough they are."

"Tell us then," implored Ronsard. "What can we do?"

"Remember, too, that we will have greater numbers before long. The council continues to meet, and we may expect help soon, I think," said Theido hopefully.

"That we must not count on," said Myrmior. "What I will propose now will serve us for the time we have to wait, little or long."

"Well said. Begin then. We are ready to hear what you would suggest."

"Are the soldiers of your country familiar with the bow and arrow?" asked Myrmior.

"Why, of course!" laughed Ronsard. "It is a useful thing, but hardly a weapon to be relied upon in the field. It is highly inaccurate, and it has not a chance against the steel of a knight's hard shell."

"It is more suited for annoying forest creatures and for striking from a distance in seclusion. It is not a weapon for a knight," agreed Theido. "The bow cannot be managed from the saddle of a galloping horse."

Wertwin only harrumphed. "Bows and arrows! Umph!"

"At least you have such weapons," said Myrmior quickly. "Do not condemn the plan before you have heard it fully.

"I do not propose to take archers onto the field with us, but neither do I propose that we take the field again. I will speak most bluntly. You were lucky today; your gods smiled on you. In all the times I have been with Lord Gurd, he has shown pity to no one and has never left the field if there was the smallest chance of victory.

"What he did today is rare, but not unheard-of. He gave you a chance to regroup and ready yourself for another battle, because more than the battle itself, he loves a skillful opponent. To him it is no sport to kill a weak and defenseless foe. That is mere slaughter, and there is little immortality to be gained from taking a weak life.

"You stood against him, and he respected you for it. When you retreated, he recognized a most resourceful foe, one whose death would bring him much blood honor. He wanted you to regroup so that he could savor the satisfaction of your defeat.

"Like the vinemaster who carefully tends the fruit of his vines, the warlord was testing you and found a match worthy of his art."

"What does all this have to do with bows and arrows?" asked Wertwin sullenly. His heart was shrunken within him, and a black mood twisted his features.

"They are the means by which we will snatch that savored victory from the warlord's foul maw."

"Defeat him with children's toys? Ha!"

"Hold, sir!" said Theido. "Let him speak! For I begin to see something of his meaning."

Myrmior bowed to Theido. "You are most astute, Lord Theido. I propose that we do not take the field against the Ningaal—at least not yet, not for a long while. Instead, we will harry them by night, raiding their camp and raining arrows upon them when they move to chase us.

"If we refuse to meet them face-to-face, Gurd will burn with rage. If we are very fortunate, his rage will consume him."

"Where is the honor in that?" Wertwin shouted. "To skulk around by night like lowborn thieves, shooting arrows at shadows. It is foolish and absurd, and I will have no part in it!"

"This war will not be won by your honor. Your men died with honor today, and tonight they lie cold in their graves. How can that help you now? Hear me, my lords! Cling to honor and you will lose your land—more, you will lose your lives."

"Myrmior is right," said Ronsard slowly, glaring at Wertwin as he spoke. "There is no honor if your land is lost. Even if we die with valor, who will remember? Who will sing our praises in the halls of our fathers?

"We will do well to look first to the cause at hand, and lastly to our good names. I would stay alive to see Mensandor freed of this menace— however it may be done."

"I agree," said Theido thoughtfully. "But I am troubled by one thing. What you suggest is well and good for meeting this warlord with his contingent. But what of the others? Do we allow his brothers to roam unchallenged through the countryside?"

Myrmior shook his head slowly. He rubbed his bristly chin with a sallow hand. "This is the most difficult part of the plan, my lords. It would be well if your council would speedily send the troops we need, but as it is, I can see nothing for it but to proceed against all the warlords as I have suggested—one at a time. The plan will work, I think, as it does not require a great number of men to carry it out. But we will need archers."

"Most of our knights are trained to the bow, though few will read-ily admit it. We can obtain more archers if we send to Askelon—which we must do to supply ourselves with the bows and arrows."

"Then let it be done at once. In the meantime we will withdraw and stay just ahead of the Ningaal until we have weapons enough to begin our raids."

"What? Are we to do nothing to impede the Ningaal? Are we to sit by and allow them to march free over our fields?"

"They have been doing so for a month or more, Wertwin," said Ronsard. "If we must bear it a little longer to secure our purpose, so be it. We will have to risk that much, at least. Besides," he added with a mischievous smile, "it may make them wonder what we are up to."

"Yes," agreed Myrmior, "it will increase his wrath. What we attempt to do is worry them so greatly as to make them angry enough to commit a foolish blunder, an error of strategy which we can seize and turn against them. And all the while we will wear away at their numbers bit by bit, like water dripping upon the stone, eroding it over time."

Theido stood and stretched; it had been a long day. "Your plan is a good one, Myrmior. I will send a courier to Askelon at once. Tomorrow we will begin schooling our knights to this new way of fighting. I only hope we have enough time to make the change."

"It must be made regardless. Believe me, my friends, there is no other way."

Wertwin scowled at his comrades and growled as he stalked out of the tent.

"Do not mind him overmuch," said Ronsard. "His heart will mend, and he will be staunchly with us soon enough." He, too, rose and stretched.

"Thank you, Myrmior. You have given us wise and well-advised counsel this night. I think that, like Wertwin, I should not have believed you if I had not encountered the foe today and felt his cunning strength. I know now that you are right, and like Theido, I pray we are not too late."

"It is no doubt that you were a faithful minister to your monarch," Theido added. "He must have valued your services very highly, but no more than we do now. Before this is over we will have cause to reward your craft and loyalty as it deserves. Perhaps one day you may return as king to your own country."

Myrmior turned large, sad eyes toward them. "I can never go back. The land that I knew and loved is gone. Here I have chosen to make my stand, as I should have long ago in my own country. Then I was afraid, but no more. I have daily lived through death too horrible to tell, and it can never terrify me again."

The three men stood looking at one another for a long moment. No one spoke. A close bond of friendship had formed between the two knights and the man from Khas-I-Quair, and all three were cheered by its warmth.

"Good night, brave sirs." Ronsard yawned and rubbed his eyes. "Tomorrow I take up once more the weapon of my youth. For that I will need my rest, I think."

Theido and Myrmior laughed and went to find their own tents for the night.

CHAPTER 34

Dumbstruck, Quentin stared slack-jawed at their host. He had expected a warrior commander, or at very least a knight well acquainted with battle and the needs of fighting men and their weapons. The person scuttling toward them across the expanse of the hall was quite the opposite of Quentin's mental image.

Inchkeith, the legendary armorer, was a small man with a thin, puckered face and sinews like ropes standing out in his neck as if to keep his palsied head from quivering off his thick shoulders. He was slight and bent at an unnatural angle; Quentin saw at once that this was because the master armorer's spine was curved grotesquely. He walked on spindly legs in a kind of rolling hop, and not at all in the slow and dignified tread of the man Quentin had imagined.

But his hands were the hands of a master craftsman: broad, generous, and deft. They were strong hands and sure of movement, graceful and never still for a moment. These remarkable hands were attached to powerful arms and well-muscled shoulders—the shoulders of a young man. It appeared to Quentin that some cruel jest had been played upon the old man with the spindly legs. The brawny arms and chest of a plowman or a soldier had been placed upon the frail body of a deformed scullery servant.

"It has been long since I have had the pleasure of your company,

Durwin. But here you are, and I rejoice at the sight of you." Inchkeith spoke with a deep voice, contrasting strangely with his wizened appearance. In two hops he was in Durwin's arms, and the two men were embracing each other like brothers long lost.

"It is good to see you again, Inchkeith. You have not changed a hair. I have brought some friends with me that I would have you meet."

"So I see! So I see! Good sirs, you are welcome in Whitehall now and always. I hope you will feel free to stay as long as you like. We do not have many guests here, and your stay will be cause for celebration." The master armorer made a ludicrous bow and winked at them. In spite of himself, Quentin laughed out loud.

"Master Inchkeith, you do us honor. I am certain your hospitality is most gracious."

"This is Quentin and his companion Toli," said Durwin.

"Ah, Durwin, you travel in good company." Inchkeith rolled his eyes and held his hands up to his face in a show of respect. "Both of you are well-known here. Your deeds are sung within these walls often, as are the great deeds of all brave warriors."

Quentin blushed and bowed, acknowledging the compliment. "The stories do not tell all. I did what any man would have done, and not at all bravely."

"Yes, but it was you that did it and not another." Inchkeith jabbed the air with a forefinger. "That is all the difference!"

At that moment a door was thrown open at one end of the hall, and a troop of young men came marching in as if they were soldiers drilling in step.

"Come!" cried Inchkeith, hobbling away. "You must meet my sons. I know they will want to welcome you as well."

The travelers followed their host; Quentin and Toli, grinning with pleasure, were irresistibly drawn to this peculiar man—so unlike the exact and scrupulous order around him.

There were seven sons, all handsome young men and well mannered.

They did not speak, except when their father directed a question or indicated that a reply would be welcome. Quentin greeted each one in turn, as did Toli, and remarked that they were all like images of one another: soft brown hair and eyes, full lips and brown cheeks, high, strong foreheads. And they all possessed strong, straight limbs; none had inherited their father's deformity.

"These are my army; my treasure, my pride," said their father, beaming down upon them as they took their places at the table.

"And these are my gold and jewels!" Inchkeith turned and waved his hand and, as if on signal, a tall, handsome woman entered from the near side of the hall, followed by five beautiful young women. "My lady and my daughters."

The young women tittered behind their hands as they approached, their plain muslin gowns swishing pleasantly as they moved together. But when each was introduced to Quentin, she held out her hand like a highborn lady and curtsied. Although he felt foolish, he kissed their hands, to the glowing approval of their mother. Toli felt obligated to follow Quentin's example.

"You are most welcome in our home, my lords," said Inchkeith's wife. "If you need anything, my household stands ready to serve you."

"You are most kind . . ."

"I am Camilla," she said, holding her hand out to Quentin. He kissed it, and she curtsied. He noticed that the woman was younger than her husband; he wondered if she had borne all the offspring he saw gathered before him. It was possible—they all had her dark coloring; but if so, she had retained a most youthful appearance.

"Thank you for your kindness, my lady. I already feel welcome here, and we have but arrived."

"Then let us not tarry another moment," said Inchkeith with delight, rubbing his hands together as if to warm them. "Be seated, good guests, and partake with us of our bread."

Inchkeith took Durwin by the arm and drew him to the head of the table with him, leaving Quentin and Toli in the care of the young women. They settled together across the table from the young men and all at once began talking, asking questions about what was going on at court, what the fashions were in Askelon, what news of the larger world they had brought.

So inquisitive were they that Quentin could hardly keep up with their questions, many of which forced confessions of ignorance from him, as he knew less about some of their interests than they did themselves. Their questions spoke of a firm knowledge of the world and its ways, despite the seclusion in which they apparently lived. As the meal ended, he had formed the firm impression that this was by far the most remarkable family he had ever met.

When they had taken their fill of meat and bread and broth and fruit, the sons of Inchkeith trooped off together, and the daughters, along with their mother, began helping the servants clear away the trenchers and serving vessels. Quentin and Toli moved to the head of the table, where Inchkeith and Durwin sat talking. Inchkeith had taken out a long pipe and was lighting it.

"Though I am grateful for the pleasure of your visit, I know that you did not come just to see old Inchkeith. There is business to be done, aye?"

"So it is." Durwin nodded. "We do have some business to discuss with you."

The craftsman took a long pull of his pipe, his cheeks caving in completely. He blew them out again in a long, thin blast of smoke. "I like nothing better," he said. "But perhaps your business is not so urgent that it will not wait until I have shown you some of my latest works."

"By all means," urged Quentin. "I would very much like to see some of your achievements."

"You twist my arm, sir!" laughed Inchkeith, getting up from the table. "Follow me and you will see something to suit your fancy, I daresay."

They left the gleaming hall by a side entrance and were at once in a low, dim room where rank on rank of polished armor stood emptily at attention, waiting for their knights to lend them life. It looked the very armory of a king, so many swords, bucklers, helms, and breastplates did they see.

Through this low-beamed room they came to another, smaller than the first and darker. It contained lances and spears of all sizes and description, and halberds without number. The long-shafted weapons were all bound together in neat piles like new-mown sheaves of grain, bundled and waiting to be threshed. In the gloom Quentin could see the steel points of lance and spear, and the smooth, sharp blades of the halberds glimmering as they passed.

"Ah! Here we are. Watch your step. There. This is my only true home—my workshop," shouted Inchkeith above a new din.

For they had stepped down into a room warm with the fires of the forge and loud with the clangor of steel on steel. The room was easily as large as the great hall, if not larger, and it was filled with the bustle of industry as the sons of Inchkeith, and various servants, went about their work of forging steel and iron into weaponry. There were tables and odd-looking devices that defied adequate description all over the place, from one end of the oblong room to the other. At each table, and surrounded by curious trappings, a man labored over his craft: here a blade being affixed to its hilt and handle, there a wooden shield receiving its hide veering, and over across the way, a truncated knight was acquiring his breastplate.

Quentin was dazzled by the display, for it was totally unlike anything he had ever seen. Inchkeith led them through the maze, pausing at each table to impart some finer point of craft to the workman there. And wherever the eye chanced to wander, it glanced upon a shining example of the armorer's art. Quentin doubted whether in all the world there was anything to compare with Inchkeith's workshop.

Quentin looked upon the table and saw, among an assortment of strange tools whose purposes he could but guess, a long, broad sword, a mighty thing, fully a span in length. The hilt was jewel encrusted and gold, and the scabbard was silver engraved with scenes of the capture of a bear. It was every inch a work of excellence and skill.

"Do you like it?" asked Inchkeith, following Quentin's gaze.

"Like it? Sir, it is the most handsome of swords. A treasure."

"Here. You may examine it more closely."

With his left hand, and lamenting that he did not have the use of his right, he drew the sword from its sheath and heard the cool whisper of the sliding steel.

It was made to be used with two hands; yet it was not much heavier than its shorter cousin and was superbly balanced. Even with his left hand Quentin could feel the lift of the blade and the almost effortless way in which it followed the movement of the hand. Quentin passed the weapon to Toli, who made it sing through the air; he saw the light of admiration leap to the Jher's dark eyes.

"The blade is of a special steel I have begun making. It will shear iron. This one"—he spoke as if it were but one fish of a thousand in his net—"I have made for King Selric of Drin. It is all but finished." He carefully replaced the sword and turned to them with a twinkle in his eye. "Now I will show you my masterpiece."

Inchkeith hobbled from his table to a low, arched door set in a recess in the wall nearby. As he passed the end of the table, he took up a lamp and lit it from a taper. After adjusting it, he proceeded to heave aside the heavy bolt that secured the door. "This way," he said, and he disappeared inside the blackened doorway.

The three followed their stooped guide into a small, round chamber, and it was a moment before their eyes could adjust to the darkness and the dim lamplight. When Quentin raised his eyes, a gasp escaped his lips. Before him stood the most handsome suit of armor he could have imagined, but that alone was not what took his breath away.

Quentin saw before him the very armor he had seen in his vision.

It was real. It existed and was flashing in the light of the lamp as if it were wrought from a single diamond. Polished, smooth, bright as water, it shimmered before his dazzled, unbelieving eyes. Without heeding the others, Quentin moved toward the place where it stood on its stanchion, as if the object had beckoned him closer.

The armor, pale and shimmering silver in the lamplight, was without ornament or device of any kind. All its surfaces gleamed like gemstones, flat and clean, reflecting a luminous radiance.

The helm was magnificent, having a simple slotted visor and a crest that was nothing more than a thin ridge from brow to crown. And, quite unaccountably, from the shoulders hung a cloak of the most exquisite chain mail Quentin had ever seen. He could not resist touching it. He reached out a tentative fingertip, and the mail rippled like liquid silver, sparkling and dancing in the flickering light. The tiny, individual rings sighed like the fall of the snow upon frozen ground as they quivered beneath his touch.

"It is as light as goose down," said a voice close to his ear. Inchkeith was standing at his shoulder, his face lit with pleasure at Quentin's unutterable amazement.

"Who is it for?" Quentin managed to croak with effort.

"Ah, there is the wonder of it!" The craftsman's voice was but a sigh. "No one—at least not yet. I fashioned it after a design that came to me in a dream. I saw it and knew I must make it. I believe the owner will come to claim it one day. Until then . . ." His voice trailed off.

"I notice that it does not have a sword," Quentin remarked suddenly. "Why not?"

Inchkeith the master armorer cocked his head to one side and frowned. "You have touched it there, my lord. I saw no sword in my dream and so made none."

"Then come, Master Inchkeith," said Durwin. "It is time we talked."

CHAPTER 35

Eskevar paced his inner chamber with long, impatient strides. He held his hands clasped behind his back and cast his eyes to the floor. "The fools! The fools!" he said under his breath. "They will bring the kingdom down."

He had been two days in his tower—pacing, worrying. He had eaten and slept little; and his features, now more lined and tightly drawn than ever, bore the effect of his distress. Often he had occasion to anguish over the stubbornness of his nobles, but now he saw clearly that the fate of the nation lay in their hands, and they seemed oblivious to the threat.

Once and again he lamented the power, or lack of it, that stayed his hand from more drastic action. In days of old he would have ordered his lords into battle with but a wave of his hand; they would have had to obey or lose their lands and privilege. In days older still, in the time of the first Dragon King, the kingdom had been ruled by the will of the all-powerful monarch; then there had been no lords to question the command of the king.

Ah, but before that had been the time of the northern kings, when each man, by the point of his sword, could become king in his own eyes, and the realm was divided into tiny territories of scratching, biting, self-important despots who swaggered about their principalities spoiling for a fight and a chance to increase their holdings through the overthrow of a neighboring monarch.

Then the kings of the north had united and formed an alliance, and had established order throughout much of the realm, for they had all acted in harmony and for the best interests of the realm, and no one dared to oppose them, for to deny one was to deny all, to bring war on one was to declare war on all. The petty kings of the south could not stand against them. Eventually, over many long years, the power had become consolidated in the north, and there it had stayed.

Eskevar turned these things over in his mind as he paced the length of his chamber or sat brooding in his great carven chair. He paused before his window, shutters drawn wide to the glorious summer day. He sighed, gazing out across the familiar landscape of green, rolling hills and the darker blue-green of forest. He saw the slow curve of the Herwydd flowing in a lazy silver arc away to the south, moving in its own unhurried time toward its own unchanging destination.

"The cares of kings and kingdoms are nothing to you, great river. Perhaps they are nothing at all."

The messenger who knocked and entered the room behind him found him still standing at the window, staring far away. "Your Majesty, there are lords without who wish to speak with you."

Eskevar seemed not to hear; so the page repeated his message. When at last the king turned to the perplexed youngster, his weary face bore a sad smile. "Allow them to enter my outer apartment. I will attend directly."

They have arrived at a decision, Eskevar thought. *What will it be?*

Outside the rain fell steadily; the sound of its splattering in the courtyard was punctuated by the rumble of thunder marching across the heavens to do battle with the mountain peaks. Quentin imagined that the mountains were giants and the thunder the voice that they raised to him. They were calling him, taunting him to come and take from them their secret—if he dared.

It had been a long time since anyone had spoken. Toli was curled like a cat in a huge covered chair by the hearth. Durwin sat with hands folded across his stomach, head down. Quentin himself sat slumped in his chair with his chin in his palm. Only Inchkeith still seemed alert and active. He hunched forward with his hands clutching his long pipe, puffing a cloud of smoke around his head and glancing periodically at his guests.

"I will do it!" he said at last, leaping up. "By the god's beard, I will do it!"

The suddenness of the outburst startled Quentin and brought Durwin's head up with a snap.

"What?" Durwin shook his gray beard. "Oh, Inchkeith, you startled me. I must have dozed off a little. It has been a long day. Forgive me."

"I have thought the matter out most carefully; be assured of that," said the master armorer. "I will go with you to seek the lanthanil, and I will make the sword. How can I refuse, eh?" The misshapen craftsman smiled, and Quentin saw the relentless energy of the man burst from that smile.

"It is the opportunity of a lifetime—of many lifetimes. If you are right and the mines can be found, I would pay any sum to work with lanthanil. You offer me the craftsman's greatest dream. Yes, by all the gods that may be, I will do it."

"I knew we could count on you, Inchkeith. We will find the mines, I am certain. The prophecy is being fulfilled." Durwin waved his hand toward Quentin.

"I care not for prophecy, nor whether Quentin here is this priest king you speak of. But I care that our realm is set upon by barbarians. By Orphe! That I do. And if this sword that I shall make can strike a blow against them, if it can turn the battle, then I will make a sword such as no man has ever seen. I will make the Zhaligkeer!"

Quentin listened to the two talking and said nothing. All evening he had listened, saying little. His restive mood was on him again, and this time he perceived its cause: his arm.

Durwin seemed to forget that Quentin, the one designated to play the most important part in raising a sword against the enemy, had a broken arm, and maybe worse. Secretly, Quentin suspected that it was worse, that his injured arm was more severely damaged than the broken bone. It had been a long time since he had felt any sensation in the arm at all; it seemed numb, dead.

He did not speak of his suspicion to anyone. Not even Durwin, on the night when his arm was reset and bound properly, knew that he felt nothing at all, for he had grimaced and moaned—mostly out of nervous fear—as if it had hurt him a great deal. There was something seriously wrong with his arm; he was forced to face it now when all the talk of swords and prophecy filled the night.

As he brooded upon this unhappy fact, the thought occurred to him that perhaps he was not the one after all—not the mighty priest king foretold in the legends. Perhaps the Most High had never intended for him to be the one; it was to be some other yet unknown.

Unexpectedly the thought sent a wave of relief through Quentin's frame. Yes, of course, that was it. One could not very well wield the fabled sword without an arm to do so. The prophecy, if it were to remain true, pointed to another. Perhaps Eskevar was the one favored by the prophecy—he was king, after all. The old oracle's prophecy had said that a king must wield the sword. That settled it.

When at last they arose to take themselves off to their beds, Durwin came near to Quentin and said, "You were very quiet this night, my young man. Why?"

"Do we not have enough to trouble us, Durwin?"

"Aye, more than enough. But I perceived this to be a vexation of a different sort." Inchkeith approached them now with a light burning brightly in a finely made lamp. Durwin accepted it and said, "We will find our own way, good sir. Thank you. You need trouble yourself no further on our account."

"The trouble, sir, is just beginning!" Inchkeith laughed. "But I chose long ago on whose side I will stand. Get your rest, gentlemen. I will be ready to join you on your journey in the morning."

"So it is. We will leave as soon as possible, but not until we have dined once more at your excellent table."

"It is a welcome change from Toli's seeds and berries," joked Quentin. "But we will not wish to linger overlong."

"Strange, I have never known you to refuse a mouthful," quipped Toli, who had woken up and now came to stand with them. "The rain will stop before morning, but the stream will rise through the night. I shall go out at daybreak to see if it is passable."

"No need, sir. By morning the flood will have eased. It always does. Have no fear. We will start our journey dry tomorrow, at least. And do not trouble about your horses. I will have all in readiness tomorrow. My sons will see to it. Now, good night."

Inchkeith, taking up the candle on the table, hobbled across the darkened hall, the sphere of light going before him like a guiding light.

"A most extraordinary man," said Durwin.

"Most extraordinary," agreed Quentin. And they all shuffled off to their beds, where they were enchanted into sleep by the distant sound of rain on the stones of Whitehall.

CHAPTER 36

The massive palace ship of Nin the Destroyer, Immortal Deity, Supreme Emperor, Conqueror of Continents, King of Kings, rocked gently in the swell. The waves rose and fell like the rhythmic breathing of an enormous sea beast. They slapped against the broad beams of the palace ship's sides and made soft gurgling noises along the mighty keel.

The ship was square-hulled, with three towering masts and two great rudders amidships. It was truly a seagoing palace, outfitted with costly timbers and exotic trappings from the various countries Nin had subdued. The decks were teak and rosewood from the Haphasian Islands. Brass fittings, which gleamed like red gold from every corner, came from Deluria and the Beldenlands of the east. Silks and shimmering samite fluttered from delicate screens on deck and in the honeycombed quarters below; these had come from Pelagia. Thick braided rope and the vast blue sails were made in Katah out of materials procured in Khas-I-Quair.

The ship itself had been built in the shipyards of Tarkus under the direction of master Syphrian shipbuilders. Its makers had anticipated every necessity, foreseen all desires of the ship's chief inhabitant, and had accommodated them in ingenious ways. Nin lacked nothing aboard his ship that would satisfy his many voracious appetites.

The ship rode low in the water. The slightest swell could rock it gently, but a raging tempest could not overturn it. And if it moved slowly and ponderously, like its master, what of that? Time meant nothing to the Immortal Nin.

The Emperor of Emperors lay stretched upon a bed of silk cushions, listening to the even breathing of the sea, rocking with the slight roll of the deck. His immense bulk heaved and swayed dangerously, now tossed one way, then the next. The motion was making him feel ill and irritated. With each movement of the ship, his huge, oxlike head lolled listlessly, dull eyes staring outward in mounting misery.

Nin, with a supreme effort of will, prodded himself up on one elbow and grasped a mallet that hung on a golden thong near his head. With a backward flip of the wrist, the mallet crashed into a gong of hammered bronze. As the reverberating summons filled the room, he collapsed back onto the pillows with a moan, dragging one huge paw across his forehead in a gesture of enormous suffering.

In a moment a timid voice could be heard, muffled as it was by the owner's prostrate posture, saying, "You have summoned me, O Mighty One? What is your command?"

Nin, with an effort, turned his head to regard the pathetic form of his minister. "Uzla, you lowest of dogs! What kept you? I have been waiting for hours. I shall have you flayed alive to teach you haste." The large eyes closed sleepily.

"May I say, Your Omnipotence, that I regret my tardiness and the blindness which prevented me from anticipating your summons. Still, I was but two steps away and now am here to do your bidding."

"Arrogant swine!" roared Nin, coming to life. "I should have you lick the decks clean with your festering tongue for presuming to address me so."

"As you wish, Most Generous Master. I will obey." Uzla made a move as if to leave and begin scouring the decks of the palace ship.

"I will tell you when to go and when to come. Did I not summon you? Hear me."

"Yes, Immortal One." Uzla's voice trembled appropriately.

"Has there been no word from my warlords?"

"I regret to inform Your Highness that there has been no such word. But as you yourself probably know, there is perhaps a message on the way even now."

"Nin does not wait for messages. Nin knows all! You fool!"

"It is my curse, Great One. You would do me kindness to have my tongue torn out."

Nin rolled himself up on his elbow once more and teetered there like a mountain ready to topple at the slightest touch.

"Shall I send for your chair bearers, Supreme Conqueror? They shall hoist you to your feet."

"I grow weary of waiting, Uzla." The sleepy eyes narrowed slyly. "I do not wish to remain here anymore."

"Perhaps you desire to be somewhere else, Master of Time and Space. Shall I make your desires known to your commander?"

"I have been patient with this desolate country long enough. The conquest is taking too long." One pudgy hand rubbed a sleek jowl with impatience. "We will go up the coast to the north to make ready to enter Askelon, my new city. I have spoken. Hear and obey."

"It shall be done, Master. I will tell the commander to set sail at once."

"I feel like a common thief," growled Lord Wertwin under his breath. "I would much rather lead the mounted assault of the camp."

"We have been through all that, my lord," Theido explained patiently. "Ronsard is better suited than either of us for such duty. He has experience in the Goliah wars to aid him."

"I was in the Goliah wars too," whined Wertwin.

"Yes, of course. However, before this night is through, and before our campaign is ended, we will both be thankful for Ronsard's bold blade. I will tell you plainly that I would not welcome a ride into the camp of the Ningaal."

"Hmph!" Wertwin snorted. He trudged off to his appointed station with his men, now armed with longbows and arrows and hidden in a bushy hollow.

The army of the Dragon King, such as it was, had been training with their new weapons and reclaiming rusty skills. They were now ready to try them in combat with the Ningaal and had, with extreme care and cunning, moved to within a stone's throw from the camp of their enemy. The archers lay hidden behind trees and bushes, in hollows of furze and within gorse hedges. Despite the grumbling that had accompanied the announcement of the proposed change in tactics, there was a tingling of excitement in the air as the men readied themselves for the ambush.

"Theido, are your archers in place?" asked Ronsard, bending to whisper from his saddle. It was very late; the moon was low in the western sky, slightly above the horizon. The knight's face shone faintly, but his features were barely discernible.

"They are." The two men looked at one another briefly. Theido reached a hand out and gripped his friend by the arm. "Take no undue risks. This business is risky enough."

"Do not worry. Surprise is on our side—this once, at least."

"The Most High God goes with you, my friend."

Ronsard cocked his head slightly. "Do you suppose he cares about such things as this?"

"Yes, I believe he does. Why do you ask?"

"Well, I have never prayed to a god before a battle. I did not consider it meet to invoke the aid of heavenly powers on earthly strife. It is man's fight and should be settled by man's own hands."

"The Most High is concerned with the well-being of his servants. By his hand alone are we upheld in all we do."

Ronsard straightened in the saddle, pulled the reins back, and wheeled his steed around. "I have much to learn about this new god, Theido. I hope that I may have time to learn it!"

The knight returned to the place where his men were waiting, already mounted and eager to be about their task. He glanced around at all of them, checking each one for readiness. In order to move more quickly in the saddle and more nimbly, Ronsard had required his raiders to don only hauberk and breastplate, leaving the rest of their armor behind. They each carried their long swords and small tear-shaped bucklers upon their forearms.

Ronsard nodded, completing his inspection. "For honor! For glory! For Mensandor!"

With that he turned and led his men into the wooded grove wherein the Ningaal lay encamped.

Theido saw his friend disappear into the darkened wood; he thought he saw his right hand raised in salute. The fifteen horses and men, Ronsard's bravest, slipped into the darkness. Theido offered a prayer for them as they passed, and then he took his place, sword in hand.

He waited. The night seemed to grow suddenly still. He could hear nothing save the night wind sighing in the trees and a nighthawk keening as it soared among the scattered clouds.

And then it came: a startled shout, cut off short. And then more shouts interspersed with the cold ring of steel on steel. Then the sounds became confused—horses whinnying and men giving voice to their battle cries. In a moment he heard the sound of horses crashing back through the wood, much more loudly than they had gone in.

"Here they come!" shouted Theido to his archers. He raised his sword high above his head. In two heartbeats a charger came pounding out of the darkness, its rider low in the saddle. The rider did not stop when he reached the ranks of hidden archers, but continued on down the dale.

"Draw your bows!" Theido shouted. Instantly there came a whisper of arrow shafts against the bow. More knights were now thundering out of the wood, and there was the unmistakable clamor of pursuit.

"Hold steady!" cried Theido as the last knight dashed by him but a pace from where he crouched waiting. He bit his lip—he had not seen Ronsard emerge from the wood.

They waited, bowstrings taut.

Then suddenly the knight appeared at the opening in the wood where he had entered only moments before. He paused and waved his sword. The shouts of his pursuers now filled the wood and echoed in the dell beyond. Theido could see torches, blinking as they waved through the wood. "Get on! Get away!" muttered Theido under his breath. Ronsard spun and galloped into the clearing and away down the dell as the first of the Ningaal came running out behind him.

"Let fly!" shouted Theido, and instantly the night was filled with dark missiles.

The first rank of Ningaal stumbled forward and dropped to the ground without a sound. Their comrades boiled out of the wood behind them and hesitated, uncertain what had become of those just ahead. In that moment's pause, death fell upon them as arrow after arrow streaked to its mark.

The enemy was thrown into confusion and dropped back into the cover of the dark wood with shouts of terror and cursing. But as the first force was joined by others from the camp, Theido thought he heard the coarse, authoritative shouts of the warlord himself. Almost at once Ningaal broke from the forest, but this time they crouched low to the ground and held their shields around them, making very difficult targets for Theido's archers.

"Get ready, men!" ordered Theido. The Ningaal were now moving more quickly over the ground between them. "Let fly!" shouted Theido, and his words were answered by the rattling scrape of arrow points upon the Ningaal shields. But some of the arrows found a home, and cries of shock and outrage stabbed the night as the shafts bit deep.

"Retreat!" cried Theido a moment later. He had seen the warlord upon his horse jump into the clearing, surrounded by his bodyguard.

The knight and his archers did not wait to welcome the newcomers with feathers. Instead they jumped up and ran yelling into the dell, just as Ronsard and his knights had done. A mighty shout arose from the throats of the Ningaal, who now believed that they had the king's army on the run. They bolted after the fleeing archers, treading over the bodies of their comrades.

Theido led his men down the slope and into the dell, across the small brook at its bottom, and up the other side to disappear just over the crest of the hill beyond. The triumphant Ningaal, bellowing praises to their destroyer god, dashed after them, heedless of the darkness that lay upon the land. They rushed headlong, recklessly, into the valley.

As soon as Theido and his men vanished over the hill, the first Ningaal were fording the stream with shouts and curses of anger. Hundreds more of the dark enemy were pounding out of the wood after them to gather in the dell, stopped momentarily by the obstacle of the brook. And once more, in that moment, whistling death streaked out of the skies as Lord Wertwin's archers, hidden all along the sides of the narrow valley, loosed their sting upon them. The Ningaal shrieked in pain and horror, as terrified beasts mortally wounded by an unseen assailant.

Arrows hailed down upon them from every side. Ningaal running out of the woods fell upon their comrades and trapped those trying to flee from the deadly ambush. Those who went down never rose again.

In a moment all who had thrown themselves down into the valley lay still. No more Ningaal came from the forest. No one moved.

"Let us escape now, while we may," whispered Theido. "The victory is ours if we do not long remain here. They will be back, and soon."

Ronsard gave a silent signal, and the men, knights, and archers began melting away into the night as quickly and as silently as the shadowy clouds before the moon. Lord Wertwin's force joined them, and they left the field in an instant, leaving it to the fallen Ningaal.

That night warlord Gurd lost five hundred. The Dragon King did not lose a single man.

CHAPTER 37

The rain-washed sky arched high above like a limitless blue dome. The air was cool and fresh, scented with balsam and pine and the damp of earth. The grass still sparkled with raindrops, glittering like diamonds in the early-morning light. The party had eaten a fine meal at Inchkeith's table and had, thanks to the master armorer's sons, set off without raising a hand—except to down goblets full of Camilla's excellent mulled cider.

Quentin, well fed and rested, had quite forgotten his apprehension of the night before. He had convinced himself that his arm was better—and that it would surely fully heal. But he still could not see how he could be expected to wield a sword before his bones had knit. Thus the awesome prospect of his being the mysterious, legendary priest king seemed remote and almost ridiculous. In the dazzle of a brilliant new day, he felt ashamed and embarrassed for having had the audacity to presume himself to be in any way central to fulfilling the prophecy.

Of course, it had been a presumption fostered by Durwin, Biorkis, and, for all Quentin knew, Toli. But he had allowed them to lead him into thinking that the prophecy might indeed point to him. The whole thing was foolish, preposterous. Quentin could see that now. He told himself so, and he believed it.

The horses had clattered out of Whitehall's courtyard at first light. Through the cleft in the ridge wall, golden rays of sunlight sliced the violet shadow of the canyon like a blade. It appeared to Quentin as they rode through the gatehouse and out onto the broad meadow, their horses cantering in high spirits, that they moved upon a trail of light all golden and green and shimmering. Everything that came into view, every tree and rock and mountain peak, seemed clean and new and vibrant with life. It was as if the world had been created anew during the night, and the old world had been cast off as a pale, pathetic parody of the true thing. Quentin imagined that he was seeing it all for the first time and that this was how it had looked when the world was young.

He heard a strange whoop behind him and turned to see Durwin's face radiant in the golden light, mouth open and head thrown back, laughing. And then suddenly he was laughing too. Toli started singing, leading them all in a song which he called *"Pella Olia Scear"* or "Song of the Morning Star."

They sang, and their voices soared up the sheer rock face of the ridge wall and fell whispering back. Beside them, as they neared the cleft, the rock stream cascaded with renewed vigor, leaping over its stony bed and splashing fire gems into the air. The stream, called Rockrace by Inchkeith, spread out like a road of flowing silver as it rushed to meet the day. They followed Rockrace for a long time among the fragrant firs, and then, as the sun mounted higher, crossed it and headed toward the Fiskills' barren foothills.

"How far from here are the lost mines?" asked Quentin after they had ridden for some time in silence. Durwin rode just ahead; he cast a backward look over his shoulder and laughed. "If anyone knew that, my friend, there would be no need of going. The lanthanil would be long gone by now."

"You know what I mean, you old sorcerer!" shouted Quentin back.

"So it is! How impatient you are. I think that before ten suns have set, we will look upon the entrance to the lost mines of the Ariga. That is, if the mountains are not greatly altered since those maps were made. Just the same, it will be no easy task to find them."

"We have the riddle," reminded Quentin.

"Yes, there is that. But you know as well as I that riddles are meant to conceal as much as they reveal. We will have a time of it, I think. The Most High will have to show us very plainly."

Inchkeith had been listening and now turned toward them and said, "You know, Durwin, the first time we met, you were gabbling about these lost mines of yours. You were full of questions about the lanthanil; you wanted to know if I had ever seen it or worked with it. Do you remember?"

"I remember it well. And I also remember your answer, though you may not. You looked at me with the greatest pity and said, 'If I had ever touched the metal of the gods, do you think I would still wear the cloak of a hunchback?'"

"Mine was a foolish question, I admit. But you must remember I had only discovered the existence of lanthanil and knew nothing of its full properties."

Inchkeith smiled strangely. "Craftsmen like myself have our own tales of lanthanil, though how much truth is in them I cannot tell."

"I have on rare occasions heard the elders speak of lanthanil," said Quentin. "To the Ariga, it was prized more highly than gold or silver. The craftsmen who worked it were almost treated as priests. But I never heard it referred to as a healing agent."

"Khoen Navish," Toli reminded him. Quentin turned to see that Toli had dropped back and was now riding beside him, intent upon the conversation.

"Yes, the Healing Stones."

Durwin looked quizzical and said, "Can you not guess the answer?" Quentin frowned and thought and at last shrugged. "Well, think a moment," replied the hermit. "The Ariga had no need of healing from any ailment. They lived in perfect health and never fell to disease, and none were ever reported to have been injured in any way. Healing is not mentioned as a property of the stone, although they probably knew about it if Toli's story is true. Its healing properties were seldom mentioned because they had no need of it themselves.

"As for the craftsmen being priests, they were—of a sort. The Ariga craftsmen were skilled in every art; they were poets, you might say. They worked in metal, wood, and stone as our poets work with words. And to the Ariga it was reckoned as almost the same thing. I say 'almost' because the Ariga rejoiced in a thing well made, for even in the smallest utensils of everyday life, they saw the face of the Most High. So craftsmen were priests in that they allowed the people to see something of their god in the objects around them. And they were greatly respected."

No more was spoken for a long time. Quentin rode along and thought about Dekra and realized he missed his friends there; he wondered what they were doing and whether they missed him as well. He also wondered what Yeseph would say if he knew that his protégé was now embarked upon a quest for the lost mines of the Ariga. What would Yeseph say if he knew Quentin was to play a role in the forging of the Zhaligkeer?

Eskevar slouched in his thronelike chair. His gaunt visage showed his displeasure quite openly. The lords of Mensandor, now gathered before him, clenched their fists at their sides and scowled determinedly.

"What of the others, my lords?" asked Eskevar, making no attempt to moderate the malice in his voice. "Do they propose to sit round in the field and join in the slaughter with whichever side carries the day?"

"We know not what other lords propose to do, Sire," said Lord Benniot in measured tones. "But we have come to offer you our swords and those of our knights. We will ride with the Dragon King."

"To the death, if need be," added Lord Rudd. "By Azrael, I will not see my king do battle alone while I have a blade beside me. My men are yours, Sire."

"And mine!" said another. The others declared their loyalty also.

"Well done, my lords," said Eskevar at last. Though he did well appreciate the decision of these, his loyal nobles, the king was enflamed against those—a sizeable party led by Ameronis and Lupollen—who had, after two days of heated contention, remained unmoved in their decision to withhold support for what they considered the king's war.

"We will go at once to muster and arm our troops. We will march as soon as we can." Lord Fincher placed his hand to the hilt of his short sword as he spoke. "It will be a pleasure to ride beside the Dragon King again."

"It will be no pleasure, my lords. Make no mistake!" said Eskevar slowly and carefully. "I believe this will be the utmost test of our might and endurance. If we fail, the world will grow dark. Freedom will die."

"Then let us fly, Your Majesty. We will return in three days," said Lord Rudd. "And we will march out with you to meet Theido and Ronsard and Wertwin's men in the field."

"Yes, fly at once. And remember, my lords, spare nothing. If we fail, there will be nothing left worth claiming in the end. I will speak again to the others to see if my words may yet prevail upon them to change their decision. We will need every strong arm before this war is over, I fear.

"Be on your way. I will await you here, ready to march at once."

There was a rustle of fine brocaded clothing as the nobles bowed as one and went out, each to ride with his train to his lands and there to prepare for war.

When they had gone, Eskevar called for Oswald and said, "Fetch me the armorer. I will speak with him at once."

Oswald appeared doubtful and frowned deeply, his old features crinkling up into a web of lines and creases.

"Do not look at me so! Fetch me the armorer at once, I say!"

Without reply the chamberlain bowed and went out. In a little while there was knock on the king's chamber door. Oswald came in, followed by a swarthy man with muscles that bulged and rippled as he moved.

"Tilbert, Sire." Oswald presented the man and left without looking at the king.

"Tilbert," the king said. The man nodded and remained at attention, his face stern and alert. "Ready my armor and my weapons. I will need both soon—within three days. Ready yourself and any tools you think best; you will be needing them."

At that moment the chamber door swung open without a knock, and Queen Alinea came into the room. Tilbert bowed to the queen.

"My lord," said the queen with a curtsy. She was slightly out of breath. "Why is this man here?" She indicated Tilbert, who looked puzzled.

"I am speaking with him."

"And about what I can guess. My husband, certainly you do not entertain any false notions of going into battle."

The king moved to dismiss Tilbert with a quick wave of his hand. The armorer bowed from the waist and started out.

"Wait!" said the queen. She turned once more to the king and fixed him with a smoldering stare. "Durwin is gone and so you think that you may now do as you please, is that it? You are still very weak, Eskevar. Think of your health."

"You may go now, Tilbert," said Eskevar. The man left the chamber quietly. Alinea crossed to the king's chair and fell to her knees beside Eskevar, seizing his right hand in both of hers.

"I pray you, my king. Do not go! It will be the death of you!"

Eskevar scowled furiously at his wife; her actions offended him. "The rascal Oswald told you."

"What does it matter? My darling, you are just up from your sickbed, and you have not your full strength. Wait at least until you feel stronger."

Eskevar put a hand to her lovely head and laced his fingers in her hair.

"My lady, I would that I could stay. But I cannot, nor can I wait one day longer than it takes to assemble an army to march."

"But why? Let your lords serve you in this. Theido and Ronsard would tell you the same if they were here. They are on the field now; let them assume command." The queen's voice quivered on the edge of tears.

"It may not be," he soothed. "The larger part of the council still opposes the call to arms that I have sounded. They are not convinced there is sufficient reason for them to march in war upon the whim of their raving monarch.

"Do you not see? They believe me ill and of troubled mind. They think I joust at shadows. I must go ahead of my army and convince them I am fit to command and that my judgment is unimpaired. Maybe then they will join us. I pray they do before it is too late."

"But is there no other way?" Tears ran freely down Alinea's cheeks and fell in dark spatters upon her blue gown.

"I must go. It is the only hope we have," the Dragon King said gently.

"Oh, my lord," cried Alinea. "It is an evil day that takes you from me thus."

"That it is, my queen. Most assuredly it is."

CHAPTER 38

The Wolf Star could be seen glinting cold and bright as soon as the sun slipped below the western rim of the sky. It rose before the other stars and set last of all. The people of Mensandor, if they had not noticed it before, now were wary of it. Doomsayers went from city to city, spreading rumors of death and destruction and prophesying the end of the age. The weak-minded believed these rumors and fled to the temples, seeking the shelter of sacred soil where the gods would protect them. More stout-hearted citizens stood their ground and waited and watched. But all listened to the wind and paused in their daily tasks to lift their eyes to the far horizon as if they expected at any moment the approach of something they dared not name aloud.

Theido and Ronsard, having weakened the army of warlord Gurd, turned their attention to the army of the warlord Luhak, who was advancing at a fast pace to the north. Arriving late at night, having traveled ten leagues that day with little rest, the king's forces struck once more on their midnight raid. Once again they caught the enemy by surprise and slew many.

On the next attempt, however, a confused signal almost defeated the Dragon King's army. The warlord's troops were waiting in a wooded draw, and Ronsard's knights met them. But before Ronsard and company could disengage and break free, the archers attacked, and many good men fell by friendly hands. The king's men withdrew from the field, leaving the Ningaal exultant.

As for Quentin and his party, the four ascended the empty foothills of the ragged mountains and labored up into the dismal heights. The way proved slow and difficult, even with sure-footed animals and Durwin's knowledge of the more passable routes. They lost their way and spent three arduous days crossing and recrossing the same trail and finally gave up, camping that night in the same spot where they had camped three nights before. One of the pack animals threw a shoe straining over the rocks and had to be set free. Many supplies were abandoned in order not to overburden the remaining animals.

The dark cloud had deepened its shadow over the land. Mensandor seemed to be a country quivering on the edge of the abyss. The roads were filled by day with travelers hurrying from here to there in an effort to find escape. The temple courtyards became choked with peasants seeking sanctuary. At the high temple above Narramoor, the trail leading to the temple had blossomed into a tent city from the base of the plateau to its crown. All along its narrow length, people huddled in their tents and waited for what they had been told would come: the destroyer god, descending to earth to slake his thirst with their blood. And at night, all over Mensandor, men watched the star grow brighter and cowered in fear at the impending destruction thus proclaimed.

Steadily, despite Theido's and Ronsard's best efforts and most valiant and courageous fighting, the Ningaal drove further north toward Askelon. The king's knights were solidly outnumbered, and the enemy soon grew wary of the crafty defender's tricks, becoming more and more difficult to lure into traps and ambushes.

On and on the enemy pushed and at last achieved the very thing the Dragon King's army feared the most: the four warlords joined their forces. The soldiers of Boghaz and Amut forged through to meet Gurd's remnant and Luhak's fairly intact regiment at the outer fringes of Pelgrin Forest. No invader had ever pushed so far inland in recent memory. No enemy had ever defied the Dragon King's knights as did the Ningaal, whose combined forces shamed the stalwart defenders.

Under Myrmior's inspired strategy, the Dragon King's army fell back into the forest to wage a war of ambush and retreat among the paths they knew so well. This increased the rage of the enemy, and that rage induced him to make mistakes and lose men. But the relentless push to Askelon continued, slowly and surely and with mechanical precision. It seemed as if nothing would stop the cunning invader.

"We cannot continue this way," said Theido wearily. It was the end of another long day of sting-and-run among the oaks of Pelgrin. The commander sat in Ronsard's tent, ashen-faced in the fluttering torchlight. "We are giving up too much ground, even though our losses in men are lower than we could have hoped, thanks to Myrmior.

"I think it is time to send word to Askelon for the king to make ready for a siege. Though I hoped it would not come to this, they should begin preparing the castle for our return."

"It would seem that in time we could bear these Ningaal if we but had more men," observed Ronsard. "Could we not send Wertwin to the other lords to entreat them to take up arms? Now is the time if ever there was. They cannot fail to recognize the danger now."

"Abandon any hope you may hold of persuading those jackals to join us. They have had every opportunity. Why, we are but ten leagues from Askelon now!"

"Even so," Lord Wertwin offered, "allow me to ride to Ameronis and the others. They are not cowardly men and will be reasonable once they know the need. I will bring them around."

"Go, then, my lord. Do what you can. But go with all speed. There is little time left. Each day we are pushed farther back."

The nobleman stood and, though weary to the marrow and reeling on his feet, said, "I will leave tonight and take but two of my own with me. The others I will place under Ronsard's command." With a quick bow he left, and the others returned once more to their nightly exercise led by Myrmior, who listened intently to the reports of the day's forays and then applied himself to creating some new strategy for the next day. He seemed to have a gift for anticipating the movements of the enemy and for diversions and surprises that allowed the king's men to hound and harry the plodding Ningaal.

"From what you have told me," Myrmior said, gazing at the map skin before him, "the Ningaal have tightened their divisions and march with a vanguard of their fiercest warriors. That is good—it means our raids are starting to worry them—but it also means that they will be much harder to trap and impossible to ambush from now on."

"As if it were not difficult already," said Ronsard. "I believe our time of nibbling away at the enemy's strength is at an end. Yet we dare not meet them face-to-face. If we could be assured of fresh troops soon . . ."

"I cannot think what we may do," replied Theido. "But you are right. We cannot charge them with lances or meet them toe to toe as we are often wont to do. I will defer to Myrmior's counsel yet a little longer."

"Lords, you flatter me," Myrmior said. "I have no secrets here, and I freely tell what I know so that you will know just how perilous is our position. It is very grave for us, my brave friends. I do not see a weakness that we may exploit; they have countered all our tricks this time."

He looked at the map, head bent down, eyes red-rimmed from sleepless nights of studying and pondering the movements of the foe as reported to him by the assembled commanders.

"How far are we from this river?" he said, stabbing his finger at the map.

"Let me see," said Theido. "That is but a branch of the Arvin which lies two or three leagues to the west. It is not so large as it appears on the map, I assure you."

"Nevertheless, I have found a plan which may gain us but a little more time." Myrmior smiled triumphantly. "A very subtle plan."

CHAPTER 39

The cold wind whipping off the sharp snags of rock stung Quentin's face, and the howl deafened him as it ravaged the bare peaks and screamed down into endless empty places. He kept his cloak turned up to cover his ears and wished that he had brought warmer clothing. Though only four days had passed since they had reached the elevations of the Fiskills, it now seemed ages since he had felt the warmth of the sun and seen the green of summer-filled hills. In every direction, wherever he turned his eyes, he saw the same thing: an infinite vista of jagged gray-and-white peaks jutting sharply against the blue sky.

Each day was much the same: cold and windy, without respite. At night they camped under a star-filled sky on ledges, in crevices and fissures out of the wind, but the rock was cold and hard. In the morning they awoke to the harsh, white light of a sun that shed no warmth upon the day—unless by chance they happened to find a spot hidden from the wind where they could stop and eat a bite before continuing. Then Quentin would feel a brief bit of warmth seep into him, tingling on his skin like dancing fire.

But those respites were rare and never long enough, for Durwin, sinking more and more into silence and a dour mood, pushed a merciless pace along the crag-bound trails. The party, at first so full of goodwill and high spirits, now dragged along dolefully, each one lost to himself and his own thoughts, their faces as gray and cheerless as the bare rock around them.

Quentin's thoughts turned toward Theido and Ronsard and the battles he imagined they were waging far away. More than once he wished he could be there beside them, instead of floundering here, lost in a world of dull rock and white light and severe blue skies—as often as not clouded with gray, wispy clouds that shredded themselves on the tors and spilled a damp, chill drizzle to thoroughly quench any spark of hope that they would see the end of their seemingly endless journey.

At night he lay awake and watched the dread star bend its fearful beams through the thin air of high altitudes. It now filled its quadrant with light and was the brightest object in the sky at night, save the moon itself. Quentin even began to believe that the star would grow and grow to consume the world and set off the conflagration that would prepare the earth for the new age. These thoughts, and others like them, filled Quentin with a sense of hopelessness he had never known before. And as the search among the high rocks continued day after day, he began to think that doom was certain and that it was already too late to forestall the inevitable.

One morning Quentin was shaken out of his gloomy reverie by Toli, who had gone ahead to check on the trail, which threatened to narrow beyond the ability of the horses to maintain their footing.

He heard a shout, looked up, and saw Toli, red-faced with excitement and the exertion of running, flying down the rock-strewn path.

"Beautiful!" Toli shouted when he was within range. "Come and see it! A valley . . ." He puffed breathlessly. "It is wonderful! Come!"

Instantly Durwin's face lit. "So it is! I believe we have found it at last!"

But Durwin was already toiling up the path behind Toli, who sprang lightly as a mountain goat over the flat slabs of rock, pointing and waving ecstatically.

Quentin turned to look at Inchkeith. "Well, a fair sight would be welcome to these burning eyes, I would reckon," said the hunched armorer. "Even if it is not our journey's end."

"Then by all means let us view this sight!" grumbled Quentin. "It must be a fine valley indeed—Toli has not said that many words in as many days."

Inchkeith turned, ignoring Quentin's comment, and began scuttling over the rock, barely keeping Toli, now disappearing over the crest, in sight. Quentin marveled at the deformed armorer's strength and agility; for in spite of his misshapen body and hobbling gait, Inchkeith somehow managed to grapple his way along the most unnerving passages.

Quentin glumly fell in and began trudging up the steep path, a narrow cut in the rock formed by a rivulet that carried away the spring melt. By the time he neared the top, none of the others were to be seen. He reached the summit and walked a few paces down the opposite slope before he thought to raise his eyes.

The sight before him so stunned Quentin, he sat down.

Across a vast and limitless gulf of silver mist, he saw an enormous bowl rimmed round with snowy peaks like white teeth. And the bowl, with gently curving sides, was a scintillating mountain green; all soft and mossy, the color of emeralds when struck by the sunlight. Carving through the center of the beautiful valley in graceful, sweeping undulation ran a river, gleaming like molten silver, filling the basin at the near end to form a lake shaped like a spearhead. The lake was deepest blue crystal and reflected the white-capped peaks rimming the fathomless blue sky above.

All this Quentin took in moments later. In his first, rapturous gaze, all he saw was the awesome splendor of the towering, frothing, magnificent falls that fed the river and formed the lake. "It is the Falls of Shennydd Vellyn," Durwin told him later, "the Falls of the Skylord's Mirror. The lake is the mirror, of course, and the Skylord is another name among the Ariga for—"

"Whist Orren. I know," said Quentin in a voice lost in wonder. "I have heard of Shennydd Vellyn. But I never thought . . ."

"Yes," said Toli quietly, as if he feared to break some spell of enchantment, "it is hard to believe that such beauty still exists in the world of men."

"Harder still to believe that beyond these forsaken mountains men are fighting and dying," said Inchkeith strangely. Of them all he seemed to be least affected by the sight before him.

All that was to come later; now, Quentin was overcome by the most dramatic vision of natural beauty he had ever seen. The falls plunged in three great leaps as they poured from some hidden crystal spring in the mountainside. This was the source of the silvery mist that floated over all like gossamer and charged the thin air with shimmering radiance as if rainbows hovered ever within reach.

Looking down upon it, Quentin could well believe that the Ariga had once sat where he sat and had seen it as he was seeing it. In that instant, he felt as if the immense barrier of time separating him from that happy time when the Ariga had walked the earth had been rolled aside. Inexplicably, the constant longing for a glimpse of that vanished time was suddenly stilled within his breast. Here it was at last, that which remained from of old unchanged.

The next thing Quentin knew, he was running down the precipitous grade toward the crystal lake, laughing and shouting with joy.

It was a tearful farewell with which Alinea sent Eskevar to meet the assembled armies of his lords. As much as she wanted to show him a brave front, she could not. In all her life as queen, she had never sent him off with tears in her eyes; no matter how much she might have cried for fear and loneliness later when he had gone, she did not want his last memory of her to be one of sorrow.

This time she could not contain her feelings. The tears welled up from her heart and overflowed down her cheeks, glistening in the morning light.

Eskevar, so used to the bold face his wife had always before maintained, seemed bewildered by what he considered a sudden change.

"My lady, do not be forlorn. I will return as soon as I can. It is nothing we have not faced before, my love."

"I fear it is, my lord." She dabbed at the corners of her emerald eyes with a bit of lace. The king took the handkerchief from her and poked it down inside his breastplate.

"I will keep this near my heart so that I will not forget the tears you shed in my absence. It will remind me to hurry here and dry your eyes as soon as I can." He lifted a gauntleted hand to smooth her auburn hair and looked deeply into her eyes. "This will be the last time, Alinea. I promise you I will never leave you again."

She looked at him, standing in the small courtyard of the inner ward just before the postern gate, and through her tears it seemed as if the years had been rolled back once more and the young Dragon King was looking down on her with brightly blazing eyes, eager to be off to defend his realm.

"Go, my lord. But do not say it is the last. For I know that you must be where harm threatens your kingdom. But go, and with no regret for me. Only promise that you will hasten back when your labors have restored peace to the land."

When she had finished speaking, she threw her arms around his neck and kissed him. He held her stiffly, her soft flesh pressed against his steely armor. "Farewell, my queen."

She turned and hurried away through the small arched door in the wall. Eskevar watched her go and then turned to the warder, who stood with averted eyes, holding the reins of his mount. The king ascended the three stone steps and swung himself into the saddle. The warder dashed to the ironclad gate and pushed it open. Outside, the armorer and the king's squires were waiting.

Without a word the king led them through the postern gatehouse, over the plank and down the long, winding walled ramp that formed the rear approach to Askelon. They crossed the dry moat and rode out across the plain to meet the lords of Mensandor and their assembled armies where they stood amid pennons and glinting steel, waiting for their king.

"Yonder comes the Dragon King!" shouted Lord Rudd as he scanned the plain, eyes squinting in the sun. "Sound the call!"

A trumpeter raised the battle horn to his lips and blew a long, clear note. At once a shout went up. "The Dragon King! He is coming! The Dragon King rides with us!" The knights gathered on the plain rattled swords upon their shields in noisy salute and shouted with joy.

"It is good he comes," said Lord Benniot, bending close to Rudd. "The rumors that he was dying had near taken the fighting heart out of my men."

"And mine," said Lord Fincher, riding up. "But now they will see that he does not hide in his tower, nor lie wasting abed. By the gods, it is good to see him astride a horse once more."

The three nobles watched their king galloping toward them across the plain. Behind him his squires carried the billowing standard with the king's unmistakable device: the terrible, twisting red dragon. On the crest of his helm he wore a crown of gold that shone in the sun like a band of light around his head.

Eskevar rode into the midst of his army to the cheers of all the knights and men-at-arms. Such was the clamor of his reception that it was some time before he could quiet them enough to make himself heard. But at last the army—more than two thousand in all—grew silent, waiting expectantly for what he would say.

"Loyal subjects, men of Mensandor!" More cheers. "Today we march to meet a great and deadly foe. Messages from those already engaged against the enemy indicate that he has reached the borders of Pelgrin Forest but ten leagues to the east." Murmurs of shock and disbelief rippled through the throng. "In his wake the enemy has destroyed our towns and villages and has slain the innocent." Cries of anger and revenge coursed through the crowd.

Eskevar looked out over the upturned faces of the host before him, many kneeling, their right hands clutching the hilts of their swords. He drew his own sword and raised it high.

"For Mensandor!" he called in a bold voice.

"For Mensandor!" came the clamorous reply.

"For honor! For glory!" the Dragon King cried.

"For king and kingdom!" the soldiers answered.

With his sword pointed to the east, Eskevar spurred his horse through the assembled armies. A way parted before him, bristling with raised swords and spears, and walled with shields and colorful snapping pennons. Along this panoply the Dragon King passed to the wild hurrahs of the soldiers. Behind him the way closed as the knights and footmen took up their weapons and followed their king into battle.

CHAPTER 40

"This makes the task of getting here worth every step," said Quentin. He sat on a grassy knoll, dangling his bare feet in the cold, clean water of Shennydd Vellyn. "This is a most fitting reward." He felt the weariness of the harsh trail and the fatigue of the seemingly endless days in the saddle, and then lastly on foot leading the horses, drift away in the soothing water. He felt revived.

"So it is! But we have not yet found the mines, though I believe we are at least at a place to begin looking." The hermit was bent once more over his maps and scribbles, searching for a clue to a sign that might spark the discovery.

Toli strode up, buoyant and brimming with good cheer, fairly intoxicated with the beauty around him. "I have set the horses free to graze. Look at them run!"

Indeed, the horses were gamboling like colts in the balmy air of the great bowl of a valley. They galloped and bucked and pranced over soft, thick turf as green as the first delicate blades of spring.

"We shall have a time of it trying to catch them again," mumbled Inchkeith. Quentin and Toli looked at each other. He had been mumbling darkly ever since they discovered the enchanted valley. While their spirits had risen on wings of joy, his seemed to have fallen lower by equal degrees. He was now quite sour.

"Do not worry on it, Master Inchkeith. They will come running to Toli's whistle without fail. He has a power over them; you will see." Inchkeith said nothing, turning his face away.

"Now then," said Durwin. "Listen to me. Here is the riddle once more. Think, now!

'Over tooth and under claw wend your way with care.

Where mountains sleep, sharp vigil keep, you shall see the way

    most clear.

When you hear laughter among the clouds and see a curtain made

    of glass

Take no care for hand nor hair, or you shall surely never pass.

Part the curtain, divide the thunder, and seek the narrow way;

Give day for night and withhold the light

And you have won the day.'

Durwin raised his eyes to meet blank stares all around. "Well," he said, pursing his lips in a frown. "As I thought. It is not so simple now, is it? Now the time has come to solve the mystery—"

"Past time, if you ask me!" said Inchkeith sharply. "It is folly to roam these wasted rocks, chasing a dream. Look at us! We are up here babbling like children over riddles and nonsense. Down there"—his hand flung wide in a gesture of anger and frustration—"down there men are dying. The blood of good men runs hot upon the ground while we potter among the clouds."

Quentin's brow wrinkled, and his eyes narrowed as he silently listened, somewhat shocked by the armorer's denunciation of their quest.

At last Durwin spoke, breaking the silence that had fallen over them with Inchkeith's rancorous outburst. "Could we serve them better by taking up swords and throwing ourselves into the fight? Would our blades matter very much, do you think?"

"Does this matter? Riddle guessing! Breaking our bones over these accursed rocks! And all for a dream."

"I thought you were with us, Inchkeith," put in Quentin. "I thought you believed as we did in the importance of our journey. You did! I know you did!"

"Maybe I did once. But I have had time to think. It was a mistake to come here; I do not belong here. I should be back at my forge and anvil. There is a war on, by the gods!"

Then Durwin, speaking softly as to a child, said a surprising thing. "Do not be afraid, Inchkeith. To others it is appointed to fight, and, yes, to die. To us it is appointed to find the sword and bring it to the king. And if there is even the slightest chance that the sword will be the Zhaligkeer, I believe our efforts could not be better spent than in searching for it, though the whole world wade in blood."

Do not be afraid.

The words struck deep into Quentin's heart. Yes, that was it. Inchkeith was afraid of failing, or never finding the lost mines. Perhaps he was even more afraid of succeeding, and forging the legend-bound sword, afraid of believing the prophecy could come true. Better for him not to put it to the test. And this was the way of Quentin's heart, as well.

Quentin, at first swept up in the excitement of great deeds and the promise of glory, had with growing reluctance come to view the enterprise as possessing little merit insofar as he himself was concerned. It was one thing to dream about being the long-awaited priest king, but quite another to actually set off in search of the means to make that dream reality. The aura of mystic fantasy had evaporated on the trail in the howling of the wind and in sleepless nights on the cold, barren rock under the glare of distant, unfriendly stars. And with every step that led him closer to the promise, he had grown more afraid.

Do not be afraid.

Although the words had been meant for Inchkeith, they stirred in

Quentin a peculiar swirl of emotions. He wanted all at once to scream at Durwin. *Why should I not be afraid? I have every good reason. I never asked to be this new king upon whose shoulders the world will rest. I never wanted it.*

But Quentin said nothing. He turned his face away and looked out across the sparkling water of the Skylord's Mirror.

That night they camped beside the lake, the white-topped peaks to the east glowing rosily across the green bowl, which was now immersed in shadows of deepest indigo. The Wolf Star burned fiercely in the sky and was reflected in the crystalline depths of Shennydd Vellyn.

Quentin sat alone—silent, brooding. He stirred only when the light tread of Durwin's feet signaled the hermit's presence. "So it is!" said the hermit, his voice seeming to resonate the water. "You have come to it at last."

Quentin regarded him with a questioning glare. Durwin, gathering his robes, squatted down beside him. "You have come to that dark and narrow place through which every servant of the Most High must pass."

Quentin flipped a pebble into the lake. "I do not know what I have come to."

"Oh, I think you know very well. And that is what is bothering you. It has been gnawing at you ever since we left Askelon. It was worrying you that night at Inchkeith's. I saw it then most clearly. I even spoke to you of it, but you evaded my question."

"Is it not possible that we may all be wrong about this prophecy? If you ask me, I am not the one. And if I were, would I not know it somehow?"

"Yes, perhaps we are mistaken. It is possible we have misread the signs. But whether you are the one or not does not matter very much."

Quentin cocked his head sharply; he had not expected the hermit to say that. "No," Durwin continued. "What does matter is whether you are willing to follow the Most High, even in your unbelief."

"I—I do not know what you mean."

"Certainly you do. All your life you have served the gods in one way or another. Of the old gods you soon learned only to demand those things which they were capable of providing—an insignificant sign or two, a small favor vaguely asked. Then you met Whist Orren, the Most High God, the One True God of All. You have served him faithfully these many years and have learned much about his ways. But now is the first time you have ever really had to trust in him, to place yourself totally in his will, and you are afraid."

Quentin started to object, but Durwin held up his hands. "Yes, afraid. You must now put your faith to the test. And such a test! With lost mines and flaming swords and prophecies fulfilled."

"Why should I fear that?"

"The reason is not so hard to guess. It is the same with every man. You fear testing your faith, because it means testing the Most High. Deep in your heart you fear he will fail. If he fails, you are utterly alone in this life and beyond; there is nothing you can believe in anymore."

Quentin shook his head. "No, Durwin. That is not my fear."

"Tell me, then."

Quentin drew a deep breath, glanced at the hermit and then quickly away again. "I am afraid of being the priest king. I cannot say why, but the mere mention of swords and mines fills me with dread. Look at my arm! How can I wield the Shining One with an arm as dead as firewood?"

"It is the same thing in the end, is it not? You fear to accept something the Most High has chosen for you."

"How is that the same thing?"

"Most assuredly it is. To accept the crown of priest king would mean placing your trust totally in the Most High. It means that you must trust him to know what is best for you, to know you better than you know yourself. It would mean trusting him beyond all trust, even when the way is unclear—especially when the way is unclear.

"When you trust like that, you necessarily test the god's ability to keep you. You are—we all are—unwilling to make such demands of our gods. If we trust but little, we will be disappointed but little, eh?"

"If I do not believe, but follow anyway, does that not mock the Most High and defeat his will?"

"On the contrary, my friend. To follow without seeing the end—in unbelief, as you say—is really the highest form of trust."

"It is but blind trust," objected Quentin. The words of the hermit made sense to him, but he still felt as if he must fight acceptance.

"Not blind trust. Not at all. Those who trust the powerless gods of earth and sky—they trust blindly.

"Quentin, look at me," the hermit commanded gently. "You cannot serve the Most High without trusting him totally, for there always comes a time when he will put you to the test. He will have all of you or nothing at all. There can be no middle ground. It is a demand that he makes of his followers."

Both men were quiet for a moment. The great bowl of the valley had deepened into violet dusk. The western peaks still had the faint glimmer of flame at their summits, but that, too, was dying fast.

"Look at it this way," said Durwin. "Why should you be afraid to test the Most High? He invites it! You see your injured arm as proof against his will. Cannot the one who created the bones also heal them? And if he chooses to raise an orphan acolyte to the crown of the realm, what is to stop him?"

Quentin smiled at the appellation. "You mean that I should go along with this strange business regardless of my own feelings about it."

"Exactly. Do not seek to hide your doubts and fears, or mask them in any way. Give them to him. Let him take them. They are, after all, part of you."

Quentin thought for a long time, and then said, "What did you mean earlier when you told Inchkeith not to be afraid?"

Durwin smiled. "More or less what I am telling you now. We must not fear for the Most High; he can take care of himself. We must only look to ourselves that we remain faithful to his call. I know it is much to think about in one piece. It has taken me years to understand these things, and I am asking you to comprehend them in but a few moments.

"Inchkeith does not know the Most High, but he is not an ignorant man. He still feels the fear of believing that something so good and so powerful can exist. And that, as I said before, is the place where most men turn aside.

"But if you go beyond your fears and doubts, and follow anyway—ah! Strange and wonderful things can happen. Yes, orphans can become kings, swords can sprout flames, and great enemies can be laid low at a stroke."

Quentin did not hear when Durwin left him, so lost in thought was he. But upon looking up into the night sky, now alive with blazing stars, he knew he was alone. His thoughts roiled and swarmed inside him; and rather than soothing his troubled spirit, Durwin's words had only served to increase the confusion—or so it seemed.

Quentin lay down and wrapped himself in his cloak to watch the glittering stars and to ponder the words of the hermit. He lay for a long time thinking and then slowly drifted into a troubled sleep. As he lay beside the glass-smooth Shennydd Vellyn, he dreamed a dream filled with things both strange and wonderful.

CHAPTER 41

The muddy little tributary Myrmior had indicated on the map lay across the path of the advancing Ningaal. It was, as Theido had advised, not a particularly large stream, but it was deep and lay below steep tor-bound banks in a most dense part of Pelgrin. If anyone ever spoke of it at all, it was called Deorkenrill, because of the air of darkness and gloom that surrounded it. Its gray and turgid waters slid quietly along a ser-pentine course through noisome bogs and stagnant pools until at last it emptied into the mighty Arvin many leagues to the north.

As unwholesome as it was, it was at this very place that Myrmior proposed that the army of the Dragon King make a final stand to try to halt the invaders' inexorable drive toward Askelon.

The plan was simple, designed to separate the amassed Ningaal into smaller groups that could be nettled more effectively by the defend-ers. But like most stratagems of war, Myrmior's plan was not without its element of risk. The weary defenders closed their eyes to the dan-ger, thinking that as it was likely to be their last hope of stopping the Ningaal before they reached the plains of Askelon, no risk was too great.

For many leagues to the north and south there was only one fit place for an army to cross the Deorkenrill: a hollow at the bottom of a slight hill where the stream flattened out slightly to form a natural ford.

"This is better than I could have hoped," said Myrmior when he saw it. "It was made for our purpose."

"Well," remarked Theido, casting an eye around the wood in the gathering dusk, "it is not a place where I would willingly choose to do battle. Let up hope that the Ningaal think the same and do not suspect an ambush here."

"They have become wary indeed. Their scouts now push far afield and ahead of the main body and are harder to elude," pointed out Ronsard. "And Theido is right. This is not a place to do battle. Look around you: mud, trees, vines. A man can hardly draw his sword."

"Brave sirs, that is precisely why this place is best suited for us. Whether they suspect or not, they must cross this water. I propose to make it as difficult as possible. But we must get busy. There is much to be done before first light tomorrow. We will need to work through the night."

"Very well," said Theido resolutely. "We have had our say, and have no better plan. We put ourselves at your command. What will you have us do?"

Myrmior looked around him in the misty twilight. A malodorous vapor was rising from the swampy banks of the Deorkenrill to drift slowly among the gray boles of trees.

"There!" He pointed out into the hollow through which the enemy must march to the stream. "We will begin by opening a channel into the hollow. We will fill it tonight and drain it in the morning. The mud should be very thick by then. And have some men start carrying water to that far bank. I would have that slippery with mud as well."

And so they began. Though they had come unprepared for excavating and carrying water, the Dragon King's forces turned whatever implements they had to the task. Knights more at home on horseback than on firm ground slogged tirelessly through mud and stinking water, digging with their noble swords or with bare hands, cutting a channel to bring water to the hollow. They worked by the glimmering of torches, listening to the forlorn cries of owls and other creatures drawn by the unnatural activity.

Others climbed the taller trees along either side of the bank and began building platforms of branches and limbs from which archers could rain arrows down upon the enemy. Ropes were wound with vines and stretched from one tree to another. And for Myrmior's supreme surprise, three of the largest trees growing at the edge of the near bank were chopped to within inches of falling and their upper branches were tied with ropes to other nearby trees and filled with mud and leaves.

This activity continued through the night, and by the time the sky glimpsed through the irregular patches overhead began lightening, Theido, Ronsard, and Myrmior stood on the far bank, looking at their handiwork.

"All that remains is to drain the hollow once more. And we will need hot coals to use with the arrows," said Myrmior, very pleased with what he saw.

"Then we wait. We should have a few hours to give the men a rest before the first of the Ningaal come through here," observed Ronsard.

"I am for it. We have done a labor this night. Let us pray that it has been to good purpose," replied Theido in a voice strained and rasping from shouting orders through the midnight hours. "We will do what remains and then deploy our men to their appointed places."

So saying, the lords turned at once to finish their tasks. Then, as the thin light of the morning filtered down into the murky dell, all fell silent. All was ready and there was not the barest hint that everything was not as it should be, that it was not all it seemed. An army waited among the ferns and in the trees and behind the turfy hillocks and was invisible.

The first of the Ningaal to come through the hollow were the scouts. They crossed the ford and passed on unaware of the army lying in wait on either hand. The next to pass were rank upon rank of horsemen, and just as Myrmior had hoped, the horses churned the hollow into a mud pit and made the far bank, already slick with the muck

Ronsard's men had created, a treacherous slide. But they, too, passed on unaware.

Tension seeped into the air. Theido could not understand why the enemy did not feel it, too. His stomach was knotted, and his nerves felt stretched as tight as bowstrings. Though he could not see them from where he hunched among the musty ferns, he knew his men must feel the same. Willing himself to remain calm, he waited.

The sun had marched to midday when the first of the footmen started across the ford. Hundreds of men, line upon line, waded through the waist-deep water and slithered up the far bank with difficulty. Theido could see them as they poured into the hollow and noted with satisfaction that the soldiers moved more slowly now as the mire deepened and sucked at their feet.

He heard a sound and a swift shout, and suddenly a horse and rider appeared at the edge of the ford. It was a warlord on his black steed, and Theido could tell he was unhappy with the time it was taking the soldiers to cross the stream. Without understanding the crude language at all, Theido knew that he was ordering his men to move along quickly; it was exactly what he would have done in the same situation.

The warlord sat straight in the saddle and looked long up and down Deorkenrill. Theido held his breath. Had the warlord spotted something amiss? Was their trap discovered?

But the grim lord swung his horse around and shouted once more to the scores of footmen trudging through the fen. Then he plunged through the stream and disappeared on the other side.

Nin's soldiers were crossing in masses now, a hundred at a time. They staggered muddily to the ford and plunged in, then flung themselves up the far bank like fish flopping out of water.

Another warlord appeared, surrounded by twenty horsemen. He waited, as the other had, watching the men cross the stream, and then splashed across.

The forest echoed to the sound of something ponderous and heavy crashing through the underbrush. *The wagons!* thought Theido. *Get ready!*

The wagons were what they had been waiting for. According to Myrmior's knowledge of the movements of the Ningaal, they most often traveled with their weapons and supplies in the wagons, half of their troops going before and the rest after. It was the second half of the Ningaal host that the defenders would attack.

Theido peered cautiously through the man-high ferns to see the first of the heavy wagons mired nearly to its axles in the hollow, now trampled into a swampy bog by the hundreds of feet of men and horses that had passed before. Around each wheel twenty or so footmen grunted and strained to push the wagon along, and the four-horse team leaned into the harness to the cracking whip of the driver.

Theido's hand sought the hilt of his sword. He knew that even now a thousand arrows were being notched to their strings in anticipation of the signal that would not be long delayed. Each archer readied his cannikin of live coals and arrows with shafts wrapped in cloth soaked in *palbah*—flammable spirits. Myrmior, seeing Theido's unconscious move, placed a hand on his arm and whispered, "Not yet. Give the others time to move up into position, and allow those who have passed on to distance themselves from the ambush."

Theido took his hand away from his sword hilt and drew it across his perspiring face. He let his breath escape between clenched teeth.

The Ningaal, by sheer force of numbers, had succeeded in hauling their wagons to the brink of the ford, but now other wagons were entering the hollow and succumbing to the morass. Shortly, the hollow was filled with wagons hopelessly enmired and hundreds of soldiers clustering around them in an effort to budge them along.

"Now!" whispered Myrmior shrilly. "Do it now!"

Theido drew his sword silently and stepped calmly from the ferns. He raised his sword, knowing that all eyes were now on him. He dropped his arm, and suddenly the air was filled with a sound like an enormous flock of birds taking flight from the treetops. The dim air of the dank dell was instantly alight with darting flames arcing to earth like stars falling from on high.

A confused cry of alarm went up from the unsuspecting Ningaal as the flaming arrows found their marks: the wagons. In moments the wains were afire and the befuddled soldiers were overwhelmed with terror. The Dragon King's archers then hailed down arrows upon the enemy without mercy. Ningaal dropped where they stood, never seeing their assailants nor hearing the sting that felled them.

The rout had only begun, however, when it was turned by the appearance of the two remaining warlords. One came pounding out of the wood, his bodyguard with him. Shouts rang out and orders flew, and in moments the chaos had resolved itself, though still the larger part of the Ningaal did not have weapons, confined as they were in several of the burning wagons.

That was soon remedied. A group of soldiers, in response to one warlord's command, rushed upon one of the burning wagons, jumped into the flames, and began hurling weapons to their comrades. When one was overcome by fire, another leaped in to take his place.

The other warlord with his mounted bodyguard pointed his sword across the stream, and his warriors came galloping across the ford toward where Theido and Myrmior waited with a dozen knights. Arrows took two from their saddles at midstream. Another came on, and Theido found himself suddenly ducking savage thrusts that chopped the ferns and sent greenery flying.

He threw up his sword to parry the slicing blows and grabbed the enemy horse's bridle, pulling its head down. The animal went to its knees, and Theido lunged at the rider, knocking him from the saddle. Theido's poniard did its work before the warrior could disengage himself from his thrashing mount.

The murky wood now rang with the sound of battle. Men shouted their battle cries and fell to with a fury. Swords struck upon shield and helmet; axes whirled and bit, splintering anything that sought to stay the deadly blades. Theido stepped away from the riderless horse beside him and saw a dozen Ningaal axemen splashing toward him—some screaming, the handles of their axes still smoldering in their grasp.

He caught the first one in the throat as the warrior raised his axe. But he had not withdrawn the blade when a second was upon him. He saw the glint of the blade swing up, and he raised his shield, expecting his arm to be crushed by the impending blow.

But the blow never came. Theido dodged aside and saw Ronsard's familiar face beside him, grimly determined, his sword streaming with blood as the wounded man at his feet writhed in agony. Behind Ronsard a host of knights stormed out of the wood where they had been concealed.

"I will take a warlord!" shouted Ronsard, leaping into the saddle so recently vacated by the rider at Theido's feet.

The lord high marshal cut down two charging Ningaal as he flew across Deorkenrill; the dark water now bore the corpses of the enemy by the score.

The warlord, wearing a helm of white horsehide with a plume of a horse's tail, whirled his mount around to meet Ronsard's charge with lively skill. Ronsard's sword flashed and flashed again; each time the warlord met his thrust and turned it aside. Neither could gain the advantage, and soon Ronsard, surrounded by enemy footmen, was forced to break off the attack and scamper once more across the stream lest he be hauled from the saddle and stabbed through a crease in his armor.

The archers poured their arrows upon the battlefield in a deadly rain. Flight after flight streaked down, and Ningaal fell by the score. The unhappy waters of the Deorkenrill flowed red with the blood of the dead. And on the far bank—that slimy incline of a death trap—the fallen lay like corded wood. In the quagmire of the hollow, the living surged ahead over the bodies of their comrades.

Myrmior had planned the fight well, and the Ningaal struggled in vain to gain the advantage. Myrmior dashed along the far bank, calling out orders and strengthening the position of the defenders where necessary and directing the archers to new and threatening targets as they emerged from the dim wood. Had there been more time, or had the Dragon King's forces been larger, it would have turned out a day of victory for the stout-hearted defenders. But it was not to be.

A mighty shout went up from behind the defender's position. It rang in the dell like thunder, and even the most dauntless among the knights felt his blood chilled. It was the howl of the raging Ningaal who had passed over Deorkenrill, now returning, summoned by the sounds of battle. In moments the Dragon King's forces were surrounded and would have been swept away instantly; but Myrmior, ever alert to the unexpected, had saved one last trick.

The bearded seneschal, heedless of danger to himself, mounted a small hillock on the far bank and there stood waving his hands. At first it seemed there would be no response to his signal; no one seemed to heed the commander presenting himself so foolishly in the thick of fighting. But then there came a groan as if the earth were rending, tearing out its very bowels. A hush fell upon the startled invaders as they stopped still to listen and look around them.

In the silence another gargantuan groan trembled the earth, and another, filling the wood with an eerie thunder accented by shuddering pops and horrible creaks as if some ancient beast were shattering the bones of its gargantuan prey. And then the sky itself seemed to pitch and sway.

The first tree crashed to earth square upon the bodies of a troop of Ningaal too startled to move. Their comrades dodged aside, screaming, only to be met by the second tree, which fell at an angle to the first and stilled many voices as its branches crushed and pinioned all beneath it.

To the terror-stricken Ningaal, it seemed as if the forest were crashing down upon them. Many dropped their weapons and fled back across the river and into the forest, where they were dispatched with arrows. The third tree crashed down across the ford and blocked the retreat of those who sought to return once more the way they had come. A cohort of defenders chased the fleeing Ningaal and slew many as they ran screaming through the wood.

The terror inspired by this last trap was short-lived, however. Soon the iron-willed warlords had their men back in close command. With terrible efficiency the warlords bore down upon the sturdy knights, cutting through their faltering defenses, and the tide of the battle turned against the Dragon King's forces. Still, though outmanned and exhausted, the staunch knights held their own through the middle hours of the day.

Teams of Ningaal, some with axes and some holding shields over their heads, began cutting down the trees wherein archers lay hurling death at those below. Thus protected, the Ningaal were able to fell the trees, if not completely stop the archers, who escaped at the last moment by swinging away on the ropes they had concealed among the vines. But the menacing warlords turned their attention to the armored knights now pulling their lines together along the far bank.

"It is time to flee," said Ronsard breathlessly. He was bleeding from a dozen shallow wounds, and his face, beneath the blood and grime, was gray with exhaustion. "We have done all we can."

Theido nodded. "Go now. Lead your men away. I will remain behind to cover your retreat and then follow you as soon as you are free."

Myrmior appeared, white-faced and holding his arm while a crimson stain spread down his sleeve. "It is too late, my lords. Alas! I have just made a last survey of our position. We are surrounded on all sides. There is no escape."

"We are completely cut off?" asked Ronsard. The strength seemed to go out of him, and his sword fell to his side.

"I feared as much. There are just too many of them." Theido turned his grim face away and called in a strong voice for the defenders of the realm to rally to him and prepare to make their dying stand.

In a few moments the remnants of the exhausted fighting force were dragging themselves together around the hillock where Theido stood with upraised sword. The Ningaal fell back to gather their numbers for the final onslaught. For a brief moment the clangor of battle died away.

"Brave knights of Mensandor," said Theido, "you have fought well this day. You have proven the honor of your king and country. Your courage this day will be sung by men as long as deeds of valor are remembered." The knights, some kneeling around him, raised their faces to his. Theido continued calmly.

"Let not the moment of death cheat you of the honor you have earned. It is but a little hurt, and then will come rest and sleep, and you will never again know pain. Have no fear, and stand boldly to the end."

"For glory!" shouted a knight.

"For honor!" shouted several others.

"For king and kingdom!" shouted a chorus led by Ronsard, who came to take his place at the head of the warriors.

The knights raised themselves to their feet, lowered their visors, and turned to meet the enemy for the last time. The Ningaal, watching them from every side, paused for a moment. Then the four warlords raised their curved blades, and with a ferocious cry the Ningaal sprang forward once more into the fray.

"It's better over quickly," said Ronsard as the attackers swarmed them. "I have no regrets."

"Nor I, my friend," answered Theido, "though my heart is heavy at the thought of our country falling before these barbarians. But I have done all any man can."

"Good-bye, brave friend," said Ronsard. "Is this the dark road you warned me of? How long ago it seems now."

"It well may be. But wait!" He turned and mounted the crest of the hillock. "Trumpeter!" he cried. "Sound your call! Sound it until your last breath! Do you hear? Sound it, I say!"

He turned, his face shining and eager once more.

"Fight on!" he cried, throwing himself into the clash. "Fight on!"

Ronsard plunged after him, guarding his left, and the two men drove ahead, swords singing in the air as if they would single-handedly drive the invader from their shores. The knights around them, heartened by the example of their dauntless leaders, put their shields together and dug in. If death came now, it would find them brave soldiers to the end.

CHAPTER 42

Quentin rose and stood looking across the polished surface of the Skylord's Mirror. The deep of the night was upon the fair valley, and the moon now crouched low behind the western peaks of the Fiskills, firing their snowy caps with a white brilliance that reflected in the fathomless lake. Also reflected with startling clarity were the myriad of stars burning like pieces of silver fire in the black vault of heaven's dome. The bright green of the valley was now gray in the subtle moonlight, and the leaping falls flowed down like liquid light, sending their ghostly mist to curl and eddy on the night air.

Across the distance Quentin could hear the falls splashing among the rocks at their base in a sound like laughter carried on the wind. It was the only sound that could be heard, for the valley was silent. Toli, Durwin, and Inchkeith were asleep, wrapped in their cloaks; they looked like lumps of earth or stone, so still and silent did they lie.

How long he stood looking, Quentin did not know. Time seemed to hold no particular meaning in the valley. But Quentin was suddenly mindful of another sound, or rather the impression of a sound, which had been present for some time. Perhaps it had awakened him.

The sound was a thin, high-pitched tinkling like needles dropping onto a stone floor. Or, he imagined, the sound of ice forming on a winter pool—if one could only hear it. The sound seemed to be coming from far above him. He turned his face to the sky and saw the Wolf Star, now shining directly overhead, filling the sky with blazing light, a light so bright it cast shadows upon the earth. The light made him cold, and Quentin pulled his cloak more tightly around his shoulders; but he could not take his eyes off the star.

It seemed to be moving, stretching, growing thinner and pulling other stars into its dance, for it swirled and shimmered in the blackness of the sky like a living thing. The stars melted together into a single shaft of light, cold and hard as ice. A thin, tapering shaft that stretched from the east to the west, from one end of the night to the other.

The tinkling was, Quentin realized now, the music of the stars, and the flashing shaft of light was the blade of a mighty sword.

In a twinkling Quentin realized he was seeing it: the Zhaligkeer.

The sword, its hilt of glittering golden stars with lordly jewels embedded—ruby, amethyst, topaz, and emerald—began to rise slowly, tilting upward as a sword lifted in triumph. Then the tip dipped and slipped and began falling through the black void of heaven, spinning as it fell, and flashing fire into the darkness.

The Shining One arrowed to earth in an arc of white fire. The brilliance of that plunge dazzled Quentin, but he looked on without flinching. The sword came to rest just above the peaks at the farther end of the valley where the Falls of Shennydd Vellyn poured out of the steep mountainside. It hovered there for an instant and then slid slowly down, as a sword sliding cleanly into its scabbard. There it remained for a moment, its glow diminishing rapidly and fading away in the sweeping mist.

When Quentin came to, he was staring at the falls, and the night lay deep around him. The mountains were sleeping, and he heard only the laughter of the rumbling water. But burned into his brain was the image of the sword. And without a whisper of doubt, he knew where he would find it.

"Durwin! Wake up!" Quentin whispered hoarsely. "Please wake up, or it will be too late!" He jiggled the sleeping hermit's shoulder and then stood to look once more into the wreathing mist.

"What is it?" said Toli, rising up silently. "What has happened?"

"I have seen it—Zhaligkeer. I know where we will find it. Look! The falls! Do you see?"

Durwin mumbled and raised his head. "Oh, it is you, Quentin," he said groggily. "It is bad luck to disturb the sleep of a hermit. I thought you knew that."

"I have seen the sword. Zhaligkeer! I know where it will be found."

"I do not see anything," reported Toli, still looking toward the falls.

Quentin whirled and pointed with his left hand. "It is there. I—" A look of deep disappointment bloomed upon his face. "No, it has gone now. But it was there, I tell you! I saw it!"

Quentin was striding away hurriedly. "Wake Inchkeith, Toli." The hermit sighed. "We will follow him. We seem to have no other choice."

"Inchkeith is awake," said the armorer. "What is the meaning of this fracas?"

"Quentin had a vision," explained Toli as they leaped after him. "He says he has seen the Shining One and knows where it will be found."

Quentin was leading them toward the falls along the grassy bank of the lake. The moon was down behind the mountains in the west, but their path was illumined by the unnaturally bright light of the Wolf Star. Quentin did not take his eyes from the falls ahead; it was as if he did not trust himself to remember what he had seen if he looked away for even an instant.

The others hopped along behind him; Toli darted back and forth from running beside Quentin to urging the others to a quicker pace. A breathless hour's travel brought them near the base of the falls. Quentin was standing at the foot of the towering cascade when Durwin and Inchkeith came puffing up.

The roar of the waterfall did not sound like laughter now. It was a mighty rumble that inundated them and set their bones to quivering.

Quentin turned to them, his face glistening with the spray, mist curling around his shoulders and beading on his cloak like pearls that gleamed in the starlight. "There!" he said, pointing his good hand. "The entrance to the mines is up there."

Durwin pulled on his chin. Inchkeith frowned. "Impossible! What do you propose to do? Swim up the falls like a salmon?"

Toli said nothing—only looked at the swirling, splashing water and at Quentin shrewdly. Durwin eyed Quentin closely. "I do not doubt what you saw. Let us see whether it answers the riddle. Let us see . . ." He put his finger in the air and opened his mouth to speak.

"'When mountains sleep, sharp vigil keep; you shall see the way most clear.'"

"Yes, I have seen it! The sword fell from the sky and disappeared into the falls."

"I thought you were not listening, but that is very good. Yes, and it fits, too. 'When you hear laughter among the clouds.'"

"I heard it. The waterfall sounded like laughter."

"Some laughter!" shouted Inchkeith. "I can hardly hear a word you are saying over the roar!"

Quentin ignored the remark. "'Among the clouds' . . . See how the mist forms the clouds. What else could it be?"

"Hmmm, yes," agreed Durwin. "'And see a curtain made of glass.'"

"The water is a curtain!" cried Quentin, his face shining and eager in the white light. "'Take no care for hand or hair,'" he recited, thrusting out his hand. "It is wet!" He rubbed his hand through his hair. "And my hair is dripping, and so is my cloak. I am soaking wet."

"So it is!"

"We are all soaking wet, and fools for it!" grumbled Inchkeith.

"'Divide the thunder and seek the narrow way,'" continued Durwin. "Go through the waterfall? Do you suppose?"

"Of course! Yes! That is what I have been trying to tell you."

"'Give day for night, and withhold the light, and you have won the day,'" quoted Durwin. He looked around. "Well, it is night. But it could also mean that the entrance could only be seen in the darkness or that entering the mine in darkness would—"

"I see it!" called a faint voice somewhere above them.

"Toli!" said Quentin. "Where is he?"

The three looked around, but could see the plucky Jher nowhere. He had disappeared while they were puzzling over the clues of the riddle.

"Here!" he called again. They looked to the falls and suddenly Toli was there, stepping out of the tumbling water as from behind a shimmering curtain. He seemed to be standing on the sheer rock face of the cliff, or walking on the mist. "Come up here. Do not mind the water!" he said, and disappeared again.

Quentin was already running after him. Durwin and Inchkeith traded doubtful stares. "It seems all chances of a peaceful night have vanished," sighed Durwin.

"And a dry one," grumbled Inchkeith. "We may as well have our bath and be done with it."

The two followed Quentin around the rocky edge of the pool at the base of the falls, where the water gathered churning and bubbling to spill into the stream that fed the pool in the center of the valley. The rocks were wet and slippery, making the way slow and laborious for the two older men. Quentin fairly skipped over the rocks and soon came to stand at the edge of the plunging torrent. Durwin saw him smile, look back over his shoulder at them, and then step into the churning water.

In a few moments they heard his voice calling down to them. "Do just as I did. I will wait for you."

"After you, good hermit," said Inchkeith. "I will follow in your wake. It's only fitting. This is your expedition, after all."

"So it is!" said Durwin. He took a deep breath and stepped into the glassy curtain of rushing water.

CHAPTER 43

Courage, men!" Theido cried. "Fight on! Our deliverance is near!"
The trumpet sounded a valiant note, piercing above the din of battle
and the shrieks of the combatants.

And then a voice called out from above on the hill behind them. "It
is the Dragon King! He has come! The Dragon King has come! We are
saved!" The trumpeter, his grinning features shining and eyes wide with
wonder, raised his trumpet once more and began to blow a strong and
steady note of hope.

Those below him on the hill heard his words and turned their eyes
to the dim wood beyond. A murmur passed among the beleaguered
defenders like a spark through dry kindling. "The Dragon King is coming! We are saved! The Dragon King!"

Theido, too, raised his eyes to the wood. Faintly, as in a dream, he
saw the glitter of gold and scarlet flicker among the shadowy branches
of trees like dancing light. And then suddenly he saw it full and fair: the
writhing, angry dragon, the king's blazon, floating swiftly toward them,
darting through the trees.

Others saw it, too. "The dragon! The king!" they shouted. And the
dark wood rang with the sound of trumpets and the crash of knights on
horseback surging through the forest. The Ningaal, surprised by this
unexpected turn, fell back, breaking off the attack. One warlord wheeled

his troop around to face the battle on the newer front. For a moment the Ningaal were divided.

"Strike, bold knights!" cried Ronsard. "Strike! Now!"

The knights, bruised and beaten and greatly reduced in number, surged ahead upon the points of their swords and sheer determination. The Ningaal before them, unable to meet the attack from both sides at once, scattered like leaves before the storm. In moments the stalwart band of defenders was surrounded, not by the enemy, but by comrades-in-arms. The bloodied knights lifted their swords with weary arms and cheered their king, while the fresh forces of the lords of Mensandor charged into the confused Ningaal.

Theido and Ronsard, battered and bleeding, stood leaning on their swords. "You are alive, thank the gods!" They looked up and saw Eskevar grinning down upon them from his great white charger.

"Yes, we had all but given up hope," said Ronsard. "But Theido here thought differently." The knight turned to his friend. "Another premonition?"

"No—well, perhaps in a way, I suppose. At first I thought it might hearten the men to hear our trumpet sound the call. And if there was a chance that anyone was passing near, they would hear and come to our aid. Where I came by that idea I cannot say."

"However it was," said Eskevar, watching with knowing eyes, "your clarion guided us to you forthwith." He jerked his head around, and Theido caught a glimpse of the man that used to be—eager, strong, and quick to the heart of the battle. "You and your men fall back through the wood. We will take these and put an end to it here and now."

"Sire!" The voice was Myrmior's; he came running up from the thick of the fighting. Theido and Ronsard had not seen him since he had stood with them on the hillside. Once again he had unhappy news. "The Ningaal across the river are swarming over the barriers, now there are no archers to hold them back. Do not think you will crush them so easily. Even now they are working to gain advantage on two sides."

"What?" Eskevar wheeled his mount around and rode a few paces away. In a moment he was back. "By the gods! These warlords are cunning wolves."

"Unless you have brought more men with you than I see, I suggest we retreat while we have the means and the strength to do so."

Eskevar glared at the panting seneschal. The afternoon light slanted sharply through the trees, but served only to heighten the dimness of the battlefield, most of which lay under gathering shadow. Clearly he did not like the idea of retreating from the first contact with the enemy; it rankled his fighting spirit. But his head wisely overruled his heart. "As you say, Myrmior. Theido, Ronsard, get your men behind us and take yourselves away toward Askelon!" The king shouted this last order over his shoulder as his charger sprang away.

Theido and Ronsard gathered the tattered remnant of their once-powerful force and left the field. The shouts and clamor died away behind them as they pushed back through the forest along the path Eskevar and his knights had forced through the wood. Though bone-weary and no longer able to lift their swords, the knights doggedly placed one foot in front of the other and dragged themselves away.

After they had walked nearly half a league, the forest thinned, and they came to a fresh-running brook. There they stopped to kneel and drink. Several of the knights among them knelt down, but could not rise again. Others stood teetering on their feet, afraid to stoop lest they, too, be unable to overcome the weight of their armor and succumb to exhaustion.

"We must press on," said Ronsard, casting a worried eye around him. A few soldiers had splashed across the creek and now lay gasping on the other side. "If we tarry much longer, they will bury us here."

"If we had horses, we would have a chance," Theido said. "When Eskevar sounds the retreat, they will soon pass us by. A knight on foot is no knight at all. This armor was not made for marching."

"I do not welcome the thought of being left behind when the army comes by. But look, Theido,"—Ronsard pointed across the brook to a clearing where a line of wagons rumbled toward them—"you have only to speak your mind and it is done. Today is your day, my friend."

"It certainly seems so."

In moments Eskevar's surgeons were scurrying among them, removing gorgets and breastplates, greaves and brassards and mail shirts, attending to the wounds of the knights. The armor was collected by squires and taken to the waiting wagons. Other knights began calling for squires to come and help them strip off their armor, and once unburdened, they splashed their way across the brook and made for the meadow.

The sun was westering when Theido and Ronsard stepped into the lea. They had waited until all their men had been tended and had either walked out of the forest or had been carried out and placed in a wagon. Just as they stepped out of the wood, a cheer went up from the soldiers. Looking around, they saw several men leading horses. Unbelievably, they were their own chargers—the animals, separated from their riders during the fight, had headed toward home and had been collected by the squires. Many of the knights found their own mounts; others took the mount of a fallen friend.

"Be mounted, men!" shouted Ronsard happily. "To Askelon!"

They turned and rode west through the forest once more and were joined by the first of Eskevar's retreating army, grim faced and sullen. Soon knights were streaming from the wood. Theido identified the devices and colors of the various lords: Benniot's silver-and-blue double eagle; Fincher's gauntlet of gray on a crimson field, clasping thunderbolts of white; Rudd's red ox on sable; Dilg's green oak above the crossed maces on a yellow field.

"I do not see Ameronis, Lupollen, or their party," said Theido.

"Nor do I. Perhaps Wertwin will convince them yet. Let us hope so in any case."

Theido swiveled in his saddle. "Where has Myrmior got to? I would thank him for his valor and sharp wit on the field today."

"His will be the last blow dealt, if I know him at all." He turned in the saddle and spied a rank emerging from the wood. "Here, Theido! Yonder comes Eskevar, and, yes, Myrmior is with him, and the lords."

In a moment the other lords had caught the two knights. "Is the enemy pursuing?" asked Theido.

"Yes," answered Rudd unhappily. Clearly he did not like retreating any more than the others, probably less. "But they are afoot for the most part. If we continue, we should outdistance them shortly." He issued a challenge with his eyes to the others around him. "I say we should rally in the wood ahead and wait for them. We could—"

"We could foolishly allow ourselves to be cut to ribbons in the night," said Myrmior savagely. Fire glinted in his dark eyes. He was angered and turned his horse away from the others and rode away after glaring at those around him defiantly.

"He speaks the truth," sighed Eskevar. "We have underestimated this enemy from the beginning. We will do well not to try doing it twice in one day. Retreat to Askelon is the only cure for our malady, my lords. We will have little enough time to prepare for a siege; let us make best use of it."

The march back to Askelon was somber and silent. It was dark when the army reached the plain below the castle, and though the moon had not yet risen, the ominous Wolf Star was burning brightly, shedding a chill light upon the land. That night the armies of the Dragon King felt the sting of that cold light. All regarded it bleakly, and strong men quaked inside with fear, for they knew an evil day had come.

CHAPTER 44

Stepping through the waterfall was like stepping through a glass curtain. At the extreme edge where they entered, the tumbling water did not have the force it did in the center of the falls. Once through, the explorers found stone steps cut into a rock face that inclined away from the vertical plunge of the mountain wall. And though the steps were wet, and slimy with black moss, each was carefully carved, wide and broad so that with care no one need fall.

The steps led up under an overhanging roof of rock to a landing of sorts—a natural bartizan. There Durwin and Inchkeith found Quentin and Toli waiting for them as they came lumbering up the stairs.

"This is the lost mine, the secret of the Ariga!" exclaimed Quentin, his voice sounding hollow in the great mouth of the tunnel. "Look!" His left hand pointed ecstatically toward the near wall. In the near-total darkness Inchkeith looked and saw strange figures carved in stone, glowing with a pale golden light. He could not make them out; they appeared to be shapes of letters in some unknown hand. But looking at them made him think of men and mountains and the waterfall churning and rivers and trees and the fullness of the earth.

Durwin stepped to the wall and began tracing the inscriptions, which were deeply carved and looked fresh, as if the scribe had just laid away his chisel. The lines were straight and well formed, untouched by the weather or age.

Durwin began to read. "'These Are the Mines of the Ariga, Friends of the Earth and All Living Things.'" Durwin turned to the others, smiling. "There seems no doubt but that we have found what we seek. Shall we go farther or wait until daylight to bring our provisions and tools up here?"

It was a needless question. The piercing look of bright expectation on Quentin's face, and Toli's quiet excitement, were enough to answer. "Very well, we can start at once. But we will need a light first. Someone must go back for the torches, so we may as well bring all the supplies at once."

Quentin's face fell a fraction. "Toli and I will go. You and Inchkeith may stay here, and we will return at once."

Before Durwin could suggest another plan, they were off, dashing down the slippery steps of the falls two at a time. "We may rescue some sleep from this night yet," observed Durwin with a yawn. "They will be gone a goodly time. We may as well rest while we can. I think it will be our last for a long while to come."

They settled down against the far wall, and Durwin fell asleep almost at once. Inchkeith pulled his coat around him and breathed the cool, musty air of the deep earth that rose up from the mine shaft somewhere away in the blackness beyond. But sleep had abandoned him completely; he was wide awake and could not take his eyes from the wonderful inscription shining softly from the opposite wall. Even though it merely marked the entrance to a mine—such an ordinary thing—Inchkeith thought he had never seen anything so inexplicably beautiful.

A shout brought both men to their feet. Durwin rubbed his eyes. "So soon? So it is! I feel as if I just dozed off. How did they manage so quickly?"

He and Inchkeith hurried, with careful dignity, down the steps to the filmy curtain of water and stepped out into a night fading into a pearly dawn. The quick splash of cold water brought Durwin fully awake. "Brrr! Such a rude awakening!" he sputtered, clambering slowly down the rocks like an animal roused from hibernation.

Quentin stood untying bundles from a horse, and Toli was leading the other, loaded down with packs and tools. "I should have guessed," said Durwin. "This night their feet would have wings. Well, let us begin. Our labor is before us."

Inchkeith only nodded. He had been strangely silent since entering the mine.

In another hour's time they had carried up all of the provisions and tools they would need. Quentin, with only one useful arm, had carried the most, making more trips than the others, so eager was he to begin the search. He had no idea what lay in the depths of the mine below, but it greatly heartened him to be once more where the Ariga had been and to see again the works of their long-vanished hands. Being here, his thoughts turned upward toward Dekra.

They piled all the baggage in the mouth of the mine and began dividing up the packs they would each carry. Inchkeith insisted on carrying his fair share, despite his deformity. Durwin allowed that he would need his strength to forge the sword and therefore should conserve his energy while he could—the way would be difficult enough. But Inchkeith would have none of it. In the end he gathered up his various implements, saying, "I carry my own tools, at least. No one touches this master's tools but the master himself." The anvil, bellows, and heavier items belonging to the forge were left behind at the mine's entrance. The party was finally ready.

"Now, one thing more and we will begin," Durwin announced. "While I light the torches, I want each of you to go back outside and look at the valley in the dawn. Unless I am far wrong, it will be some time before any of us sees the light of day again. I want you all to fill your hearts with a pleasant memory against the time when darkness crowds our way."

They all went outside and gazed upon the bright green bowl of the peaceful valley. The morning light struck the curling mist with a golden radiance, and the mountains seemed crowned with flames of red gold. Shennydd Vellyn lay smooth and deep and undisturbed, mirroring the limitless blue of a clean morning sky brushed with the lacework of wispy white clouds.

The thin mountain air smelled sweet and fresh, vastly different from the dank, stale air of the mine. Quentin, though he appreciated Durwin's suggestion as a wise one, was anxious to be off. While he gazed about him intently, his mind was so full of new excitement that he saw little. When they finally turned to go back into the mine, Toli was the last to tear himself away from the beauty before him.

One by one they ascended the tumbled rocks, wet with spray. One by one they approached the thunder of the falls. One by one they parted the shimmering curtain and stepped inside, into the darkness of the fabled mines.

Esme and Bria stood on the high barbican overlooking the gates of the castle and the town below, its buildings clustered like a flock of timid sheep in the shadow of its great protector. On this fresh morning, the narrow, cramped streets were rivers of moving color, all surging at flood stage toward the gates below. Out on the plain, as far as Pelgrin's dark border, threads of travelers could be seen weaving their way to the city to join the streams moving into the castle.

"Those poor, weary people," said Esme, her voice softened with awe. "There must be whole villages of people down there."

"True," replied Bria. "Fear is a swift messenger, is it not? Two days ago the lords returned from battle. Now look. Some of them have traveled day and night to get here. I would do the same in their place—what else can be done?" These last words were uttered with such hopelessness that Esme turned to her and took her by the shoulders.

"Bria, we are friends, you and I. Are we not?"

"Yes, of course. Why—"

"Then I must tell you something—as a friend would." Esme searched her companion's face and looked her in the eyes. Bria was startled by the directness with which this dark-haired beauty addressed her.

"Speak freely," said Bria.

"We are women now, Bria. Royal women. There is no more room for girlish indulgences. You have eyes; you have seen. We are to endure siege here not many days hence. We must put away all thoughts of ourselves and begin thinking of others first. It must be done. We must be strong for the men who fight, for the people who will look to us for hope and encouragement, and only lastly for ourselves. For the sake of the kingdom this must be; our courage must be a flame which can kindle the hearts of those around us. That is a woman's duty in time of war."

Bria's green eyes fell, ashamed. "Your words pierce me, fair friend. What you say is true. I have walked in proud misery these past weeks— ever since Quentin left. I have been selfish. I have shown myself to be afflicted by the fate that took our loved ones from us—though others had better claim to such recourse than I." She raised her eyes once more to her friend's.

"But no more, Esme, no more. You have spoken the truth as a friend ought. I will put away girlish airs and simpering. I will be strong that those around me will take strength, too, and not be at pains to cheer myself when there is more important work to do. I will be strong, Esme."

Bria threw her arms around Esme's neck, and the two young women embraced each other for a long moment. "Come, let us do what we can to see to the accommodations for the villagers seeking refuge within these walls," suggested Bria.

They turned away from the barbican and began walking along the southern battlements. "I feel such a fool, Esme. Forgive me."

"No, do not chide yourself. I did not speak so to reproach you, for you are far more tenderhearted than I."

"If that were so, I should have been comforting you, Esme. You are far away from home, and no news has come of the fighting there or of your family. You must be worried."

"I am, though it was part of my father's plan to send me here and thus remove me from the threat of war. I honor him by holding to the course he set for me, though I am sure he scarcely guessed that mighty Askelon would fall under siege."

Esme threw a guarded glance to Bria, then blushed and averted her eyes.

"What? Speak if you will. What is it?"

"Well, to tell you the truth," said Esme slowly, "I have not thought of my own family as much as I have another."

"Toli?"

"Yes, Toli." She regarded Bria carefully. "Why? Is something wrong with that?"

"Oh no! Far from it, Esme. It surprises me a little, that is all. Toli is always so quiet, so invisible. I scarcely notice when he is around. But then, he and Quentin are inseparable, and since I only have eyes for Quentin, it should not surprise me that someone else sees in Toli something I do not."

"Believe me, it was the furthest thing from my mind to lose my heart so easily. I was on an errand for my father, but in those days upon the trail and—Bria, you should have seen the way he protected me when we met the Ningaal. And afterwards, when I saw him alive again, my heart went out to him. I believe he loves me, too."

Their talk had brought them to the great curtain that divided the inner ward from the outer. They stood looking down into the outer ward at the mass of people moving about, constructing tents and temporary lodgings for themselves. Cattle, pigs, and chickens had been brought along to provide food should the siege prove a long one. The warder and his men were scurrying around, directing the flow of humanity here and there, trying to keep the pathways open for soldiers who would be moving through.

"Can the castle possibly hold all these people?" asked Esme.

"I have never seen anything like it, though it is said that in the Winter's War, a hundred thousand were besieged here all winter. But that was long, long ago."

The lowing of cows and the squeals of pigs, intermingled with the general shouting and crying of peasants and villagers, created an overwhelming din. The princesses looked down upon the frightened populace and forgot their own cares, for in the pathetic confusion of the refugees, they heard small children crying.

"Are you sure you want to go down there?" asked Esme.

"I am sure. There may be little we can do for them. But that little shall be done."

With that, they entered the southern tower and began descending the spiraled ranks of stairs into the noisy chaos of the outer ward.

CHAPTER 45

The darkness was unlike anything Quentin had ever experienced. Far darker than the blackest night, it was a palpable thing, primitive and insistent. Almost as if alive, it crouched around each turn and on every side, waiting to smother all intruders in its velvet embrace. The torches they carried seemed fragile and ridiculous things, mere toys against an unrelenting foe of stupid, savage cunning.

Still, the spluttering pitch torches served somehow to keep this awesome darkness at bay, though they always seemed to be on the verge of guttering out completely and plunging their bearers into a void as black as death. Each person carried a torch except Inchkeith, who labored doggedly along, weighed down with his delving tools, as he called them. Durwin went ahead, relying on his sparse knowledge of Ariga mining lore to serve as a guide. Quentin, arm in sling but toting a large pack nonetheless, followed Durwin. Inchkeith hobbled along behind Quentin, and Toli brought up the rear, grinding his teeth with every step into the mountain's black heart.

After walking for what seemed like days on end into the darkness along a low-roofed, wide corridor of solid stone, Durwin halted the party, saying, "No doubt you young men could go on walking this way until you wore the soles out of your boots. But I think it is time for rest. A bite to eat would not be unwelcome, either."

"Take no thought for me, hermit. Do not stop on my account," said Inchkeith. But Quentin noticed he loosened his pack all the same.

"It is not for anyone but myself that I sit down, sir. My feet tell me it is time to rest a bit, and my stomach agrees."

They ate, and Quentin realized how hungry he was after all. As he munched, he wondered whether it was day or night outside. But in his mind he pictured it exactly the way he had seen it last. Durwin had been right— it was a useful thing to carry a little sunlight with one into this dark hole.

Toli ate little and said less. He had grown sullen and had withdrawn into himself, becoming, if it were possible, even more quiet than usual. Quentin pretended to take no notice of his friend's behavior, for that would have only served to make it more painful to him. He knew precisely what was bothering Toli: the Jher did not like the smothering confines of the mine. It was a supreme act of bravery for Toli, born of a people who roam the earth at will, following the wild creatures, to have even entered the hateful place, which seemed to him worse than a grave.

And there was something of the same uneasiness that bothered Quentin, too. But in him it took the form of a puzzlement. The Ariga, whose every word was a visible, tangible song, had constructed a most unappealing mine shaft. Not that Quentin had expected the brightly colored, sweeping galleries of Dekra to be reproduced below, but he did anticipate something of their remarkable flair, which usually showed in even the most mundane articles of their everyday life, to be present here. All he could see was a black tunnel of stone that glistened in patches where water seeped down its sides.

"If I am not mistaken, we are still in the entrance shaft. Soon, I think, we will reach the first level. How many levels there are, I cannot say, nor on which one we shall find the lanthanil," Durwin said. "We will search each level and every gallery until we find it. My own guess is that it lies very deep and that we must descend to the lowest level."

At that Toli made a strange grimace, as if he were eating a most bitter fruit. Quentin would have laughed if it had been anyone else, but he knew how much this experience was torturing his friend. So he turned away and said to Durwin, "You mention the lanthanil. I would hear more about it, for all I know is what little you have said and what I remember from Dekra, which is so wrapped in legend as to be beyond belief."

"Do not be certain of that. Yes, often the stories men recite about such things do grow in the telling. But the Stone of Light—that is what the word means, roughly translated—is a most fantastic substance. It has many exotic and powerful properties."

"If tales are to be believed," said Inchkeith, staring into the darkness, "hear this one. Many years ago my father was traveling the world with his father. He was but a small boy at the time, and they were seeking the secrets of weaponry and armor, of forging and forming rare metals, of setting gems in their bezels—all the craft which an armorer must know.

"In Pelagia they met a merchant who sold arms, and they became friends when the merchant saw a sample of my grandfather's work. When the merchant realized that he was talking to a great craftsman, he took them into the back of his shop—for in that country they had stalls outside covered with awnings, and inside—where the merchants and craftsmen lived and worked—they kept the very finest articles of their trade. To be invited inside was a considerable honor.

"This merchant, a well-known and respectable man—I cannot recall if I ever heard his name—took them in and led them to a very small room in his large house. He unlocked the bolt across the door to this room and then led them inside. My father said it was very dark. He remembered the walls of the room were extremely thick and the door was very heavy, for it groaned on its iron hinges like a drawbridge.

"The merchant closed the door and brought out a casket from some hidden place and put it before them on the table. The case was bound with locks and chains, though it was but a small one. When he had unlocked it, he took out an object wrapped in cloth. My father said the object was not very large, and appeared to not be much in weight, for the man handled it with ease and with great reverence.

"The merchant did not speak, but unwrapped the cloth and revealed a chalice of surpassing beauty. But most remarkable of all—the thing my father remembered most clearly until the day he died—was the way it shone in the darkness, as if lit with an inner flame. He said he cried to look at it, it was so beautiful, but then, he was a small boy.

"He reached out to touch the shining cup, and the merchant pulled it away, saying that it was enchanted and to touch it with bare hands diminished its power. He said it was very old and its power was only a fraction of what it had been, but that it was still great. He said that cordials sipped from the goblet cured at once, that the very touch of it healed all infirmities.

"My father's father then did a very unusual thing. As proud as he was of his work, he said he would give the merchant his finest dagger for one touch of the chalice for himself and his son. My father noticed the strange look which came over his father's face as his voice pleaded. The dagger was finely wrought; it had a golden handle with rubies inset. It was worth a great deal, and yet the merchant hesitated.

"But in the end he relented and let them touch the chalice. My father remembered how the light that leaped from the exquisite cup lit his father's face and seemed to infuse him with a new power of creating and a heightened understanding of his craft—though this was observed much later. When his father finally passed the chalice to him, he was afraid to touch it, but his father urged him to, and he did. He said he never felt such strength and wholeness, and nothing in his life ever moved him with such emotion after that. Though he was but a small boy, he knew even then that he would never recover that feeling or see such beauty again; so he treasured it in his heart.

"My father spent the rest of his life trying to achieve in his craft the beauty that he saw in that cup. And you know he lived far beyond the natural span of a man's years. He always said it was because of the chalice and that had his father given a hundred golden daggers, it would have been but a paltry sum for the gift of that one touch."

Inchkeith's voice softened to a whisper. Quentin, Toli, and Durwin, too, sat rapt and staring in amazement at the story the armorer told. For a long time no one spoke, but at last Quentin broke the silence. "What became of your grandfather? How did it affect him?"

Inchkeith was slow in answering, and when he at last opened his mouth to speak, he turned eyes filled with sadness toward them. "His was not a happy fate. He, too, lived long and prospered. But he became obsessed with finding another chalice, or some other object made from the mysterious metal, and when he could not, he tried to make one himself. But he was always disappointed. For though his works became the most highly prized in all the realm, he was yet unsatisfied. He died bitter and broken, consumed with despair. Some said it was the despair that killed him in the end."

"Did your father not share his fate, then?"

"To some degree, yes. He, too, was never satisfied with the work of his hands after having held the chalice. But you must remember he was a small boy. I believe his heart was yet innocent and untutored in the ways of the world. The touch of the chalice, rather than leading to bitterness in the end, inflamed him with a burning desire to seek that beauty. He died at last unfulfilled, it is true, but not unhappy for that."

"Your story is most moving," said Durwin. "I begin to see now why the Most High has chosen you to accompany us on this journey. It seems your family has some part to play here." He looked around at them all and said, "Well, we have rested and talked long enough. Let us continue our quest. Onward!"

Slowly and painfully, they shouldered their burdens once more and lifted their torches to resume their long, slow descent into the mine.

If the outer wards were filled with the frenzy of frightened citizens, the inner wards were filled with soldiers feverishly preparing for the impending siege. A steady stream of soldiers marched from the base of the southern tower, emerging from the donjon with armloads of spears and bundles of arrows. Others, bent to the task in smaller groups, labored over objects of wood, rope, and iron on the ground; they were assembling the machines of war. Still others tied piles of straw into bundles and sewed heavy pieces of cloth and skins together.

Horses were led to the stables around the ward yard, where squires sat at whetstones sharpening sword, lance, spear, and halberd. Provisions, brought up from the town by the wagonload, were stacked away in kitchens and pantries by cooks and their helpers. Dogs chased cackling chickens and honking flocks of geese, while children, uninhibited by the danger and excited by the bustle of activity around them, ran and played, dodging the footsteps of their elders and staging pretend battles.

Eskevar roamed the battlements like a shade. He seemed to be everywhere at once. His commanders looked up to see him watching them as they drilled the troops; the donjon keeper found him inquiring about the level of water in the reservoir, dipping the measuring rod himself; the squires were instructed in better sharpening techniques by one whose hand bore the royal signet. At the end of the day, there did not seem to be anyone anywhere within the walls who had not seen him.

"Sire, I must protest!" exclaimed Biorkis, clucking his tongue. "Durwin would tell you if he were here, and so I tell you in his stead— listen to him if not to me: you must rest. Your strength is but half recovered, and your ride into battle has tired you. Rest, I say, and let your commanders make ready all that is necessary."

Eskevar fixed him with a baleful stare. "You little guess the danger gathering at our gates. Who is there to see to those preparations if not the king?"

Biorkis, well warned by Durwin regarding the obstinate pride of his patient, did not flinch from his duty. "What good will you be to your people when you lie exhausted on your bed, unable to even lift your head, let alone wield a sword or shout a command? Rest now while you may."

The king frowned ferociously. "I am sound enough, I tell you! My strength is none of your concern." Even as he spoke, he tottered uncertainly.

"How so, Sire? It is now the concern of every man and child in the realm who would see his king deliver him from the hand of the enemy. You need rest. Gather your strength that the day of the trial does not find you enfeebled."

"Enfeebled! The way you talk! And to your king, by the gods!" Eskevar snapped. His face darkened in such rage that Biorkis thought it best not to press the matter further for the moment. "There is much to do, and someone must see to it that it is done well," Eskevar growled as he went out again. Biorkis did not see him the rest of the day, though he waited near Eskevar's chamber for the king to return.

CHAPTER 46

I t was strange to wake in the vast darkness of the mine. When Quentin opened his eyes, he did not know that he had opened them at all. The sensation of blindness was so overpowering that for a moment Quentin's heart clenched in his chest until he remembered where he was and how he had come to be there. Just to make sure, he winked both eyes several times, but could discern no difference. So he lay on the hard, uneven stone and waited, not inclined to bump around in an attempt to light a torch. From the deep, regular breathing that filled the chamber's towering silence, he knew the others were still asleep. He would wait.

They had made two more long marches before fatigue overtook them, and Durwin decided they must sleep before moving on. They had reached the first level shortly after they had stopped to rest and eat the first time. The corridor with the low roof had ended in a steep incline that emptied upon a room of interminable size, judging by the echoes the stony walls flung back at them when they spoke. But they had no light to see how large the room was, for the torchlight failed to illuminate its farthest dimensions.

They had crossed the great room, passing huge columns of reddish stone carved of the rock of the mountain's core, rising out of the floor like monstrous trees sweeping from the ground, their tops lost in the inky blackness above. Quentin counted twenty pillars before they reached the far end of the room, which tapered to a huge arch through which they passed. The arch bore the unmistakable marks of having been made by Ariga stonecutters. Quentin would have liked to stand and admire it, but they passed quickly on.

The next corridor was more difficult to navigate than the first. It was wider and its roof higher, allowing for more freedom of movement, but numerous shafts and galleries opened off it, often abruptly and at slight angles. It forked in several places, splitting off to the right and left. Sometimes they would pass by an opening that Quentin could not see until he felt a chill breeze on his face and smelled the dank, musty odor of stale air and stone. Once they crossed a stone bridge that arched across a wide crevice, splitting the floor before them in a sharp divide. On the bridge, Quentin felt a warm updraft and guessed that the rift was the chimney of some subterranean fire eternally blazing.

Each time Durwin came to a fork or a turn that offered a choice of paths to follow, the hermit elected to take the one that promised a downward course. He admitted he had no precise notion of what they were looking for, but had the idea that the highly prized ore they sought lay at the deepest levels of the mine.

They had rested in a curious domed chamber on the far side of the stone bridge. They talked among themselves at first, but somehow— through fatigue, or through the wearing oppression of the deep dark- ness—the conversation seemed to dry up like a trickle of water in the desert sand, vanishing slowly without a trace of its having ever been there.

Though tired, and aching from the weight of the packs they carried, they had decided to press on. The slope of the downward track increased dramatically once they left the domed chamber. With the extra weight they carried on their shoulders, the falling grade impelled them onward at a faster pace than they would have normally had strength or inclination to attempt. The result was that they reached the second level in what seemed no time at all.

Quentin knew they had been walking for some hours when they

tumbled into the enormous cavern that formed the central chamber of the second level. But time had ceased to function in its normal way. Hours collapsed and minutes stretched out incredibly until it seemed that time had no meaning at all unless it was measured in footsteps or in tunnels passed.

They had been walking in silence, each wrapped in his own thoughts as in a hooded cloak from head to toe, when Quentin felt a touch at his elbow that caused him to jump in fright, nearly dropping his torch. "Toli! You scared me. I did not hear you creeping up behind me."

"Excuse me, Kenta. I did not mean to alarm you." He looked at Quentin with large, shining eyes as deep as fathomless pools. For a moment Quentin was reminded of the time, long ago it seemed now, when he had met a young Jher in the forest, dressed in deerskins and peering at him with the soft, wary eyes of a wild creature. The look Toli gave him now was exactly as it had been then. With a sudden creeping sensation, Quentin imagined Toli had entered some more primitive state. Looking at those large, dark eyes glittering in the quavering light of the torch was like looking into the eyes of a wild and frightened animal.

"What is it, Toli? Is something the matter?" Quentin spoke in barely a whisper.

Toli stared around him in a strange, wide-eyed way. When he spoke again, it was with a quivering voice on a strange note that Quentin had not heard before in his friend. Toli appeared poised and ready for flight; Quentin feared that he might suddenly dash off into the darkness, never to be seen again. "My people do not love dark places," said Toli. "We have never lived in caves. In ages before this one, when holes and caves were home to many men, my people lived in the forest and made their homes in the light."

The way he spoke made it seem that Toli was offering a deeply personal confession. Quentin did not know what to think.

"There are still those among us who speak of the times of the cave dwellers," continued Toli. "Some even have been inside caves when they have come upon them in the forest. But I have never been."

All at once Quentin realized what Toli was trying to tell him. And he realized what strength it had taken for the Jher to follow him into this dark place. To Toli it was not a mine; it was an ancestral taboo that he was willing to put aside, out of love for his friend. But the darkness and the endless walkways of stone boring ever deeper into the bowels of the earth had at last stripped Toli of the veneer of civilization he had acquired living with his Kenta. He was the Jher prince once more, wild as the free creatures of the Wilderlands.

"We will soon be finished here, Toli. Do not fear. You will see the living land once again, and very soon." Quentin felt the emptiness of his words. The more so when Toli turned an uncomprehending, glassy stare upon him and seemed not to recognize him at all. Quentin had the odd feeling that he was looking at a stranger whose face was as familiar as his own. The Toli he knew had vanished.

"*Delnur Ivi,* Toli," Quentin murmured as they trudged along, repeating the words over and over by the flickering torchlight. He had racked his brain for some smattering of the Jher speech he could use, and that was what he had come up with. *Delnur Ivi.* Hold on . . . hold on.

Quentin rolled over in the darkness and was startled to see a faint light bouncing toward him out of the formless void. It seemed to float or swim in the darkness, and it blinked like the eye of some cave beast that had happened upon their trail and was now stalking them. He watched as the light grew brighter by degrees.

Quentin sat up, wondering whether to wake the others and warn them. He heard the shuffling footsteps of someone coming down the passageway toward the chamber where they had huddled to sleep. But even as Quentin framed the thought, the feeling of danger passed. He waited, and presently the light burst through the arched entrance to the chamber, filling the room, or so it seemed to Quentin's light-deprived eyes, with a sunlike brilliance.

"So it is! You are awake, Quentin. Come with me. I want to show you something."

"But the others—"

"Let them sleep. It is not far. Come along."

Quentin stood stiffly and found at once how sore his feet were. He padded after Durwin, who lifted the torch high so both could use it as they entered once more the main tunnel they had been following on their last march. Presently they came to a small arched entrance in the side of the passageway. Durwin stopped and said, "I have been wandering long up and down this gallery. I only saw this when I was returning to the chamber to sleep a little while ago. I decided to try it. Follow me."

Quentin, curiosity piqued, stooped and ducked under the arch. At once they were in the uncomfortably close confines of a low and narrow wormhole tunnel that twisted and turned with barely enough room for a man to stand erect.

The tunnel fell away steeply, far more rapidly than Quentin thought safe; it seemed as if the tunnel would suddenly pitch down and he would find himself falling into a bottomless well. But Durwin seemed to have no fear, lurching along as quickly as his legs would carry him. So Quentin kept his fears to himself and followed dutifully along.

They came to a narrow place at the end of the tunnel. But Quentin saw Durwin turn sideways and disappear into a crack just wide enough to squeeze through. He, too, turned his shoulders and, holding his breath, scraped through the thin opening. As he came through, Quentin felt Durwin's hand on his arm; the hermit stooped and lay down the torch so that he could see that he only stood on a narrow ledge.

Then Durwin smiled at him in the glow of torch, his face gleaming with ferocious glee. "What is it, Durwin?" asked Quentin. He felt a thrill of excitement tingle along his spine. Quentin heard his own voice fall away from him, and he knew he must be standing before an enormous chasm.

"What is it? What is it indeed!" laughed the hermit. "I will show you." Durwin's voice sounded empty and metallic as it reverberated through the dark open space before them. Quentin crowded closer to the rock wall at his back.

The hermit took the torch and with a mighty heave sent it spinning off into the darkness beyond.

"No! Wait!" cried Quentin. His cry echoed back to him across a great distance. The torch tumbled and spun as it fell and fell, and Quentin saw the reflected flash of the fire on smooth surfaces as it plunged and at last was extinguished in a splash that sounded like ice splintering on a newly frozen pond.

"Watch," said Durwin breathlessly.

Quentin could see nothing and worried about the torch. How were they to find their way back again? But then a strange and wonderful thing happened.

As he watched, he imagined that he saw the stars of heaven come peeping out, one by one, into the darkness surrounding them. At first these stars were but the tiniest slivers of light, but they began to grow. "What . . . ?" began Quentin. He never finished the thought.

Above him the vaulted roof of the enormous chamber began to shine with a soft amber luminescence that blushed pink like a winter sunrise. The far walls held glimmering green traces like liquid light streaking down. The floor of the cavern far below shone with its own ghostly light in irregular splotches here and there, in seams of blue and gold. Within moments—though to Quentin it seemed like the slow dawning of day—the vast chamber was radiating light from all sides, and Quentin was swept away with incredulous joy.

"Durwin," he whispered.

"Yes, Quentin. We have found it. It is the lanthanil."

CHAPTER 47

By the fierce light of the Wolf Star, the sentinels watched them coming. Although it was the sixth hour of the night, the cold glow of the awful star cast a light as bright as the day upon the plain. The star had grown to fill the entire eastern sky, obliterating all lesser lights. And by the light of their savage star the Ningaal came to Askelon.

A messenger was dispatched to bring the king; he had ordered that he be notified, whatever the hour, when the enemy approached. The courier had scarcely left the battlements when he was back with Eskevar, grim and glowering in his sable-lined cloak, his golden dragon brooch and chain glittering in the streaming light. The embroidered silver figure of the dragon could be seen writhing on the back of the hooded cloak as it swirled out behind him. The king was wearing tall, red boots, and his sword hung at his side; those who saw him knew that he had not been to bed that night, but had been waiting and was ready to meet the enemy.

They were still a long way off as Eskevar glared defiantly out into the unnatural light. "Come to Askelon, you barbarian horde!" spat the king Eskevar. "Come and meet your doom!"

The commanders who had gathered around him exchanged worried glances, for Eskevar's countenance burned with a feverish mien like that of a ravening wolf. He cocked his head to them and said, "Rudd, there. And you, Dilg, and Fincher. The dragon sleeps while the enemy draws closer. He is under the hill, sleeping in his hall of stone, but not for long. He will awaken and defend his home. Never has the hand of an invader touched these walls, and none ever shall. The dragon will stop them. Yes, the dragon!"

The lords nodded in silence, afraid to break in on the king's ravings. Eskevar gripped the stone crenellation with both hands as if he were holding up the walls with his bare hands. "See how they come," he said slowly, every word ringing clear. "I feel their hated feet upon the land. I feel their evil intent deep in my inmost parts. But the dragon's heart is in me; it is of iron. I am not afraid."

The lords shrank away from the Dragon King. Even those who had served in the wars against Goliah had never seen him so. His eyes started from his head and his mouth was taut; his high, noble brow shone smooth and tight in the starlight.

"This is a wonder, is it not, my lords? Look upon it. See how willingly they come to the slaughter. See the accursed marching to their destruction. But have no pity for them, my lords. They deserve what they shall receive. They shall be cut down."

"This night is chill, Sire," said Rudd. He spoke hesitantly, for a number of soldiers had gathered around and were murmuring over the king's behavior. If it was to be whispered about that the king had lost his senses, their soldiers could not be expected to fight as they should when the time came. "Perhaps we should all wait within for a little. I would talk with you about our defenses."

Eskevar turned to them as if seeing them for the first time. "Eh? What is that you say?" He passed an unsteady hand over his brow, now beaded with sweat. Rudd felt a shudder shake the king's frame as he placed his hand on his elbow.

"Yes, come with us and tell us what orders you intend for us," urged Dilg, taking the king's other arm.

The two led him away from the battlements, and the other lords followed after dismissing the crowd that had gathered, saying, "Go to your posts. We will be in council with the king." Then they hurried after Eskevar and his escort so as not to raise suspicion among those who watched them pass.

Upon reaching the turret of the western tower, they were met by Queen Alinea, stepping out from the deep shadow of the doorway. "My queen," said Rudd. She read at once the sheepish looks of the nobles.

"Eskevar, I was just looking for you. Dismiss your commanders for yet a little while; let them go to their men. Or if you will, allow them to gather in the council chamber. I would talk with you, my husband. There is much to discuss before this night is through."

"Yes, Sire. We will talk soon. Send us back to our men that we may stir them to boldness with high words."

Eskevar did not notice what was being said. He only looked at his wife, who linked her arm in his and steered him back into the tower. "Yes, go to your men. Tell them we must be ready. We must be ready." The king turned away, his face white in the glaring light of the star. The lords of Mensandor, glad to be relieved of the responsibility for the king, though sick at heart for his most unusual condition, hurried back to their posts to reassure their men that the king was sound and would lead them when the time came. But in their hearts they wondered.

They stood on the floor of an enormous vault at the very roots of the mountain. Quentin stared wide-eyed like a child, blinking in utter disbelief. The magnificence of the chamber was beyond his ability to form words to give utterance to his thoughts. Toli, too, stood by him in mute wonder at the splendor of the subterranean treasury, for treasure it was.

Inchkeith had shouted for joy and gamboled like a kid down the long, winding ledge where they had entered the vault. He still darted here and there examining first one kind of ore formation, and then another. Durwin, by contrast, seemed almost sedate and restrained. But he was as excited as the others, Quentin knew. His jubilance took the form of speech—Durwin had not stopped talking since they had entered the vault the second time, bringing Toli and Inchkeith.

Quentin turned to the hermit, who was babbling about the various devices the Ariga had used to mine the lanthanil, and asked, "What was that you said about some sort of collapse at the main entrance?"

"Collapse? Oh, yes. I found the main entrance to this room, this castle, with no trouble. Our path led straight to it. But it was blocked by a fall of stone." He turned around, searching for the entrance, spied it, and pointed out across the expanse toward an opposite wall. "There, see all that rubble? It is there the entrance lies."

Quentin saw a tumbled mass of rock slabs and boulders, some as big as houses, that looked as if the tunnel had collapsed. "What happened there?" he asked.

"I can only guess, of course, but I imagine the Ariga blocked it off for some reason. They were far too skillful as miners to have allowed such a catastrophe to happen accidentally. I think they intended it. There came a time when they decided to close off this particular part of the mine."

"This part? This is where the lanthanil is."

"So it is! They had a reason for it; of that you can be certain. What that reason was I cannot say, any more than I can say how the Ariga vanished, or where they went. But leave it they did . . . for us to find."

"But it would have taken us years to dig through that confusion at the entrance. What made you think there would be another way in?"

"I do not think they determined to keep everyone out—just the curious, the fortune hunters and desecrators."

"I would never have thought of trying that hole in the wall. It looked like a drop to certain death to me. How did you think of it?"

Durwin smiled and shrugged. "I do not know. But if you believe that it was meant for us to find it, then we would have found it in any case. If the Most High had so wished, the mountains would have opened up before us!"

Toli had been scraping around the mounds of stone that sloped up from the floor, and he came gliding back to where Durwin and Quentin were talking. "Come with me," he said, pulling them away. "I have found something!" He ran away again with Quentin and Durwin tagging after him. As they rounded the heap of stone, Toli pointed to something that shimmered in the glowing light of the cavern.

"What is it?" asked Quentin, bending to get a better look.

"I think it is an anvil," Toli answered.

"An anvil like none I have ever seen."

"That is because it is gold! And look at these." The Jher stooped and began picking up objects from the floor, where they were arrayed as if waiting for the master to return and take up his work once more.

"Let me see those." Inchkeith pushed in and took two strange-looking objects from Toli. He turned them over in his hands and tested their heft.

"What are they? Tools?"

"Exactly," replied Inchkeith. His face shone with excitement. "But such tools! These are the tools of a great master craftsman. And they are made of gold, too. Imagine—thinking so little of gold that you would make tools of it! They are of very old and unusual design, but I can readily perceive their purpose. And look—here is a hammer."

"I recognize that at least. But it must be very heavy, and much too soft for a hammer." Quentin took the hammer from Inchkeith and tried it. The golden hammer was not as heavy as he expected; in fact, it was only slightly heavier than a hammer made of iron.

"Lanthanil can be worked with tools of any kind," the armorer explained. "It is wonderfully malleable. But gold does not diminish its power. Gold is the only substance which does not transmit the power of the metal. And the Ariga no doubt used a secret alloy to strengthen the gold for use as hammer and anvil.

"It was foolish of me to have brought those." Inchkeith gestured toward the pile of baggage that lay stacked on the floor a few paces away.

"Between these"—he shook the tools in his hand—"and the forge yonder, we have everything we need."

"The forge?" Quentin looked around. "I do not see a forge."

"There, set in the wall. Mind you, it does not look like one of our forges; it is more like a shrine. But I can tell what use it had. It is a forge."

Quentin felt very small and insignificant in the magnificent chamber. He turned his eyes once more toward its huge dome, glowing amber and green, and to the walls streaked with blue and violet veins, and to the floors suffused with red-gold and rose. He felt like a thief in a king's treasury, who might be caught at any moment and thrown out.

"Now, then. Here are the tools and anvil. The forge is close by. We lack only the ore and we can begin," said Durwin.

The words shook Quentin out of his reverie. He had forgotten all about their reason for coming, so taken was he with the otherworldly beauty of the Ariga vault. "Begin?"

"Yes," Durwin laughed. "We have a sword to make!"

CHAPTER 48

N o," instructed Durwin. "These will not do." He handed two shin-
ing green rocks back to Toli, whose eyes sparkled as he looked at them.
"Neither green, nor amber, nor blue, red, nor even gold is suitable.
Perhaps for chalices and utensils and the like, but not for the Zhaligkeer.
The Shining One must be made from white lanthanil, for it is the most
rare and possesses the greatest powers."

Quentin looked around. "I wondered why so much of the precious
rock lay about. It was the white the Ariga prized most."

"So it is! We will have to delve for it if we are to fashion a sword,"
Durwin stated. "For I have not seen a showing of white since we entered
here."

"Nor have I."

At Inchkeith's suggestion they spread out, each to a different quarter, to search for a vein of white ore among all the rainbow traces of colored lanthanil. Inchkeith schooled them on what to look for and how
to go about it, so that at the end of several hours' search, they were well
acquainted with the methods of the miners. But by the end of the entire
day's search, they were no closer to having found a speck of the rare
white ore.

The next day's search brought nothing but sore fingers and knees to
the miners. The following day was the same. Quentin considered these

periods of activity to be days since they were bound on each side by intervals of rest, but how long in duration they were, he could not say. At the end of it, as they sat before the small fire Toli had made in a ring of stones, frustrated and longing for sleep, Inchkeith grumbled to himself—a habit he had fallen into of late.

"What was that?" asked Durwin.

"Nothing," growled Inchkeith. He raised his cup once more to his mouth.

"You said something about the water," replied Durwin. "I think I would like to hear it again."

"I said this water tastes as stale as stone!" Inchkeith glared at the hermit with a look of smoldering exasperation.

"I think you may be right," said Durwin, tasting his water. "Very like stone."

"What is so odd about that?" inquired Quentin. He believed they were all beginning to show signs of strain and exhaustion. "We have been drinking this water for two days."

"Yes," added Toli, "ever since we emptied the skins we brought with us."

"Where did you fill them, Toli?" asked Durwin eagerly, leaning forward in the light of the fire.

"Why, at the pool over there. Just below where we entered. But it is safe enough. I tested it myself and found no ill effect. It is stale because it has been so long in the cave, away from sun and air."

"Then the pool is not fed by a spring?"

"I should say not. If it were, perhaps the water would have a fresher taste." Toli looked narrowly at Durwin.

"Why this sudden interest in our water? We have been drinking it some little while, as Toli says. It has brought no harm." Quentin shrugged, and as a show of confidence in Toli's judgment, he drained his cup.

Durwin stood abruptly. "Take me to the pool." No one moved. "At once!"

Toli rose and led him off. Inchkeith and Quentin stared at one another, mystified. "Well, we might as well trail along after them as wait here. I am ever amazed at the notions that hermit takes into his head. There will be no sleep until he is satisfied anyway."

So the armorer and Quentin followed the figures receding in the glowing half-light of the great vault. When they caught up with them, Durwin and Toli were down on hands and knees, peering into the ebony depths of a pool whose surface looked as hard and polished as black glass.

"No, I cannot see anything," sighed Durwin. "But I think we must try."

"Try what?" asked Quentin.

"I cannot be certain," began Durwin. "But . . ." He hesitated.

"Out with it, you pesky hermit. What do you suspect?"

"Only this, and it is a forlorn guess—that it would be very like the Ariga to further conceal their prize in a way that did not altogether hinder discovery."

"You think it is in the pool?" Quentin knelt and stared into the water in disbelief.

"Perhaps," intoned Durwin. "I did not say for certainty that it was."

"Bah!" said Inchkeith. "This is seepage water, nothing else. You will find nothing down there."

"Oh, do not be so sure. Have you seen any seepage or running water since we entered the mine?"

"A little, of course."

"Very little, sir. The Ariga miners knew their craft—far better than any miner living today. Water is a constant danger in a mine. But as you yourself have seen, no such hazard threatens this mine; the Ariga had ingenious ways of disposing of it. Therefore, I am inclined to believe that this pool is here for a purpose."

"Of a purpose or no," Inchkeith said, squinting into the fathomless depths, "how do you propose to delve down there?"

Durwin shook his head and stood. "That I do not know. But let me sleep on it. Perhaps something will come to me in my dreams."

They all went back to the place where Toli's fire still burned and pretended to try to sleep. But the attempt was far from effective because each had fallen prey to the puzzle of the pool: how to remove the water. So each tossed and heaved under their cloaks and thought about nothing but the pool and the white lanthanil that might lie buried in its black depths.

At last Quentin sat up and said, "It is no use. I cannot sleep, and if my ears tell me anything, they tell me no one else is sleeping either. We may as well talk about it."

"You are right," grunted Inchkeith. "There will be no rest until we have solved the riddle of how to get ore from a puddle."

"So it is," Durwin said, rising up. "Has anyone thought of a way?"

Blank stares met over the fire. It was clear that no one had any idea of how the mining operation might proceed.

Slowly Toli got to his feet. "There is only one way," he said. "I must go down there."

Silence followed the pronouncement. Toli's features had become a mask of fear and revulsion such as Quentin had never seen on his friend before, not even in battle. "Toli, there is no need; we will find another way."

"What way would that be?" Inchkeith muttered.

"We could drain it, or . . ." Quentin could not think of another way to suggest.

"You see, my way is best," said Toli softly. He appeared as a man going to his death.

"But——," Quentin started to object.

Durwin stopped him, saying, "No, I believe Toli is right. His is the only way. I see no reason to talk about it any longer. We might as well get on with it since no one feels like sleeping."

"No!" Quentin protested. "I will not hear of it, even if Durwin thinks it is the only way. If anyone must go, let it be me. It is supposed to be my sword, after all."

"Think of what you are saying." Durwin turned a steady gaze on Quentin that made him feel like a small child. "Are you fit to swim and wield a pick underwater? With your arm, what could you do?"

Durwin continued, "Who of us better than Toli? Inchkeith? Myself? No. Toli is right. He is the only choice. Of all of us, he has the best chance of succeeding."

"Then I will go with him," said Quentin hotly.

Durwin shrugged. "You may be of some help. All right. Let us begin."

Within a short time they were ready. Toli and Quentin stripped off their clothes and, wearing only their leather baldrics—to which had been attached long ropes, tools, and on an inspiration from Inchkeith, small pieces of glowing lanthanil so that they might be seen as they descended and worked in the inky depths—they stood on the brink, looking morosely into the pool as if Heoth himself waited below to embrace them in his icy grasp.

Durwin and Inchkeith held the ends of the ropes. "Remember, you have but to tug on the rope and we will pull you up in an instant. Do not try to swim—save your energy and lungs. It will allow you to work longer. The weight of the tools you carry should take you down quickly enough. Save your strength, both of you."

Toli said nothing. His countenance had hardened into features as cold and unreadable as the stones of a castle wall. Whatever he felt inside had been pushed far back into some remote corner of his being.

"This is a brave thing you are doing, my friend." Quentin put a hand on Toli's shoulder and felt the tenseness of the Jher's muscles. "Do not worry. I will be beside you."

Toli nodded briefly, never lifting his eyes from the pool. Then he took one step, and sank out of sight with scarcely a ripple. Quentin took a deep breath and followed, clutching his injured arm to his chest so that it would not float awry.

The shock of the icy water upon his bare skin almost caused Quentin to gasp at once. It felt like ten thousand dagger points tearing at his flesh. He swallowed air into his stomach, and bubbles spouted from his nose. An instant later he was numb to the icy assault of the chilling water. He opened his eyes as he drifted down and down into the black, silent, dreamlike void. He looked up to see the faintly luminescent glimmer of the cavern above as it receded and dimmed with his descent.

Close beside him Quentin could feel Toli's presence, though he could but faintly see his friend. At three spans or so below the surface of the water, they reached a sharp overhang and felt along this shelflike projection with their feet, almost walking along it, until it dropped off again. Underneath the shelf was a great hollow, or that was the impression Quentin received, for he could see nothing at all. Even the dim glow above was now obliterated beneath the overhanging rock ledge.

It was with some surprise that Quentin's feet touched smooth rock once more. Whether it was another rock ledge or the bottom of the pool he could not tell. But here it was that Toli decided to begin searching for the elusive white ore. Quentin felt a slight swirl of movement beside him and knew that Toli was inching forward toward the wall that he imagined was directly before them.

Quentin made to follow and immediately stubbed his toes against a lump of rock. The sudden pain caused him to lose some of his air as he stumbled awkwardly and slowly to his knees. With grace and ease he righted himself and weightlessly followed Toli, whose belt of glowing lanthanil he could just see before him.

Toli had reached the rock wall, and with a jarring bump Quentin reached it too. They had only been underwater for a few moments, though already it seemed like hours to Quentin. He wondered how Toli was taking it. Another swirl of movement, followed by a small clink, and he realized that Toli had wasted no time or motion and was already picking away at the surface of the rock face with one of Inchkeith's handpicks.

With his good hand Quentin fumbled at his baldric for a tool and followed Toli's example. He picked blindly away with the slow, cushioned movement of the swimmer. He could hear, like the clink of coins struck together, the tap of their tools upon the rock. After but a moment of this exertion, Quentin's lungs began to burn, and he reached out to signal to Toli that he was going up for air. Toli acknowledged his signal with one of his own. Quentin tugged on the rope and stepped back away from the rock wall. All at once he began ascending rapidly—so much so that he had to kick furiously in order to avoid the overhanging shelf above.

With a fizz of bubbles and a gasp, Quentin bobbed to the surface. Durwin and Inchkeith were peering down at him intently. "It is c-cold as ice down th-th-there!" Quentin chattered involuntarily.

"Can you see anything?" asked Durwin, ignoring the temperature report. "What is down there?"

"There is a rock ledge three or five spans below me here. Just under that is a space large enough for a man to stand and work. Whether it is the bottom or not, I cannot say. Toli is still there, but he should be up for air shortly."

"That sounds as good a place as any to begin looking," said Inchkeith eagerly. Quentin thought the old armorer would gladly have changed places with him if offered the chance; his face gleamed in the soft light of the vault with a glaze of intense anticipation.

"Toli is staying down too long," observed Quentin. He ducked his head beneath the water, but could catch no sign of Toli's glowing belt surfacing. Inchkeith still held Toli's rope slack in his hands.

"I shall fetch him; he has been down long enough."

"Yes, go and see what is keeping him. No need to overexert his lungs, even if he can swim like a fish." Durwin began paying out rope again, and Quentin dropped at once back into the cold, silent viscid world of the pool. Once below the rock ledge, Quentin could see the dimly shining belt of Toli just below. He pushed on as quickly as he could and approached his friend in long, weightless strides.

Quentin felt in the water for Toli's shoulder and, touching it, turned the Jher around. But Toli turned away again, and Quentin felt the swirl of motion and heard the odd, faraway clink that meant Toli was continuing with his picking.

Quentin, becoming worried for his friend, thought to grab Toli's rope and tug it himself and so get him hauled to the surface whether he wanted to go or not. As he reached for the rope, he saw something out of the corner of his eye.

He turned and saw a very faint spidery crack appear in the rock wall, as if a shining web of delicate silken strands was glowing there. He took up his own pick and, following Toli's lead, began chopping away at the rock before them, leaving Toli to his own judgment.

In a moment the black wall of rock before them crumbled away with a flash of silver, and there before them, blazing like the sun with cold brilliance, opened a vein of white lanthanil two hands wide.

Toli, quick as a snake, reached out and placed his hands on the radiant stone, and Quentin saw, in the inundating glare that so suddenly shone forth, Toli transformed. It seemed to Quentin, feeling so cold and unnatural in this watery grave of a place, that Toli suddenly appeared larger, stronger, and more noble.

He had little time to wonder about what he saw, for Toli was already hammering at the stone and breaking off a big chunk of the precious rock. Quentin had hardly blinked his eyes when Toli offered him a huge piece of white, shining ore. Quentin looked at it, strange in this underwater world, and at Toli, who was grinning in spite of himself. Already Quentin's lungs were beginning to burn again—it was time to surface. He wondered with amazement how Toli could remain submerged for such a time.

Quentin reached out to grasp the stone Toli offered him, with no more thought than to take it up to the surface for Inchkeith and Durwin to see, to tell them they had found their treasure at last. But as Toli tumbled the stone into his hands Quentin felt the shock of heat sear through his body like a flame. He tingled all over as if he had been struck by lightning, but the burning passed in an instant, leaving behind a warm glow of peace and well-being. Even the ache of his lungs vanished in that instant. He suddenly felt more alive and whole and at peace than ever in his life.

In that very same moment—though Quentin was never really certain, for it all happened so fast—he felt a long shiver course through his right arm. The arm tingled as if needles pierced it all over. And then, deep within his arm, in his very bones, he felt a strange warmth that grew and grew until he thought his bones were on fire.

But the fire left just as quickly, to be followed by a rush of soothing cold, as if water were running over his arm. This startled Quentin as much as the fire had, for it was the first time he had experienced any feeling in his arm in many long weeks. He looked at Toli in the weird, shining light, and Toli grinned knowingly back at him. He stretched out his hand to touch Toli's face, and the hand obeyed him once again. The fingers flexed, and the arm swung freely, though encumbered somewhat by the splint still attached to it.

Toli broke off another piece from the vein of blazing ore and jerked his hand upward, signaling for them to rise. Quentin had quite forgotten they were underwater; the urge to return to the surface had vanished the instant he touched the stone. But now he was eager to show their find to the others. So, quite forgetting to tug on the ropes, they began swimming to the surface.

Durwin and Inchkeith, growing apprehensive over the unusually long time the two had been down, were discussing whether to pull them up—especially Toli, who had not come up for breath at all.

Suddenly Durwin shouted, "Inchkeith! By my lights, look there!"

The armorer looked where the hermit was pointing and saw two bright objects, like the glowing white eyes of some monstrous sea creature, rising rapidly toward the surface. With a hop Inchkeith jumped back a step and threw his hands out before him, so strong was the illusion of a sea monster boiling up out of the pool.

But next the hermit's voice split the air like thunder that rolled and echoed through the vast cavern. "It is the lanthanil! Praise be to the God Most High! He has shown us his high favor! We have found it!"

Then, quite unceremoniously, Durwin began to hop about in a wild dance with Inchkeith while the two water-soaked, happy divers looked on.

CHAPTER 49

Upon the straining backs of groaning slaves, Nin advanced along the old river road from Lindalia on the western coast toward Askelon. Fifty thousand footmen followed in his train. The Arvin here ran bold and deep, and wide enough for those who could find boats—and even those who could not—to escape to the other side as Nin's terrible caravan passed by.

He had sat in his palace ship waiting just beyond the island, where the river mingled its waters with bright Gerfallon's. But his rage had flared and burned while he waited for word from his warlords that Askelon had fallen. When it was not forthcoming, the Supreme Deity of the Ningaal had decided to go himself and see to it that the end came swiftly.

He ordered his standing army of fifty thousand foot soldiers, waiting in their ships, to disembark upon the western coast, and then he had ordered his throne to be carried ashore. There he mounted his throne over the prostrate bodies of his slaves, and with a wide, generous sweep of his hand, ordered them ahead. Like an army of locusts, they cut down everything standing in their path: crops of fields, the hovels of peasants, small villages. Nothing deterred them, and no one lifted a hand to prevent them.

By night and by day they marched, tirelessly, relentlessly, inexorably drawing nearer and nearer to Askelon.

By night and day the evil Wolf Star shone in the heavens. By day it could be seen shining low on the horizon, a bright spot appearing as a tiny second sun. By night it nearly assumed the brightness of the sun itself, transforming night into an eerie, mocking reflection of the day just passed. Unnatural shadows stood upon the land; birds fell silent in the trees, and animals huddled in the fields, uncertain whether to sleep or graze; the masses, crouching in temple courtyards and castle wards across the land, wailed with fear and covered their heads.

And Nin marched on toward Askelon.

In Askelon the lords met secretly and discussed the strange behavior of the king. Some said it was the star that had driven him mad, that it had touched him as it had touched the people cowering within Askelon's mighty walls. Others said his illness was upon him again. They all worried together what would happen if their knights and soldiers should find out that the Dragon King would be unable to lead them in battle, for none of them held the slightest hope that they could long endure the siege. Sooner or later they must meet the enemy on the field to defeat him. Desperately they hoped Eskevar would be recovered in time to lead them, if only for a show to the men, for they were certain the fateful battle was drawing swiftly nearer.

"Is there any word?" asked Eskevar anxiously. He seemed composed and in his right mind, resting peacefully in his bed. Biorkis and the queen stood by him as the lords entered his chamber.

Lord Rudd, who had taken it upon himself to speak for the rest of the lords, approached the king's high bed.

He knelt, saying, "Sire, we have had no word, and now the opportunity for such is gone. The warlords of Nin have surrounded the castle on all sides. They occupy the plain below the rock and have taken the town as well. They have as yet not dared to draw near the ramp, but that will come soon, I have no doubt. Askelon is besieged."

"So it has begun," sighed Eskevar wearily. "I had hoped a messenger might come from the lords to the north to bring word of their decision to join us."

"It is too late, I fear. Even if a messenger came now, he would not get through the enemy. But even so, the lords might still come." Lord Rudd glanced at his peers and hastily added, "We would seek a boon, Sire."

"You shall have it," replied Eskevar. "Ask it and it is yours."

"We would have you come and speak to the knights and men, Your Majesty. There are rumors . . ." Rudd fell silent, feeling he had said too much.

"Rumors? Ah, yes, what are they? You need not fear to anger me. I know full well the rumors voiced about."

Rudd looked nervously to the others for help.

"Well?" demanded Eskevar, his temper rising. "Speak, man!"

"Some say that you are changed, Sire. That you do not have the will to fight—"

"They say that I am insane! That is what you mean. Say it is so!"

"It is so, my lord." Rudd lowered his head.

Eskevar made a move as if to leap out of bed. "Please, Sire!" Biorkis jumped to life. "Stay abed but a little and regain your strength."

"Listen to him, my lord," pleaded Alinea, rushing up. She threw a dark, disapproving look at the unhappy lords, who made a move as if to withdraw at once.

"No!" Eskevar held up a hand toward the priest and his queen. "Do not hinder me. I will go with my lords to speak to the soldiers. They must have no doubts, nor harbor despair in their hearts for their king. I will show them I am neither ill nor afraid."

He turned to the lords. "Assemble the knights and men in the inner ward. I will speak to them from the battlements of the inner curtain and will pass among them when I have spoken to quell their fears and apprehensions. They will see me and will know I am with them and will lead them."

The lords, anxious to be away from that room, bowed as one and rushed out to begin bringing their troops together. When they had gone, Biorkis and Alinea came close to the king and helped him up.

"You are so weak, my king," Alinea sobbed. Tears filled her green eyes and ran freely down her cheeks.

"Let me tell them you will come tomorrow," suggested Biorkis. "Rest just this night, and you will feel stronger."

"No, it cannot be. Tomorrow may be worlds away. I must go at once. The rumors must not be allowed to persist if I can stop them, for they would eat away my soldiers' hearts. A soldier needs his heart if he is to fight for his homeland. I must go."

Leaning heavily on their arms, he stumbled toward the door. When they reached it, Eskevar squared his shoulders and raised his head. "I will walk alone," he said, and went out.

When he had gone, Alinea turned tearfully to Biorkis. "He should never have gone into battle, Biorkis. He was just getting better. He exerted himself overmuch and has not recovered his strength, and . . . and, oh, now I fear he never will!" She buried her face in her hands. "If Durwin were here, he would know what to do," she sobbed.

Biorkis wrapped one arm around her slim shoulders and comforted her. "Yes, Durwin would know what to do, but he is not here. We will have to think what he would do in our place, and then do it."

"I am sorry," sniffed Alinea. She raised her eyes to the kindly old priest's. "I did not mean to belittle you. Your help has been most valuable. I just—"

"Say no more. I, too, wish Durwin were here. He has far more knowledge of the world and men than I. I have been too long on my mountain, removed from the ways of mortals, and I feel old and useless. Let us hope that Durwin will return soon."

"Let us pray that he does."

"Yes, my lady. By all means let us pray that he does."

Eskevar went out from the eastern tower and strode along the battlements in the cold, mocking light of the star. His great cloak swept like a huge, dark wing after him, the silver dragon device glittering in the strange light. Theido and Ronsard marched gravely by his side, and when they had reached the midpoint along the inner curtain battlements, Eskevar stopped and looked down at the ranks of soldiers that had been assembled to hear him speak.

As he looked down upon them, seeing their fearful faces turned upward to his, seeking strength there, and wisdom and assurance, he felt very old and tired. They were sapping him, he thought, and it was as if he felt his strength ebbing away even as he gazed down upon them. He felt too tired, too used up, to speak.

But they were waiting, watching him. His men were watching and waiting for him to banish their fears. How could he do that, he wondered, when he could not banish his own? What words were there? What magic could make it happen?

Without knowing what he would say, Eskevar opened his mouth and began to speak, his voice falling down from on high like the voice of a god.

He spoke and heard his voice echoing back into the small places of the inner ward. Murmurs arose in response to his words, and Eskevar feared he had said something wrong, that he had run afoul of his own purpose. But he spoke on, oblivious to the words that tumbled from his mouth unbidden. *They are right*, he thought bitterly. *The king is insane. He is babbling like an idiot from the battlements and does not know what he is saying.*

The murmurs changed gradually to shouts and then to cheers. As Eskevar's last words died away, the inner ward yard erupted in shouts of acclaim and hearty cheers and battle cries. Then suddenly the soldiers were singing an ancient battle song of Mensandor, and somehow he,

Eskevar, was moving through the thronging soldiers, touching them and being touched by them.

The Dragon King stood among his troops, bewildered by their cheers and high acclaim. He was humbled, realizing he did not know what he had said; he was gratified, knowing that his words had been the right ones.

The cheers and songs had not run their courses when they were interrupted by a sound not heard in Askelon for five hundred years. *Boom!* The sound rolled away like hollow thunder. *Boom! Boom!* It came again, and all around the Dragon King became silent. The cheering stopped; the singing shrank away. *Boom! Boom! Boom!*

The Ningaal had brought a battering ram to the gates of Askelon. The siege war had begun.

CHAPTER 50

I can scarcely believe it still," Quentin said, flexing his arm. "It is as if it had never been injured at all. Better even! And look; the skin is not withered, and the muscle is firm."

Toli, standing near as Durwin unwrapped the bandages and removed the splints, replied, "I can well believe it. The stories of old were true ones. The Healing Stone still exists."

The two glowing lumps of rock shimmered like fiery white coals fresh from the fire as they lay beside the black pool. Durwin finished examining Quentin's arm and satisfied himself that, indeed, it was whole and healthy once more. "So it is!" the hermit said, still prodding Quentin's arm with his fingers. "Your arm is healed most wonderfully. If I had not set it myself, I would say that it was never broken."

Durwin cocked his head to one side and observed Quentin closely. "I see nothing now that would prevent you from lifting the Zhaligkeer. Do you?"

With a thrill like the touch of a spark to the skin, Quentin remembered all his old misgivings, which he had succeeded in putting far out of his mind. In an instant they all rushed back upon him like a flood, quenching his excitement of the moment. Something like fear grabbed him in his gut and squeezed with an iron grip.

"Do you still think I am the one?"

"Why do you fear? You have already chosen to follow the Most High. This is the way he has set for you. Do not turn away from it."

Quentin stood looking at the blazing stones. "But the prophecy . . . It is . . ." Words failed him.

"You think that you will be alone? Is that it? Ha! You will not rid yourself of us that easily. We will be ever at your side. Do not think the Most High makes his servants tread only lonely paths. His ways are more clearly seen with the help of others of like spirit. He has given us to you, as you have been given to us, that we might help each other."

"Take it, Quentin. It is for you." Durwin threw out a hand toward the white stones, and Quentin slowly, reluctantly bent toward them and picked them up.

"Yes, I will take it. I will claim the Zhaligkeer." So saying, he lifted the stones high over his head as if he already had a sword in his hands. "Inchkeith! Let us begin. Time is drawing short. There is a sword to be made!"

But when they looked around, Inchkeith was not to be seen.

Boom! Boom! The sound of the ram against the gates thundered on and on. The peasants who had crowded into Askelon to escape the enemy screamed in terror at every dreadful knell. The outer wards were roiling in panic.

Archers had mounted to the gatehouse barbican and were endeavoring to pick off the Ningaal plying the massive battering ram against the drawn bridge of the castle. Occasionally an arrow would strike home, and an enemy warrior would tumble off the narrow plank they had thrown over the chasm that divided the end of the ramp from the castle; despite this annoyance the Ningaal were not greatly hindered. They were protected by the ironclad roof over their implement, and any unlucky wretch who chanced to show himself too openly was replaced in a trice by another. So the drumming continued on and on and on.

"Call off the archers," said Theido, gazing down from the battlements. "We may as well save our arrows. They are not going to prevail against the gate. No one ever has."

"We could pour fire down upon them," suggested Rudd, wearing a worried expression. "That would get rid of them."

"And it would also burn down our own gates!" snapped Ronsard irritably.

"I do not think even fire would harm those gates," mused Theido, shaking his head. "But I could be wrong. Still, it would be better not to take an unnecessary chance. We will wait to see what they try next.

"They cannot tunnel beneath the walls, for they rise out of solid rock, and the mountain is stone as well. The postern gate is well protected, and the maze of walls leading to it prevents the use of a ram such as this. Our archers can keep them at bay there, too. My guess is they must find a way through that gate and that gate alone, for there is no other way into Askelon Castle."

As he finished speaking, the Ningaal took up their pounding again. *Boom! Boom!* The timbers of the gate shuddered with each massive blow, but held firm.

Theido turned away from the battlement, and Ronsard followed him, after instructing his officers to bring him word if the situation should change in any way.

"Theido, I would talk with you awhile," he said, falling into step beside his friend. "Let us go inside where we may speak freely."

They strode to a nearby barbican and went inside, ascending to a higher platform of the round turret to look out over the plain and the city below. From that lofty vantage they could see the better part of one side of the castle and a portion of the second side. The Ningaal had indeed surrounded the castle on all sides, being most heavily deployed around the main gates and throughout the town. They had set fire to sections of the city, and the smoke swept up in black columns to streak the sky above.

"It is an evil day." Ronsard turned a careworn visage to his friend. "How is Eskevar faring?"

"He is the same. No change."

Eskevar had nearly collapsed when the sound of the ram commenced. It was as if each blow had been so aimed as to strike directly at the king's heart. It was only with difficulty that the two knights had led their sovereign away without the soldiers witnessing his fall. Upon gaining the security of the tower, they had all but carried him to his chambers. Biorkis and Alinea had been in attendance since then, and the knights had returned to watch through the day-bright night as the Ningaal strove to batter down the doors.

"Will he ride, do you think?" asked Ronsard.

"Why do you ask me? You have stood with him in battle enough times to know. But we are under siege! Why does everyone insist upon talking about battlefields and riding?" Theido snapped. After a long, silent moment in which Ronsard merely looked back at him sadly, Theido sighed. "Forgive me, my friend. I am tired. I have not slept in three days—one cannot even tell day from night anymore! I am tired."

"Go and rest. Let me take your watch. You yourself have said that nothing will happen soon. Have something to eat, and lay yourself down a little. You will feel better."

"Yes, perhaps I should do that." Theido turned his eyes away toward the north. "They should be coming. They should have been here by now."

"They will come. And do not forget that Quentin, Toli, and Durwin are abroad. Theirs is some errand that will make good; of that I am certain."

"So I believe. I only hope they are in time." He smiled briefly and gripped Ronsard by the shoulder. "Thank you. I will rest a bit as you suggest. It has been a long time since I endured a siege. I have forgotten my manners almost completely."

"You have forgotten nothing, my friend. Go now, and I will send for you if anything changes."

When Theido had gone and his footsteps descending from the barbican could no longer be heard, Ronsard settled himself against the stone crenellation of the turret. He looked long and hungrily to the north for the shining armies he hoped he would see riding to their rescue. But the far vista shimmered instead with the heat of the summer sun. Nothing moved out on the plain.

Still, the knight watched and waited, and his thoughts became a prayer, turning toward the new god he had so recently elected to serve.

"God Most High," Ronsard mumbled, "I do not have the knowledge of your ways that others do. But if you need a strong sword, here I am." There was a long lapse before he spoke again. "I know not how to pray in seemly words. I have never been a man of prayers. But I believe you helped me once, long ago, so I pray you will listen to me once again. Lead us against this terrible host which gathers at our gates and seeks to destroy us. And if it is my lot to die, so be it. But let me face the moment like a true knight and seek to save another's life before my own."

He prayed on, pouring out his heart as the words came to him, and would have continued praying but for the alarm that brought him instantly to his feet and sent him off to meet a new disaster.

CHAPTER 51

They found Inchkeith huddled behind a hill of stone far away from the pool. All wondered at his odd behavior in hiding and the look of fear that twisted his features as he raised his eyes to meet them.

"What is wrong, Inchkeith? Why did you disappear like that?" asked Quentin. The master armorer peered at his discoverers with a distrustful look. His hands trembled as he worked up the nerve to speak.

"Do not make me touch it! I beg you, sirs! Do not make me touch it!" He hid his face in his hands once more, and his shoulders shook as if he were sobbing.

"This is very strange," remarked Quentin, turning to Toli and Durwin. The hermit gazed with narrowed eyes upon the huddled body of the deformed man.

"I think I know what ails him. He is afraid to touch the blazing white lanthanil; he has seen its power and what it can do. He saw your arm healed, and he fears what it might do to him."

"But," Quentin spluttered in amazement, "certainly you are wrong here, Durwin. If anything, he should rejoice and rush to take it into his hands that he might be healed of his crippling deformity. I would, and so would anyone else, I think."

"Would you?" asked Durwin. His bushy eyebrows arched high as they would go. "Think again. His twisted spine cripples him, yes. But he has lived his life with it and has come to accept it and himself for what he is. His spirit has risen above his physical limitations in the beauty of his craft. There is strong pride in that."

"To be healed, to be made strong and whole again—what can be the harm of that?" Quentin shook his head slowly from side to side. The thing was a mystery to him.

"Quentin, have you never had a flaw of some sort, a hurt that you carried with you?" Quentin's brow wrinkled sharply. "You cursed it and fretted over it and longed to cast it aside, and yet you secretly caressed it and held it close lest it should somehow slip away. For that weakness was part of you, and however hateful it was, it defined you; you took strength from it. With it, you knew who you were; without it, who could say what you would be?"

Quentin answered slowly. "Perhaps it is as you say, Durwin. When I was a child, I held many childish flaws and weaknesses as virtues. But I put them away when I became a man."

"Ah, yes. But your weaknesses were not of the same kind as Inchkeith's. His is not so easily put aside. How much more must he fear losing the thing—ugly as it is—that has given him such comfort all the long years of his life? It is no wonder that he shrinks away from the Healing Stone. For though he would give anything in his power to be made straight and strong, he would give much more to remain as he is."

Quentin turned to regard Inchkeith where he sat a little way off, still huddled and trembling. There were no words to describe the pitiful picture that met his gaze. Sadly, he turned away from it.

"Go and ready yourselves for another dive," suggested Durwin. "I will talk to him a little and convince him that whether he touches the stone or not, the decision is his. We will not think less of him for refraining if that, in the end, is how he chooses. Go on, now. We will be along directly."

Quentin and Toli did as Durwin told them and returned to the pool. "Look how they shine, Toli," marveled Quentin as he knelt before the two lumps of glowing rock. "Have you ever seen anything like it? It is as if they burn with an inner fire. They should be hot to the touch, but they are cool."

"They possess very great power. Of that there is no doubt. I understand now why the Ariga closed off the mine and concealed what was left of the white lanthanil in the pool. The temptation to wield such power must drive men mad."

Quentin nodded silently. "I wonder what else the stone can do?" he asked at last. His bright face shone in the aura of the stones.

"We shall see, Kenta. You have been chosen to carry the Shining One; you will find out."

In a moment Durwin came, leading a sheepish Inchkeith toward them. "Very well, shall we continue? We have much work to do and have only begun."

"One moment, Durwin. Please, I would speak." Inchkeith held up his hand. "I am ashamed of my behavior, and you would do a kindness to a foolish old man if you would banish it from your minds. I am sorry to have embarrassed my friends so. I promise I will embarrass you no further."

"Think no more on it, Master Inchkeith," replied Quentin happily. "I assure you, it is already forgotten, and you shall never hear of it from our lips again."

They all returned to work as before and threw themselves into their labors. The energizing force of the ore-bearing stones that Quentin and Toli brought up allowed the two divers to remain underwater for greater periods of time, and before long a fair-sized pile of the shining stone was heaped beside the pool.

When the heap had grown to the size of a pyramid half a man high, Inchkeith called a halt to the diving. "This is enough for our purpose, I believe. If this magic stone is similar to other ores I have worked, we should have enough to make a sword and a scabbard and chain, too."

Quentin and Toli dragged themselves out of the frigid water and dried themselves. Inchkeith left them to hobble to the forge at the far end of the cavern. "Bring the lanthanil when you are ready. I will begin firing the crucible."

Filling Inchkeith's empty tool chest with ore, Quentin and Toli carried it to the forge, where, using fuel he had found neatly stored away beside the forge, Inchkeith had a fire roaring and ready. Durwin busied himself preparing food for them, as it appeared there would be no sleep for any of them for some time.

When Toli and Quentin had filled the crucible with ore, it was rendered into the fire, where a curious transformation took place. The stones did not crack and release their ore as the stones bearing copper and iron do. Instead, they were slowly melted away like ice in the spring when plunged into running water. Using a long rod, Inchkeith poked and stirred the molten lanthanil, causing the impurities to flame into hot ash and ascend to the chimney of the furnace. With long tongs he introduced new ore into the crucible and kept his ceaseless vigil at the fire, maintaining a constant temperature.

This activity continued for a long time, during which the others watched and dozed and ate by turns. At last Inchkeith pulled the crucible white-hot from the flames and gingerly set it down.

"Quickly, now!" he shouted. "Take up the forger's yoke and lend a hand. Step lively!"

Quentin was nearest at hand and took up the tool Inchkeith had indicated—a long iron utensil with two handles and a circular bulge in the center. Inchkeith took the yoke and placed it over the crucible, directing Quentin to take one of the handles and carefully follow his instructions. Quentin did as he was told, and they proceeded to pour out the molten ore, now a shimmering pale blue like liquid silver, into four long, narrow molds that Inchkeith had arranged along the floor. There remained a fair amount of the precious metal when the four molds were filled, so Inchkeith poured the rest into a sheet mold, and then they sat down to wait for the metal to cool.

Waiting for the glowing lanthanil to cool was like waiting for an egg to hatch, Quentin thought. But at last the four rod molds were judged cool enough. Inchkeith took up a dipper of water and poured it over the still-hot metal, sending billows of steam rising into the dimly luminescent air of the cavern. He then broke apart the molds and, with tongs, and heavy gloves on his hands, drew out four square rods nearly four feet in length.

The master armorer hopped to his anvil, took each rod, and pierced one end; then he joined the rods together by passing a rivet cut from the sheet of lanthanil he had made.

"Now, then. I have done all I may do," he said, holding up the four newly fastened rods for the others to see. "Durwin tells me that you must do the rest, Quentin."

Quentin rose to his feet. "Me? You jest! I know as much about making a sword as I would know of making a tree!"

"Then it is time you learned. Come here." Inchkeith held the rods in the tongs and indicated for Quentin to take them. Quentin stepped forward, looking to Durwin for approval. Durwin waved him on, and Quentin took the rods.

"Now, do not think for a moment that I will allow you to mar my greatest masterpiece, young sir. I will guide your hands to even the smallest movement. I will be your brain and your eyes, and you will do as I direct to the utmost. Do you understand?"

Quentin nodded obediently, and they began to work.

Under Inchkeith's watchful eye he took hammer and tongs and began to braid the still malleable metal, one rod over the other, in a tight square braid. When he had finished the task, sweat was dripping from his face and his bare arms. He had long since stripped off his shirt and tunic and wore only his trousers.

The braided rods were then thrust into the pit of the forge among the burning embers, and Quentin turned the core—as Inchkeith called it—constantly, while the armorer plied the creaking bellows.

Soon the core began to glimmer blue-white once more, and Quentin pulled it from the fire, his own face glowing red and flushed. Taking the core, he placed one square end into the square hole in the side of the golden anvil and with the tongs began to twist the braid together.

He twisted and twisted, winding and winding until he could twist no more. Then Inchkeith let him stop, and the core was plunged back into the pit of embers and heated to blue-white once more. Then came more twisting and still more. Quentin was exhausted and feeling more so all the time, but the rhythm of the work began to steal over him, and he found he entered a free-floating state where he moved in concert with the master armorer's wishes—so much so that he began to feel as if it were Inchkeith's will directing his hands and muscles and not his own.

The braided core was twisted again and again until, by the very tension of the coils, it began to fuse together. When it had fused completely, Inchkeith had Quentin cut the long, thin core in two, for it had nearly doubled in length with all the twisting. One half was then set aside, and the other half was pounded flat on the golden anvil with the hammer of gold. Every time Quentin struck the core, dazzling sparks showered all around and a flash like lightning was loosed.

The flattened core was heated and pounded, heated and pounded time and again until it was very thin and flat. Then it was set to cool. Toli was given the task of dousing it with water numerous times to cool it more quickly.

Taking the length of twisted braid that had been set aside, Quentin thrust it into the forge pit to reheat it. He then began twisting it again and again, drawing it out into a thin rod. This rod was pinched in half as well, and these two pieces, along with the cool flat piece, were thrust into the burning coals once more as Inchkeith explained that the repeated heating and cooling of the metal tempered it and made it stronger, as did the braiding of the original rods. "You have then the strength of four blades, not just one," he crowed. "This is how the legendary blades of old were made. There is a tension in the twisting of the braid that is never undone.

This tension is what makes the sword leap to the hand and sing in the air. No common blade forged of a rod and flattened can stand against it."

When the three long pieces were once more burning with blue brilliance and crackling with sparks, they were withdrawn. Quentin was so absorbed in his work it seemed as if he walked in a dream; all his surroundings blurred, becoming faint and insubstantial as he toiled on. His eyes had sight only for the flaming blue metal turning under his hands.

The three hot pieces were placed precisely upon the anvil according to Inchkeith's exacting specifications. With quick, sure hammer blows, Quentin welded the two rounded pieces to the flat one. This action resulted in a very long, flat piece with a rounded ridge in the center. When that was done, Inchkeith sent him to plunge the core into the pool and leave it there until it could be handled freely.

Quentin hurried off, so absorbed that he nearly stumbled over the curled figures of Durwin and Toli rolled in their cloaks, fast asleep.

After a time Inchkeith came and settled himself down beside Quentin to wait. "You are doing a master's job, sir. A master's job. If you were not spoken for, I would take you in and teach you the armorer's craft. You have the heart for it and the soul; I have seen how you look upon your work. You know what I am talking about, eh?"

"It is true. I have never done anything like this, but it is as if I feel in my hands what the metal would have me do, and I do it—though you must take credit there, for I would not begin to know what to do. But when I lift the hammer and I see it fall, a voice says 'Strike here!' and it is done." Quentin lifted the core from the pool. Water slithered down its pale blue surface and slid back into the pool in shining beads. "It does not look very like a sword yet," remarked Quentin.

"Oh, it will. It will. The work is just begun. Now we will see how this metal works. Now will come the test!"

Inchkeith and Quentin worked on and on, pausing to take a little food now and then, and to rest only in idle moments, though there were few of those. Toli and Durwin looked on and uttered words of encouragement when such words were needed, but mainly kept themselves out of the way and silent, allowing the master and his eager apprentice to work on undisturbed.

There was much heating and cooling, hammering and shaping of the gleaming metal. It was chiseled and chased, beaten and burnished, until at last the blade of a sword could be seen emerging from the long, flat length of metal. A hilt and handle were fashioned from the solid sheet that had been put aside. From this a flat piece was rolled and flattened, and it, too, was twisted and twisted and then joined to the emerging blade.

The blade was fired and refired. Each time it was scraped smooth and filed again and again with long, careful strokes. Inchkeith bent his face over the hot metal and directed Quentin's fingers here and there along the length, pointing out minute flaws that only he could see. If his young apprentice's strength and enthusiasm flagged, the old master's never did. With praise and threats and stubborn demands, Inchkeith challenged Quentin to better and higher work, at one point taking Quentin's hands in his own and guiding them over the blade to do the job he knew must be done.

And then it was finished.

Quentin sat exhausted on a large rock and looked at his handiwork as it lay across the golden anvil. Inchkeith studied it carefully, nodding and puffing out his cheeks alternately. Durwin and Toli were nowhere to be seen. Quentin's eyes burned in his head, and though tired, he watched Inchkeith's every wink and frown with breathless anticipation.

At last the master craftsman turned to Quentin, his face beaming, his chest swelling with pride. "Yes, it is finished." He hesitated, seeing Quentin hungrily grasp at his words. "And it is a masterpiece."

Quentin leaped and shouted for joy. "We have done it!" he cried. "We have done it!" He grabbed the old man and began dancing around the forge where they had lived and worked and sweated for what seemed years on end. They were so caught up in the relief and exultation of the moment that they did not hear Durwin and Toli return.

"Does this unseemly exhibition mean that you two have finished your labors at last?" Durwin called, bounding forward to clap them both on the back. He stopped, and a look of reverent awe lit his eyes. Toli, coming hard on his heels, stopped and began speaking in his native tongue.

"It is——" Durwin searched for words. "It is indeed a thing of fearsome beauty." His hands flew up toward his face as if he feared the sight would burn him.

"It is the Zhaligkeer," said Toli. "It is the Shining One."

Quentin took it from the anvil and held it in his hand, lifting it toward heaven. "This is the Shining One of the Most High. Let it move as he alone directs. As I am his servant, let it be filled with his power, and let our enemies fly before its terrible fury."

"So be it!" shouted the others. Durwin stepped up and brought out a vial from the leather pouch at his side.

"I have kept this for this time. It is oil which has been blessed in Dekra. With it I will anoint the blade of the Shining One."

Quentin held the sword across the palms of both hands as Durwin opened the vial and poured the holy oil along the length of the blade, which shone with a pale, silvery blue light. The sword was indeed a thing of dread beauty. It was long and thin, tapering almost imperceptibly along its smooth, flawless length to a gleaming point. The grip and hilt sparkled as if cut from gemstone.

As Durwin poured out the oil, he blessed the sword, saying, "Never in malice, never in hate, never in evil shall this blade be raised. But in righteousness and justice forever shall it shine." Then he took his fingers and rubbed the oil over the finely worked blade.

As he touched the shining metal, Durwin felt the power of the lanthanil flow through him, and it was as if the years fell away from him; he was a young man again and marveled at the sensation, for he had quite grown used to his numerous aches and pains. When he turned to the others, he was the same Durwin as before, but vastly changed in aspect. He appeared wiser, stronger, and more noble than before. He laughed out loud and pointed a long finger at Inchkeith, who gazed at him with some alarm, seeing the sudden change that had come over the hermit.

"Look there, Inchkeith, my friend. The blade has worked its enchantment upon you as well, I see."

Inchkeith, aghast, sputtered, "What are you talking about? I never touched the stone, nor the blade. What do you mean?"

Quentin looked at the hunchbacked armorer and saw that he was standing erect and tall; he seemed to have grown several inches. How or when it had happened he had not noticed. Perhaps when the master had placed his hands upon Quentin's, the power had gone into him; but they had been so completely absorbed in their work, they had not noticed until Durwin pointed it out to them just at that moment.

"Yes!" shouted Quentin. "You are healed, Inchkeith. You are whole."

A look of stunned disbelief shone on the craftsman's face; he squared his shoulders and raised his head. It was minutes before he would believe that his hump had disappeared, but when that belief finally broke in upon him, he sank to his knees and began to cry.

"Your god has done this, Durwin!" he cried as tears of happiness streamed down his face. "I believe now. I believe all you ever told me about him. Blessed is the Most High. From now on I am his servant."

They all rejoiced together, and the high-domed roof of the great cave echoed with their voices. The halls of the Ariga, deep beneath the mountains, rang with joyful sounds such as had not been heard in ten thousand years.

CHAPTER 52

When Ronsard arrived at the gatehouse barbican, he was met by the worried glances of his officers and Lord Rudd. "What is it?" he asked. "What is the alarm?"

"I ordered it," explained Rudd. "Look down there. They are bringing some machine up the ramp."

Ronsard looked down and saw that what Rudd had said was quite true; two hundred or more Ningaal were laboring with ropes and poles to drag an enormous device up the ramp. The battering ram had been taken away, and this lumbering object was being wheeled with great exertion to assume its place before the gates.

"What is it?" a perplexed Ronsard asked. "I have never seen anything like it."

"I cannot say I have seen such a machine in war either. But I can tell you I do not like the look of it, whatever it is."

"Direct the archers to hinder them as much as possible. I have no doubt it would be better if it never reached the gates. I will fetch Biorkis; I would have him look at it. Something tells me that thing down there belongs more to his ken than ours."

Shortly the lord high marshal was back at the battlements, dragging a blustering priest behind him. "What do you make of that?" Ronsard asked as they peered over the stone ramparts onto the activity below.

"It is a strange thing indeed!" said Biorkis, pulling on his braided beard. "Very strange."

His old eyes gazed upon the massive black object inching its way up the long incline under a hail of arrows. Its black skin shone with a dull luster in the sunlight, and two great arms thrust forward, palms upward as if to receive the supplications of the castle dwellers. It stood with the legs and torso of a man, one leg thrust forward, bent at the knee, the other stretched straight behind. But its face and head were its most distinguishing features, next to its size, for it bore the head and mane of a lion and the gaping maw of a jackal with a jackal's sharp fangs bared in a furious, frozen snarl of rage. Two huge black horns swept out from either side of its hideous black head, and its unblinking eyes stared angrily ahead as it groaned forward under its immense weight.

Ronsard's archers were causing much consternation among the enemy, but not as much as Ronsard would have liked; for no sooner had one rope-bearer fallen than another sprang forward to take his place. Soon those in the forefront had been provided with shields that they held over their heads to fend off the deadly rain, and the arrows rattled harmlessly down, striking only at random and seldom causing any mortal hurt. Ronsard called for the arrows to cease, but for the archers to remain alert to any target careless enough to present itself. Still the thing inched forward.

"Well?" asked Ronsard. "What say you, Biorkis?"

"Undoubtedly it is an idol of some sort. But to which god I am uncertain. I have never seen it before, and the thing that puzzles me is this: what kind of idol is it that it is taken into war to do battle with men? What kind of god do these Ningaal worship?"

"Why should that puzzle you? Men are always calling on their gods to lead them in battle, to deliver the victory into their hands, as you well know. This is only slightly more obvious, I will warrant, but it is the same."

"Yes, it is the same, and not the same at all. This is more primitive and more savage. It is a thing unholy and evil. Even the gods of the earth and sky are offended by such as this. It belongs to a long-distant time and place, back in man's darker past. It is evil, and it breeds evil."

"But does it have any power?" asked Ronsard. Biorkis looked at him oddly. "You know what I mean. Of itself—is it a thing of power?"

Biorkis thought for a moment before answering. "That I cannot say with certainty. Your question is perhaps more difficult than you know." He fingered his white beard as he gazed at the monstrous thing.

"An idol is but wood or stone," the priest continued. "It is the image of the god it represents. Images do not often have power, except for the ones who worship them, and then the power can be very great indeed."

"This one has power," said a gruff voice behind them. Ronsard and Biorkis turned to see Myrmior standing behind them. "And, yes, it is evil. Well I know it, for I have seen it work often enough. It is an idol, yes. But its purpose is far more coldly cunning than you suspect. It is foremost a machine of war, known in other lands as Pyrinbradam—a fire-breather."

A glimmering of understanding appeared in Ronsard's eyes. "If that is true, I will order water to be brought up at once."

"It would be wise," Myrmior assented. "Wet skins, if you have them, might offer some protection."

Ronsard called his officers to relay his orders and see that they were carried out. Water was to be poured over the gates and wet skins draped across them in an effort to reduce their flammability.

"Is there nothing else that may be done?" he asked.

"Nothing but to wait. Wait and pray," muttered Myrmior.

The waiting began and lasted for twelve long days. And each of those days was filled with ceaseless labor as water was hauled in buckets to the top of the drawbridge gate and poured over the great wooden planks. By night and day the water cascaded down the gates, and skins of cattle were soaked and spread only to be retrieved, soaked, and spread again.

The fire-breathing idol spewed flames from its mouth and nostrils in a never-ending torrent, scorching wood and stone, and heating metal until it glowed with a ruddy cast. The Ningaal tore apart the dwellings of the townspeople to fuel the monster at the gates. Into a cavity at the idol's base they threw the timber and oil that sent the flames and sparks gushing from its white-hot mouth.

On the evening of the thirteenth day, an officer approached Ronsard timidly. The knight rested on his arm and watched with weary dread as the flames and water did battle one with the other, clouds of white steam resulting from the conflict.

"Lord Ronsard, I—" The man hesitated and fell silent.

Ronsard swung his tired gaze toward the man. "Yes? Say anything but that we are running out of water." The thought had occurred to him often during this long vigil.

The man's face went white; his mouth hung slack.

"By Azrael! I meant it as a jest! Speak, man!"

"What is the trouble?" Theido said as he strode up to relieve Ronsard at his post. He was fresh and rested, eyes alert and tone confident.

"I am trying to find out, sir," said Ronsard hoarsely. "It seems the news he brings steals his voice."

"Well? Speak, sir. We are stout enough to hear it." Theido looked furiously at the officer and folded his long arms across his chest.

The man licked his lips and worked his jaw, but it was some moments before any words tumbled out, and when they did, it was in a tangled rush. "Lord Rudd has sent me . . . the water . . . supplies too low . . . we cannot last the night."

Ronsard needed to hear no more and sent the man away. "That cuts us to the quick. What are we to do now? Wait until our gates crumble away in flames, or until we die of thirst? Which would come first, I wonder?"

"We have our wits about us yet. But we have been too slow in comprehending this menace, and that may be our undoing. I have an idea I should have had days ago, but may work yet. Quickly, send some of your men to bring ropes and grappling hooks. Tell them to hurry, Ronsard, and bring all they can find. There is little time."

Theido took his place on the barbican directly over the flame-throwing idol. After soaking a long rope in water, he tied a three-pronged grappling hook onto one end and, leaning as far out over the wall as he dared, held only in Myrmior's and Ronsard's steely grasp, he lowered the hook toward the monster. The Ningaal, guessing his intent, howled with rage at the sight as above them the long length of swinging rope snaked down the face of the castle wall.

After several futile attempts, Theido swung the hook out and by a chance it caught on one of the iron beast's fangs. He called for a group of men to take the rope and pull it tight as he readied another rope and hook. In the space of an hour he had another hook lodged in the idol's horns. The Ningaal were now in a maddened frenzy, helpless to prevent what they feared might happen. They screamed in frustration as a third and then a fourth rope snagged the fire monster.

"That should suffice," said Theido as he scrambled back to safety on the battlements not a moment too soon, for the howling Ningaal had begun launching rocks and flaming debris from slings and mangonels.

"Do you think it will work?" asked Myrmior. He eyed Theido's web of ropes and hooks suspiciously.

"We will soon see. I can think of no better course."

"Then let us hope this one does not fail," replied Ronsard. He signaled to the men, three hundred in all, who were holding the ropes to begin pulling. With a mighty groan they all heaved at once. There came a resounding roar from the enraged Ningaal below as they saw the ropes pulled tight.

"Heave, men!" shouted Ronsard. "Heave!"

A few of the enemy, braving the arrows that still whistled through the air on occasion, threw ropes of their own over the ropes that Theido had fastened to the idol. Now they skittered up these like spiders, armed with knives that they carried in their teeth in the hope that they might somehow cut the ropes binding their fire-breathing god that threatened to overturn it.

The king's archers managed to keep the ropes of the Ningaal unoccupied, though at great price, for the warlords had appeared on the scene and were directing the efforts to save their endangered machine. The first act of the warlords was to order the mangonels to be filled with flaming coals from the idol and these flung aloft into the archers' faces. More than one bowman fell screaming to his death after being struck with the flaming debris.

The ropes were pulled and pulled with force, but the iron image did not move. Three hundred more men were ordered to the battlements, and the ropes were lengthened to accommodate them. They heaved and pulled, straining to their task until their hands bloodied the thick lines. But still the idol stood.

"It is not working," observed Myrmior. "We need more ropes."

"We have no more," reported Theido. "At least not the length we need."

"Then we must tie them together, and our cloaks and shirts as well. Your plan will work if we have more ropes."

"Wait! I have just thought of something," announced Ronsard. "What about chains? There are long lengths of chain in the gatehouse below. Let the ropes be fastened to the chains and the chains to the windlass of the drawbridge and the counterbalance."

"Can such a thing be done?" wondered Theido. "It might mean disengaging the drawbridge."

"It is a chance we must take. Send for the gatekeeper!"

What Ronsard had proposed was done without great difficulty. The massive drawbridge of Askelon was operated by not one but two windlasses and a system of counterweights. It was quick work to release the chain and allow the ropes to be bundled and threaded through a large iron ring. Then, with the counterweights once more in position, a dozen brawny men were placed on the windlass and they began to turn.

The chain wound around the windlass and disappeared into a hole in the stone floor of the gatehouse. Theido and Ronsard dashed back to the battlements to see the effect of their labors.

"It is working!" shouted Myrmior as they came panting up. "You lazy geniuses! It is working. May the gods be praised!"

They looked down to see the ropes stretched tight as harp strings. The iron idol teetered ever so slightly as the ropes pulled it upward.

"I pray those ropes can hold," said Theido.

"They will hold—you shall see," replied Myrmior. "By all that is good and right, they will hold."

No sooner had Myrmior spoken than he was nearly proved wrong. One of the ropes snapped; its ragged length sang through the air and lashed four Ningaal to the ground as it struck like a whip. "Bring grease!" cried Theido.

"Stop pulling!" shouted Ronsard. The chain stopped moving as the men at the windlass obeyed the marshal's order.

Grease was brought up from the gatehouse in buckets and smeared on the ropes and on the ledge of the crenellation where the ropes passed over the stone. Two men were stationed to swab the grease onto the ropes as they passed over the stone, and the windlass began turning again.

In a few moments the flaming idol was slowly lifted up off the ground, and then began to swing forward toward the gate. A tremendous knock sounded as the enormous iron image banged into the drawbridge; smoke from its fire rolled up the walls, stinging the eyes of the men on the battlements.

"Keep turning!" shouted Ronsard to the men below at the windlass. The Pyrinbradam inched slowly up the drawbridge, its snout pressed against the bridge's planks, which began to smolder.

"The gates are burning!" cried a voice from below.

Ronsard shot a quick glance toward Myrmior and Theido. "I did not foresee that."

"Do not turn away now," said Myrmior. "Stay with your plan."

"Yes, just a little while longer," agreed Theido, peering over the battlements.

"Bring water to the gates!" barked Ronsard. "Continue turning!"

More water was poured down the outside of the gates to quench the fire that had started. White billows of steam rose with the black smoke of the flames.

The idol rose a few more inches and then stopped. The men at the windlass strained; the windlass creaked.

"The cursed thing is caught on something," called Theido. "I cannot see what it is."

"Keep turning, and perhaps it will come loose," suggested Myrmior.

"Put more men on the windlass! Keep turning," ordered Ronsard.

A dozen more strong men were added to the windlass, and they fell to with all their might. The windlass creaked in loud complaint, the ropes stretched, and the chain moved but one link.

"It is not working," reported Theido. "Call them off. The gates have caught fire again."

Ronsard moved to relay the orders below when there came a whooshing sound, and the ropes went slack. A thunderous crash was heard, and everyone dashed to the battlements to see the flaming monster teetering on the edge of the ramp. The ropes had burst under the strain and had dropped the iron image back to the ground, where it had rolled to the edge of the ramp and was in danger of toppling over the edge into the dry moat below.

The king's men saw this and began to cheer wildly, urging the thing onto its own destruction. Ningaal warriors, half-crazed with anger, leaped to the dangling ropes in an attempt to haul it back from the brink. It appeared they would succeed.

The image righted and stopped rolling with two of its six huge wheels spinning over the chasm. Hundreds of Ningaal were now swarming to the ropes and were tugging it back inch by inch. The cheering from the battlements now abated.

"Well, we are in for it now, I fear," sighed Theido. "No better off than before."

"It was a good idea, my friend," said Ronsard. "It almost worked. At least we did not let the monster destroy our gates without a fight."

The enemy had placed long beams under the wheels and were attempting to rock the ponderous image in order to allow the rearmost wheels to be pulled back onto the ramp. But the rocking loosened one of Theido's hooks, and it broke free.

"Look!" cried Myrmior. "We are saved!"

Ronsard and Theido turned in time to see fifty men tumbling down the ramp, grasping the end of a falling rope. The snap of the rope caused the towering statue to lurch violently, teeter once, and then plunge over the edge, dragging a hundred men with it, still clinging to the lines.

The terrible idol spewed fire as it spun slowly in the air, ropes snaking after it with men attached like insects, plummeting to their deaths. The idol landed on its wicked head and crumbled in a shower of sparks, one arm breaking off and opening a great hole in its chest where flames leaped up and showed those looking down from the battlements that the monster was indeed ruined completely and many of its wretched keepers as well.

"We are saved to fight another day!" shouted Ronsard happily.

"Yes, but how many days will we last without water?" asked Theido, the short-lived triumph dying in his eyes and his features giving way to the black cast of despair.

CHAPTER 53

The council was held in Eskevar's chambers with the king sitting up in bed, frowning furiously and darting quick questions to his advisors. Though he appeared even more gaunt and pale than ever, his eyes burned intensely and his hands were steady as he turned the sword that lay across his lap.

"This is not good!" he shouted. "It leaves us no choice but to fight them on the plain. The siege can kill us one by one as we drop from thirst."

"We have a little water left, Sire," put in the warder weakly.

"How little?"

"Three days. Four."

"So we prolong the agony that much longer. No, I will not see soldiers weakened by thirst attempt to hold off the fall of Askelon. If Askelon falls, it must be on the field of battle. If the end is to come, let it come. But let us have our wits about us, and let us die with our swords in our hands.

"We can at least give these barbarians a fight they will long remember. This Nin will live to regret the day he set foot upon the soil of Mensandor, even if every one of us perishes."

This fiery speech of the king greatly heartened several of the lords in attendance. Rudd, Benniot, and Fincher had grown restive during the siege. Not men of patience, they itched to take up arms and meet the foe in a fair contest, even though—as greatly outnumbered as the king's forces were—there was nothing fair about it and not much of a contest. Still, the idea of taking once and for all a stand worthy of brave men appealed to them. They were ready to fight.

"What say the rest?" asked Rudd when he and the others had spoken their support of the king's plan.

Theido was slow in speaking, and as he stepped forward, all eyes turned toward him. "Sire, what you propose is the last desperate act of desperate men. I do not think we are pressed that far just yet. I say we should wait a few days. Much can happen in that time, and we are safe within these gates. The Ningaal have done their worst and have failed. I think we may yet prevail against them if we but wait a little."

"The time for waiting is over! It is time now to act. We have waited these many days, and we are no better for it. I am with the king; let us fight and die like men, since we have no better choice." Rudd threw a defiant look around the room and gathered support for his position with his fearless tone.

"I am much inclined to agree with you, Rudd," said Ronsard. "And when the time comes to stand toe-to-toe with the enemy, you will find me in the foremost rank; but there is good counsel in waiting. Three or four days may mean much. The lords of the north may yet appear at any time, and we would do well to be ready in that event.

"I say let the time be spent in readying ourselves to fight, but hold off fighting until we must." Ronsard's logic cooled several heads that had been hot to rush into battle that very moment.

"What do you say, Myrmior?" asked Eskevar. "Your counsel has been invaluable to us these last days. Speak. Tell us what you would have us do."

Myrmior looked sadly at the king and at those around him. His large, dark eyes seemed wells of grief, and sorrow tinged his deep voice.

"I have no counsel to give, my lord. I have said all I thought best, and it has brought us to this extremity. I will speak no more but rather take my place alongside these men worthy to be called your loyal subjects and raise my blade with theirs against the hated Nin."

The effect of Myrmior's words was like that of a pronouncement of doom. He had said in a few words what most of them felt but resisted giving words to: There is no hope. We must prepare to die.

"Sire," said Theido, coming near the bed, "let us not act hastily in this matter. Let us rather withdraw from here for a time and search our hearts before pressing for a decision."

Rudd, too, stepped up, shouting, "And I say we must not wait. Every day we stand by, our men will grow weaker and our chances worsen. Now is the time to strike!"

The room fell silent as everyone looked to the king to see what he would do. "Noble lords," he said gravely. "I will not force you to a decision. Neither will I tax you further with waiting which can belabor a man's spirit."

They all watched intently. Theido noticed the set of the Dragon King's jaw and knew what was coming before the words were spoken. "Therefore, I say that we will ride out tomorrow and engage the enemy, that what little advantage there may be in surprise we may carry with us. Go now and look to your men. See that they are well fed and made ready. Tomorrow at dusk I will lead them into battle."

The lords murmured their approval and left at once to begin preparing for combat. Theido and Ronsard lingered and spoke to the king in an effort to change his mind. But he turned a deaf ear to them and sent them away. After they had gone, Queen Alinea came in to spend one last night at the side of her king.

Eskevar had chosen dusk to lead the attack, because reports from his sentries had it that the enemy's watch on the postern gate was reduced at that time, while the Ningaal took their evening meal. It was a bold move and a clever one. It was assumed that an attack by the castle dwellers would issue from the main gate—here it was that the warlords had positioned their greater strength in anticipation of such a move. The postern gate—being smaller, and the long, crooked ramp that led from it being walled and narrow—permitted knights to ride but three abreast.

These things Eskevar took into consideration and decided the result was favorable. He would achieve a fair measure of surprise in such a maneuver, and he would catch the Ningaal unprepared and in the wrong position to begin a battle. They would mass quickly as the call to arms was given, he knew, but by that time he hoped to have his own men ranged upon the plain and ready, having already dispatched a goodly number of the foe.

The Dragon King and his army spent the day preparing and positioning men and horses to move through the postern yards and through the gates as quickly as possible.

When all was ready, a hush fell over the wards and yards where the men waited. The sun sank in the west, a great, crimson orb, and the Wolf Star shone fiercely in the east, shedding its cold, harsh light upon all who huddled beneath it. The villagers and peasants gathered to send their champions forth, and to pray to all the gods they knew for the victory. Women cried and kissed the brave knights; horses snorted and stamped their feet; children stood stiff-legged and stared round-eyed at the men in their glittering armor.

At the far end of the ward yard, a commotion arose, and those at the near end craned their necks to see the banner of the Dragon King lofted on its standard and waver toward them as a path opened before it. And then there was the king himself, sitting erect upon a milk-white stallion that pranced in trotting steps toward the gate. Over his silver armor he wore a royal coat that had the dragon emblem worked in gold. His helm bore no crest but the simple gold circlet crown. Flanking him on either hand, two grim knights—one astride a black charger, the other riding a sorrel—gazed resolutely ahead. The shield of the dark knight bore the device of a hawk; the blazon of the other showed a mace and flail held in a gauntleted fist.

Behind them rode Myrmior, who, after the fashion of his own people, wore no armor, but carried only a light, round shield and short sword. Ronsard, however, had prevailed upon him to don greaves, and a brassard for his sword arm at least. He had refused a helm, complaining that it was impossible to see out of the iron pot.

They passed through the yard to the gate, followed by ranks of nobles and knights three abreast. When they reached their position, the king raised his hand and the procession stopped. He looked to the gate-keeper, who, peering down from the barbican, nodded in return, declaring that the Ningaal had moved off the gate, leaving only a small force to watch. Then Eskevar, his face gray and hard, his eyes gleaming cold in the evil light of the star, drew his sword with his right hand. It whispered softly as it issued from the scabbard, but the sound soon filled the ward as the movement was repeated a thousand times over. The heavy iron portcullis was raised and the plank let down over the dry moat. And the Dragon King rode out to battle.

The Ningaal at the postern gate were scattered as chaff on the threshing floor. Several of them foolishly drew their weapons and were cut down before they could lift their hands; the rest ran howling to sound the alarm that the defenders had broken free and were in pursuit.

Eskevar turned the attack not toward the town, where the main body of the enemy waited, but to the more lightly manned cordon that had been thrown around the castle. This tactic proved successful, for the thundering knights easily routed the ill-prepared foe and dispersed a great many who could have formed a second front if given the chance. No sooner had this been accomplished than the knights wheeled to face the charge sweeping down around the castle rock behind them.

The full force of Eskevar's army met this hastily assembled attack and drove through it with little hurt. They then moved quickly on to thrust into the larger of the Ningaal's many siege camps, where several thousand of the enemy had gathered to eat and sleep that night. The sight of three thousand knights charging through their camp banished all thoughts of food and slumber from their barbarian minds as the camp instantly became a boiling cauldron of confusion and terror.

The Ningaal were caught unaware; the alarm had not reached them before the knights' fierce attack. In moments the scene was one of fire and blood, rearing horses and slashing blades. Many of the Ningaal fled from the camp rather than face the fierce justice of the king's swords. And for a fleeting moment it appeared to the defenders that the Ningaal would be overcome and crushed.

But that notion faded with the appearance of two warlords astride black warhorses, rallying their panic-stricken troops with cool control.

The knights had encompassed the camp and had driven through the center of it. Seeing the warlords bringing their scattered regiments together, Eskevar sent a company of knights against them to quell that opposition before it could materialize in force. The rest strove to keep the Ningaal running and confused, not allowing them time to coalesce into a unified front.

But too soon the body of knights surrounding the camp was out-flanked by a larger ring of bellowing Ningaal led by the two other war-lords. These began pressing forward, pushing the knights inward, shrinking the diameter of the circle by force of superior numbers. It seemed that no matter how many of the enemy were killed, there were more standing than had been there before.

Eskevar realized that the position was indefensible. With Theido on his right and Ronsard on his left, the Dragon King led a withering charge toward a weak section of the circle. There was a tremendous clash, and many knights fell into the wall of Ningaal axe blades, never to rise again. But the circle bowed and broke, and the king led his soldiers out upon the plain.

When they reached a place in the center of the plain half a league from the castle, Eskevar halted and turned to face the enemy, which was now massing for the final assault.

CHAPTER 54

The warlords, perceiving that the victory was theirs to be won, did not rush at once to the attack. They waited, gathering their forces and ordering their troops for the final conflict. This gave the Dragon King time to position his knights as well, placing them in stout ranks around scores of footmen with pike and spear who had joined them from the castle.

The first clash with the Ningaal found the Dragon King ready and waiting at the forefront of his army. The bellowing mob, with battle-axes swinging, rushed down upon the Dragon King's forces from the upper plain, led by two warlords. The two remaining warlords held a vast number of their foul flock in reserve.

Amut and Luhak rode with the charge and were met with a wall of steel. The Dragon King's knights, fighting with a strength born of desperation, held the line against the warlords' fearsome bodyguard and reduced that number effectively. The Ningaal axe men boiled onto the field like a tempest-driven flood. Though they beat against the armored knights with terrible blows of their cruel axes, the defenders withstood all.

Thwarted and repelled, the attack broke off and the warlords withdrew—to the cheers of the knights—leaving the field with the blood of their fallen.

Theido, astride his charger on the king's right hand, lifted his visor

and looked over the battlefield. "We have made a good account of ourselves," he said. "What is more, we have not suffered much loss."

"Even one man is too many in this fight," Ronsard retorted from
his place at the king's left hand. "Do you fail to see it? They mean to
wear us down one by one to the last man."

"By Azrael!" said Eskevar. "It is the only way they will take Askelon.
But we are far from defeated yet. And I have a plan that may confound
them. Theido, gather the commanders. I would speak to them before the
next attack."

They met on the field, and the king spoke hurriedly, finishing just
as the rolling whoop of the advancing enemy once more filled the air. As
the Ningaal closed on the defenders for the second time, there was a stirring within the king's army, and the attack met not a solid wall this time,
but a rank that gave way before them. The enemy was instantly drawn
inside the ring, like water into a flask, and then the stopper replaced, cutting off the axe men from their leaders, who were now inside. Thus the
battle began with the Ningaal herded together within a palisade of stinging blades.

No one in the enemy's camp noticed the small force that broke
away from the rear of the Dragon King's army and made its way back to
the castle.

Once more the king's knights stood to the task, hewing down the
enemy before them. The pikemen worked among the flashing hooves of
the horses to bring the warlords' bodyguard down, where they were
pierced with spears. The Ningaal axe men, separated from their commanders within the palisade, ran screaming around the outer ring, throwing themselves ineffectually upon the unforgiving lances of the knights.

Warlords Gurd and Boghaz, watching from a distance, soon realized what had happened and readied a second wave to smash the outer
ring of the king's defenses, and thus lay open the battle for a speedy end.

Mounted upon their sturdy black steeds, they swept down into the
fray. They had nearly reached the field of combat when their attack fal-

tered and broke apart amid a deadly flight of arrows. The Ningaal fell in such numbers that the warlords pulled up short of engaging the king and swerved to meet the archers who were now running to join their comrades on the plain, having staved off the second wave. The archers, who had been left behind to defend Askelon in its last need, were led by Myrmior and several of the boldest knights. They had been sent to bring the archers as part of Eskevar's plan to divide and confuse the enemy.

The charging Ningaal could not draw within blade range of the archers and were at last forced to retreat and regroup. The archers reached the plain with ease, and the air sang with their killing missiles. Within moments of their arrival, the Ningaal withdrew once more and left the field to the Dragon King.

"We have not fared so well this time," said Theido, once more surveying the carnage around him. "We have lost many good men. Perhaps too many to withstand another charge."

"Withstand we must!" shouted Eskevar. "We must hold."

"We have surprised them twice. I do not think we will again," said Ronsard. "But we have stood them a battle that will be sung in the halls of brave men everywhere. That is something to take with us. Yet I begin to think that if we last this day, we may yet turn the tide of battle in our favor."

"If Wertwin were as good as his word and brought the armies of Ameronis, Lupollen, and the others with him, I would agree with you," said Theido. He turned his eyes to the north but saw nothing on the horizon. "But even if they came now, I think it would be too late."

"Do not talk so!" charged the king. "We will prepare to meet the attack with courage."

"As you say, my lord." Theido looked at his king, and his noble heart swelled within him almost to bursting, for he seemed to see a dark shape, like the wings of a raven, hovering around the king's shoulder. When the knight spoke again, it was with a voice choked with sorrow. "You have ever shown us courage, my king. Lead us, and we will follow through the gates of death itself."

Eskevar's face shone fierce in the strange white light of the star, shining as bright as day. But when he spoke, it was with a gentler tone. "You have served me well, brave friends. I have trusted you with my life on more occasions than a king ought, but I have never found you wanting." He stopped and looked at each of them before continuing.

"This is how I want to be remembered—turned out in my finest armor at the head of loyal men and brave. This is how I would enter the rest of my fathers."

Ronsard raised a hand to protest, but Eskevar waved him silent. "Enough of dying," he said. "Now to arms! For the enemy once more draws near."

Across the broken battlefield, now slippery with the blood of the dead and dying, the Ningaal advanced, slowly this time, behind a vanguard of horsemen with flaming pikes. The four warlords had positioned themselves so as to command a phalanx of troops ahead and behind them. This time there would be no force held in reserve, and there would be no tricks, for they moved over the plain step by step, wary of the slightest shift among the soldiers of the Dragon King.

The baleful Wolf Star burned down upon the scene with its hateful light, bright as noonday sun, casting shadows all around. It seemed to grow larger and to fill the sky, making the forlorn moon rising in the east a pale and insignificant thing.

Eskevar turned his face to the Wolf Star. "Surely that is an evil thing. I feel its fire in my bones. How it burns. Ronsard, Theido"—he turned to them both—"do you feel it?"

"It is the heat of battle I feel, Sire," offered Ronsard.

"Aye, that too," agreed Eskevar. The king seemed to come once more to himself and looked out across the battlefield, now rolling in the smoke of the fiery pikes of the Ningaal.

"If they think us slow-witted enough to wait here like cattle for the slaughter, they are mistaken," said Eskevar as he glared out over the field. "Assemble the commanders!" he called. A trumpeter sent the message ringing in the air.

"We will charge them there—in the center," said the king, pointing with his long sword toward the advancing body of the enemy. "We will show them how the knights of Mensandor value their lives."

"Aye," agreed the gathered lords, their armor battered and bloody but their faces still eager in the light of the hateful star.

"And we will show them how the knights of Mensandor value their freedom," shouted Rudd. "For glory!" The nobleman raised his voice and led them in a rousing battle chant.

"Go back to your men," instructed Eskevar. "Be ready, and wait for my signal." Eskevar took his place at the head of his knights. Theido and Ronsard stayed at either side.

Theido, guessing the end was near, looked across to his friend Ronsard and offered a wordless salute. This was the long, dark road he had seen so long ago. Now that it stretched before him, he did not fear it, though it saddened him. He wanted to speak some final word to his friend, but none would come. The salute said all.

"Farewell, brave friend," said Ronsard as he returned the salute. He closed the visor of his helmet and raised the point of his sword to Theido.

"For Mensandor!" cried Eskevar suddenly. His voice sounded clear and strong as thunder as it carried across the plain. He raised his sword and spurred his courser forward, and with a roar the army of the Dragon King leaped as one into furious motion.

The shock of the clash as the charging knights met the stubborn Ningaal shook the earth. Horses screamed and wheeled, plunging and plunging again. Knights cut the air with mace and flail; swords flashed and spears thrust and bowstrings sang.

Eskevar's white stallion could be seen dashing straight away into the thick of the fighting. Ronsard, bold and bright, defended his king's left with a tireless arm. Time and again the champion's sword whirled through the air, dealing death with every blow. Theido guarded the king's right and strove to keep himself between his lord and the bloodthirsty axes of the barbarian horde.

Here and there amid the furious melee, the standards of the Mensandor lords could be seen, as the islands of defenders, surrounded by a sea of enemy fighting men, labored to remain abreast of one another. But one by one the standards fell, some never to rise again, as the long night of battle wore on.

The daring attack of the Dragon King produced at length an unexpected result. So fiercely did the king's army fight, and so well, that they succeeded in punching through the center of the Ningaal formation. Despite the enemy's superior force, the defenders cut a wide swath through the heart of the warlords' offensive and in time came together behind the Ningaal lines.

"This is unexpected!" cried Eskevar, breathing heavily and leaning forward in his saddle. "Our cause is not yet lost. Look there! See, Rudd drives through to join us, and yonder Fincher and Benniot."

Theido looked at the swirling maelstrom before him and separated the shapes of the Dragon King's knights from the darker forms of the Ningaal. The din of the fight rang loud in his ears, but he did not see the faintest glimmer of hope that the battle could be won, as Eskevar had said. Their charge had scattered the larger part of the Ningaal and had divided them like a wedge. The warlords of Nin circled around the outside of the battle storm and sought to rejoin their troops, but in vain. The enemy was falling away in droves.

"Is it true?" shouted Ronsard, throwing his visor up to view the contest.

"Yes!" agreed Theido. "See how they crowd toward the center—their own numbers crush them. If we direct a sally there, we can further divide them."

"Good eye, man! You are right. Trumpeter! Rally the men. Onward we go!" Eskevar urged his steed once more ahead, and the Ningaal felt the heat of his blade like a flame kindled against them. The king's knights formed a spearhead that drove through the milling mass and cut it down. Ningaal warriors forgot their discipline and ran screaming from the battlefield in great numbers; their commanders slew many deserters with their own hands in order to stop the rout.

This second charge was successful, and the defenders took heart that they might indeed carry the victory. With jubilant whoops and courageous battle cries, they stood shoulder to shoulder and fought, urging one another to greater deeds of valor.

By the time the sickly moon had advanced two hours' time, the army of the Dragon King had for the first time taken the upper hand in the battle. The warlords were fighting a defensive action, seeking a retreat whereby they could regroup their lagging regiments. But Eskevar and his commanders, though suffering from fatigue and the terrible attrition of their numbers, doggedly struggled on to put the invaders to flight.

At midnight an entire Ningaal regiment broke and ran from the field. The sight of the beaten enemy dragging itself away from the combat greatly heartened the defenders, who sent a cheer aloft that reached Askelon and was echoed by the fearful refugees who peered anxiously from the battlements of the fortress.

"We can seize the day!" shouted Eskevar. "The barbarians have lost the heart to win."

"Sire, let us pursue them and drive them from the field," said Ronsard. "But you remain here where your soldiers can see you. Gather your strength."

"Yes, my lord," agreed Theido. "Let your commanders earn some glory. Do not endanger yourself further. Rest a little and regain your strength."

Eskevar glared dully at his knights as he sat hunched in his saddle, unable to sit erect any longer. His visor was open, and his face showed white with exhaustion. He shook his head wearily and replied, "I will rest when the day has been saved—and not before. If my knights wish to see me, they must look toward the heart of the battle, for that is where I will be."

Theido and Ronsard exchanged worried glances. They would have preferred to have their king stand off from battle at least for a time. Theido was about to protest further when Eskevar closed his visor and jerked the reins, plunging once more into the clash. The two trusted knights had no choice but to surge after him and protect him however they could.

For a moment it appeared as if this final assault would indeed shatter the Ningaal strength, for the howling axe men of the warlords melted before the defenders' blades as snow before the flame. And for a moment the Dragon King and his knights stood unchallenged on the hard-won battleground as the enemy roiled in retreat.

But the illusion of victory was fleeting, for there came a sound that seemed to tear out of the ground as if the very earth were rending. It filled the air and soared aloft to shriek across the plain. Those who heard it quailed in its presence; even the stoutest among them trembled.

All eyes turned toward the south, and for the briefest instant the rolling smoke parted to reveal a solid wall of warriors stretching across the plain. Nin the Immortal had arrived with his fifty thousand.

CHAPTER 55

The battle-weary defenders watched in horror as the conquest, so nearly won, dissolved in bleak futility, and certain doom swarmed in to take its place. The cheers of triumph turned to bitter wails of despair as the Ningaal, seeing their sure salvation, halted their retreat and turned once more upon the Dragon King's battered army.

Eskevar had but little time to rally his flagging troops before the enemy surged around them like a flood whose waters rose to overwhelm all. At once the hapless defenders were surrounded on every side and cut off from any possible retreat. The warlords urged their warriors to fight in a frenzy, and one by one the Dragon King's brave soldiers fell.

Ronsard and Theido fought to keep abreast of the king and protect him to the very end. But a sudden rush of the enemy swirled up before them and drove them apart.

Three black-braided, howling Ningaal, mouths foaming, eyes wild and faces smeared with blood, leaped up and grabbed the reins of Theido's mount. One of the attackers instantly lost a hand in a crimson gush; another dropped dead to the earth, his axe in Theido's chest, and the knight felt the blade bite deep as his armor buckled and parted. He reeled in the saddle, falling back beneath the force of the blow, which would have killed most men.

The Ningaal attacker, still clutching the haft of his axe, was pulled off the ground as Theido's courser reared. Theido swung his buckler down upon the enemy's head, and his opponent fell sprawling to the earth, where the warhorse's flashing hooves made short work of him.

Theido, by some miracle, remained in the saddle and wrenched the axe from the crease in his chestplate. He knew himself to be grievously wounded but turned to look for Ronsard and Eskevar. The current of battle had carried them far apace. He saw Ronsard engaging four or five enemies with flaming pikes and swords, trying to keep them from reaching the king, when suddenly a warlord, charging into their midst with his black cape flying, struck into the fight.

Instantly the warlord was met by the lightly armed figure of Myrmior. The seneschal, his face a mask of hate, thrust himself between the king and the warlord. Theido saw Myrmior's sword flash in the starlight in a shining arc. The warlord raised his blade; Myrmior's sword shattered with the force of his mighty blow. The warlord struck again and beat angry Myrmior's shield. Theido watched, helpless, as the warlord's cruel and curving blade flicked out and buried itself deep in Myrmior's unprotected chest. Myrmior clutched at the blade with one hand and pulled, even as the warlord sought to withdraw it, jerking the battle lord forward in the saddle. In the same instant Myrmior brought his broken sword up and slammed it into the warlord's throat. Theido then saw the two men topple to the earth.

So quickly did this happen that Theido scarcely lifted the reins to send his mount forward and it was over. From his vantage point the knight saw Ronsard, who had killed three of his assailants, lurch away and drive once more to the king's side. But in that momentary lapse, worlds were lost, for Theido, already pounding to his aid, saw Eskevar pulled from the saddle to sink into a boiling mass of Ningaal with pikes and axes.

Ronsard reached the spot where his monarch went down first. He killed two with one stroke and four more in as many passes. Theido's arrival sent the rest darting away as Ronsard, heedless of his own safety, flung himself from the saddle and knelt beside his king.

Soon there were shouts all around. "The king has fallen! The Dragon King has fallen!" The defenders swarmed to his side, forming a wall around the body of their beloved ruler.

Ronsard held Eskevar's head in his hands and carefully removed the king's helmet. "It is over, brave friend," Eskevar gasped. "I shall lift my blade no more."

"Do not say that, Sire," said Ronsard, tears seeping out of the corners of his eyes to run down his broad cheeks. He tore off his own gauntlet and thrust a corner of the king's cloak into a bleeding wound at the base of Eskevar's neck.

"There is no pain . . . no pain," said Eskevar, his voice a whisper. "Where is my sword?"

"Here, Sire," said Theido, placing his own weapon into the king's grasping hands.

Eskevar clutched the weapon to his breast and closed his eyes.

Those watching from the castle ramparts and battlements saw the king fall, and a cry of grief and dismay tore from their hearts as from the throat of a mortally wounded beast. But the cry had not yet died in the air when someone shouted, "Look to the east!" All eyes turned their gaze eastward, where the forlorn watchers beheld a strange and wondrous sight.

It appeared to those watching, and to the soldiers crouching over the body of the Dragon King, that lightning flashed out of the east with the brightness of the blazing sun, for there was a sudden blinding flare that seemed to fill the sky, outshining even the light of the Wolf Star.

Another burst of brilliant light struck the sky, and surging Ningaal paused to look up from their bloody work to view with alarm this new marvel.

Suddenly all anyone could see was the form of a knight on a white horse bolting out of the east. In his upraised arm he carried a sword that blazed and flashed with living light.

All the earth seemed to fall silent before the approach of this unknown knight. The thunder of his charger's hooves could be heard pounding over the plain as he flew as on eagle's wings into battle.

"Zhaligkeer!" someone shouted. "The deliverer has come!"

A murmur swept through the ward yards and towers of Askelon. Alinea, Bria, and Esme, holding vigil in the eastern tower, looked out through tearful eyes to see this strange sight. The soldiers of the Dragon King, standing shoulder to shoulder around their fallen lord, raised their visors in astonishment.

The sword in the knight's hand seemed to cast a beam of light toward heaven as he rode swiftly onward. The Ningaal, amazed at this unheralded apparition, looked on with gaping mouths. Even Nin, Supreme Deity of the Universe, struggled to his feet from his throne upon his platform to better see what was happening.

Quentin, astride the speeding Blazer, saw the remnant of the Dragon King's army surrounded by the enemy upon the plain. With Toli at his side, he had no other thought but to rush to their aid and take his place beside them. In his dash he had seen the standard of the Dragon King fall beneath the flood of the enemy. He had then drawn his sword and with a battle cry he launched himself straight toward the place where he had marked the banner's fall.

Zhaligkeer burned with the brilliance of a thousand suns, throwing off bolts of lightning that seared the air. For the Ningaal, transfixed by the unearthly vision, this was too much. Unafraid of bold earthly warriors, they were terrified at the appearance of this heavenly foe. The barbarians threw down their weapons and fled before him. Quentin drove into the center of the reeling horde and rode untouched into the midst of the Dragon King's awestruck army.

Quentin glanced down and saw his friends Theido and Ronsard kneeling over the body of Eskevar. He read the sadness in their eyes and knew that the Dragon King was dead.

Without a word Quentin wheeled Blazer around and leaped after the fleeing Ningaal. An unspeakable grief seized his mind, and Quentin had no thought but to drive the hated enemy before him, to ride until he could ride no more, to the sea and beyond. In his mindless grief he drove straight toward Nin the Destroyer and his fifty thousand panic-stricken warriors. The Ningaal parted before the invincible knight with the flaming sword, as waves before the tempest.

Quentin saw nothing distinctly; it was as if he had entered a dream. Pale shapes moved before him, rolling away on either side like clouds; the night sky was filled with a burning white light. Then there was a darkness before him that rose up in a seething mass.

Zhaligkeer flashed in his hand. Quentin raised himself in the saddle and flung the sword skyward with a mighty shout. The sword spun in the air, and it seemed that as it reached the apex of its arc it suddenly exploded with a blinding crack that showered tongues of fire all around.

The sky went white, and every man threw his hands before his face to save his eyes. It seemed to Quentin that he entered his vision, for he was once more the knight standing upon a darkling plain, wearing the shining armor and lofting a blazing sword that burned into the heart of the darkness gathered about.

There was a shudder in the air, and he felt the fire rush through him. Though the lightning danced blinding waves around him, he opened his eyes and saw the darkness roll away, revealing a city splendid and beautiful, shimmering in the light as if carved of fine gold and gems. The exquisite sight brought Quentin off his horse and onto his knees.

He threw his hands before his face to blot out the vision, and the tears came rising up as from a spring. In that moment he felt in his inmost soul the hand of the Most High God upon him.

When Quentin raised his head, he was alone, and the night was dark. The Wolf Star had disappeared in a great flash. Some said that the Shining One had reached up into the sky and smitten the star and extinguished it, for it vanished in the same instant that Quentin had thrown the sword.

Zhaligkeer had fallen to earth and was found buried to the hilt in the obscene body of the Immortal Nin. The Conqueror of Kings lay dead, pinned to the ground like a serpent. His unhappy minions, witnessing the swift miracle of their cruel lord's death, fled screaming over the plain. Their pitiful cries filled the night as they sought to escape the justice that would soon overtake them. The warlords of Nin fell upon their swords and joined their loathsome sovereign in his well-deserved fate.

Quentin returned to the place where Eskevar lay. Together with Theido and Ronsard and the lords and knights of Mensandor, he picked up the body of the king and, lifting it upon his shoulders, bore it away to Askelon.

CHAPTER 56

The funeral of the Dragon King lasted three days, and his mourning continued for thirty. During this time Wertwin and the armies of Ameronis, Lupollen, and the others arrived—greatly saddened and contrite, for the news of the king's death had overtaken them on their way. They were in pursuit of the Ningaal who were fleeing back along the Arvin toward the sea, where their ships still waited. The lords slew many of the enemy in their flight, and the rest were driven into the sea at lance point.

Eskevar's body was taken at once to the castle, where it was placed upon his own bed. Durwin, aided by Biorkis, came to minister to the body, washing it and composing it for entombment. Inchkeith worked long hours over the king's armor, pounding out the dents inflicted upon it in the last battle and shining it bright as new. Queen Alinea herself dressed her husband in his finest garments; Bria and Esme adorned him with his most treasured jewels. And then he was taken to the great hall, where he was solemnly laid upon his bier.

The king's body lay in the great hall for two days, guarded by a sorrowful contingent of knights and nobles throughout the day and night while a steady procession of tearful subjects filed past the litter. The miserable, wailing peasants filled the ward yards, and afflicted citizens roamed the streets of the town, inconsolable with grief. The great

Dragon King had passed; no one had ever thought to see that dark day.

Quentin remained in his chamber and would see no one. He did not even venture to the battlements to watch the funeral pyres of all the brave dead of the king's proud army as they burned upon the plain. He held himself to blame for the king's death, reasoning that if he had arrived but a few heartbeats sooner, Eskevar would still be alive. Quentin would neither eat nor sleep, but sat slumped in a chair before the darkened, empty hearth.

At midnight on the second day, Quentin bestirred himself and crept quietly to the great hall. The mourners had gone, and no one lingered in the hall except the ten knights standing as statues of stone around the body. Torches burned on standards at the four corners of the bier, casting a soft, hazy light over the pall. Quentin moved closer, mounting the flower-strewn platform to kneel beside the body.

In the lambent glow the king's features were relaxed and calm; except for the unnatural stillness, he might have been asleep. Gone were the traces of illness that had so wasted his noble frame. Gone, too, were the lines of care and concern that had creased his features in the last few days. The years seemed to have been rolled away, and Quentin saw a younger Eskevar than he had known. His hair was dark and swept back over his temples. The high forehead was smooth, the nose straight and well formed above a firm but not ungentle mouth. The hard jut of the jaw had been softened, revealing a man at peace within himself, and the deeply cleft chin spoke of the unflinching purpose of the man who had been. The king wore his armor and held his helm nestled under his left arm. His sword lay upon his chest, where it was held at the hilt in his right hand. The writhing dragon device on the king's breastplate seemed to twist and wink in the firelight. A cloak of royal blue edged in silver and gold was fastened at the throat by a golden chain and the king's favorite dragon brooch. Eskevar appeared ready to leap to his feet and ride once more to the trumpeter's call.

Quentin bowed his head, and hot tears fell upon the bier. He recalled so vividly the time when he had seen his king just so, held in the evil Nimrood's spell. Then, by an impossible miracle, the necromancer's enchantment had been broken and the Dragon King freed to live again. But it was a far more powerful sorcery that embraced the king now, one that claimed all men in the end and from which there was no release.

Quentin heard a soft step behind him, and he felt a light touch on his shoulder. He glanced up to see Queen Alinea, dressed all in sable, looking down on him, her green eyes deep pools of sorrow, but shining more beautifully for the compassion with which she regarded him.

"I have sought you these past two days, my son." The queen spoke softly, and the tone eased Quentin's troubled heart. He did not speak.

"You must not blame yourself, for in the end he chose his own course, as he ever did. It was his wish to die serving the kingdom he loved. And of all his loves, this one, his love for his realm, claimed his highest devotion. He was a king first and a man only second."

"Thank you for your words, my lady. They do soothe me well. I will not blame myself, though I did at first. I know now that his course was set for him long ago. He would not bend to another."

"Not and remain Eskevar for very long. Look at him, Quentin. See how peacefully he slumbers. Death held no terror for him; he had conquered it many times. The thing he feared and hated most was that his realm would fall before him, and he would not be able to save it. That gnawed at him; it poisoned his last days. But he conquered that, too, in the end."

"How well you knew him, Alinea."

"Knew him? Perhaps I knew him as well as anyone could, and I loved him with all my heart; he loved me, too, in his way. But a king does not belong to himself, or to his family. He belongs to his kingdom. Eskevar felt this more intimately than any I have known. He died for Mensandor as he lived for it.

"But there was much that even I did not know of him. The long years of war, years away from his home, took more than time away from us. Many was the night I cried out in loneliness for my husband and would have had a strong hand to hold my own. There was none. Eskevar was away, fighting for his kingdom. Even when he returned, he never rested; he was always turning his eyes here and there, searching every remote corner of Mensandor for any sign of weakness or trouble.

"He once told me—by way of apology, I think—'If you seek to know me, know first my kingdom.' He was Mensandor; its life was his."

Quentin looked upon the dead monarch, realizing there was much he would never know of the man who had adopted him to be his own. "Now that he is dead, what will happen to his realm?" he wondered aloud.

"It shall live on in the life of the new Dragon King," murmured the queen softly. She bent over her husband's body and removed the dragon brooch and chain. She then turned and drew Quentin to his feet. "You will find this to be far heavier than the weight of its gold, my dear one. But he wanted you to have it, and all that goes with it."

Quentin shook his head slowly, fingering the golden brooch the queen had fastened on his cloak. "I was never his son. As much as I love you both and am grateful for your kindness to me these many years, I am not fit to be king."

"Who would be better?"

"His trueborn son, perhaps."

"You know he had no male heir. But I shall tell you something. I have always thought it strange that a man who valued his throne so highly would have—"

"Given it away so freely," muttered Quentin.

"No, he did not give it away at all, Quentin. You see, Bria was born just before Eskevar went to war with Goliah. When he learned that I could have no other children, and his offspring was female, I expected him to be angry. I offered to relinquish my crown so that he could take another, but he would not hear of it. He said he was content, that he would trust whatever god that ruled him to provide an heir when the time came. He never spoke of it again.

"So when he asked you to be his ward, I knew he had found his heir. How he knew, I cannot say. But he saw something in you that pleased him very much."

"It seemed a kingly whim to me, my lady. Not that I was not over-joyed to receive his high favor. But as much as I loved him and Askelon, Dekra is my home. He must have known that."

"It did not matter. He wanted for you only your happiness. He knew that when the time came, you would fulfill his hopes and expectations, so deep was his trust."

"I hope he was not mistaken. I pray he was not," said Quentin. Alinea looked upon the still form of the king and, drawing a long breath, turned away at last, offering Quentin her hand.

"He was not mistaken, my son. All is as it should be—as he would have had it. You will see."

Quentin cast a glance toward the body and withdrew with Alinea on his arm. Their footsteps echoed in the darkened hall, and when they had gone, silence again reclaimed her own.

The next morning the body of the king was taken to the Ring of the Kings, the ancestral resting place of the Mensandorean monarchs established within the green walls of Pelgrin Forest.

The funeral cortege, made up of knights and nobles on horseback and loyal subjects on foot, wound through the hastily cleared streets of Askelon. Townspeople stood among the ashes of their ruined city to pay a last farewell to their sovereign. Quentin rode on Blazer, next to Alinea and directly behind the funeral wain. Bria and Durwin followed and were in turn followed by Theido and Ronsard, who led the procession of noblemen. Others came on in turn, riding beneath their colorful devices and banners. At the head of the cortege, the Dragon King's own standard carried his red dragon hung with pennons of black.

The king rode to his tomb on his bier beneath a sky of radiant blue sown with tufts of white clouds. A cool wind freshened the summer air and bore sorrow far away, though here and there a tear still sparkled in an eye. The sun shone down upon the body of Eskevar fair and full, and the wind ruffled his hair as his armor glinted hard and bright in the sun.

Eskevar was placed in one of the beehive-shaped barrows within the Ring—the very barrow Quentin had found him in years before to rescue him from Nimrood's fell scheme. The barrow was clean and well ordered, having been swept and appointed by Oswald, the queen's chamberlain.

With much ceremony and dignity, Eskevar was laid to rest upon his stone slab, which had been spread with fur coverlets from his bed. His most highly prized possessions were placed about him, and when all had looked their last upon the king, the tomb was sealed and the entrance filled in with earth. Quentin assisted in this work rather than stand by and watch. And when it was over, he turned away and did not look back.

As the funeral party emerged from the green silence of the Ring of the Kings, they were met by a party of lords led by Wertwin. The noblemen bowed in their saddles and gazed down at Quentin, who still walked beside the queen, holding her arm. "We are told," began Wertwin, "that you are to be the king's choice to succeed his throne."

"I am," Quentin said flatly. No one could determine from his tone how he felt about the matter.

Wertwin appeared disconcerted and glanced at the lords around him. "We mean to offer you our fealty," he explained.

Quentin only stared at them. "He who wields the Shining One is our king!" said someone from among them. A chorus of hearty approval endorsed this statement. From somewhere nearby Toli appeared, bearing a sword in his arms. Quentin smiled at his friend and took the sword.

He felt the quick warmth of its grip as it touched his fingers, and he heard the blade whisper as he drew it forth. Then suddenly the forest glade was awash in a brilliant light as Quentin lofted the sword for all to see.

The assembled lords dismounted at once and came forward to gather around him and to kneel. Quentin held the sword high and said, "May the god whose power burns in this blade burn in me as well. I will accept your fealty."

The forest rang with cheers and shouts of acclaim. Theido and Ronsard shouldered their way to his side and clapped him on the back, and then he was borne away on the shoulders of loyal subjects.

A jubilant parade returned to Askelon, in marked contrast to the one that had issued from the gates earlier in the day. Although the official period of mourning would continue for many more days, from that moment the healing process throughout the ravaged land was begun. In Eskevar all the dead were buried and the old order laid to rest. In Quentin the new order was present with a promise bright as the future that shone like the light of the Shining One at his side.

A new age had dawned, and a new king had been chosen to lead the way. And of all those who reveled in it and welcomed it, only Durwin, the faithful hermit of Pelgrin Forest, knew it for what it was: the priest king had come at last. The promise of the ages had been fulfilled.

The Story Continues in Volume 3,
The Sword and the Flame,
of The Dragon King Trilogy

THE SONG OF ALBION TRILOGY

Picture a world intricately entwined with our own yet separate, pulsing with the raw energy and vivid color of Celtic myth come to life.

ROBIN HOOD.

THE LEGEND BEGINS ANEW

It is the ultimate QUEST
for the ultimate TREASURE.
CHASING A MAP TATTOOED ON HUMAN SKIN,
ACROSS AN OMNIVERSE OF
INTERSECTING REALITIES, TO UNRAVEL
THE FUTURE OF THE FUTURE.

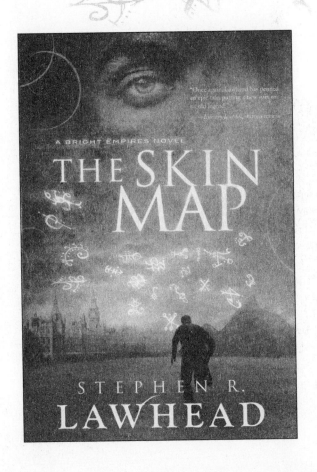

A BRIGHT EMPIRES NOVEL

THE SKIN
MAP

"Once again, Lawhead has penned
an epic tale, putting a new spin on
an old legend."
—*Publishers Weekly*, starred review

STEPHEN R.
LAWHEAD